THE PRAGUE
CONNECTION

ALSO BY THE AUTHOR

Apocalypse Watch (A Brandt Swindon Novel, Book 1)

The Exocus Hour (A Brandt Swindon Novel, Book 2)

THE PRAGUE CONNECTION

A NOVEL

A Brandt Swindon Novel

Will Steadman

HMB Press

The world will ask you who you are,
and if you don't know, the world will tell you.
—Carl Jung

Prologue

Dusa Benik took Fedot's warning seriously. In the fall of 1989, political upheaval was spreading through the East European Soviet Bloc with volcanic energy. All the Russian satellites speculated how Moscow would react. Dusa and the Russian, Fedot, had become close friends despite Fedot's position in Soviet Army Military Intelligence. Both held the rank of senior lieutenant, Dusa an artillery officer in the Czech People's Army. Together, they were responsible for protecting entry to the nuclear storage bunkers. When it came to nuclear weapons, two-man control was the standard procedure. Heavily guarded, fenced-in bunkers in the Prague countryside could only be accessed by a combination of a Russian and a Czech officer. Fedot's warning was about the third man who had recently arrived from Moscow. He wore the uniform of a GRU military colonel, but everything underneath the wool said KGB.

"I don't trust this so-called colonel," Fedot whispered to Dusa. He looked at the three guards escorting them. "When I go in with the colonel, laugh and say you have to relieve yourself and go into the trees and wait. Be prepared for trouble. If something happens, save yourself."

Dusa did as Fedot said and positioned himself behind a large linden tree to wait. Early morning frost sparkled on the tree-shaded ground cover and fallen leaves. He glanced back at the bunker. Two guards had slung their weapons over their shoulders and were hopping on their feet, trying to get warm. The third one crept close to the bunker to avoid the wind and leaned his weapon against the wall before lighting a cigarette. Fedot exited the bunker ahead of the colonel. His face had a grim look, as if inside he had confronted the mythic forest *hejkal*. The shot that killed him came from the KGB-favored PSM pistol behind him. Dusa hesitated, not sure if what he saw was actual or a deception. When the KGB man ordered, "Shoot the other one," he decided it was time to run.

The unprepared guards gave Dusa barely enough time to reach the dark shade of the deeper forest before bullets began to zing past him. He moved like a snake through the woods, using trees and scrub oaks for cover as he headed up a hill. Without a clear target, the shooting became random, then stopped. An adrenaline boost helped him outdistance the three pursuers to the chain link fence surrounding the bunkers. He climbed a bent elm with a long, thick branch that allowed him to drop across the fence. He avoided open fields and stayed in the tree line, stopping often to listen for noise from pursuers. Hearing nothing but the wind rustling through branches, he started to feel safe. But when helicopters began circling with troops fast-roping to the ground, he looked for a place to hide. A hunter's cabin with a sod-covered roof offered out-of-sight height and concealment. He used a stack of logs and the edge of a rain barrel to climb up and then burrowed between the stalks of tall shrub grass and leafy wild boxwoods. A spread of elm and oak leaves covering his body hid him from eyes on the choppers. He froze and listened as soldiers broke into the cabin to search, then moved on without checking the grassy roof.

Thoughts of his family plagued Dusa. He feared his wife and son were already dead. The KGB had read the tea leaves. Moscow's grip on their satellite countries would soon be gone. They knew it was time to act. West Germans were already gathering at the Berlin Wall, preparing to tear down a ruthless landmark. Doors had had to be closed, loose ends eliminated, and like the Nazi SS, the KGB needed to brace for impact.

1

Gazing down at the World War II debris from his Frankfurt hotel room, Brandt thought the tail section of the RAF bomb sticking out of the mud looked like a student art project. He'd give it a D, though it probably deserved an F. It was like watching the opening scene of a movie and guessing what would come next: an explosion with thick smoke, torn flesh, and flying glass, or safety and a cryptic view of mortality being excavated. His binoculars gave him a closer look at the men in white forensic suits, who looked like extraterrestrials as they moved cautiously through the bomb rubble. Leftover pockets of slick, gray snow, thick mud, and icy chunks of cement made each step an acrobatic balancing act. They were digging and searching for bones, skulls, and souvenirs—Wehrmacht soldiers, civilians, even POWs could have been buried under the debris. When human remains were uncovered, the spot was photographed and the pieces then labeled and carefully placed in a plastic box. Brandt set down the binoculars and held his head like a sympathetic mourner. The solemn display had a macabre quality: potter's field to a priest, charnel ground to a poet, boot hill to a bar full of drunks. Final destinies were like that.

The scene was another reminder to Brandt that death had its own timetable—never late, never hasty. He listed the close calls he'd had since Deke dragged him into the CIA: Chernobyl, Bosnia, Istanbul, Prague, Munich, Stockholm, Helsinki, Amsterdam, and an old abandoned German defense tunnel near Cologne. For a long time after his wife succumbed to cancer, he didn't care if he lived or died. Morgues, cemeteries, and black-robed visitors made a nightly appearance in his dreams. That had changed. Casey was the genesis of his rebirth. She was next to him in all those places. She brought with her a sweetness to life.

The Explosive Ordnance KMBD van had left, indicating the thousand-pound British bomb was now safe and ready to be hauled away. The disposal crew pulled mud from below the bomb until they were able to slide thick webbing straps underneath for the lift and carry. A second truck, also part of the *Kampfmittelbeseitigungsdienst*, was waiting for the bomb to be set safely on the flatbed trailer. Residents and workers were beginning to return to their homes and offices while the bone diggers continued their grim work.

There would be more bombs—Brandt knew the count. Even in the spring of 2019, an estimated five thousand were expected to be found annually in Germany for another decade. Berlin knew it too. The Allies never ran out of bombs.

He moved to the room's coffee machine and made a cup of espresso. A shot of caffeine would take the yawn out of the day's mission. In his mind, finding covert spots in travel agencies for CIA agents to use for cover was as futile as looking for Māori tribesmen in Siberia. Someone in Langley should have hit the delete key.

The bomb removal setting stayed with Brandt while he watched the cup fill. The foamy crema swirling on the coffee's surface acted like a muse urging him to put the scene on one of his abstract canvases. He never understood the crema-to-art connection, but it had happened before. A mystical link for Picasso, who claimed Red Sea coffee opened his eyes to a deeper world. He envied Picasso's experience. When his own soul mumbled stuff like that to him, it never did speak clearly. It didn't matter—the task was impossible. Bright colors weren't part of death. Blacker than black was the whole story.

He sipped and turned to the scene again, watching as the bomb was slowly lifted a few feet out of the mucky soil. Next, the two-man crew tried to adjust the sling around the muddy nose. One man lost his grip on the webbing strap and fell into the thick slime. He shouted a curse while his partner laughed.

A light tap of knuckles on his hotel room door shifted Brandt's focus. "It's me, Tig."

Abrupt noises, even friendly ones, raised an alert. At six-four, Brandt needed to lean down to peek through the peephole and ensure he was only letting his new CIA bodyguard inside. Since the Haystack mission, the terror group Sword of Allah had been a continual threat. Bodyguard, side arm, safety phrases, and a Glock 26 on the nightstand were all part of his life now.

Brandt let him in, and Tig asked, "Ready for breakfast?"

Brandt pointed out the window to the disposal crew. "As soon as they haul that thing away."

"It's been defused, right?"

"Safe enough to sit on. Ummm, maybe not sit on."

Celebrities had their guards in black suits looking like gangsters, but not the CIA. Someone who needed a bodyguard meant someone important. Attention, limelight, and notoriety are hazardous for a spy. Tig had done his homework and mastered an unassuming appearance. Prissy styled Vuarnet sunglasses kept his gray eyes hidden while he scanned for threats. Never a suit; instead, a European leather jacket purposely too large for his sinewy frame to make him appear smaller, shoes that kept him three inches shorter than Brandt. The best part of the camouflage was the studious legal satchel holding extra weapons. Celebrity bodyguards never carried a briefcase.

Casey had been Brandt's first bodyguard, and now that they were a loving couple, she had checked Tig out for him. "He's good. Very good. File reads like a superhero. West Pointer. Ivy grad school. Ranger. Three tours with Delta Force in unfriendly places. Krav Maga savvy, so he's excellent in close. Better shot than me. He needs to improve his threat awareness, though. He missed a few things on the tapes. I told him forget the desert, threats are subtler here."

Brandt wondered why Tig had transferred to the CIA. "Bodyguard seems like a career-killing assignment for a West Pointer. Why the switch?"

Casey answered with a shrug, "Said he needed a change."

Brandt shared the binoculars with Tig, and they watched the crane swing the bomb toward the truck bed. The nose strap began to slip. They both held their breath while the crew rushed to adjust the webbing again.

Brandt noticed Tig had added a knotted Parisian floral scarf and a gold earring stud on his left ear that morning. "I like what you've done with your outfit. Is this a *GQ* day?"

The question brought a predictable shot of pain. A floral scarf and earring to a West Pointer was like waving a white flag. "Langley's idea. Ask them."

Tig's hair was long enough to cover the top of his ears; a chin beard and connecting mustache formed a bookish oval under a stubby nose. The scarf and gold stud finished an image that said: *I'm only a poet.* The bright colors drew eyes away from his one battle wound: the top of his left ear was missing a half inch from a Special Ops assignment in Libya. Brandt was still sizing up his new bodyguard. Trust came easy with Casey. Tig's would take time.

A crew member signaled the crane operator an okay and the bomb rose again. A crowd had formed to watch the procedure, as if waiting for a curtain to rise. Few, if any, of the spectators had been alive when the RAF dropped it on Frankfurt. A thousand-pounder would have taken out most of the block then. The projectile hovered above the flatbed for a moment while the operator shouted to a crew member for help centering the load. The delay caused the strap webbing around the muddy nose to slip again. The crowd, fearing a fatal demolition, turned and scattered. The strap completely lost its grip and swung loosely in the air, and the bomb's nose hit the trailer bed, splintering the wood. The tail followed with a metallic thud.

"That went well," Brandt mocked.

Tig handed the binoculars back to Brandt; his face resembled a big question mark.

"What?" Brandt said.

"Before we left London, Deke told me you were only a floater. I was shocked . . . hard to believe. I wanted to know how a CIA temp rated a bodyguard. He laughed, said to ask you."

"He likes to dodge the tough ones. Some people in Langley consider it favoritism. They accuse us of abusing our friendship."

"Are you?"

"More like self-abuse. Deke and I have known each other since we were both smoke jumpers in college. Casey and I have been together since the Haystack mission. Come to think of it, maybe they're right. We've always been pretty good at bending rules."

"Bullshit. I hear rumors all the time. The coffee shop talk in Langley says you've saved our ass more than once."

"Fake news. Starbucks is where truth goes to die."

"Deke also said you're an insufferable smartass."

"He's one to talk."

"But a floater? Casey is a trained field agent. Shouldn't you be one too?"

"Casey has to deal with the Langley bureaucracy. Because I'm a lowly floater, I only have to deal with her." Brandt briefly raised his eyes toward heaven in gratitude. "You're a combat vet. Geared for action. Medals for valor. Think of me next time you have to sit through a boring HR lecture."

"Yeah, those are scary stupid."

"Absolutely lethal. Total soul killers."

"The book says floaters are one-time mission add-ons . . . sort of movie extras. But you're, like, permanent." Tig wouldn't let it go. He had the perseverance of a beaver.

"Nothing in this world is permanent." Brandt read a text. "Grayson is coming to see us."

"Wonder what it's about?"

"First flight from London. That can't be good."

§

Despite the cool spring morning, Café Wilhelm's outdoor seating was nearly full. Germans were ready for winter to be over. Cherry blossom trees were no longer barren from the harsh winter but budding with hope. Sun filtered through the limbs of willows, turning clear glass into colorful prisms that danced shadows on the flagstone. Brandt snatched two *Frühstück* menus from the hostess stand, and Tig grabbed seats at a wrought iron café table next to a row of shrubs bordering the trees. A waitress in yoga pants and a thick wool sweater poured their coffee and took their orders. Brandt balanced a healthy cup of fruity low-fat yogurt with a buttery croissant and jam. Tig went big—a four-egg omelet with feta cheese and tomatoes and, on the side, pomegranate-avocado cream cheese and grainy whole-wheat brötchen.

"So it's a travel office search-and-destroy mission today?" Tig joked.

"We'll see what Grayson has to say, but that's the plan. Our first stop is Rhein Reisebüro. Some good friends there."

"And this is the director's idea?"

"One hundred percent. He likes my tour guide cover. Thinks he can use it in travel offices all over Europe."

"Will it work?"

"In Germany? Not a chance."

"So what will you do?"

"See if any of my old guide friends are still around. Have a cappuccino, chat 'em up. Drink some beer over lunch maybe. Then I'll pass on that none of them are interested in a new American partner. That should kill it."

Tig nodded, sipped his coffee, and said, "You're my first assignment. I need this to go well. Anything waiting for you out there I should know about?"

Brandt's eyebrows squeezed in surprise over the question. "The crazy Bosniaks. You know about them, don't you?"

"Yeah, yeah . . . Sword of Allah. I got them covered."

"Remember, they're Islamic but still European. They don't look like they're fresh out of the desert."

"I got it. No problem. Here comes Grayson."

Brandt turned his head and watched him approach. Grayson was on Deke's Langley team during Haystack. He had the natural ability to hide in plain sight: a mediocre five-ten height, an indistinct everyman's walk, common hazel eyes, and a brown hairstyle found in church choirs . Grayson was a newly promoted field supervisor under Deke, recently assigned to London Station after a tour in Riyadh. The Saudi job made looking average easier for him; too much time in a desk chair had turned him sluggish and heavy, and his once-beefy shoulders now showed a puffy loss in muscle tone. Brandt had confidence in him. Grayson had impressed him with his intelligence, judgment, and skill in Haystack. Brandt would never forget Grayson handing him the L-pill postage stamp. *"Lick the back of Lincoln to get the cyanide."* It didn't sound any better now than it had then. When it came to postage, peel off/stick on was the way to go. Since this was probably Grayson's first mission as a field supervisor, Brandt imagined Deke would break him in on a simple one. Most likely low on the danger, high on the monotony scale.

"I'm impressed you found us," Brandt said.

Grayson slid a chair next to their table and nodded toward Tig. "The beauty of microchips."

"I thought that stuff was for movies," Brandt said.

"Not since they created a nano version."

Tig pointed to his side, under his left arm, and made a tortured face. "Nano, hell. It feels like a rock in there."

"Yeah, well, floaters don't get chipped," Brandt said. The aroma of a mixed plate of Bavarian sausages at the next table reached him, and he eyed them with lust. A jerky breeze rose up, sending loose paper napkins fluttering to the ground while staff chased after them.

"I don't need help, so you're here to check up on Tig's first assignment? He can be a pain in the ass, but take it easy on him. He turns thirty-one on Friday."

"Tig gets a pass. There's a plane in Wiesbaden waiting to take us to Brussels," Grayson said. "Not sure what it's all about."

"NATO, huh? Deke won't like it."

"Naw, he suggested you. Said it's right up your alley. He's there now."

"Now I'm really concerned. Erding?"

"Dead. Rudolf Sturm is his replacement. Officially it was a heart attack. But the NATO cafeteria food has been known to kill."

Tig turned his gaze back from watching two men enter the café. "Explains the short lines."

"Casey too?" Brandt said.

"There's more, but no Deke and Casey. Deke has her in Finland and is putting me in charge of this one."

The waitress brought their food, and Grayson ordered café au lait. Locals began to pick up briefcases, grab newspapers, and leave for jobs. On the other side of the tree line, a group of preschoolers and teachers marched on the sidewalk in single-file silence. Brandt wondered how the teachers arranged the stoic peace. In America, he would expect screeching, yelling, and laughter. Kids poking other kids, trouble on the horizon. The somber walk made him feel a bit sad for the little *kinder*.

"Can you tell us anything?" Tig asked.

"Find out when we get there. That's all Deke said."

Brandt slumped in his chair, suspicious of the change. Without Deke and Casey, he felt like both arms were missing. They had always been part of his missions. *Real* missions—not hunts for office space.

Whatever Brussels had in mind would have to be something he could agree to. Floaters could say no, and he wondered if he should refuse. Deke had pulled him into the CIA to help with the Haystack mission. At the time, he was a reluctant volunteer. When it was over, he found he missed the clear sense of purpose the mission had given him. The good-versus-evil thing can be like a drug, tempting some to puff up their chest and wave the flag. Living together in London with Casey was a bonus, and there was something about England that made his paintings take a huge leap. New techniques and materials were only part of it. He'd found a place inside himself that guided his brush with authority and spared him the curse of English art—the dreary landscapes and fox hunt oils found in the museums. Assignments like this surprise trip to NATO were beginning to crimp his psyche. The CIA meant duty, mission, and personal satisfaction. Art meant delight and creative fulfillment. Maybe it was time to pick one.

2

Grayson left for the airport while Brandt and Tig walked back to the hotel to check out. As they neared the Euro Tower plaza, a familiar face brought Brandt's caution a notch higher. Aaron was a diminutive Mossad agent no more than five-seven, but trouble came with him like a pack of street dogs.

Brandt pulled Tig into the doorway of a stationery store. "Wait here. I think something's going down."

"What's up?"

"Looks like GSG 9 is on to something. Those two guys that got out of that big-ass green van. One of them is Aaron, the Mossad chief here. Don't know the other one. If he's with Aaron, he's part of the German anti-terror force."

"What do we do?"

"Nothing. Just watch."

More men exited the vehicle one after another like clowns from a circus car, only these men carried Heckler submachine guns. Polizei cars appeared at both ends of the street and blocked traffic. Officers began herding people inside and away from the scene. A uniformed officer approached their doorway.

Tig pulled out his NATO identification and flashed his Glock. "We're part of this."

The officer moved on.

Brandt and Tig extracted their Glocks and turned the safeties off.

The men from the van took up positions facing a three-story building across the street. Gunfire erupted from the first floor. A group of men exited the building, firing at the van. The GSG 9 force returned fire. One man ran out a side doorway, dodging bullets as he snaked his way toward the van. When he was steps away, he set off the explosives strapped to his chest. Glass shattered and rained on the street, the van rose slightly and shook, loose debris flew like shrapnel. The display window for the stationery store fractured and collapsed. The blast momentarily halted gunfire, and bodies lay on both sides of the street. Three men rushed out of an adjacent building, obscured in the smoke and shielded by female hostages. They slanted across the street toward a parking garage next to the stationery store.

Brandt and Tig had the best angle on them. Tig waited for a clear shot and dropped two with his Glock, leaving the hostages safe. Brandt didn't think he could have pulled off a shot like that. The third man and his hostage were steps away from the safety of the garage when Brandt raced out of the doorway and, like a linebacker, knocked him hard to the asphalt with his shoulder. The hostage stumbled away, then fell to her hands and knees. Brandt regained his balance while the man searched for his pistol and tried to get up. Brandt gave him a kick to the head that flattened him. The man tried to rise again, and Brandt whipped his Glock across his head, knocking him flat. He watched to be sure the man stayed down and then helped the hostage into the garage. Tig had picked up the man's loose pistol and was waiting there for Brandt with the other two hostages.

The explosion took the energy out of the battle, leaving sporadic gunfire that killed the rest of the terrorists. Brandt and Tig kept the hostages safe in the garage until the ambulances arrived, signaling the fighting had stopped.

The hostage Brandt had rescued went from silent shock to tears. In between sobs, she repeated, "*Danke. Danke. Vielen danke.*"

Aaron and the GSG 9 officer brought paramedics into the garage for the hostages. "Brandt Swindon! I thought that might be you. Nice work," Aaron said. "Who's the expert shot?"

"That's my new sidekick, Tig. Moving targets don't faze him. Learned to shoot ducks in a carnival booth."

"That's only partially true," Tig said.

"Whatever. Head shots. Impressive. Some great shooting."

The GSG 9 officer took the hostages' information while paramedics wrapped them in blankets to keep them warm and gave them a choice of water or peppermint schnapps. Except for some scrapes from the pavement, they were unharmed.

"Can you tell us what all this was about?" Brandt asked.

"Pretty straightforward. I've been keeping an eye on this cell for months. Houthis and Syrians. Iran is doing the funding. They were planning an assault and takeover of the Euro Tower today. I alerted GSG 9 and they took it from there."

"Casualties?"

"Five wounded GSG 9. Only one looks serious. Nine bad guy KIAs including the bomber."

The officer had finished with the hostages. "The women are most grateful for your rescue, and so is the Republic. This could have been much worse."

"Right place at the right time," Brandt said. "Unusual for me."

"I'll need you to come to headquarters for the report. My men will drive you."

Tig stepped up and flashed his ID again. "Sorry, we have a plane to Brussels to catch."

Aaron looked at the officer. "Save yourself a lot of trouble. Thank them for their help and let them leave."

3

Brandt had two impressions of Brussels. In time, they became visions he could reproduce whenever he chose. The first picture had modern European Union and NATO headquarters buildings filled with bureaucrats in shabby shoes and ugly neckties. Soulless and depressing. The preferred version was La Vieille Ville (Old Town) with epicurean bakeries, famous Belgian fries, and spring floral baskets. Postcard quaint and colorful. He tried his best to ignore the petty tourist crime in Park Royale.

Deke met them at Brussels' Chièvres Air Base. As the CIA European deputy director, he was there to balance the power structure and make sure NATO played by the rules. Tig, Brandt, and Grayson crammed into the second-row seat of a white NATO Yukon SUV for the twenty-five-minute drive to the meeting. From the front passenger seat, Deke turned to face them. "You'll meet with Sturm today. He's a tweedy, mawkish sort of guy, enamored with the Brits. Doesn't like us much. Refers to us as 'the cowboys' when we're not around. He'll give you the mission outline. Tomorrow, you meet the Russians."

Brandt and Grayson looked at each other in silence. Tig squeezed his lips and lifted his eyebrows.

"Russians, huh?" said Brandt. "Is this a Putin attempt to make nice?"

"Or get some agents inside NATO?" Tig said.

"He's got too many in there now. Moscow Center is looking at a cutback. Keeping them here is expensive. Langley and Vauxhall are looking at agent costs too. Robots and algorithms get all the funding. As far as Putin, I don't think he knows the meaning of nice."

"Then what?" Grayson said.

"It's about nukes. That's why I got Brandt involved."

"Theirs or ours?" Brandt said.

"Theirs . . . sort of."

"Nice to have that cleared up."

Sturm's office was in the underground Intelligence and Security section of the new NATO headquarters building. After a security and ID check, an aide brought them into the conference room connected to Sturm's office. The room had a musty, moldy odor thanks to recent heavy rain and the Senne River flooding. Energy bars, apples, and water bottles sat on a side table. Concrete walls and a lack of windows suggested a castle crypt. Flat-screen TVs used for intelligence work doubled as an attempt to offset the dreariness. Gone were the old-style photographs of tanks and fighters, replaced with scrolling screen mockups of laser armaments and hypersonic weapons in development.

Sturm entered, followed by his aide carrying a large file box. Sturm was a few inches taller than a floor lamp, gaunt, with a pencil-thin face and jutting jaw that reminded Brandt of a Great Lakes pickerel. He wore a disheveled herringbone coat and heavily wrinkled slacks as if believing no one would notice. He removed a briar pipe from his lips, forced a lethargic smile, and muttered a feeble, "Good morning. Hope your flight went well." He paused to spread a sheet of notes on the table. "Let me begin with how this started. In 1997, Dr. Alexie Yablokov, science advisor to President Yeltsin, testified to your congress about the existence of Soviet Special Atomic Demolition Munitions. SADMs or portable one-man atomic bombs, if you will. He received the information from officials of the Twelfth Directive responsible for overseeing the Russian nuclear program."

"Yablokov? Is he still around?" Deke asked.

"Died in '17. We think natural causes."

"Polonium is natural. Lethal too. Moscow uses it to fix people problems," Grayson said.

"Yablokov testified that of the one hundred and thirty-two SADMs reported to have been manufactured, only forty-seven had been recovered. If he was right, that leaves over eighty of Moscow's nuclear weapons unaccounted for. We have information now that the weapons never left their former East European allies."

"So the Russians left them sitting around old porches like broken refrigerators," Deke said.

Sturm puffed up and made a crooked sitcom face, giving the impression of someone who preferred to be at work, where he was important; at home, the dachshund outranked him. "After the testimony, there was talk about looking for them, but with Russia in chaos, nothing happened. It stayed that way until Lena Averin, a Russian physicist, left the Twelfth Directive as part of an exchange with your Atomic Energy Commission. She raised the issue again and supplied evidence that Yablokov was right, not just blowing Cold War smoke."

"The Russian army is responsible for safeguarding the nukes. What do they say?" Grayson asked.

"Very little. While it's true the GRU is responsible for their atomic weapons, they insist some never came under their control. The SADMs were a KGB design. Something they could smuggle into a major city or installation in the West."

"In a suitcase?" Tig asked.

"No, not really. Suitcase bombs are journalist folklore. They are more like backpack bombs, weighing anywhere from twenty-five to thirty kilos. They still pack a punch. One kiloton is certain. Yablokov said some larger ones were produced for a full three kts. The problem is, no one knows what happened to them. Including Moscow."

"Don't worry about them," Brandt said. "Backpack or suitcase, after more than twenty years those things are useless as a weapon. They need tritium to make them go boom, and tritium degrades faster than a political promise. Forget about those things."

Sturm turned to his aide. "*Ich wünsche.*"

"What was that? I didn't get it," Deke said.

Brandt was quick. "He said, 'I wish.'" His tone challenged Sturm. "Explain the urgency, *bitte.*"

"I apologize. We didn't make this up or discover the problem. Until recently, Moscow denied their existence, insisting Yablokov was bribed to lie to Congress and it was more Western propaganda. Lena Averin made a difference."

"What changed?" Brandt asked.

"Couple of things. Averin brought old files from the Twelfth Directive with her to the US. She pored over and analyzed the data and concluded one of the SADMs was hidden in a Benedictine monastery in Poland and informed the Pentagon. When they searched, they found it in an abandoned root cellar, hidden underneath hemp mats. You're correct about the tritium. Only Averin is afraid the tritium has been replaced, possibly in all those unaccounted for. The Twelfth Directive did an inventory of their tritium stockpile when one of the nuclear plants producing it had to be shut down. It showed a rather large unexplained shortage."

Brandt thought, *No surprise.* Everything got pilfered, stolen, or miscounted in Russia. Maybe some warehouse employee thought he could sell it to farmers for their tractors.

Sturm continued, "Here's what panicked Moscow. Igor Petrov was the KGB colonel in charge of the SADM project, a physicist and a superpatriot who wanted to destroy the West. He constructed the weapon based on a stolen design of the American version. He died in 2002, but he had a son." Sturm passed around a folder with photos. "I'm sorry about the picture quality, but it's all we have. Ilya was part of the Twelfth Directive after finishing university and disappeared the same day the tritium inventory was completed. According to Lena, he bought a new car, cut his hair, shaved his beard, called in sick, and took off. It's not difficult to see why Moscow and the Pentagon are worried. If he's responsible for the tritium losses, there's a good chance his father taught him everything about the SADMs, including who has them and where they are."

"What about terrorists?" Tig said.

"The Chechens and Palestinians claimed to have grabbed a couple when the Russians took their missiles home, but it's been twenty years so we discount that. If they get wind of missing Russian SADMs out there now, they could become a problem."

"So what are we supposed to do?" Brandt said.

"Help the Russians find them."

4

Deke and Brandt waited on the headquarters steps while Tig went for the car. Deke had stopped doing triathlons since being posted to London but managed frequent visits to the embassy gym. Building muscle replaced his endurance obsession. Barbell presses and ab crunches, he joked, would grow his hair back. No such luck. The horseshoe of wispy strands that circled his dome got thinner, but his shoulders expanded.

"Sturm reserved rooms for us at the Rocco Forte Hotel Amigo," Deke said.

"Best hotel in Brussels. Doesn't sound like NATO."

"He's aware of your travel connections and wants to be sure you're happy. The Russians are at the Hilton."

"How many?" Brandt asked.

"Not sure. Sturm had the good sense to keep Averin separate. She's at the Rocco with us."

Tig pulled up with the car and they climbed in the back.

"Casey told me the Nottingham show went well," Deke said.

"Very well. Sold a lot of paintings. I hated to miss it. The London gallery brought everything on hand for the show, even stuff I thought was garbage. Some of that sold too. I think they must have got the patrons liquored up."

"How does it feel to be a success in the art world?"

"Like a fraud—I still can't draw. Casey said to donate the money. then I'd feel better."

After checking in, Brandt unpacked, then called Casey but was sent to voicemail. He wondered if her mission was solo or a team effort. There was no sense asking Deke. That was like rubbing a magic lamp and hearing the genie say, "Fuck off." He'd throw "You don't have a *need to know*" at him. It didn't matter what Casey was doing. She could be counting the steps in front of the Russian embassy. Deke would be difficult with Brandt just for the fun of it. They had played mind games, practical jokes, and one-upmanship since they first met in college. Haystack had given Brandt a big lead.

He was checking emails when Deke called. "Meet me in the lobby in ten minutes. We're going for a little walk."

§

Tig provided security in his poet outfit as they started up rue des Brasseurs, then turned left on rue Duquesnoy, passing shopkeepers tending their sidewalk displays. The choice outdoor tables at popular cafés were already taken—prized spots for espresso, Italian spritzers, and Belgian beer. Deke brought them to a curved stone bench in Square de la Putterie. Tig leaned against a wall across the square, under the famous grand white mulberry tree where he could cut off an attack from either direction.

"Hotel rooms bugged?" Brandt asked.

Deke opened up a newspaper and spread the pages across his face. "In Brussels, between NATO, the Russians, Chinese, and the EU, it's impossible to find one that isn't. When we sweep, we find ours all the time." He pulled out a section from the paper and handed it to Brandt. "Read this while we talk. There's more Chinese lip readers here than hookers."

Brandt hid behind the newsprint. "My French is shaky, but according to this, Macron's approval numbers in Paris are in single digits."

"The EU is shaky."

"We're all shaky these days."

"It could get worse."

"I'm listening."

"Tomorrow you meet your travel companions. Major Dimitri Mokolov, aka Moky, Moscow claims is part of military intelligence in charge of all the Russian nukes. Karyi is the driver. Gleb is the muscle. KGB, FSB, SVR . . . he's been in all of them."

"Hell's Angels?"

"He'd be tossed out for cruelty. Sturm is sending a car for Averin. She was quick to agree to help us find the rest."

"So we've got some superspy watching us and an egghead Russian scientist. You sure Netflix isn't here with cameras?"

Deke's head sagged. "Get serious. These are Russians. Everyone watches everyone. Especially Lena. She's something else . . . centerfold qualified. But don't let that fool you. She has a Mensa card."

"Does she know where they are?"

"Just where to look. The KGB destroyed all the GRU reports, but she got a hold of interesting Twelfth Directorate files and cross-checked them against Petrov's solo visits to the satellite countries and KGB intelligence reports."

"Where do we start?"

"She's being cagey about that. She's got Soviet street smarts. Keeps it all in her head. Doesn't trust the Kremlin."

"Hardly unique." Brandt was certain the Russian word for trust was *nev'r*.

"She's afraid they'll jump ahead and grab them before we get there. She let Sturm know Prague is first. We suspect she knows more than she's telling. She and Petrov had an intimate relationship when they worked together."

"Prague, huh? Hope this is more than a lover's spat."

"Putin wants a do-over. Insists they belong to Russia and need to be returned. Langley thinks he wants us to help find them, but once they're in Russian hands, he'll turn around and hide them across Europe. Nothing like having a bunch of small nukes to stick inside NATO."

"Nuclear Trojan horses, huh?"

"Yeah, the Greeks only needed one."

"What about the locals?"

"We're not sure how the new governments will respond if they find out Soviet nukes are there, so it's locked up tight. Top Secret, SCI level required, and NATO Cosmic. Of course, when it comes to secrets, NATO has a weak bladder . . . everything leaks. So be ready. Warsaw believes the one found in the monastery was only a training device."

Brandt let the newspaper droop. "So now the Russians are our friends, but our real allies are kept in the dark. Machiavelli would be proud."

"It's why this is covert. Clandestine with a capital C. If you find them, the weapons will be moved in commercial trucks. DHL, FedEx, something like that. Not even a hint of military being involved. We can't risk a finders-keepers diplomatic blowup with our new East Europe allies over these weapons. If they discover we snuck nukes out without informing them, it won't be pretty. Liable to cost some important people their jobs. So don't get caught."

"Wouldn't it be simpler to find them ourselves with Lena's help and destroy them? The Russians have enough nukes."

"When the Russians pulled out of East Europe, we agreed they could take all the nuclear weapons with them. They're holding us to that."

"And Petrov?"

"We *all* want him. He's the pucker factor."

A black-winged bird hopping along the ground caught their attention. Its head bobbed like a doll. The bird picked up a piece of tinfoil, then exchanged it for a white plastic tab before flying off to its nest.

Brandt said, "I'm looking for the high moral ground in this. Where is it?"

Deke smirked and wagged his head. "I didn't say this would be easy. You know the drill. Washington, Moscow, and Brussels will be watching closely. Failure could be unpleasant. You don't want to be part of any fallout. Floaters make excellent scapegoats."

"I'm not sure I even want to be part of this. I have second thoughts about this whole CIA thing anyway." There were days he didn't want the brush to leave his hand, his CIA role something in the background. He wondered if his hesitancy was the result of the commercial success he was beginning to enjoy or the gnomes, fates, and tricksters again. They found a home with him and were always throwing questions at him, hoping to force a wrong turn.

"That's just fucking great," Deke said. "Now that the director broke the rules and paid to send a floater to London so he could be with his new love, you decide to be an asshole."

He wondered if Deke was right, but *asshole* did seem a bit harsh. "Look, you were born to do this," said Brandt. "It's in your DNA. My whole CIA career has been two missions. I'm just asking the standard 'is this the right path for me now' question."

"Maybe it's a clinically depressed widower travel agent. You were good at that."

"Now *you're* the asshole."

"You're right. I'm sorry I said that. But it's a hell of a time for the 'who am I, where do I belong' bullshit. Talk to your sister. She makes her living treating the troubled and confused."

Brandt held his tongue. His therapist sister had told him the CIA and art questions were only a symptom of a deeper issue that would be there waiting for him. She was always telling him he had "deep issues," but he wondered if she was right this time. He felt like a carrier pigeon lost in the clouds. He sighed in a huff. "Does Grayson know all this?"

"He's in Sturm's office going over the reports and files now. The old Soviet satellite countries know me too well. Grayson is an unknown, so he's the right guy for this mission and so are you. You're just a travel guide."

A tough mission, Brandt thought. *Like eating liver. Raw liver.*

Deke stood to leave. "And I thought Tig was the one with a problem."

That caught Brandt by surprise. "What's with Tig?"

"We should move before the dealers and hookers show up."

They left the open square and made a short walk to the Mont des Arts, a long park of short hedges, tall conifers, and bushy lilacs. A whiff of jasmine floated out of a flower shop. A clerk in a bow tie handed passing women white narcissus in an attempt to coax them inside. Traffic noise rose with rush hour.

Deke glanced behind to see if Tig was in earshot. "Tig . . . there's issues with him. The director assigned him to you as a favor to some White House big shot. He's in a bad place now, kind of lost his way. We thought working with you could give him a lift. An easy mission checking out those travel offices. Drinking beer with you and your old travel buddies might do the trick."

Brandt's voice rose two levels. "And you didn't feel it important enough to tell me my bodyguard was a Section Eight? Does Casey know this?"

"His file's been scrubbed and this SADM thing with NATO just came up. I was waiting to get you both together to fill you in."

"What's his problem?"

"Tig was leading a Delta Team supporting a Kurd unit near Al-Bab. According to the French advisor, Tig lost his nerve. The Kurds got smoked. Tig got the blame."

"Is it true, or the usual Paris bullshit?" The French version of battlefield events was no better than a glossy press release. Always a courageous image—accuracy and truth were just another casualty.

"His team said he did the right thing. The mission was hopeless. Poorly planned, shaky force estimates. The Kurds waltzed into an end-of-life trap thanks to the French guy. But Tig took it personally. His wife filed for divorce after he came home a train wreck."

"So I'm supposed to be his shrink?"

"Well, get your sister to fix both of you."

"I dunno. If this mission is so important, why have Tig?"

"He's got the skills and training, he's battle tested. We're just not sure how he'll react now if something goes south."

"Maybe I don't care anymore. My reviews say I'm a hot artist now." He almost choked on "hot artist." It was like believing he could fly with the pigs.

"I know better. Give Tig a try. If you see a problem, I'll look for someone else."

"Get a list ready. I had the impression Sword of Allah slipped his mind. I'm not gonna give him any rope."

Streetlights came on with a cottony effect on twilight, and the dipping sun left an alpine glow on the tips of office buildings. They walked back toward the hotel in a heavy silence. Smiling Belgians walked along carrying groceries to their homes. Guest workers from Turkey hurried home to relax with their hookahs. The iconic tiny European neighborhood tapas bars where people stood to drink were crowded two deep.

Tig stopped them in the lobby. "Never seen this before. You guys must be very popular. You had two teams on your ass. A really good European team, three men and two women. Different ages. Pros all the way. Used the Dutch box technique with a woman carrying an H&M bag as the lead stalker. The three kung fu guys weren't as good. The Chinese just don't get human surveillance. They might as well have a sign saying 'spy' on their back."

Brandt wasn't surprised. Beijing had been emboldened by their success in electronic espionage and felt it only natural that human intel would follow. Ian Fleming books were as mandatory as tai chi for MSS agents. For every ten students admitted to the Ivys, Duke, or Stanford, six had gone through the first stage of spy training. Fraternities, sororities, casual sex, booze, recreational drugs, and Wall Street jobs became a problem. No one defected. They were just absorbed in American culture and stopped reporting. Forget the Silk Road, Ming Dynasty, and Confucius—craft beer brought enlightenment.

5

Sturm and the Russians were standing by the refreshments, drinking coffee and chatting in the basement intelligence center before the meeting started. The previous day's snacks had been replaced with international pastries in glass-topped cake stands: Belgian craquelin brioche, Danish kanelbulle, Lisbon tarts, Italian pasticciotto, and American cornbread. Brandt scanned the offerings, then touched his squishy middle and turned away.

After introductions, Lena Averin smiled and walked up to Brandt. "In those jeans and black turtleneck, you remind me of Steve Jobs. I met him at a Zurich conference. An interesting man."

"I liked his style, simple and effective. Eliminates wardrobe worry," replied Brandt. "Unfortunately, I'm dumber and a lot poorer."

"But you're taller. And your blue eyes sparkle more than his brown."

"Wouldn't know. Steve and I never met."

Her smile turned sultry. "The curl around your ears is engaging. Very tempting to women."

Lena was becoming scary. "So I've been told."

Her hair was a statement. Forget the PhD. A playful look for a professor, a deep red French ombre that gave way to blonde ends styled in a twisted, tangled, layered look. She favored black jeans with expensive labels that could have been specially tailored for her Playmate curves. A classic white shirt with corset-style lacing at the waist emphasized her bust. Metallic silver high-fashion sneakers bred in Paris. A short Versace scarf tied close to her neck that matched her gray-blue eyes finished the look—edgy, sexy, like a supermodel who could explain quantum theory.

"I like turtlenecks on men. It's a virile, confident look." Her tongue slid along her lower lip.

"It's all I wear. My sister says I'm compensating for a long list of inadequacies."

"I bet you drive a Porsche."

"Uber mostly. But there's a ten-year-old Saab that balks at starting and a Land Rover the agency loans me for missions."

Moky spoke up. "Anti-Russian missions, I believe."

While Brandt's tone carried the bass of a TV news anchor, Moky's voice was the high side of midrange, harsh, brassy, harpy-like. He tried to hide a scowl that was building under a forced smile over Lena's flirting. "Moscow graciously allowed NATO to bring you in to be our guide and cover."

"And to help us with the locks," Lena said.

Brandt tried to hold back his surprise. *Locks on nukes again?* Neither Deke nor Grayson had mentioned that his training and experience would be needed. Locks on nuclear weapons were what got him dragged into the CIA initially. Keeping the nuclear arsenal safe from jihadists, anarchists, and nutjobs who believed a few mushroom clouds could fix everything was his Army job. He left that all behind when he and Anne moved to the Bay Area and opened the travel business. After Anne's death, Deke had convinced him to be the bait to locate a missing warhead with the lock still on. The Bosniaks who had the weapon never forgave him for destroying their plan and were still out for revenge.

Deke shifted his weight as if standing at attention. "Brandt solves two problems. We need an expert travel guide to keep the locals from asking questions . . . one who can be discreet and who knows the devices. He might be a little rusty with locks, but he'll get the job done."

Lena's head wobbled approval. "I'm sure he will."

Lena had an earthiness that gave her intelligence a stylized, sensual quality. Brandt could imagine her starting a party in a garden shed or attending a Lincoln Center gala, but he wasn't so confident about the locks. The twenty-plus years that had passed convinced him if they needed his help with a lock, they were in trouble. He had forgotten what a SADM lock even looked like.

As everyone sat down, Deke asked Moky, "Major, how did all this happen?"

Moky attempted to minimize the dilemma. "Moscow considers it an inventory problem. Thankfully, Lena has the information to correct it. Originally, they stored them from Estonia to the Ukraine. With perestroika, a few anti-reform KGB sensed the end coming and began gathering them up." He paused as if uncertain how much to divulge, then turned toward Gleb, who pretended not to notice. "Those that were not returned to Russia, we believe were hidden by these criminals among our satellite friends."

Brandt thought Gleb was the one to worry about. Russia dominated Olympic wrestling, and Gleb looked part of the team. He had a barrel chest, and his shoulder muscles made his neck disappear. His murky gray eyes were like a cobra's, ominous from birth. He soaked up every word as if prying into the team's private thoughts like a determined shrink. He had yet to utter a word, satisfied to let Moky grapple with the Americans.

"What's with the locks?" Brandt said.

Lena did an about-face. The playgirl professor was gone. Mensa scientist took her place. "We need to know if these weapons have been compromised and are capable of detonation. I have an instrument to measure the tritium level, so we'll learn if it's been replaced. The locks need to come off for the gauge to work. If it's been refreshed, then Petrov has been able to remove the locks and rearm the weapons. I'm sure you understand what that could mean."

Brandt did. Small, armed backpack nukes in the hands of the son of a KGB superpatriot could disturb sleep world leaders' sleep for a long time. The urgency of the Russians that led them to ask for help made sense.

"Since the locks are copies of the ones your Army uses, new security will have to be installed for transport back to Russia," Moky said.

There was something peculiar in his face that Brandt couldn't identify.

Gleb bent down and lifted a box. The dark stubble on his unshaven face spread across the top of his plain head like a burr. He extracted a three-inch-long cylinder with a combination dial at one end. "These are the replacements,"

The man can speak, thought Brandt. If pit bulls could talk, they would sound like Gleb. "You have the combination for the old locks, right?"

Moky shifted his eyes away. "Moscow is working on that."

Brandt reached toward the cylinder. "May I?"

"Of course."

The SADM locks began to come back to him. The replacement lock in his hand was bigger than he remembered. He twisted the dial, testing its specificity, looking for clear, obvious clicks on numbers. It was like a spinning wheel, no obvious clicks making it very difficult to pick. He looked for the small slot where a lockpick tool might be inserted but failed to find one. The Russians weren't taking any chances with the new locks. Without the combination, no lockpicking, no entry.

"What about Petrov?" Deke asked. "Have you found him?"

"We believe he's still here in Europe," Moky said.

Tig looked around the table. "I dunno. We look like a bunch of spies complete with a decoy."

"Don't worry about that. There'll be one more on the team tomorrow," Sturm said. "He'll make a difference."

§

Midmorning, they walked out to a landscaped courtyard to escape the dismal confinement of the basement for some sunlight. A coffee bar allowed access from a patio. NATO staff personnel sat on benches underneath Japanese maple and kousa dogwoods. Moky lit a cigarette.

Lena grabbed Brandt by the arm and pulled him out of range of the others, the flourish to her walk seductive, her face evasive. In a nightclub, she could pass for an arousing twenty-six; in a physics lab, a white-coated professor of thirty-nine. She handed him a lighter for her cigarette. Unlike creamy-skinned Russian women, Lena was tan, beach tan, typical of oligarch wives and mistresses. Brandt lit her cigarette and watched her exhale toward a budding maple, then smile.

"Please forgive my flirtation. I don't mean to be taken serious. Moky and I have an unfortunate history. I don't want him thinking it can be renewed. I thought if I showed an interest in you, he would realize he has no place in my life. I'm afraid I went too far. Please forgive me."

"So I'm not virile and confident?"

"Of course you are, but I haven't slept with you, and I made the mistake of sleeping with him when I was young and foolish."

"I'll bet vodka was involved."

"Sober would not have been possible."

"Not a great start for a collaborative mission."

Lena shrugged. "We're Russians. We do things differently."

"That's what the French say."

"Your man Tig, is he military?"

"Something like that."

"I don't think he and Gleb will get along."

A buzzer sounded, and office staff lined up at the doors to return to their cell-like cubicles—proof that Pavlov was on to something. Moky kept glancing toward Lena as she smoked and talked with Brandt. Finally, he stuffed his cigarette in a container, glared at Brandt with brutish insecurity, and stomped back inside. Brandt noticed the parts of Moky's face that caught his attention earlier. Along with a stout chin at the end of a firm jaw and a forehead that sloped like a ramp, Moky had an eye bulging out of a smaller socket, making it look oversized, like the eye on a Muppet.

The discussion resumed with a roadblock, a big one for NATO. Moky wanted to bring in Russian trucks as soon as the weapons were found, without waiting for the civilian-disguised NATO escort. "Since they belonged to the Russian people, they should be under Russian control," he argued. Grayson refused. The bickering continued through a working lunch of baguette sandwiches and puff pastries.

Brandt let his attention drift through lunch while they argued. He saw the squabble from a different angle, like two kids with hickory sticks banging at a piñata to see who would be first to the prizes. How would two countries who were satisfied to be in constant conflict come together for a common goal with nuclear weapons at stake? An unnatural coupling of interests, like one of his sister's therapy groups. Gleb and Tig were warriors, too much alike to put competition aside. Grayson and Moky would be good at pretending to cooperate. When trouble with one of the host nations arose, a test would come. Lena . . . well, Lena was Lena. Too intelligent to be called free spirited, with a vein flowing with indifference and a frivolous past she was trying to leave behind. He had the sense that politics bored her. She was both above it and below it. A complicated woman. Yet he grasped something below the surface driving her. NATO credited her vigilance for discovering the threat. What had made her keep digging until she put it all together? Whatever it was brought Lena to a different level.

About his place on the team, he wasn't certain. Babysitter, tour guide, and go-fer. Water boy seemed to fit best.

By late afternoon, Deke had had enough. Back-and-forth, ping-pong arguments that went nowhere were for political talk shows. He broke the logjam by threatening to pull out of the mission and let the host countries know there were Russian nukes inside their borders.

"I see," Moky said with a smile cold enough to form ice. "If that's the way it has to be, let us proceed."

A cooling-off period was in order.

"It's late. We can pick up again in the morning," Sturm said.

"I've had enough of this basement dungeon," Lena said. "Let's find a café or bar."

Grayson stood. "I know a place."

The black Audi behind them was unnoticed all the way there.

6

The Dupont Café was a short drive from NATO. A large green awning slanted down to a lattice frame attached to a row of wood planters filled with tall, cone-shaped evergreen thujas. A well-designed barrier protected outdoor picnic tables from glaring pedestrians and noisy traffic. The inside was old and worn without being rustic or charming: cabinet facing that had lost luster and color, chairs that wobbled if someone passed by, dreary faded tile the color of old mustard. Patrons believed what it lacked in charm was offset by Ingrid's theatrical talent. She brought in customers as if she were a Vegas lounge act. Slow with your drink order, she became an insulting Don Rickles. Compliment the food, she became Top Chef. Complain about service, you met Hannibal Lecter.

Inside, the Americans and Russians sat on opposite benches at a picnic table. The top was scarred, carved, and chiseled with names and vulgar sexual references. Deep scorch marks from a blowtorch obscured swastikas. A complex Thelonious Monk piano set played in the background.

Ingrid came to take their order. "The Russians are having cheap vodka. What about the rest of you?"

Deke said, "Scotch. Ardbeg if you have it."

"Ardbeg, eh? A man with taste. I think from you I need cash up front." Her face became a sour-faced emoji. Her voice had a scratchy fine-whiskey-and-bootleg-cigarette edge to it. "You remind me of my ex-husband. Twelve euros, please."

"Smart," Brandt said. "He has that effect on people."

Ingrid shifted her aim. "You're one to talk. Lose the turtleneck. Steve Jobs you're not."

Grayson ordered a beer, then looked across at the Russians. "I have something for each of you in the car. I'll be right back."

Grayson smiled at Ingrid, who gave him a quizzical look, then went out to the Yukon parked in front of the café. He opened the passenger door behind the driver's seat. An Audi that sped out of nowhere clipped the edge of the door, slamming it into his left shoulder and legs like a hammer. His head banged against the roof while his legs were smashed against the undercarriage panel. He slid down and spread out on the street, bleeding from his forehead and only semiconscious. Two cartons of Marlboro cigarettes lay scattered around him. Three NATO troops in camouflage uniforms, exiting a bar across the street, rushed over to help him. One soldier called for an ambulance.

Ingrid walked to their table. "Something just happened outside. Maybe one of you should go check on your friend."

§

The ambulance pulled away with the CIA team following in a replacement Yukon, headed for the Army hospital with Grayson alive but in bad shape. Brandt guessed mangled shoulders, concussion, and shattered legs. Grayson was in for a long recovery. They needed a backup.

From the back seat, Brandt tapped Deke on the shoulder. "Is this an omen or a sign?"

"That would be superstitious. I'm assuming it's an accident. Drunk driver, something like that. The two soldiers saw the car speed off . . . black Audi."

"Will this delay the mission, or do we go short handed?" Tig said.

"No, the Russians would get too pushy. I'll have to bring someone in to replace Grayson."

"Anyone in mind?" Brandt asked.

"I know what you're thinking."

"Why not? Casey would be perfect. You know we work together well."

"Well, despite having little to work with, she does bring out the best in you."

"Another woman would improve our cover," Tig said. "Better visuals with two women."

Brandt sensed an opening. "It's either Casey or put Gleb in a dress. He's got KGB stamped across that huge forehead. Besides, you said Grayson was an unknown. So is Casey."

"Keeping the locals from screaming KGB when they see Gleb and Moky would be a plus. Let me think about it."

Deke answered a call from Sturm as they parked at the hospital. He listened mostly, agreed with him, then hung up. "The Capital police found the car already. Dumped only a few blocks away. Audi with a broken headlamp and banged-up left fender."

"Stolen?" Tig said.

"Of course. Makes us wonder if it wasn't an accident. We decided you might need more firepower."

Brandt looked out the Yukon window. It had never occurred to him that it was anything other than an accident. An actual attack altered his thinking. Maybe they would be putting Casey at risk and replacing Grayson wasn't such a great idea. If someone wanted to take out the team leader, Casey would be next. The thought chilled him. "You have anyone other than Casey that could take Grayson's place?"

"That was quick. Why the change?"

"I didn't want to take her out of an important mission just to be with me."

"Bullshit. You realized there may be risk now."

"It crossed my mind."

"I'll check with the Chief of Stations, see who might be available."

§

When the morning session started, Brandt was surprised to see Sturm accompanied by a brown-robed monk walk in. In the presence of men of the cloth, Brandt became a saint with angelic eyes and folded hands, searching for forgotten prayers. He was the only one. The Russians looked as if Rasputin had just walked in.

"Please welcome Brother Al. He might be the most important member of your team." Deke gazed at Brandt trying to be Saint Brandt. The holy veneer had to be lost on Deke, who had extensive knowledge of Brandt's sins, shortcomings, omissions, lies, and bad behavior.

Moky let out a foul laugh. "A papist? Is this NATO's idea of help?" His tone was filled with sarcasm and disdain usually reserved for drunks, prostitutes, and low-ranking soldiers.

"Major, I don't need any shit from you," Brother Al said. "The Twelfth Directorate wants my help. Talk to them."

Brandt dropped sainthood upon hearing the monk's response. He liked him already. Al could be a bigger piñata stick.

"You knew?" Moky challenged Lena. "Has America turned you into a Popov Cossack?"

"I might have forgotten to mention it," Lena said. "Marshall Grovsky loved the idea. Save your childish insults for him."

Moky appeared to be looking for a place to hide. He eyed Deke and sniggered.

"A religious is Lena's idea," Sturm said. "When the church was kicked out, the KGB moved in and looted the abbeys, monasteries, and convents. That gave them excellent places to hide SADMs. Like the one found in Poland. Brother Al is part of your mission now. He can get you into religious sites you wouldn't have a chance of searching without him." Sturm eyed Tig. "Al will be a big help with cover too. He could be leading a pilgrimage."

Brandt scanned the filled seats. *More like a crusade than a pilgrimage.* He had some experience with monks. An Iowa monastery built beautiful wooden caskets he'd helped deliver as a teen. All were hand built without power tools; the workshop floor was usually covered with wood chips from an adz or hand planer. He remembered the odor from varnish reached the parking area. The monk craftsmen drew their energy from the abbey vineyards, and empty wine bottles lined the top of the benches as if forming a glass wall. Al didn't look like a casket craftsman—more like a CEO than a monk. He stood erect, confident, and his face looked carved from stone, every angle or slope distinct, with a spiritual depth in his blue-green eyes. The way he brushed off Moky and his stately presence indicated that Brother Al—pious monk aside—was not one to be messed with. He appeared to be a man without an addiction, and that bothered Brandt. People without failings reminded him of his own.

Al smiled at Sturm, then looked up and said. "Please call me Al. Only the pope calls me Brother Al. I'm grateful, as are all my Benedictine brothers, to be a part of anything that will support world peace. I will do my best to make this a successful mission for you and the world."

Gleb showed his disinterest by walking over to the snack table. He took his time before picking out two croissants and a Danish kanelbulle.

Al waited until Gleb sat down. "Some background and rules to start. You need to be aware that many of the religious facilities we will be searching are hundreds of years old, built during times when monarchs were notably mercurial when it came to religion. It was not difficult to find both piety and sacrilege in the same royal house. Tunnels, caves, and hidden passages were there for safety. Some church sites will be small and obscure, even inside caves. I have visited and prayed in many of these places. We will be given access, but please remember these are still houses of devout worship."

Brandt detected a trace of drill instructor in Al's voice and the same loping walk as a blade-thin marathon runner. He was taller than Moky but shorter than Brandt, and his bulky brown tunic and long scapular effectively hid his bony frame. The garments lacked the large cowl and hood, indicating a monk who had not made final solemn vows yet. Brother Al was still thinking about it.

"Lena suggested Prague as the place to start," Al said. "There are two monasteries the KGB occupied that we need to search."

Brandt mentally pictured a swath of East Europe. The mission was shaping up to be an extended assignment, and he wondered how the different personalities would stand up under pressure of a lengthy secretive mission.

Moky looked withdrawn. Lena gave Al a curious stare. Deke mimicked a blank page. Tig and Gleb glared at each other. Sturm glanced around the table, then said. "Anything more?"

"I think we're done," Deke said. "Casey is wrapping up in Finland. She'll replace Grayson as the new mission supervisor."

7

Casey scanned the silvery gray-and-blue motif of the Helsinki hotel room for the third time. Waiting was always the worst part of these missions, a paranoia trigger. She'd been taught to expect the targets to be late. They planned it that way, to make her fret and worry they weren't coming or had been caught before the exchange could be made. When they finally arrived, she would feel relieved and let her guard down. *They're being careful,* she told herself, *making frequent taxi switches, quick stops in and out of buildings, turning shop windows into mirrors, using escalators to reverse direction.* Anything to feel secure they weren't being followed.

She slid a desk chair by the window to look out Hotel Kämp toward Helsinki and caught a glimpse of her auburn hair in the reflection. The reflection seemed to distort the off-the-shoulder length, and she nervously adjusted it with her fingers. She thought she looked thin, too thin. As a self-defense instructor, she had always been in shape, but not like what she saw in the glass. If it wasn't more distortion and she really was too thin, it was the result of English food.

Much of Europe was in between seasons. The esplanade park below still had moguls of snow in the tree-shaded paths. The early spring melt had turned sidewalks a mossy color. The open areas of lawn began to sparkle green in the sunlight. It struck her how nature's green worked outdoors, unlike the startling kelly green shade on the walls of her and Brandt's new Westminster townhouse. Homes in London's Zone One were expected to be tasteful and subtle, like the monarchy. Not a color more befitting a Boston bar. They both thought it something earthy but mild, certainly not the decorator's fêng shui favorite deep gray that matched the English weather. Her son, Eric, was trying to decide on his favorite Premier League team for his room colors. The move to England had worked well. Eric's outlook and behavior had improved; playful humor replaced sullen defiance. He even teased his mother by handing her a red penalty card for fussing at him over his teen clothes.

She was anxious for the exchange to be finished so she could go home. The couple wanted the money, were willing to be labeled traitors in the Kremlin. The CIA and Pentagon wanted the tech. Moscow would suffer, its big lead in AR (augmented reality) would disappear overnight. The price in euros was in a roller suitcase on the floral bedcover. She had unzipped the top but left the lid closed. Inside were thick stacks of euros in only one denomination—twenty pounds of five-hundred-euro notes totaling five million dollars. Deke had laughed and snickered over the couple's Faustian trade. Money for souls was a spy game staple.

Two agents from Helsinki Station were along for backup. Bronfman was in the lobby, behind one of the marble columns, having drinks with one of the staff secretaries recruited from the embassy. He was the early warning. The dark-haired secretary was better cover than pretending to read a newspaper. Kerr was in the connecting room to Casey's, with headphones and a Glock on the nightstand next to him. Casey had two microphones transmitting in Mont Blanc ballpoint pens, one on the desk and one in the pocket of the blazer that hid her Sig 40.

Bronfman alerted her. "They're here. Waiting for the elevator. Kiril's carrying a small black case by the handle. Looks plastic. Should be our package. Lyudmila looks nervous."

The anxiety left Casey. Langley had sent an animated video showing what the device would look like—pretty simple, dark eyeglasses like Clark Kent wore, maybe a bit thicker. Scan the glasses with her CIA iPhone sensor and wait for Langley's okay before she let them leave with the money. Everyone was suspicious because Kiril had insisted on a female for the switch. The assumption was a female agent wouldn't be as formidable. A mistake on his part. A deceptive five-seven with subtle aqua eyes, Casey was more dangerous than a pit viper. She'd taught Israeli Krav Maga self-defense to the FBI before joining the agency and had experienced enough combat across Europe to be awarded two hostile action citations. If it were up to her, she'd be waiting for Kiril in martial arts leggings and a sweat top. The tan knit slacks and stretch white turtleneck were fine, but the blue blazer was too restrictive.

"Copy that, Kerr?" Casey asked.

"Roger, I'll be standing by the door."

When Casey let them in, Kiril pointed to the suitcase on the bed. "Is that the money?"

"Let's not rush things," Casey said

Kiril was scruffy. Puffy face, watery eyes with large pupils that went with hard drugs. His wife, Lyudmila, was the healthy one.

Petite, a head shorter than Casey with blonde hair treated in a salon. Shopping for her size two was her addiction. Most likely she was anxious to see the designers' collections on Avenue Montaigne in Paris and the Quadrilatero d'Oro in Milan.

"What have you brought me?" Casey said.

Kiril and his wife sat on the love seat and opened the plastic case on the coffee table. He handed the black eyeglasses to Casey for inspection. The thick temples on the glasses suggested a bargain pair like a gas station might offer. Casey set them on the white desk blotter as instructed and began to scan them with the special smartphone program. All sides, every angle, top and bottom, front and back.

"It will take a few minutes for the okay. You have the flash drive and backup disc?"

Lyudmila pulled a multicolored envelope from a shoulder bag and handed it to Casey.

"I assume you have plans for the money," Casey said.

Lyudmila's eyes brightened. "We're going to Monaco first."

Kiril shoved his elbow into her side. "Stop. We talked about that."

Casey read the text from Langley. "It's good. The money is yours. Count it if you like."

Kiril went to the bed and examined the currency stacks. The bills were fresh, wrapped like bricks. He picked one stack out of the middle, thumbed the bills like a deck of cards, then stuffed the stack in his coat pocket. Lyudmila was busy counting the bricks. While Kiril was occupied with his new wealth, Casey turned her back to him at an angle and made the switch. She slipped the high-tech version into a blazer pocket and then made sure Kiril saw her put a cheap copy back in the case. She raised the case up by the handle in front of him. "Thanks for doing this. I hope all goes well for you both. *Do svidaniya.*"

Kiril zipped up the suitcase and they left without another word.

"That was textbook," Kerr said in her earpiece. "I need to pack the gear up. I'll meet you at the safe house."

"Don't forget my suitcase. I'm going down to meet Bronfman."

Casey opened the door slowly and peeked to each side of the empty hall. After turning the corner to the elevator, she faced two men rushing at her. She threw the plastic case in the face of the first man, then kicked the second one in the groin. He bent over in pain, and she shoved him head first into a metal door. The first man recovered and threw a punch at her that she blocked with her left arm, and then she used her right palm to smash his nose. The second guy grabbed the plastic case and they both ran to the stairs.

"Two coming down the stairs. Let them go," Casey said to Bronfman. It went exactly as Deke said it would.

She called Deke from the safe house, a third-floor flat above Frazier's Café halfway between Stockmann's and the train station. "Everything is in the embassy pouch. Langley will have it tomorrow. I have a flight home tonight."

"Plan on a short stay. I need you in Brussels with Brandt ASAP."

Casey's shoulders sagged. If she was heading for Belgium, painting the townhouse would have to wait.

8

Brandt met Deke next to the Escalade in the NATO basement parking garage.

"Sturm pulled out the spare tire, jack, and tools and refitted the storage," Deke said.

Brandt opened the lift gate and the steel plate covering the new space. Hecklers, Colts, Glocks, Sigs, military tech, and high-explosive pyro were laid out like a jigsaw puzzle. He looked up. "Where's the war?"

"Tig likes to be well armed."

"And if we get a flat?"

"Call Triple AAA, I guess. Dumb-ass Sturm removed the electronic bugs from the Russians' car. Claimed it ruined trust."

"What trust?" Brandt was certain Sturm would have sent Custer out with picnic baskets.

Deke pointed to the side of the SUV where *Swindon Travel Adventures* and a logo showing a plane circling the globe were painted on the side as part of their cover.

Brandt's smile curved up at the corners like a happy jack-o'-lantern. "So I'm back in the travel business. I like it . . . I feel alive again. Tell Langley I quit."

"You have to be full time to quit."

"Shouldn't Tig be here?"

"Picking up Casey. He was at the armory before first light to choose the weapons and tech. He wanted to take out the third seat to load some HK grenade launchers."

"First light, huh? Maybe he can't sleep."

"The Russians are satisfied with what they have. Makarovs and Parabellums."

"I think Gleb is all they need. More powerful than a locomotive. Bends steel with his bare hands." Brandt paused in thought, unable to shake his doubts after the attack on Grayson. The image of a bull's-eye on Casey's back left him concerned for her safety. "Langley figure out who hit Grayson?"

"An accident. Some Turk kids stole a car and went out for a joy ride. Sturm is beginning to waver too. Says since they could have killed him but didn't, maybe Langley's right."

"You buy that?"

Deke shrugged. "Normally, I'd be the first to blame Moscow, but there's something else going on with the Russians. Moky would never attempt to sidestep the agreement without Moscow's approval."

"So Putin's scheming. What a surprise."

"I'm thinking whoever hit Grayson might be tied to one of the groups that followed us to the hotel," said Deke. "They were on our ass for a reason."

"You're like honey to a bear. They see you, they follow."

"Let's see if they follow me to back to London tonight."

Brandt read a text. "Casey just checked into the hotel."

§

The morning drive out of Brussels was like *The Fast and the Furious* in French, German, and finally Czech. Tig complained all the way to Prague about how the car handled on the twisty, choppy Czech roads. Poor tires and the weight from a load of hidden weapons covered in steel plate made the back end squirm like an aroused eel. When they reached the city, Tig was thankful Al was along to guide him through the medieval narrow lanes and one-way streets of Prague.

The Russians dropped out somewhere near Pilsen and never answered Casey's calls. Having no high-tech listening devices in their car made it easy for them to go their own way. Brandt cursed Sturm's naïveté.

Prague had been one of Brandt's favorite tour stops in his guiding days. He understood why Hitler loved Prague so much he planned to retire there. The castle complex was the largest in the world, including government offices, medieval military quarters, historic noble mansions, and even a tropical garden. Malá Strana (Lesser Quarter), an area with quaint streets, boutique shops, and trendy international restaurants, overlooked the Vltava River. Old Town, on the opposite bank, had the tourist hotels, a short walk to the famous Charles Bridge, and a spectacular view of the floodlit castle at night. Initial trips to Prague favored staying in Old Town, near the astronomical clock. A second trip meant Malá Strana, below the Hradcany Castle District and its Golden Lane alchemist shops. He knew the best place for the group to stay in Prague, the Golden Well, a small boutique hotel underneath the walls of Prague Castle, away from the Old Town tourist crowds and close to the highways leading to the monasteries.

Brother Al agreed to stay with them one night in the hotel since it was too late to impose on a parish or monastery. He would have to adjust to a step up in luxury. Benedictines and Franciscans were famous for avoiding earthly opulence. In the days before cars, they'd traveled on mules rather than horses. Brandt pictured Al sleeping on the floor to stay true to his vocation.

Al looked up at the top floors of the hotel and turned to Brandt. "I know this place. It's one of the best in all of Europe. If my fellow brothers discover I spent the night here, I'm afraid I'll be in trouble."

"Certain risks can't be avoided," Brandt said.

"The local abbots are not aware of my role. In the morning, I'll have to speak to the Emmaus Monastery prior, Brother Kremov, for permission to look around."

"What are you going to tell him about us?" Casey asked.

"The monks distrust anything government or military. Between the Gestapo sending them to Dachau and the communists torturing them, we have to be careful. I have a letter from the superior general asking the monasteries to help and assist us."

"Will they go along?" Casey said.

"Put it this way. Without the letter, it would be impossible."

"Are you familiar with the monastery?" Brandt said.

"Just the church. By medieval standards, it's quite modern. The spires had to be rebuilt after an American bombing in '45. The bridges were supposed to be the target."

"Poor aim on a windy day?"

Al smiled. "The bombing is a popular café topic with the old men of Prague. They wonder about the targeting too. Was it a deliberate miss to save the historic bridges or the vengeful aim of a pissed-off Catholic?"

"I'll stick with the wind."

Tig watched the bellman retrieve the luggage to be sure the weapons locker wasn't tampered with. When it was safe, he unlocked the steel plate and extracted a battlefield camo laptop. He whispered to Casey, "I'll check on the Russians first."

§

Inside their room, Casey turned to Brandt. "This place is perfect." She lusted over the Renaissance ambience, hardwood floors, a Bavarian writing desk with a marble surround bordering a crimson leather top, a rich blue-and-ivory gentry rug, and a seventeenth-century hand-carved Italian armoire. "I think I could live here." When she opened the curtains to the Prague skyline, the tile mansard roofs stood out like a patchwork quilt of terra cotta.

"As soon as Moky gets here, I'll make reservations at Hergetova Cihelna on the river," Brandt said.

The bellmen arrived with their luggage and Tig on their heels. He waited until the bellmen left, then opened the laptop. "Guess what. The Russians played it smart and ditched the iPhones Sturm gave them. Must have their own now. It's why they never answered Casey's calls."

"So much for trust. What about ours? Can they track and listen to us?" Brandt said.

"Ours are encrypted but nothing's sure these days. I'll get backups from the car."

After Tig left, Brandt and Casey uncorked a bottle of cabernet sauvignon, opened the balcony doors, and moved two chairs to gaze out toward Prague. Brandt dug out his sketchpad and began to convert the city skyline into abstract shapes. He never carried a sketchpad and colored pencils before moving to London with Casey. They were having an outdoor lunch of fish and chips along the Thames where they could watch the London Eye, the giant Ferris wheel that gave riders a sky-high view of London. The scene was made to order for an abstract; he took some pictures but wished he could sit there and sketch it all. The arches supporting Westminster Bridge, the linear flow of the river, Big Ben's vertical thrust, the circular Ferris wheel provided all the modern shapes. Just fill in the colors and repeat the geometry in different sizes, hues, and colors. Overlapping created character, and be sure to add some gold leaf for splash. That afternoon, he purchased an eight-by-twelve sketchpad and a packet of artist pencils with an instruction book on learning to draw.

Casey watched his pencils move. "Congratulations on the Nottingham show. I'm proud of you."

"It feels good. Confusing, but good." He loved the clarity of the CIA. Get out of bed each day and fight the bad guys. Art was different. Foggy but filled with exciting possibilities.

"What do you mean?"

"I thought being a CIA floater and living with you in London would be perfect. But since my art took off, I keep getting these nagging doubt darts. The kind that start in your head and end up in your gut. Secret agent one day, Jackson Pollock wannabe the next." Brandt set his sketchpad down. "It makes me wonder if I should be devoting more time to art."

"One show and you're ready to turn your life upside down again?"

"Maybe I'm just going with the flow."

"So was the *Titanic*."

"Remember, Deke dragged me into this. I never saw myself as part of the CIA. It was supposed to be over once we got the nuke back in Haystack."

"You should thank Deke. Before Haystack, you were thinking of jumping off a bridge."

"Not just any bridge. The Ponte Vecchio. I wanted a bridge with class."

Casey covered his hand with hers. "It's really not something to joke about."

"I dunno. Laughable. Moronic, if you think about it. I stumbled into art out of grief therapy. And 'floater' sounds like a bad career choice."

"What do you want to do?"

"Both. Neither. Sit on the fence and moan."

"You're becoming an expert."

"Maybe that's progress."

"If your goal is bipolar. You're just torturing yourself with unanswerable questions."

Brandt hesitated for a moment. "Maybe you're right."

Unanswerable questions were life's Gordian knot. He had no trouble leaving unanswered questions about his art alone. He never knew what his paintings meant besides simple expression in color. The critics claimed to know everything, assigning metaphors, allegories, and obscure analogies to his colorful abstract canvases. His agent told him they needed critics for the bullshit. Wealthy collectors wanted a chronicle, a narrative they could use to impress their friends. When an art critic from Stockholm tried to explain one of his paintings as a contra-sexual interpretation of gender and politics, Brandt had frozen him with, "You need help."

"CIA is kind of like being a cop. Maybe I'll try fireman next," Brandt said.

"Working out of London together has been more complex than I imagined. But if you quit to paint full time, we wouldn't be sitting here drinking a glass of wine, gazing out at the Vltava. And there's other benefits, special benefits to consider."

"Such as?"

She traced her index finger across his hand with a carnal smile.

"I need to be reminded of those."

"I'd be happy to. I'm very talented."

He helped her up by the hand and led her to the bed. Moist lips met with intensity. "Have I ever told you how intoxicating you can be?"

Pleasure led to an easy warmth that settled in and kept them close while their breath became shallow. Casey turned playful, reaching over and brushing curls off his ear. Brandt tickled her side in return.

"Stop!" she giggled.

"I need to be reminded again."

"I like the way you think."

Brandt rose above her and waited for her to guide him.

§

While they dressed for dinner, Casey asked how Tig was doing.

"No problem. Why?"

"Bronfman in Helsinki passed on some things that concern me. Stuff not in his file."

Brandt refilled their wineglasses. "Yeah, I know. Deke filled me in."

"He said be careful. Tig can change in a flash—lost his inner compass. He can flip from passive to aggressive, wimpy to gutsy, in the blink of an eye."

"Steroids?"

"More like PTSD with your death wish."

"Ouch."

Casey sipped her wine, then said, "Just keep it in mind."

"I guess Moky won't be here for dinner."

§

The Hergetova Cihelna restaurant's interior blended modern lighting, brown leather seating, and sleek maple accents with historic stucco Roman arches boasting intricate scrollwork. The riverside tables offered the best view of Charles Bridge and the famous spotlit statues. A popular choice with locals and tourists, the menu spanned the Atlantic from American burgers to East European potato dumplings.

"Al is skipping dinner here," Brandt said at the entrance. "Way too gourmet for a simple monk, and too many people in Prague would recognize him. He wants us to bring him some bread and a bowl of their goulash soup."

The maître d' recognized Brandt from his tour guide days and gave them a riverside table for three.

Tig ordered grilled veal loin and crispy sweetbreads. Brandt had the baked sea bass and lobster bisque. Casey ordered the two-course vegetarian of salt-baked celeriac, portobello mushrooms, beans, broccoli, and potato puree.

"Mixed vegetables, huh?" Brandt said. "I better let the sommelier choose the wine."

"Why do you think the Russians left us near Pilsen?" Tig asked.

"No idea. But I'd bet it was a planned stop," Brandt said. "Moky won't get out of bed without an okay from Moscow Center."

"Lena wanted Brother Al to ride with them," Casey said. "I don't think she was looking for spiritual guidance."

"Sturm nixed it. I think she was hoping for a buffer with Moky," Brandt said. "Al's a bit of a surprise. Shut down Moky like he enjoyed it."

"Probably did," Tig said, then dropped his gaze. His voice lowered to a whisper, airing self-doubt. "The guy has guts."

"We have some company sitting at the table by that column. The two of them show more than a casual interest in us," Casey said.

Tig reached across the table for bread and got a better look at the pair. "Both are armed."

"Local Russians or Czech BIS?" Brandt said.

Casey refused to look at the pair again. "Could be BIS. We're both in their files after Haystack."

"Maybe we should reach out to Andrej then?" asked Brandt, referring to the Czech intelligence contact. "If it's BIS, he'll know."

Casey shook an emphatic no. "Sturm said no contact with intelligence services. Deke didn't argue either."

"Let's see what they do when we leave," Brandt said.

"Tig, skip dessert and find a place to hide outside," Casey said. "See if they follow us to the hotel. Then wait for the Russians to show up."

9

At two a.m., Brandt's phone woke him and Casey.

It was Tig, still in the lobby. "Lena just got here. She's alone and shook up pretty bad. The Russians ditched us."

Brandt turned to Casey lying in the bed next to him. "Tig says the Russians dropped out. Lena's here but a wreck."

"Tell him to bring her up. Get some clothes on."

Sitting on the room's love seat, Lena looked ragged, as if she'd been thrown from a car and had bounced on the pavement before landing in a dumpster. Her billowy silver jacket was torn and marked with dried mud down one arm and across the back. Sweat and Czech forest dirt created an organic, earthy odor common to a landfill. Her fluffy tussled tresses had gone flat—wet strings of hair hung down her face next to mascara streaks. Her eyes radiated hatred. "A gang . . . monsters," she said.

"Spetsnaz?" Brandt said.

"Worse. Black Berets."

"What happened?" Casey said.

Brandt grabbed his Ardbeg scotch he brought with him and poured Lena a drink. Casey sat next to her and rested a hand on her shoulder. Tig and Brandt stood waiting for the details.

Lena gulped the scotch down and raised the glass for Brandt to pour another. "Those fucking pigs. Putin's special *vyrozhdat'sya*. Gleb turned off the main highway toward Pilsen and we ended up on a dirt road in the woods. Gleb's buddies were waiting for us in a gray trailer. They took my phone and told me to wait in the car while they began passing vodka around like old friends happy to see each other again. I knew what I could expect next from that scum. While they were busy drinking, I slipped away. When they saw I was gone, they came after me. I had a big lead, but one was very fast and knocked me down and climbed on top, laughing. He stopped laughing when I pulled his pistol out of his holster and smashed his head with it."

"Do you still have it?" Brandt asked. He guessed Lena's inner warning buzzer had saved her. For Russian women it was as necessary as food and water for survival.

Lena brought a PSM pistol out from her jacket.

"How did you get here?" Casey asked.

"The highway wasn't far. But I was afraid they would look for me going toward Prague, so I started walking back toward Germany. I tried to stay in the woods alongside the road and dodge car lights. When I finally reached an open service center, I had to walk through a dark parking lot full of trucks. One driver thought I was a prostitute. I flashed the gun toward him and he backed off. Inside the café, the manager and his wife had one of their staff drive me here. I've never been so grateful in all my life."

"Brandt, call Deke," said Casey. "I'll stay with Lena."

Lena raised up. "Is Al okay?"

"Sleeping in his room."

Lena settled back in the love seat.

Brandt went into the bathroom, turned on a faucet, and filled in Deke back in London.

"Langley won't like this, but I'm not surprised," Deke said. "Moscow is up to something. Looks like Lena is the key. Is she all right?"

"Shook up but fine. She could kick Rambo's ass."

"Be careful around her. Remember, she was part of the Twelfth Directorate. This still could be a Moscow setup."

"According to her, we have the Black Berets to deal with."

"Figures. I'll let you know what Langley and NATO decide. While you're waiting, be sure to read the *Post* today."

"Why?"

"There's an article that has Langley in a twit. Reporter claims we're helping Russian intelligence infiltrate our East Europe allies. Suggests we sold out our friends. Supposedly SVR and GRU agents are moving in and buying real estate with our help. No evidence, just rumor on top of innuendo."

"Moky and Gleb looking for property, huh? Can't see it. More fake news. What about the SADMs?"

"Not by name, by implication. The director made sure I saw it. He knows the *Post* is after his ass for shutting down access."

"Whatever happened to truth in journalism?"

"Doesn't matter anymore. Just an inconvenience. It's all about gathering eyeballs to sell ads. Go with the popular narrative. Keep the boss happy."

"Greed over truth . . . journalism's age of darkness."

"History will not be kind to the media for their manipulation and indifference."

"I hope they name names," Brandt said and hung up.

Casey sent Brandt across the hall to sleep in Moky's empty room. Brandt pulled Tig in and asked him about the two from the restaurant.

"They knew what they were doing. Very cautious. After they followed you and Casey back to the hotel, they waited outside for over an hour in case you came back out. When they did leave, they tried to be sure they weren't being tailed too. Standard stuff—switchback streets down to the river, leapfrogging each other, circling back through alleys. I lost them for a bit but caught up with them at the river and saw them grab a taxi and leave."

Brandt wondered how Tig had lost them. Between what Deke told him about Tig's problems and Tig letting Sword of Allah slip his mind, the bodyguard was still a worry. "Sounds like pros. I had hoped they were only thieves."

"Definitely pros."

"Could be the Prague BIS. They like taxis because they never pay for them."

§

Brandt and Tig were at breakfast when Casey came in.

"Lena?" Tig said to her.

"She's fine, just has no clothes to wear. I have to buy her something before she can go out to shop."

"Brother Al already left to talk to the prior. We're supposed to meet him on Charles Bridge in front of the statue of Saint John Nepomuk at ten. He won't come near the hotel anymore. You can grab something for her after that," Brandt said.

"She wants an outfit she won't be embarrassed to wear while she shops on Pařížská Street."

"She's more than a fashionista after last night," Brandt said. He wondered if she could shoot too.

"I called Deke before I came down," Casey said. "See if Langley or NATO changed their minds about continuing on."

"What's the verdict? Do we abort?" Tig sounded caught up in hope, as if he were on trial.

"Continue on without the Russians," Casey said. "Langley, State, and NATO are afraid if they warn the host countries about the Russians and SADMs, they'll end up with an Old West–style land grab for nukes, every head of state on TV boasting to their countrymen that they're now a nuclear power. The last thing the world needs is a half dozen more."

Brandt was more concerned. "Any found in Ukraine would probably end up as mushroom clouds in the Kremlin within days."

"What about Lena?" Tig said. "Is she going back to the States now?"

"It's up to her. She volunteered. She can quit any time," Brandt said.

"No way she's quitting after yesterday," Casey said. "She said she was afraid Moscow might pull something like this. They were counting on her to lead them to the weapons ahead of us. By escaping, she really stuck it to them."

"Mensa card with guile," Brandt said. "Perfect."

§

Brandt knew why Al had chosen the statue of Saint John Nepomuk—a Czech mix of myth and history. The Benedictines of 1393 were partly responsible for the saint's torture, death, and martyrdom. Politics stayed wrapped in religious cloaks in those years but were as lethal as any castle poison. In John's case, the seal of confession was to blame. Either he refused to tell the queen's secrets, or he did. Historians weren't certain how to label the injustice. His toss into the Vltava was at the very spot on the bridge where his statue now stood. Legend claimed when he hit the water and life left his body, five stars rose in the sky, and the statue's wire halo with five shiny emblems circling his bronze head honored that fable. The Benedictines remembered their treachery and used the spot and the statue to remind themselves to be honest, contrite, and humble.

Brother Al was waiting for them in front of the saint's cast effigy. Al's proud nose and warm smile gave him an air of nobility. A prince, if not a king. "This is a good place to start our search. Czech folklore has it if you touch the shiny scene of John on the base, it will bring us good luck." He pointed to a second glossy metal etching on the left side. "But stay away from this one. Rubbing the queen brings bad luck."

"Cost some of her lovers their heads," Brandt said. He forced himself to rub John's metal square. He found religious statues about as interesting as tree stumps. They had populated old Europe like rabbits. "You got anything that will bring an army of angels?"

"Who do you think got us here safely?"

"Tig's no angel . . . unless fallen counts," Brandt said.

"Where's Moky? Meeting here too Catholic for him?"

"When the Russians turned toward Pilsen yesterday, Moky met up with some of Gleb's comrades," Casey said. "The vodka flowed, and we don't know where they are now."

"Lena?"

"She escaped. She's back at the hotel with Tig," Casey said.

Al's face wrinkled, his concern was apparent. "Is she okay?"

"Fine and more than willing to help us now. I need to get her some fresh clothes."

"Moky made it a race then. I'm not surprised."

Al is right, Brandt thought. *It is a race. But they have the lead and the sprinter.*

"Spetsnaz, I expect?"

Brandt was startled by Al's question. "Lena said the Black Beret division. How do you know about them?"

"If you're a Benedictine, you know. Spetsnaz and the Black Berets rattled fear in all our monasteries. I figured Gleb as a Black Beret."

"Do we have permission to search the monastery?" Casey said.

"We're too late. Two people claiming to be from Czech security searched it two days ago. These old monasteries have basements, tunnels, cellars, and junk rooms that go on forever. Like dungeons . . . stairways to hell. You could fill a dump or a museum with the stuff stored in them. The KGB counted on that. Some of the burial chambers date back to the seventh century. Rooms filled with stone sarcophagi."

"Great places to hide SADMs," Brandt said.

"The two found a couple of crates with a Soviet star on the side, in a catacomb alcove buried under barrels full of horseshoes and boxes of broken pottery. They told Brother Kremov the crates were filled with explosives and needed to be removed for their safety. We went through everything to be sure there weren't others."

"They can't be Moky. Who were they?" Brandt said.

"If it really was Czech BIS, Andrej will know. We have to talk to him now," Casey said. "I'll see if I can get it cleared with Deke."

"There are two more monasteries here we should search. I have friends at Strahov, so we'll go there next," Al said. "But I'm afraid we're too late. Get the car and pick me up in front of the KGB museum on Vlašská in an hour. The Russians will stay clear of there."

Brandt turned to Casey. "Keep Tig with you while you shop with Lena. She's the one we need to protect now."

§

Brandt made his way to the KGB museum in the Escalade. He wondered about Tig. Shopping for clothes with Lena in Prague would test his mettle. Could even break him.

When Brandt pulled up to the curb, Al climbed in wearing a new beret. "It's midday in Strahov's canonical hours, so the monks will be at Sext prayer. Then lunch," Al said.

"Don't they have a brewery?"

"Saint Norbert's is famous across Europe. We can eat while we wait."

The brewery beer boasted *Antidepressant* on the label, and Brandt agreed. Maybe over lunch it was time to seek a little guidance from Al. The life decision to become a monk had to be a difficult one. Modern secular societies eliminated religious life as a dumping ground for royal and noble families with extra children. If you became a minister, priest, nun, or monk now, it was your decision rather than something ordered by the family patriarch. Al had to have insight and guidance into difficult life decisions, and Brandt needed answers.

The waiter brought their lunch and Brandt said, "What motivated you to become a monk, Al?"

"I get that question a lot. Often from people struggling with change."

"The world is a tricky place. Everyone needs help and guidance."

"Tricky?" Al set his beer down "An understatement. Every day, evil is out there looking for victims."

Brandt let his head sink in agreement. When it came to discussing evil, he felt sure he was outgunned. Religious vocations, especially priests in confessionals, faced off with evil like homicide police.

"I was older when I came to the Benedictines. My life was like a broken window. I was caught in what Jung called the vortex of questions and uncertainties that ultimately transform us. An easy thing for him to write about, but not so easy to live through."

"That part I understand."

Al appeared locked in the past, intense eyes with flesh sagging at the corners. "I was Humpty-Dumpty with too many pieces and not enough glue. I needed something stable and safe in my life. The Benedictines offered me that."

"Any regrets?"

Al perked up. "Now you're getting into my soul. You're not allowed there yet."

"Sorry. But you don't have the cowl. You haven't made your final solemn vows. The question seemed obvious."

"It's also obvious that you are struggling enough with something to ask these questions."

Fair enough, thought Brandt. "Okay, I thought that with being a floater with Casey in London, my life was settled. But it doesn't feel that way. It's like two parts of my life that are important to me don't seem to fit well together. Like purple next to yellow. Makes me think I should pick one." Brandt leaned back and put his fork down. "These dumplings are delicious. Fluffy, not as heavy. Wonder how they do it."

Al smiled. "I knew you would like this place." He set his fork down and leaned back in his chair. "You're fortunate to have such a pleasant problem. Life isn't so easy for many."

"Hey, fuck the guilt trip. I lost my wife to cancer. I didn't feel fortunate then."

"That took some balls. But you're right. That was preachy. I apologize. The choice between two goods? A timeless question. The seed of an existential crisis. Philosophers and social scientists love that one. A career builder, if they get it right. The practical answer is to weigh the utility of each and choose the heavier one. Doesn't always work, though. People often choose the lighter version anyway."

"Why is that?"

"Pascal had the most eloquent answer. *'The heart has its reasons of which reason knows nothing.'* Science hates that one."

"I can see why."

Al smiled weakly.

Brandt's mouth opened as if to form a comment, but he held back. Al knew his way around Catholic saints, honored philosophers, and the giants of psychology. He spoke their language as if he were born with it. Brandt had more in common with sinners. Deke was proof of that.

A monk walked in and waved to Al, who waved back. "Brother Thomas is available now. We'll continue this another time. Get your gear from the car."

He met Al in the visitor lobby with tools to pick a SADM lock. He also had a GS meter/gamma ray detector strapped over his shoulder.

Al moved some brochures from a table and unfolded a map of the monastery. "I was right. The two men claiming to be Czech security have already been here. They knew right where to look. Finished in less than an hour. Very rude, according to Brother Thomas."

"Did they find anything?"

"They carried out three large duffel bags. Told Brother Thomas they were full of personal items, tools, and old Russian communication equipment left behind. We'll drop down to the bottom level and you can turn on that gizmo. Maybe they missed something."

"There's not much to detect from a SADM. For this to work, we'll have to be sitting on one."

10

Moky felt as uncomfortable with Gleb's old friends as he did with Sturm and the Americans. They were Spetsnaz like him, but part of the special Black Beret division that had more in common with a Mongol horde. Excessive violence came easy to them. Very useful to Moscow in Chechnya, Crimea, and Ukraine, but everyone knew to keep their wives and daughters away. He kept looking out the tiny window over the trailer's sink, hoping that Lena would come walking up yet afraid she would. The team's trailer was a credible likeness to a trash truck. It stank of stewed cabbage, boiled potatoes, bad sausage, and acrid Tajik cigarettes. An excess of garbage overflowed the container, spilling bottles, cans, and condoms onto the floor. Huddled in the corner of one bed was a Black Beret recovering from the beating Gleb and the others inflicted on him over his failure to watch Lena. Her escape was a setback. All they had now were some KGB notes.

Moky went outside to smoke. With all the explosives and ammo lying around, it wouldn't take much to blast a meteor-size hole underneath the trailer.

Gleb was creeping toward him with fish-faced Karyi; the muddy stone path had them stepping carefully. They were dressed as common laborers in baggy wool pants and coats stuffed with cotton, peaked worker's hats on their heads. They were returning from a meeting with Grekov, the Pilsen SVR Station Chief.

"We're too late, but so are the Americans," Gleb told Moky. "The weapons were in Emmaus Monastery. Two men removed them last week."

Moky cringed. "Does NATO have them?"

"We're not sure. The men were either Czech BIS or imposters. Grekov's sources at BIS say they don't know anything about them."

Moky kicked over a plastic chair. "Moscow Center's intel. Worthless shit!"

"Grekov called it an emergency since we lost Averin," Gleb said. "He's flying back to Moscow to brief the president and security council."

11

The clouds circling Old Town Prague were an ominous purple and black, like a painful bruise. A brittle wind sent gusts threatening to unleash biblical rain and hail but stopped short of exploding. Kiosks took precautions with strips of heavy plastic curtains that were unrolled and hung down to the cobblestones.

Lena went about shopping like a celebrity diva with managers and clerks forming a Hollywood-style entourage. Someone had to point out what was current chic and carry all her purchases. If it didn't say Hermès, Gucci, Cucinelli, Burberry, or Givenchy, it remained untouched. Casey stayed with Lena, talking to Deke and her mom over the phone while she followed the escorts. Tig had stationed himself near the front, shifting his gaze from Lena to the entrance. By the time she was finished, Tig carried two large bags, Lena and Casey one each.

Lena thanked the staff and gave each one a generous tip, then turned to Casey. "I have enough to get by until I get to Paris. Let me buy you both coffee for helping me and being so patient."

"There's a fun place by the square," Casey said. Lena had risen up in her eyes. After everything Lena had been through the day before, she still managed to treat the staff with grace and style. As a narcissistic pop diva, she would be a failure.

Kafka Coffee was a pleasant memory from Casey's first trip with Brandt. The café looked the same, black-and-white harlequin tile floor and a bakery case full of strudel and kolaches. The tourist attraction was a famous rock star's signature underneath cracks in a large mirror behind the counter, the result of a saucer transformed into a Frisbee. They sat around a tall café table next to a window. Lena ordered the Russian favorite of cappuccino, Tig, coffee Americano, and Casey, latte.

"I want you both to know this SADM business is important to me," Lena said. "When I was with the Twelfth Directorate, someone very special to me was pulled out of his car by the secret police and taken to Lubyanka prison. Leonid was released months later, a shadow of a man. He stepped in front of a subway train two days later."

"What was behind it?" Casey asked.

"When Petrov came back from a trip west, Leonid asked him about it. He joked about the KGB and SADMs. Petrov made it sound like espionage and passed it on to the FSB."

"That's awful," Casey said.

Lena's tone turned reflective. "We had talked about marriage."

"Do you have someone special back in the States now?" Casey asked.

"No. No one. American physicists are usually married and boring. Not my taste."

Tig saw a chance to connect. "Are you looking for a poet or a warrior?" A pig searching for truffles was less obvious.

"In Russia, we love and honor our poets and warriors the same. Americans need to learn that." She looked down and traced her index finger over the Kafka Coffee imprint on the cup, then raised her eyes. "Life has a way of forcing women to look at men differently over time. Our dreams get shattered by realty." She turned to Casey. "When I was a child, I read *Doctor Zhivago* and fell in love with him . . . a poet, a doctor, and a soldier in the Great War. A typical teen fantasy. I think I've been looking under rocks for my Doctor Zhivago ever since."

Casey's eyes were full of empathy. "I think you'll find him."

"When the FSB took Leonid, I began to lose hope. They're no better than the KGB was. But Petrov is the one who made it happen."

"So it's time for payback," Tig said.

"It's why I'm here with the CIA."

Casey noticed a call coming in. "It's Brandt. I'll take it outside."

"Al and I are done," he said. "Nothing in the monasteries. Our two friends from Emmaus were ahead of us again. Al's thinking there's a place in Krakow to check, but it's up to Lena."

"Lena is all in on this. Highly motivated."

"I suspected that in Brussels."

When Casey returned, Tig and Lena were laughing together. A small step toward relationship drama they didn't need. "Brandt and Brother Al are finished. Too late again. Al suggested Krakow but left it up to you."

Lena nodded slowly. "He's right. Petrov loved the salt mine."

§

They all were an hour outside of Krakow when Tig announced, "This is fucked. We're being followed."

Brandt turned to look behind them. "I don't see anyone."

"It's not a car, it's a drone. I'm guessing a small military version. It just follows above us while we drive. If I tap the brakes, it shoots ahead then falls back."

"Who's flying it?"

"Doesn't have to be anyone. It could be tagged to the car. Once it's locked on, it can follow us like a magnet. If it goes too high, it loses contact. I saw one demonstrated at Fort Belvoir. The big problem is power. Most small ones can't fly for more than a couple of hours on batteries. If this one has been with us since Prague, it must be a tactical military model with the new hydrogen fuel cells."

"Russians again," Casey said.

"Possible. But they've been way behind in drone tech. They could have got it from the Germans. There's a company in Berlin that has developed some great hydrogen cells. I think I should pull over and shoot it down."

"No. Keep going," Brandt said, then turned to Casey. "Call Deke and have Langley track it. Maybe we can find out who's behind it."

"Is it armed?" Lena asked.

"Doubtful. It's not much bigger than a commercial fan," Tig said. "To stay with us this long, it couldn't carry much payload. Weapons are heavy."

Casey hung up. "Deke said to pull over someplace. Give him time to get the okay for Langley to zero in. Ten minutes tops."

Tig found a rest stop. A semitruck had just pulled out, leaving the gravel lot empty. A sheltered picnic table and a stone shed one-person restroom facility with a shaker roof were all the area offered. The drone hovered and elevated once the car stopped.

"I need to stretch my legs," Al said and got out and headed for the shed.

The rest stood around the car and waited their turn. A Volvo pulled in and parked near the picnic table. When Al returned, Brandt left for the shed. The two men from the car got out and headed the same way.

Casey focused on them. They raised an alarm with her: swarthy men who walked with purpose. Arabs? Muslims? Sword of Allah?

"Tig, come with me," Casey said.

They hurried to the shed before Brandt exited. The two from the Volvo were waiting just outside the door for Brandt to leave. One smiled at Casey, the other said, "Hello." Brandt came out and looked surprised by both the pair and his escort. The one who smiled replaced Brandt in the shed. Brandt started back with Casey and Tig like bookends.

When they reached the car, Brandt said, "What was that all about?"

"Have you forgotten Sword of Allah?" Casey shot back.

"Don't worry," Al said. "Those two are Mossad."

12

Late-spring snows left Poland in a gritty gray film. The mud season in Carpathian mountain towns required tractors to pull other tractors out of gushy roads and swampy fields. Hitler's invasion of Russia had to be delayed when his army couldn't get their tanks out of the deep Silesian mud. Stalin had famously said the mud in Poland was better than artillery.

"Al got us rooms in Tyniec Abbey," Brandt said. "On the Vistula, outside of the city."

"The Russian anti-religious campaign didn't get traction in Poland," Al said. "The church has always had strong support here. The Poles never wavered. They pushed back, and Moscow was forced to ease up, so the monasteries were left alone. They didn't need them anyway. The KGB and GRU found the Wieliczka Salt Mine was perfect. Nature handed them an underground fortress bunker."

"I know Petrov took pictures of the mine," Lena said.

Brandt shifted in his seat. "The place is like the Grand Canyon. You could literally hide an army in there."

"The Russians tried their best," Al said.

Brandt and Tig shared a room in the abbey's guest hall. Lena and Casey paired together in the one next to them. Al moved to the monks' wing. An informal common room at the end of the hall was a place for small groups to meet. Brandt thought his room was a treasure in its simplicity: a polished acacia floor, two steel-frame single beds, two desks and chairs, reading lamps, and a crucifix above each bed. No TV or radio. No fancy bedding, No cheap art on the wall. None of the visual distractions of a Four Seasons or Kempinski that disrupted inner life.

Tig set their bags down and gazed out the lone window at the gazebo across from the entrance. "More people arriving. Looks like a busy place."

Brandt left the door open, set his backpack on the bed, and pulled out his laptop.

Casey walked in. "Not much help on the drone. It left us when we crossed the river and flew into a barn. No cars. No one around. Deke thinks they'll wait until dark to move off."

"How about thermal?" Tig said.

"Langley said it's only a drone. Could be anyone's these days. They stopped tracking when it went into the barn. Deke couldn't get infrared authorized."

"Did you ask him about calling Andrej?" Brandt said.

"I think we're better off just calling him. Andrej will keep it to himself. I plan to ask him about Al too."

"Al's Sturm's guy," Tig said. "You think he's a monk or a NATO plant?"

"Those two at the rest stop . . . how did he ID them as Mossad?" Casey said. "None of us did."

"Aaron must suspect something to stick them on us. But I doubt he'll have anything on Al," Brandt said. "He might be a Sturm pick, but Al's for real. He knows stuff a monk would know. The answers for real-life puzzles. Quotes Pascal and Jung. If he's a NATO asset, he's a damn good one."

"How did the other monks treat him?" Casey asked.

"Like one of their own," Brandt said.

"I guess he's okay then," Tig said.

Brandt grabbed a coat. "Tig and I are going for a walk."

"We are?"

"Put your coat on."

Brandt led Tig down a steep path from the high bluff toward the banks of the Vistula. "Casey thinks you might be interested in Lena. Is she right?"

"Some laughs, that's all. What's the problem?"

"I'm asking the questions. Tell me about Syria."

Tig's chin was in danger of dragging in the dirt. "Bad shit . . . some real bad shit."

"I need more, or you go home."

Tig shook his head as if searching for answers. "The sandbox is nothing but a politically correct clusterfuck. Forget about the war. Follow orders, but don't take casualties, don't harm civilians, don't destroy infrastructure, be friendly with press, and be sure to make the brass look good."

"Sounds more like a dance. Can't be easy."

"More like impossible. I mean, how can you tell a nineteen-year-old kid from Omaha not to shoot anyone who isn't a threat when they all look alike and dress the same? Huh? Tell me how. It's all so wrong. You're not even allowed to check if there's a dynamite vest underneath a big smile and a burka. Fuck up, and you either get court-martialed or you're scraps in a body bag. It's all just bullshit. The brass is worried about the press, and the press doesn't care if we all get killed as long as they get a story and some pictures to photoshop. They think if they can make us look evil on the front page, they'll get a Pulitzer."

Brandt steered them into the orchard, a boulevard of budding but fruitless apple trees kin to the neighboring pear trees with tiny blooms. They took the middle lane, heading away from the monastery. The ground was moist without being squishy. Bohemian waxwings chirped their displeasure over the intrusion. "So what happened there?"

"We were in reserve of the Kurds. Good guys. The hajis were dug in . . . an old village at the end of a box canyon. Our intel said they had killed all the villagers and were hoping the Kurds would attack and set a trap for them. This French advisor thought different. He told the Kurdish leader the villagers were being tortured by a handful of terrorists and it was their job to save them. I agreed to be backup. I never should have said that. They might have called it off if I'd said no. Our intel is a crapshoot in that part of the desert, either dead right or bogus, so I didn't think I could refuse."

"They had it right."

"All the way. The Kurds got waxed. Alamo time. The hajis drew them in and then sealed off the canyon behind them. They were caught in a perfect kill zone. Out in the open. No cover. Hajis hidden in the cliffs. The French captain never called us in, but we started forward to help anyway. Then I stopped. It was already too late. I called in air strikes, sat down, and cried."

"What about the French captain?"

"The hajis made sure they took him alive for the ransom. The French pay big, fifty thousand euros for officers."

"It was his blunder, not yours."

"If I had only said no."

Brandt saw the fix Tig was in. Sometimes the correct decision ends badly. Life could be unfair and occasionally brutal. He was sorry it happened the way it had for Tig. "You had no choice. They would have gone in anyway, thanks to the French guy."

"Maybe. Maybe not. And what if I'd gone on the attack sooner? Stayed glued to their six all the way in? Maybe it would have been different."

"Forget the second-guessing. It's a dead end." Brandt wished he took his own advice. He kept a mental hammer handy to whack himself over mistakes.

"That's what the shrink in the States said."

"Sorry about the divorce. That couldn't have helped."

"I was broken. She was broken. Everything . . . everything had gone cold. I never knew she was so unhappy. I had been deployed too much and then to come home like that . . . I dunno. She didn't have anything left for us. I don't blame her for quitting."

"How do you think you're doing now?"

"About half, I guess. I did my best and screwed it up. It eats at ya. Sometimes I just sort of drift away. Thinking how it could have been different. I feel dead inside a lot of the time. I miss Becky and my old life. She liked to call me Van Gogh, because of my ear. We laughed about it. I still love her."

"Be careful with Lena. Don't make things worse for yourself."

"I know. I know . . . not sure I care, though. Being around her helps."

"Do this for me. Spend as much time as you can with Brother Al. There's something special about him. The guy knows some shit about life."

"There's another drone," Tig said. "A bigger one."

13

Casey noticed her and Lena's room was different from Brandt and Tig's. It had a small sink below a hazy mirror and two wafer-size bars of soap wrapped in paper. Two hand towels lay on the bed. The lone window was open, creating a chill.

"Petrov loved Krakow," Lena said and closed the window. She sat on her bed and leaned her back against the wall. "He came back with pictures of the salt mine and Auschwitz. The death camp made the wrong impression on him. He didn't see the horror. He wanted Moscow to build extermination camps too. You can imagine who he wanted to put inside."

Casey spread out a mat to do some stretches. "You think he found SADMs here?"

"I'm counting on it. The salt mines became KGB headquarters and the military stored missiles, trucks, and artillery in them. Plenty of room to hide small SADMs."

"Are they big enough for all that?"

"You have to see the mine to believe the size. Poles hold festivals inside . . . with hot air balloons rising to the ceiling. It's like God carved them out with a finger."

"Searching them won't be easy then."

"No. I'm hoping Al can get some help from the abbey."

Casey lowered herself to the mat and moved through a series of yoga poses. "You knew Petrov well?"

"Yes, we were together for a time . . . lovers when we worked in the Twelfth Directorate. I questioned whether it could become something special. Then his trip to the west . . . Poland, Hungary, Czechia, and East Germany. He came back full of anger and rage. Gorbachev and Yeltsin had betrayed Russia. Hitler had had the right idea. Russia needed to pick up the fight, and he knew how to make it happen."

"Did that cause a breakup?"

"Over time, yes. I chose to slowly separate . . . drift away. I was afraid of what he might do if I broke off suddenly."

"That was smart," Casey added.

"He didn't seem to mind, though. He was so preoccupied with his own plans. I wasn't needed anymore. I was relieved. Then Leonid came into my life."

"Lubyanka and the metro?"

Lena's head dipped. "After his death, I decided to apply for the exchange to America. I needed distance from Petrov, Russia, and the secret police."

"We're glad you were accepted."

"I have some friends high in government who like to see me happy. It was the best decision I ever made."

§

To Tig, the low-flying drone looked more hostile than the earlier one. It had a ten-foot wingspan that could handle a bigger payload. He told Brandt he had seen Tel Aviv–based IDF tactical drones fitted out with a .22-caliber Uzi-like gun, and this looked a lot like one of them.

"We should be careful of this one," Tig said. "Let's head back inside."

Brandt looked up and tried to focus on the drone. Tig was right. All it needed was fangs and claws to complete a malevolent look. They turned back toward the monastery with Tig pushing ahead. Brandt heard a muffled crack, and the moist ground in front of them thumped with impact.

"Take cover," Tig ordered.

The apple trees gave a five-foot clearance to duck under. Brandt wished the leaves had already sprouted to hide them better. Tig was in the tree in front of Brandt. The drone fired again, and twigs began to snap off Brandt's tree. Brandt understood the new computer-aided weapon systems were intuitive and could anticipate a target's flight and direction. He faked a step to the front to throw it off, then dashed to the tree behind him.

"That thing has fired six shots. I think thirty is the max and it can't reload," Tig yelled.

"Twenty-four is plenty."

"On the count of three, run to the other row on your left. I'll go right. I doubt the pilot can react that quick."

"What if he's locked on to only one of us?"

"Then I'm wrong again."

Two more shots pinged through Brandt's tree. "That's eight. He's zeroed in on me. Count and let's go."

"Roger. One . . . two . . . three."

Brandt dashed toward an apple tree in the adjoining row but didn't stop there. He ducked under one, then ran to a pear tree in the next row. Tig drew the first shots. Brandt lost count. Three, maybe four. Then the gun switched targets and ripped the ground under the apple tree he had just left.

"How many?" Brandt shouted.

"I'm not sure. Lost count."

"Terrific," Brandt mumbled.

"Five, maybe six . . . something like that. I'll run up and down in between the rows and draw fire. Try and make it inside."

This was the gutsy part of Tig that Brandt had been warned about. "That's very brave, but very stupid. Think of something else."

"Okay . . . do the same thing as before. This time, you run back and I'll go forward. On three again." Tig paused. "One . . . two . . . three."

The drone kept Brandt as the target. The first shot grazed his left calf, and a second whistled past his left ear.

"It's coming for you!" Tig screamed.

Brandt looked up. The drone was less than a hundred feet above him and still descending. He kept running a zigzag pattern, dodging fire, while looking for something better than a sparse tree to hide under. But there were no buildings or natural structures close enough to help. A rotting apple on the ground from the last harvest was on the ground, and he thought about picking it up and throwing a perfect baseball strike at the drone. He knew on his best day that was impossible. He was picking out his next tree when a blast from a shotgun startled him.

Al was standing in the middle of the row, aiming at the drone with a semiautomatic shotgun. The first shot took out one of the propellors, and the drone turned toward the river to get away. The second shot damaged the power supply, and it began to limp and sputter more than fly. It never made it across the river. The Vistula's strong spring current swept it away.

Al kept an eye out for more drones as they hustled back inside.

"Where did you get the shotgun? It's an Italian military Fabarm," Tig said.

"It belongs to the monastery. I knew where they kept it, and when that drone showed up, I grabbed it."

"Good shooting," Brandt said. Al had Jedi skill. Two shots, two hits.

"Every Czech learns to hunt ducks. They're our favorite holiday meal. I was pretty good at it."

§

Casey pulled Brandt into the common area at the end of the hall, away from the others. The fireplace was filled with ashes and partially burnt logs. Despite the charcoal scent, the room had a Vatican mood. On the walls hung a mixture of religious icons and paintings of various saints. Above the mantle was a large portrait of the Polish pope, John Paul II. Photos of Lech Walesa hung left of the fireplace; on the right, a Solidarity rally in Gdansk. A thirdhand mix of worn leather and cloth chairs huddled around a distressed square table in front of the stone hearth.

"I think a drink would go well now," Brandt said.

"Brother Al saved your ass out there," Casey said

"Yep. In that monk tunic, he even looks like Obi-Wan Kenobi."

"How's your calf?"

"Tig took care of it." Brandt settled into a worn fabric chair with thick arms. "He put on some special military patch that stops bleeding. I expect to be sore tomorrow."

Casey sat on the chair arm. "Maybe you should stay inside until we leave."

"I'm giving it careful consideration."

"You think Sword of Allah has switched to drones?"

"They've always been partial to knives. I just can't see them flying drones."

Casey stood up and shook her head in agreement. "I talked to Andrej. He insists Al is not BIS. It's a small outfit and everyone knows everyone. He's checking with the Germans and Europol to see if he's hooked up with either of them."

"What did Deke say about the drones?"

"He's got nothing. They're impossible to trace. Remember how anonymous drones shut down Heathrow? Never caught the guys. Langley stopped watching the barn, so this last one is an unknown."

"Tig's a mess. Can't leave Syria behind, but he came through in the orchard . . . sort of."

"What do you mean?"

"For a moment there, he had a death wish. Ready to sacrifice himself to save me. Al showed up at the right time."

"What about Lena?"

"Don't think he's serious. More of a diversion."

"Lena wanted to know if Al was okay. You two never came up."

"Interesting."

"'Let things happen' is your motto anyway," Casey said.

"Did you ask Deke about the Mossad guys?"

"He was surprised by them showing up. He's thinking of calling Aaron about them. Since Langley can't find the Russians, he wants us to stay vigilant."

"Keen sense of the obvious. What an ass."

"He says the same thing about you."

"That's why we're friends."

Lena came in and announced, "Happy hour is coming. Tig and Al are bringing wine and cheese."

The orchard dive-bombing meant something stronger than wine for Brandt. He went to his room and came back with scotch and a water bottle. No ice—scotch and a splash of water would have to do. Tig and Lena were standing by the fireplace. Al stood by Casey with a glass of wine. Brandt slid past the chairs to inspect the paintings. An art critic would immediately grind on about negative space, dominance, and distortion. He was more interested in the names attached to the frames: Saint Adalbert, Saint Stanislaus, Saint Andrew Bobola, and more. He admired the works without slandering them with critical comments. His Nottingham exhibition success filtered in, and he wished he had brought more than a sketchbook.

Al waved to join him. "Have you ever been to the mine?"

"Once . . . for a dance festival," Brandt said. "Must have been four or five thousand people there."

"Since the mining stopped in 2007, there are more cultural and entertainment activities now. Saint Kinga Cathedral and the lake are still the main attractions."

"How long will the search take?"

"Day, two at most. We don't have to search below the hotel rooms. That area was still a working mine after the Russians left and any SADMs would have been found."

Lena walked up to them. "Tig said you showed some expert skill with the shotgun."

"Four more and he'll qualify as an ace," Brandt said.

"Maybe I already am?" Al smiled.

"Are you?"

"Only if you count ducks. But maybe there'll be more tomorrow."

"Tig wants me to go for a walk with him so he can show me where everything happened. Is it safe now?" Lena said.

"From the drone, yes. It's getting dark and Al has given them a reason to stay away. But Tig, I don't know. That has an element of risk," Brandt said.

"Well, it won't be boring then."

Brandt grabbed Tig's arm as they left the lounge. "Remember, this is a monastery. Holy ground to the monks. Don't do anything to offend our hosts."

"Roger that."

Al added wine to his glass and watched them leave together, then sat down. Brandt grabbed the chair next to Casey. Speech was a threat that needed to be avoided while they sat with their thoughts. After a long stretch of quiet reflection, a bell rang from the steeple, signaling Vespers.

"Do you have to leave?" Casey asked. She picked up a taper next to her wineglass and used it to relight a candle that had lost its flame.

"No, I'll catch up after dinner. Compline's at eight."

"Will you eat with us?" Casey said.

"All the monks eat supper in the refectory. We sit at separate tables while postulants and novitiates serve the meals to the guests. Lunch is our main meal and supper is usually soup, bread, and leftovers. Tyniec Abbey has its own farm, so the food here is better than most restaurants in Krakow."

"Al, I'm curious how you knew those two were Mossad. Then the shotgun expertise. I keep asking myself, is he a spy or monk? Which is it?" Casey said.

Brandt didn't believe Al was a spy; he was an alpha monk. Alpha enough to become a pope. He hadn't expected Casey to come right out and ask. Maybe Tuscany Benedictine wine was strong.

"I'm still in Formation. That's all. When those two got out of the car, I heard them speaking Hebrew. I got a peek at their shoulder holsters and figured they had to be Mossad."

Brandt sensed deception. Al was hoping to ward off a follow-up. "Are you a novitiate?"

Al chose his words carefully, his head twitching as if his neck was mechanical. "Past that. In Simple Profession."

"For how long? Three, four years?" Brandt said.

"Oh, longer than that."

"How can that be? The Benedictines have a five-year limit for discernment."

"They made some allowances for me. I'm very grateful."

Al's honest answers meant he couldn't be a spy. Lie, cheat, and steal came natural to them. The tower bell rang again, announcing dinner. "I'd like to hear more," Brandt said.

§

Gleb grabbed a folding stock AK-12 assault rifle and jumped from the truck hauling the trailer. Karyi pulled the SUV behind and stopped. Moky didn't like the look on Gleb's face and decided he better join him. He was never comfortable with Gleb and his Black Berets. Too brutal and sadistic for him. Those that survived the slaughterous hazing and training became soulless cyborg tools. Murder, rape, and torture got results—that's all Moscow cared about. They used them with caution, knowing Gleb's special Black Berets considered themselves immune to the laws of Russia and the laws of God.

Gleb was looking to the sky.

Moky pointed to the weapon and said, "What are you going to do with that? Shoot some birds? We need to get to Poland. The Americans are already in Krakow."

Gleb sneered. "There's a drone up there staying on our ass. I'm going to get rid of it."

Moky looked up and located the dark spot in the sky. "Maybe it's NATO's."

"I don't care if it's Putin's," Gleb said.

"It's over a hundred meters. Can you hit it?"

"It's too stupid to move . . . just hovers like a *tochka* whore." Gleb fired on full automatic and the drone shuddered, tilted, and struggled to maintain altitude. The drop was erratic, sliding left then right but unable to slow descent until it gave up and plunged into the trees across the road.

14

B reakfast was apple-filled potato pancakes and weak coffee in a guest breakfast room separate from the religious, where Al sat with the monks. An intermittent rain settled on Poland, and Brandt hoped it would keep the armed drones away. Tig was morose, his mind in another place, maybe with his ex-wife or maybe in the desert. Lena was dressed differently, as if she'd lost her luggage. She looked like she was heading for the farmers market on Saturday in simple blue jeans and a gray cotton sweatshirt borrowed from Casey. Tight around the bust.

They left for Wieliczka from a side door that allowed them to walk to their vehicles under an old wood roof that protected delivery trucks from the rain. Al and Brother Kasmir led the way to the salt mine in a rusty Toyota truck. Tig drove the Escalade and checked the gray sky for drones that didn't mind the rain.

At the mine, they parked the truck in an open spot reserved for clergy and Tig slid the SUV next to it. He got out, opened the weapons locker in the rear, and picked out two Glocks, one for Brandt and one for him. Brandt strapped on a backpack with head lamps and tools they might need. Tig helped Lena carry some of her equipment. The clergy elevator took them down four hundred forty feet to the room where articles for church rites were stored.

Al was dressed for mine work in a pair of work pants and a clerical shirt without the white collar. "We have a few minutes before the tourists come. The cathedral is worth seeing before we get started. Take a quick look, but don't wander too far. We have a long day ahead of us."

Brandt had seen it before and stayed with Al in the chapel's doorway where they could watch the others. He knew that weddings with a thousand guests had been held in the underground cathedral. Casey uttered an audible gasp when she entered the crossing and nave. Carved from rock salt, the chandeliers were listed as a national treasure. They sparkled like the finest Czech crystal. The mosaic-pattern floor, walls, and altar had been dug out by skilled miners. Statues depicting biblical scenes had been chiseled from rock salt and mimicked the work of Renaissance sculptors. Lena patted the head of a kneeling statue, sniffed her hand for odor, then brushed invisible salt away.

Al was busy with an iPad tablet Brother Ignatius had given him with the mine's plan and diagrams. He showed it to Brandt next to him. "The rooms in purple are chambers open to the public. We can skip those. When they're finished looking, we'll take the stairs down to the lake. It never fluctuates more than a few inches. Besides the dining room, there are some storage areas around it that could hold a few SADMs. Maybe we'll be surprised. Oh, and watch out for bats on the stairs."

"Vampire bats?" asked Brandt.

"Certainly feral."

"Casey will freak out if she sees one."

"The local villagers believe they were here before the Russians. Left during the occupation and returned when the Russians went home."

"Feral and snobby."

"They like to nest around the lake. Look up and you might see them hanging."

When the group joined them, Brandt handed out head lamps and flashlights. Everyone passed on the hard hats, then started down narrow, creaky, poorly lit stairs with shaky handrails. When they reached the underground lake, sunken lighting put a blue-green cast on the walls and ceiling.

Al stopped at the bottom of the stairs and waved an arm at the setting. "Germans call it the Polish Riviera."

The stone path around the lake was eight feet wide and led past storage rooms. Older wood doors showed age but were free of the chloride corrosion released by the rock salt on the newer metal doors.

"Nine rooms, everyone take one. If you find anything suspicious, have Lena or Brandt check it," Casey said.

Brandt's room had small wood crates containing broken mining tools and plastic buckets of rusty nails, screws, and hinges. The others reported similar items. Al checked the last four rooms himself. Then they walked back up the stairs to the next level, a worked-out mine shaft with enclosed storage areas and open chambers protruding along the sides. A wall switch lit up a string of caged lights.

Al pointed to the floor rails used for the mine bucket cars. "Be careful you don't trip over these." Then he checked his tablet again. "Sixteen rooms along here." He flashed his head lamp on a corroded door. "From the look of that one, we might have a problem getting in. The map doesn't show how far the shaft goes."

"I'll find the end while the rest of you check the rooms," Brandt said.

"Stay on the main line or you'll get lost."

Brandt nodded and moved on. His progress was slow, the footing difficult with the tricky rails and floor debris. As he went deeper into the shaft, he found that many of the lights had died. If it had been a dream, he would have tried to wake up. When he came to a new wing, he would look for a switch to turn on the lights or just flash his head lamp down the passage. The shiniest rails were the most worn and kept him on the main shaft. After twenty-five minutes, he reached a spot he thought must be the end. Crates, boxes, and tarps covering old mining machines and broken furniture were piled there. Short open chambers to the left and right were like wings, holding similar materials. He wanted to be sure this was the end, and he started to move some of the lighter items away. As he moved crates, his head lamp reflected a glimpse of flat, cold metal. He moved larger boxes and was able to shove a piece of machinery aside, uncovering a door that didn't look like any of the others he'd seen—more like a vault, a thick oak door with metal plates attached over panels. Two heavy steel bars were folded across the front with oversized padlocks to hold them in place. The wood above the panels had an aged carved inscription in Polish: *Plaga*. Stenciled in yellow paint on one steel plate: *Juden*. On each corner of the door, he could barely make out a timeworn chiseled skull in the wood.

He would need more equipment than he had to open this door, so he took pictures with this phone and followed the rails back to where the rest were searching. When Al saw the pictures, he said, "I know what's inside."

Casey looked at the pictures, then handed the phone to Tig.

Tig shook his head and said, "We're gonna need a bolt cutter and a big-ass pry bar. Maybe some C-4 to blow it open."

"Easy enough in a mine," Al said. "Come with me."

Brandt led Casey and Lena back down to the lake to wait for Al and Tig to find the tools. They sat on benches placed for tourists.

"What do you think is behind that door?" Casey asked.

"Death. Has to be," Brandt said. "Crypts, coffins, vampires, and the undead . . . maybe some ghost miners. The stuff of horror flicks."

"Stop," Casey said.

"Evil. I'm sure Petrov was in there," Lena said.

"It's not the kind of door you want to open unless you have to," Brandt said.

Tig came partway down the stairs and told them to come back up. Al was waiting with a bolt cutter and handed Brandt a gooseneck crowbar. Tig had a six-foot pry bar. When they reached the door, they cleared away the rest of the crates, furniture, and machinery. Al took an oily rag from a box and wiped the dirt and dust off the door, then they all stepped back for a long look. Brandt saw a thick medieval door modified with modern steel plates most likely forged in a Krupp foundry in Essen. He wondered if it was designed to keep people out or to keep the contents inside.

Al used the bolt cutter to remove the padlocks. Then Brandt lifted the bars away. The lever handle wouldn't budge, so Brandt knelt down and inspected it. "Without the key, there's no way we open this one. We'll have to drill it out." He grabbed a high-speed drill from his backpack and began to work on the lock.

Tig used the pry bar to clear out the gaps between the door and the frame. All three took turns with the drill. Fifty minutes later, the lock handle was ready to be removed.

Brandt used his crowbar to gouge out the lock in pieces, leaving a hole. He bent down with his head lamp on and looked inside. "Can't see much."

"Before we go in, let me explain what I believe we'll find in there," Al said. "*Plaga* is the Black Death. When the plague began to spread across Europe, King Kazimierz closed off the borders and quarantined risky towns. Saved a lot of Poles. In this region, travelers, foreigners, and traders were forced into the mines to prove their health. Of course, some were sick and ended up spreading the disease to the healthy ones. We will find their remains inside. *Juden* is the work of the Nazis. They brought Jews here to work in the mine. Many, of course, died and the Nazis found it convenient to toss their bodies in with the plague victims. What's inside will not be pleasant."

Tig finished clearing the door edges. Brandt hooked the gooseneck into the hole and pulled.

"Stop," Al said. "I need to test for gas. Wait out here, please."

"Methane?"

"This isn't a coal mine. This gas is a lot more deadly."

Al put on a miner's mask and took a yellow hand meter he'd brought from Tyniec into the chamber while the rest stayed in the wings, by the door. When he came out, his face was ashen, his eyes saddened.

"Is it safe?" Brandt asked.

"No gas. But I wouldn't call it safe."

"What's in there?" Casey said.

"Bones . . . thousands . . . crates of bones. Bones all over. It's an ossuary. Imagine how catacombs look after an earthquake. And some things the KGB left. Stacks of them."

"Nukes?" Brandt said.

Al nodded. "It's them."

"Let's take a look," Casey said.

"No light switch. Take the oil lamps with us," Al said.

Tig worked on getting the oil lamps lit. Their head lamps sprayed and flickered light into an eerie, dusty cavern filled with boxes, more crates, small wood barrels, large steel drums, tarps, and rotting woven mats. Bones were scattered like twigs in a forest and stuck up out of oil drums. The shrunken cadavers were the most unsettling. The Russian SADMs were under piles of lumber, torn tarps, and bone containers. Thick industrial hoses and obsolete mining drills stood in the way. They cleared away the larger debris and uncovered open rectangular metal frames stacked three high, supporting horizontal barrel shapes.

"Looks like they're all here," Brandt said.

"No, not all," Lena said. "I only count fifty-five." She pointed to an empty spot next to the first stack. "Petrov has been here. Looks like six weapons are gone. We need to check the rest for tritium."

"These are SADMs?" Casey asked Brandt. "They look like beer barrels hanging inside the frames, not nukes."

Brandt swiped fingers across one frame, looking for a serial number or lettering under the dirt. "Yeah, almost the same as ours. Backpack size."

"I need to go back up and call Deke. He can get NATO moving," Casey said.

Brandt watched Lena extract a test instrument that resembled a metered caulking gun with a thin hose from a bag. Tig came back in and started setting out bright oil lamps.

"Looks like I'm up," Brandt said. The SADM on the top of a stack had the easiest eye-level access to the lock on the flat top of the barrel shape. Brandt spun the dial a few times to get the feel. "Just like ours." He sighed in relief, wondering if they bought them from the same manufacturer. Hoping they did.

"Can you open it?" Lena asked.

"I think so," Brandt said it like he was trying to convince himself. "Focus your head lamps on it for me. The picking slot is tiny."

Lena and Al moved closer and adjusted their beams.

"Got it." Brandt grabbed his pack, found the T-shaped slender tool, and inserted it in the slot. He began to twist the dial.

"Don't you need a stethoscope?" Tig said.

"Naw, that's a movie thing. You can't hear the tumblers fall in place. You have to feel the click."

The first number came quickly. "That was easy enough. First number is seven. Somebody write it down."

Al wrote it in the dust on top of a box lid. The second number followed just as quick: four. He dialed three point five before finding an eight and two. Brandt twisted the lock and the lugs released.

"You're amazing," Lena said.

He felt lucky, not amazing. "I should go to the casino and bet those numbers."

Tig began clearing bones and debris from the other stacked weapons.

Lena attached the cable end of her instrument to the inside of the hole left by the lock and switched it on. Her eyes never left the dial. "Empty. This one's safe."

"I'm gonna pray the others have the same combination," Brandt said.

"Russians like to keep things simple," Lena said.

Brandt dropped down to the second weapon, dialed the same numbers, and removed the lock. "We caught a break."

Lena's test showed it safe too.

They were able to repeat the procedure until the eighth stack, where the combination failed and Brandt had to repeat his picking effort. New numbers but same result for those remaining. After three hours, the weapons had all been opened and tested. The lack of tritium was comforting.

"We don't have any of Gleb's locks, but we can't leave them like this," Brandt said. "It will take time to change the combination, but it needs to be done. You guys can put the old ones back on then."

"You can do that?" Tig said.

"It's what separates me from a safecracker."

"Put in 1-9-8-9, the year the Berlin Wall came down," Al said.

"That's only four numbers," Tig said.

"Three point five is always the middle number," Al said.

Brandt froze like a statue, his eyes not moving. He knew about the common middle number procedure but wondered how the alpha monk knew it. Al raised more questions than a sixth grade sex lecture.

Casey returned to the ossuary. "Looks like things went well."

"We're done except locking them back up," said Brandt. "No tritium."

"It's a good start, but we don't have them all," Lena said.

"When will the NATO people be here?" Brandt asked.

"And what about the Russians? We're not turning them over, are we?" Tig said.

Casey replied, "Sturm is flying a C-130 in with a lead team of five to help until they figure out the rest. Three hours ETA. I'm supposed to meet them at the airport. They're trying to come up with an illusion that will work. They never thought we'd find so many so soon. As for as the Russians, right now these are ours. Moky and Gleb can beg Moscow for forgiveness."

"That won't last. The State Department will hold a press conference and special event to hand them back," Brandt said.

"What about the room? The vault door can't be locked anymore," Lena said.

Casey mumbled a familiar curse. "You and I will go get new locks for the bars and then go meet the plane. These guys will have to be guards."

"We'll need sustenance," Tig said. "I'm starved."

"Tig, go have the hotel kitchen fix up something to bring back," Brandt said.

"Beer too. Czech beer, pilsner," Al said.

15

A l and Brandt shoved the door closed and pulled the bars down. They tilted some wobbly old metal chairs with torn vinyl seats against wood crates in front of the damaged door. A gauge read 15 degrees Celsius, 59 Fahrenheit. Slivers of rock salt in the walls reflected light like chips of quartz. Feldspar cast a pinkish tone, iron in the rock left a strip of rusty brown down to the floor.

Al exhaled loudly and sat down. "I knew as soon as I mentioned the common middle number to Tig it was a mistake. I hoped you missed it, but I could tell by the way you reacted that a light went off in your head."

"No one is supposed to know the full code. That's always been the rule. The first two numbers or the last two. That's all. You knew about the three point five common number in the middle. How could a monk know that?"

Al shifted his chair to keep it from rocking on the uneven shaft floor. "My old job . . . I was a major in the Czech People's Army. Russia copied your procedure. Two-man control was the rule. That meant the same common middle number for security."

Brandt thought about his Glock. Al had suddenly switched from curious enigma to risky unknown. He felt around his pockets and belt in back for his weapon. "It's a big leap from Czech Major to Brother Al. Let's hear it."

Al let a smile sneak out. "You don't need your Glock. I'm not a spy or working for the Russkies. I truly am a Benedictine."

"I'm listening." Brandt wiggled and felt the Glock at the back of his waist. Saint John Nepomuk had trusted the Benedictines. He would be more careful.

Al pulled a black finger rosary from a pocket. "The KGB tried to get sole control of the SADMs in Czechia. I was the Czech officer in charge of security and safety. They killed my Soviet counterpart, a good friend. He had warned me something was wrong. They tried to kill me too."

"Let me guess, they failed."

Al continued to finger the beads. "It was close. I was afraid for my family. I needed to get home quickly. Back then, no one in Prague would pick up soldiers, so I ripped off my uniform jacket and managed to get a ride into the city. The KGB was already at my home. I saw them bring out the bags holding my wife's and son's bodies."

"I'm sorry. That must have been awful."

"You cannot imagine the pain I felt. Real torture. In a matter of hours, my life had become a vision of hell. I knew the monks that had been kicked out of Strahov lived on a farm on the way to Brno. I stole a bike, walked, grabbed rides, and hid from the KGB until I reached them. Only five of the original twenty-seven were left. The result of brutal interrogations, prison camps, and firing squads. I stayed there three weeks, helping them farm and instructing them on how to deal with the Russians, what to expect, what to hide. The kind of questions they would be asked and how to answer them. There came a time when my presence was too risky, and we agreed I had to leave. Czechia, Hungary, and East Germany were too dangerous. Poland was safer, closer, and the church was still able to operate in most of the country. I was given a monk's habit and told to drive a load of wheat and rye to Tyniec. The abbot there arranged for Pope John Paul II to request a visit from me. With the church truce in Poland, a request from the pope for a lowly brother was okayed without a problem. I flew to Munich with a Russian escort who asked me to pray for him, and I did while he sat next to me on the plane. Two Episcopal priests met me when we landed, and I flew on to Milan with them. The next day, we took a train to Rome."

"That's quite a story, but it doesn't explain how you got here as Brother Al."

Tig arrived with a baguette in white paper, a hunk of Swiss cheese wrapped in wax paper, and a long stick of sausage.

"No beer?" Al said.

"It's coming. One of the staff is bringing it up the stairs. I'll be back."

Al placed the bread in its paper wrapping on a crate. Brandt took a pocketknife, sliced a chunk from the sausage stick, then set the sausage and knife on the paper. The sausage went down better than Al's story. The mental picture he'd formed of Al was like a time-lapse photo that kept flipping between a monk kneeling in a church with an AK-47 strapped to his back or a papal figure in white vestments commanding a tank. The yin and yang of Al the monk.

Al unwrapped the cheese and cut a thick slice. "I think how I got here is not so interesting. I am curious how *you* got here. I don't see you as a swashbuckling, James Bond superspy."

"Funny. Neither does anyone else. I'm more the accidental agent."

"How do you see yourself?"

The question touched Brandt in an odd way. What swagger he had toward Al left him in a sigh. He shuffled some rubble with his feet, then lifted his head. His voice went soft, almost a whisper. "I guess I'm a travel guide who got lost. My wife and I had a travel business. Those were good times. When she died, I had a difficult time dealing with the loss. Deke probably saved my life. Pulled me into a CIA mission I wasn't really prepared for. It's when I met Casey."

"So now you're an agent. Quite a change."

"Sometimes I think I'm still lost."

"The saints will tell you that feeling lost is a holy place to be. Not a comfortable one, but a holy one."

The lights in the shaft went out. The dark side of the moon had more lumens.

"I left my head lamp inside," Brandt said.

"Me too. I hope Tig can make it back here with the beer."

Brandt groped for the bread and twisted off a chunk.

When a light began to bounce around the walls and rails, Al said. "We might need your Glock."

Brandt fumbled for it behind his back, then set it in his lap.

They both heard Tig say, "It's me." He was out of breath. "Moky and Gleb are here."

§

Casey and Lena drove to John Paul II airport in the village of Balice. The commercial terminal dwarfed the military and cargo zone across the field. They waited in a hangar office with two Polish corporals and two cargo checkers. A C-130 with *Air Europa Transport* on the fuselage landed and taxied to the cargo area. Casey watched the tail door open and a long panel truck drive down the ramp. Four men in civilian clothes began loading luggage and gear into the truck. *European Union Department of Mines* was painted on the side of the truck.

Casey recognized the man in charge walking toward her—Bronfman from Helsinki Station. "Hello again. How'd you get picked for this?" Casey said.

"College. Colorado School of Mines. I've been in more than a few. Langley wanted someone who knew their way around in the dark, so they sent me. I'm glad they did. All I do is monitor Nord Stream gas flows from Russia. Putting numbers in boxes and sending them to Langley. Pretty boring stuff."

"What's the plan?"

Lena approached the four standing by the truck and welcomed them.

Bronfman kept his eyes on her. "Is she one of us?"

"She's our Russian scientist."

He turned back to Casey. "Sturm and Deke are fitting out a semi to haul the weapons to some old nuke storage bunker. Deke has to come up with something that looks like a simple civilian operation—a convoy that doesn't look like a convoy. Maybe Lufthansa trucks filled with Delta Force. That's the easy part."

"What's the tough part?"

"Getting them on the truck without the Poles getting curious."

"Does Warsaw know you're here?"

"Not yet. We're staying in Krakow, away from the mine, until we have a plan."

"When will the trucks get here?"

"If all goes well, tomorrow. We better have a plan by then."

§

Brandt had hoped the Russians were drunk in Pilsen, or Prague, or Munich. Nowhere near Krakow. Secrets in NATO might as well be posted on Facebook. How else did they know to look for them in Wieliczka?

"Did they see you?" Brandt asked Tig.

"Negative. I heard someone speaking Russian in the tourist passageway. I climbed up the stairs, turned off the lights, and watched. They didn't hesitate. They went to the dining area and grabbed a waiter. Gleb got loud and aggressive with him. The rest of the staff came out to quiet things down."

"We can't let them see Casey and Lena. Go back up to the parking lot and warn them to stay away. Be sure you don't run into any Russians."

"What are you guys going to do?"

"We'll stay here. Leave the lights off. If you see them leave, let us know," Brandt said.

"I'm hoping they're just looking for us and not the nukes," Al said. "If they don't find us, maybe they'll move on."

"There's no way we can get these things out of here without them knowing."

Tig left to warn Casey, while Al and Brandt sat in the dark.

"Go ahead and finish your story," said Brandt. "How'd you end up a monk with us?"

"In Rome, I had a very brief meeting with the pope. His staff took over and found a monastery in Florence where I would be safe. I was glad to be there, but the pain from the loss of my wife and son wouldn't leave. I needed work, something to distract my mind. At first, I just helped out with the vineyard and household chores. Ultimately, I got curious about the monks' daily schedule. I hadn't gone to

Mass since I was a child, but I started going back. Occasionally first, then daily. The pain was still there. I don't think it ever completely leaves, but I also began to feel periods of relief . . . almost joy."

Brandt knew a wound like that was a scab that never healed.

"The Russians left Prague in July the next year. By the time I came back, I was attending all seven canonical hours. The monks that survived needed help. Too many had been lost. To rebuild and replenish the monasteries was a secular task, something where I could help. I lived in twelve different religious enclaves over the next sixteen years, helping them to recover from the Soviet trauma."

"When did you decide to become a monk?" Brandt was more than curious. Everything people said seemed more open and poignant in the dark, as if light increased inhibitions. Some of his most heart-felt talks with Casey were in bed with the lights out. Arguments and squabbles came in daylight. Night brought peace.

"I'm not sure that decision has been made. In 2012, I finally found Elena's and Sergei's graves. It brought all the horror back. For months, I was like a dog circling for a place to lie down. Part of me thirsted for revenge and part of me searched for peace. Brother Anton suggested I go back to Florence, to the place where it had all started, the Abbey of Monte Oliveto Maggiore. I began the discernment process to become a monk there."

"You're past the time limit," Brandt said.

"Is there any more beer? Talk and cheese make me thirsty."

The beer came in old-style porcelain flip-tops. Brandt felt around the crate and found one on the ground. "Here."

Al groped for it. "*Danke.* After two years, the abbot told me that God doesn't care about Benedictine rules and timetables. Go back to Prague and be useful until you know. That's what I have done."

Brandt decided to pry. In the dark it was easier. "What keeps you from final solemn vows?"

"An ache in my soul. It never leaves. I miss having the togetherness of a family. The sense of two people making their way through life together. The monks haven't been able to replace that experience. There's a darkness too. A troubling one."

"If you left, what would you do?"

In the dark, Brandt could sense Al shaking his head.

"I have no answer for that."

§

Tig met Casey at the car. "We have a problem. Moky and Gleb are here."

Casey looked at Lena as if she might know why.

"I never mentioned the mines," Lena said. "I don't know why they came here."

"Do you have the new padlocks?" Tig asked.

Casey lifted a plastic bag.

"I need your head lamps too."

"We can't let Moky see Lena," Casey said. "We'll hide in the cathedral until Brandt finishes."

Lena nodded. "Gleb will never go in there."

"We'll come get you," said Tig.

§

After Brandt and Al relocked the bars and they were on the way back to Tyniec, Casey called Deke about Moky.

"Didn't expect that," Deke said.

"See if Langley knows how they found us."

"Good question. Bronfman just left the consulate for the mine. Find a safe place to meet him away from the Russians."

Casey sent the text to Bronfman and read his answer. "I know Bronfman from Helsinki. He wants us to tell him where to meet."

"Send him to Kopalnia Smaku in Czarnochowice," Al said. "It's off the main highway. We should be safe from the Russians there."

Al had chosen a simple café in a rural village with a plain tile floor, a curious mix of handmade dark wood chairs, and tables topped with cut-glass shakers of salt, pepper, and paprika. The walls were barren of art, and faded dried flowers sat on a small bar with a Formica top. For Martha Stewart it would have been a room from hell, artistically bland, but with the promise of home-cooked meals that small-town diners offered.

"The Polish sample plate is excellent. Authentic cabbage rolls and pierogi," Al said.

"How's the pizza?" asked Brandt.

"It's my favorite. With kielbasa topping."

"Do they have a veggie?" Casey said.

"Never thought to ask."

The owner came over and greeted them with a smile and respectful nod toward Al, who was back in a clerical collar. They ordered two pizzas with Polish sausage and beer. Then, in Polish, Lena ordered a veggie pizza for her and Casey.

Bronfman stuck his head inside and looked around. His head was almost as round as a soccer ball, topped with Scandinavian blond hair that fit well in Finland. He had delicate eyes and fingers that stretched like snakes. Seeing Casey, he came in and walked to their table. "How did you find this place? I drove past three times."

"Local guide," Casey said and introduced everyone.

Bronfman sat and ordered a beer.

"We have a plan yet?" Casey asked.

Bronfman looked around to be sure it was safe. "Sure do. Deke pushed Sturm aside. He's running this now. Sturm just nods okay. The plan is a bit complex, mostly theatrics and scare tactics. Grayson came up with it from his hospital bed, and Langley helped put it together."

The owner brought the pizzas and plates, then said something in Polish to Lena.

"He wants to show me the mine," she said. "I told him I've already seen it."

Bronfman waited for the owner to leave. "The plan is to create a fake biohazard in the mine. The ossuary fits in perfect. We'll have a team in hazmat suits bringing up everything—bones, machines, boxes, weapons—and put them in the truck."

"The Poles won't let you close the mine down," Al said.

"We know. We'll only quarantine the ossuary and the shaft."

"The Poles still won't like it. They'll want proof."

"The proof is coming to the consulate tomorrow. Two hazmat suits, vials, and a written CDC report. *Staphylococcus* and *Micrococcus* were found in new potentially lethal mutations along with dangerous airborne fungi. The ossuary and shaft is a death trap that needs to be emptied and disinfected before it spreads to the tourist areas."

"They still won't like it," Brandt said. "They don't like the EU pushing them around."

"They'll be presented with a choice. Let us clean out the ossuary or have the site condemned and lose the UNESCO heritage designation. No one wants to risk that."

"What about the Russians?" Casey asked.

"There'll be plenty of Delta Force with the truck. The Russians won't want to risk a battle in a NATO country. Deke is loading the truck with biohazard containers that we'll put the weapons in."

"That won't fool Moky," Brandt said.

"He can't be sure what's inside them. He'll have to check with Moscow before doing anything," Lena said.

"So what happens tomorrow?" Tig asked.

"After I get the shipment from the consulate, I'll pick one of you up at the abbey to show me the way down to the ossuary. We'll do a short inspection to 'verify' the lab results, then go to the mine authority offices with the plan."

"What about the other twenty-nine?" Casey asked. "We still need to find them."

Lena was ready. "We have to focus on places where my research and Petrov's travels coincide. Potsdam, Dresden, or Rostock. One of those should be next."

§

Everyone was pleased Grayson had recovered enough to be an asset again. Over the pizza and beer, Bronfman explained how grateful he was for some real field work.

They split up for the drive back to the abbey. Casey rode with Bronfman in the Ford rental sedan, and the rest followed in the SUV.

Tig put the Glocks back in the locker but handed Brandt two Heckler submachine guns to hold for the drive back. "A nighttime precaution with the Russians around," he said.

The streets were deserted and windows shuttered with only dim lights, more like candles, escaping through the cracks. The drive to the main highway cut through the dense Niepolomice forest on a narrow two-lane road that had been chewed up, rutted, and potholed by heavy Soviet tanks as if they'd made a daily commute from Krakow. They passed the rusty hulk of a Russian Volga staff car with its doors, wheels, and seats missing. It reminded Brandt of abandoned vehicles across farm belt highways.

Lena asked Al, "Do you play *mariáš?*"

"Czechs learn as children and play for life. Mariáš, foosball, and billiards are very popular in monasteries. Gambling is forbidden, of course. Though sometimes the next day's tasks might be decided by a game. How do you know about *mariáš?* It's not a Russian game."

"A boyfriend taught me. He also taught me how to cheat."

"Then I am forewarned. We play tomorrow."

A few miles out of the village, red flares had been placed in the road to warn of an auto wreck. Bronfman and Tig slowed to a stop. The road was blocked by a pickup truck and a Skoda crossways in the road with taillights flashing warnings. Two men standing by the Skoda pointed at the truck.

Brandt called Casey. "What do you think?"

"Looks okay. But I told Bronfman to stay in the car and keep it running."

Brandt handed Tig one of the Hecklers. "Just in case."

The two men discussing the accident shook hands and returned to their vehicles.

Bronfman crept ahead, ready to pull around if the truck cleared the way, just as an RPG rocket from the tree line shot across the front of the Ford. Bronfman hit the brakes hard. A second rocket went over the roof.

Brandt said, "Woods on the left," and jumped out of the car. He sprayed his Heckler toward the trees where the rocket had exited.

Tig didn't move.

The man by the pickup crouched down and fired a pistol that put a hole in the center of the Ford windshield. Casey opened the door, dropped one foot to the ground, and shot him twice in the chest with her automatic. The second man ran into the woods.

"Tig, go around Bronfman and push the Skoda out of the way," Brandt ordered.

Tig sat stone-faced.

A third RPG rocket sailed between the two vehicles.

"Move, dammit!" Brandt screamed. He ran up to Casey's car and continued to spray wild bursts into the woods.

Tig finally pulled around Bronfman and began to push the Skoda off the road.

"You guys okay?" Brandt said.

Tig had the Skoda halfway into a ditch.

"So far. Let's get out of here," Casey said.

Brandt dived into the back seat, and Bronfman accelerated away.

§

The Ardbeg scotch was gone, and Al produced a bottle of cognac. The fireplace had been cleaned and stacked with hornbeam logs and kindling. Tig got it roaring. Most of the monastery had settled in for the night. Matins devotion began at three the next morning.

"Maybe natural gas reporting isn't so bad," Bronfman said.

"What will you do about the bullet hole in the windshield?" Brandt asked.

"I'll drop it off at the consulate and let them take care of it. Maybe they'll put in a claim to the Russian embassy," Bronfman joked.

"Those weren't Russians," Lena said.

Al nodded in agreement.

"If it was Gleb, we'd all be dead. They wouldn't have missed," Lena added.

"Way too sloppy for Black Berets," Al said. "Amateurish."

"Will the body by the truck be a problem?" Tig said.

Lena shrugged. "Polish Mafia."

Brandt stood and listened to the other four sitting around the table sharing their theories. The picture of John Paul II above the fireplace had one hand raised as if waving an all clear. He wondered if Moky was somehow connected to the drones. Lena was probably right about the Polish Mafia. It seemed like every country had their own version of a crime family. Not the Swiss, though—the government assumed that role. Could it be Sword of Allah? The drone attack made him wonder, but he still couldn't see them abandoning knives. No one abandons their signature. Best he could come up with, given that they'd missed three times, was a group who had never fired an RPG before. Plenty of extreme left or far right groups in Europe fit that description. Langley had a list two pages long—Friends of Trotsky, the Goering Group, the Marx Militia, and the Brown Shirt Brigade were the largest and covered both extremes of the political scale. Secret meetings and loose talk, but no action. Hard to fathom RPGs—weapons not readily available at Guns R Us—in their hands. The drone attack had sophistication, but the RPG misses seemed like something hastily thrown together. Then he remembered there was never a shortage of futility in battle. All the agency's and military's botched missions were proof. The RPG rockets could have been old and malfunctioned. Even battle-hardened pros made mistakes. Anyone could be behind the attacks, even a vodka-soaked Spetsnaz team.

Bronfman left for the hotel, planning to be back with a new car in the morning. The five emaining sat together, pouring cognac as if celebrating New Year's Eve. Nerves needed to be calmed. They all knew they had been lucky. Then Deke called Casey.

She went to her room to take the call, Brandt followed her. He stood close and heard her say, "Wow. This must a big deal in Moscow." She looked up at Brandt as she hung up.

"Wows" from Casey were meaningful, sometimes imperative, like bugle calls to charge. "What was that all about?" Brandt asked.

"We know how the Russians found us here. They tasked the Gagarin satellite to track our car."

"That's state-of-the-art surveillance. No need for drones with that on our ass. The Kremlin's not fooling around. Gagarin can fix on an engine signature, heartbeat, or voice pattern. Moscow Center can only request access. Approval has to come from the Executive Committee."

"Deke thinks it picked up our engine signature when we left Brussels."

"What should we do?"

"Nothing for now. Deke figures we can use this to our advantage at some point. He said to be sure to read the *Post* again today. The same reporter wrote about losing a CIA supervisor in NATO's backyard. Couched it like negligence."

"Grayson?" Brandt said.

"Who else? Deke's worried, and Langley's furious."

Brandt frowned. Reporters came in different shapes: facts-only zealots, truth sleuths, and agenda-pushing parasites. He figured this one lived in a compost pile. "Where's the *Post* get that stuff? Sturm?"

"Well, Sturm's a German first and NATO second. He has to know Berlin still has a grudge with the agency."

Brandt sat down on Casey's bed to weigh everything. "Not sure how this will go over at the White House, but I'm thinking of pulling the plug on Tig. He froze up in the ambush."

"I wondered how he did. If you think it's the right thing to do, go ahead. But the timing isn't great. Might piss off the White House connection just when the *Post* has the director's ass in its crosshairs."

"Yeah, I thought of that too. I'll talk to him and decide then."

"The trucks and Delta Force will be here late tomorrow. If all goes well at the mine, Bronfman plans to load the nukes the next day. Tig volunteered to go with him in the morning."

16

Al was already at chapel for Matins, followed by Lauds. Brandt showered and waited in the room, straddling a desk chair, until Tig came in from his morning run.

"Tig, we need to talk about what happened at the ambush. I expected more from you than a blank stare."

Tig picked up a towel and wiped sweat from his face. "I wasn't scared, you know."

"I didn't say you were, but I want to hear your explanation."

"Ambushes don't scare me."

"They do me." Brandt stood up. "I'm scared of a lot of things—snakes, pundits, experts—but ambushes top them all."

Tig gazed out the window, then lowered his head and sat on the bed. He looked up to Brandt. "I said I wasn't scared. I just didn't know what to do. I've been through much worse than that . . . real firefights . . . long ones. I was always able to make decisions then. But yesterday I drew a blank. I knew to never stop in the kill zone. Go forward or go at them. Then I wondered if leaving you guys alone was the right move. What if Bronfman was hit? Who would drive the car? And if you got shot, would I get the blame again? I just couldn't make a decision. When you yelled at me, I was glad someone told me what to do."

Brandt looked at him with concern. Tig had become a Smurf. All he needed was a floppy white stocking cap. The meek might inherit the earth, but passivity and indecision in a soldier can get a lot of people killed. "I can't have you on this mission like that, Tig. We need someone we can count on. You needed to act fast."

"I know. It won't happen again."

"How can I be sure?"

Tig rose slowly from the bed. He met Brandt eye to eye and spoke with a firm voice. "I know you're concerned, but I'm okay now. You can count on me."

"Is Lena on your mind? Are you two cool?"

"Yeah, we're cool."

Brandt hesitated, then made a funny liquid sound with his lips. "Bronfman should be here soon. Get ready."

§

Bronfman picked up Tig in the morning. He had vials, paperwork, and hazmat suits with him. They dressed in the priest's office before Tig led him to the ossuary chamber. They moved everything away from the door, and Bronfman stuck a large Day-Glo sign on a panel that read:

DANGER

DO NOT ENTER

BIOHAZARD

INFECTIOUS WASTE

A second sign repeated the warning in Polish, French, and German. Tig took Bronfman downstairs to kill time and show him the lake. On their way back up, they strung red-and-orange biohazard tape across the shaft entrance by the stairs. In the mine authority office, they had to wait to see the commissioner.

"What's in the vial?" Tig asked.

"Not sure," replied Bronfman. "But I was told to be very careful with it."

An aide eventually escorted them into Commissioner Orodsky's office. After the introductions, Bronfman instructed him on the mine problem and what needed to be done.

"We've never had any ill effects from that part of the mine. Are you certain of this?" Orodsky said.

Bronfman handed him the written report and set the vial on the desk in front of the commissioner. Orodsky read the report, then reached for the vial.

"Be careful with the vial. Open it in here and we could all be dead in forty-eight hours."

Orodsky pulled his hand back. "I'll have to get approval from the minister."

"I'll be back in the morning with a truck and a biohazard team to empty and disinfect the chamber. Be sure to tell him if he refuses decontamination, the EU Mine Authority will be forced to close the mine."

"Brussels acts like Hitler sometimes."

"When the mine is safe, you'll thank us. You can keep the vial."

Orodsky said, "Take it. I have no need for it."

When they left, Tig said, "That went well."

"We surprised him. Tomorrow could be different. I just hope they don't have time to get their people in here to test. Deke said since we let them keep the mine open while we work, they'll agree."

§

Casey got on her laptop and phone with Deke and Langley while waiting for Tig and Bronfman to return. Brandt watched Lena and Al play cards while he drank coffee and traded emails with his London art agent.

The longer Brandt watched the mariáš game, the more confused he got—only thirty-two cards, strange-looking suits. Points were won by winning tricks. He got that part. Then one hand, Lena announced a *flek* (double), followed by Al's *re-flek* challenge (double again) and Lena's final re-double *tutti*. Lena won with an enthusiastic shriek, and they both laughed. Brandt had seen enough to know he didn't understand the game and went back to his room.

After a few minutes, Casey knocked and came in. "How are things in the London art world?"

"The Nottingham sale has been a big help. There's a lot of interest in my work now. Cybil wants me back working in my studio. The market is completely fickle. She says when you're hot, you have to get stuff out there. It won't last forever."

"Hopefully we can wrap this up soon and get you back in the studio."

"That's what bothers me. I don't know which I want more. Stand in front of an easel with a brush or point a Glock at Gleb."

Casey read a text. "Bronfman is on his way here with Tig. Let's see what they have to say."

They waited in the monastery entrance as Brandt kept watch for another drone. Lena and Al came down from their card game to wait with them. Bronfman arrived, looking relaxed. Brandt took that as a good sign. "Any problems?" Brandt said .

"I think we're good. I wish the truck was here and we could get this done before the Poles have time to react. If they start asking questions, there could be problems."

"Any sign of Moky or Gleb?" Lena asked.

"Negative," Tig said. "How'd the card game go?"

"I'm winning, so it's fun. Al is going to show me around before it gets dark."

§

Al led Lena toward the agricultural area in back of the monastery. The first stop was an expanded greenhouse separated from the farm and the chapel. Al peeked in and saw two monks, one tending an herb garden, the second occupied with rows of flowers. "Let's go in."

The greenhouse odors went from peat and decay to lilac and hyacinth; the humidity could trigger sweat. The monks went about their work as if no one had entered.

"Everything is so green. They bring hope for spring," Lena said. A tall tray of chives edged a row of basil. She pointed to each section and named them. "Coriander, dill, parsley, chamomile, and cilantro."

"You know your herbs. When I was here years ago, I made the mistake of pulling up the basil thinking it was a weed. The monk in charge wanted to put me on the rack."

"They have a rack here? I thought those were a part of history."

"The monks brought it from the castle to hide it from the Germans. The Russians had modern torture methods and didn't need it. It's probably still around here some place."

The monk tending the flowers was stick thin, bent over, and shrunken with advanced age. He was checking the underside of leaves for fungus and for insects—aphids, mealybugs, mites, and whiteflies.

"You were married before you became a monk, weren't you?"

"Yes, how did you know?"

"You're comfortable around Casey and me. Monks and priests get nervous around women, a threat they don't know how to handle."

Al grinned. "The monks in Russia have a saying. 'It's easier for the stallion when a woman gets off the cart.'" He moved a hose out of their way. "Were you ever married?"

"There was a time I thought it would happen. When that ended, I no longer cared about marriage."

The monk dropped his bug inspection and shuffled to Lena, handing her a long-stemmed, bright red rose. "Red roses symbolize deep emotions, part of a beautiful soul," he said. "I hope this will bring pleasant feelings to you." He had a welcoming quality in his voice, smile, and gentle movements. An essence that comes to someone satisfied with their life as it nears the end.

"It's wonderful. Thank you," Lena said. She lifted the rose with a breezy air and sampled its fragrance.

The monk then handed Al a yellow daffodil. "I remember when you first came to Tyniec. It was a new beginning for you. Daffodils, like spring, are for new beginnings. Maybe Tyniec will be a new beginning for you again." The monk bowed his head and then ambled back to his flowers.

"This was clearly a good stop for us," Lena said.

"He left part of it out. New beginnings come after endings. Sometimes sudden, unpleasant ones."

"What did you love about her? Your wife, I mean."

"That's an extraordinary question. Most people want to know what happened but never come right out and ask. Just hint around until they're satisfied. No one has ever asked me that before. You went right to my heart."

"To go from marriage to a monastery, it had to be something tragic . . . something awful that required silence, prayer, and time."

"Are all physicists clairvoyant? Can you bend spoons too?"

Lena chuckled. "I can do parlor tricks with graphs, make them say anything I choose. First rule of physics in Skolkovo Institute is make sure your data gives you the desired result. You never worry about peer reviews in Russia. They can backfire. No one objects to your work out of fear you might be politically connected. Just be sure you give the right people the answer they want."

"Weave your hands and fingers together like you're going to pray," Al said.

Lena lowered her head, interlaced her fingers, then looked up.

"Look at your hands again." Al watched her drop her gaze. "That's what I loved about being with her. We meshed together like those fingers. Nothing could separate us unless we allowed it to. We could be miles apart and still feel joined, like your hands. It's a feeling I miss."

"I've never had anything like that. It must be awful to have had it and lose it."

"You said you almost married. What did you love about him?"

"You'll laugh. It's a strange thing to love about someone. It started with curiosity, but it brought us together."

"Something sensational, I hope."

"You'll be disappointed. I've only told my closest friend about this." Lena hesitated, as if to be sure it was safe to tell. "It was the way he moved. He was a large man, as tall as Brandt, very broad shouldered. A bit of a gut too. But he moved with such grace. When I first saw him walk past my office, I thought, who is that? He moves like a dancer. Watching him skirt tables in the coffee shop was like watching someone in the Bolshoi. I loved dancing with him. We moved so fluidly together."

"I sense there was tragedy too."

"All deaths feel tragic. If it's someone you love, the pain is endless. I'm certain you know that."

"We should leave before we get to the funeral lilies or we'll both be very sad."

17

Heading to the mine in the morning, Brandt suspected his inner con man might be needed before the day was over. Bronfman and the semi were already at the mine when Tig parked their SUV by the cleric entrance. Lena stayed in the monastery in case Moky and Gleb were around.

"Let's wait in the clergy office," Brandt said.

"I'll bring the hazmat suits," Tig said.

"The guy in charge doesn't know we're connected. Probably best if Al and I disappear," Casey said. "We'll be in the cathedral if we're needed."

Inside, Brandt left the door open wide enough to watch Bronfman and Orodsky in animated discussion in the visitor lot. Bronfman nodded and then spoke to the semi driver, who hopped in the cab and moved the rig over near the cleric entrance, sheltered behind a tree line.

Bronfman came in to put his suit on. "Orodsky wanted the truck moved right away. He didn't want to scare off any tourists. He insists I wait until the deputy minister of Agriculture and Mining arrives.

I said if we started now, we could be out of here sooner and have less chance of a tourist problem. Didn't faze him. We have to wait."

"Nice try anyway," Brandt said.

"These suits are damn hot," Bronfman said as he struggled to put his on.

"Did you bring the respirators?" Brandt asked Tig.

"Box on the table."

The deputy minister's limo arrived along with two Polish generals—the local problems Deke had warned about.

"Shit, three of them," Bronfman said. "Let's get this over with."

Brandt and Tig followed Bronfman out to the limo and tried to count heads on the way. Bronfman's team had been enlarged by Delta Force troops. More than thirty men in white hazmat suits stood around the semi waiting to help retrieve the weapons and provide security for the truck.

Orodsky turned his head toward Bronfman and said to the minister, "This is the man from the EU."

"I am Deputy Minister Sketch. Who are you and what are you doing here?" Sketch had wire-framed eyeglasses that pinched his nose like a clothespin and the manner of a bureaucrat who'd reached the zenith of his career and knew it.

"I am Professor Jamison," said Bronfman. "I'm here to save your ass, Minister."

"There is no Jamison in the EU Mining Authority," Sketch said, then nodded toward the generals as a warning. "I think you should be concerned with *your* ass."

"I'm from the Centers for Disease Control in Atlanta, Georgia, and the one who discovered your bug problem. You should be thanking the EU for sending me to save your infected mine. Keep the threats coming and I'll have this whole mine and area quarantined with a phone call. You understand?"

Brandt was impressed with Bronfman. If he ever left the CIA, he had a future in stage and film.

One of the generals said, "I am General Plestvi. Your presence here is a concern. There have been rumors the KGB left some important items in our mines that rightfully belong to Poland. I need to see what you intend to bring out."

Both generals wore mossy brown uniforms with red epaulettes shining with more stars than the Milky Way. Their cavalry boots were a polished cordovan that would fetch three grand a pair in the States. Plestvi's right arm dangled loose by his side as if in need of a sling.

"No problem," Bronfman said. "We're happy to have you see everything. We do need to take some precautions for your safety, though. Give us an hour or two. We won't bring anything out until you're satisfied."

"Do what you need to do, but do it quickly. General Straginsky and I will be waiting." Plestvi had the look of someone born suspicious, a prosecutor's eyes and the guise of an executioner.

Bronfman was ready. His next move almost brought Brandt to a LOL moment. He handed the two generals each a three-page form to fill out with their personal medical history. Sometimes bureaucracy could be as lethal as a Glock.

"Generals, I need you to fill this out before you go in. I'm sorry they're in English, but if you have any trouble with the questions, I'll be glad to help."

Plestvi scanned the first page and scoffed. "I don't see a need for this. We are both healthy."

"General, I'm sure you are both healthy. Very healthy, from your appearance. But this mutation is very dangerous . . . extremely lethal. We believe it's in the same category as Ebola found in Liberian caves. If either of you get ill and die, we need to see if any of your medical history had an influence."

Brandt awarded Bronfman an Oscar, a Tony, and a Screenwriters Guild of America lifetime achievement award.

Plestvi sneered but took the forms.

Brandt pulled his respirator mask down over his mouth for effect and picked out six of the Delta Force in their suits to follow him and Tig inside. Now that Bronfman had set the stage, he was counting on the two generals making a quick inspection and then racing out of a deadly biohazard. There were too many weapons for them to claim the SADMs were only training devices. An idea had kept rolling around in the back of Brandt's mind since Bronfman laid out the plan. Sometimes those ideas led to trouble. Those involving Deke often led to big trouble. But he had to make sure the nukes looked like something else before the generals made their inspection.

"Okay, it's on us to pull this off," Brandt said. "We're gonna need tools—wrenches, screwdrivers, hammers . . . big ones."

A soldier said, "I'll get the toolbox in the cab."

"Good." He turned to Tig. "I'll need the backpack from the car too."

§

Overnight guests from the mine's subterranean hotel lingered in one of the chapel wings. Casey and Al found a secluded pew in front of a small side altar and waited.

Al whispered. "It's never officially come up, but it's clear to me that you and Brandt have more than a work relationship. Not something I would expect in the CIA."

"Neither did I. He was my first bodyguard assignment. I really didn't want to get involved with someone I was sent to protect, but it happened."

"Almost sounds fated. Something must have clicked."

"A couple of small things at first. The basic guy things. He was honest with me and could make me laugh. But one day I woke up and just knew. There was something very different going on. I felt safe with him. Here I was assigned to keep *him* safe, and he made *me* feel safe. I guess that's one of love's tricks."

"Love doesn't have a rulebook. But I imagine the CIA has some rules about it."

"Put it this way—it's frowned upon. HR and the lawyers go crazy when it happens. But as a civilian, Brandt stepped up and risked his life to prevent a nuclear war. So a lot gets overlooked now. How about monks? You guys ever break the rules or change your minds?"

"That also happens. More common now than in the past. So many choices available to people in today's world. Too many for some. The lucky ones find a different path. I know of a Dominican friar who left and became CEO of a beverage company in Darmstadt. Has a wife and three daughters. He jokes his daughters are his penance. A Benedictine friend left, got married, didn't like it, and came back. Marriages are very difficult after a monastic life."

"Monks can do that? Leave, get married, and come back?"

"They can. Either way, it's a drastic change. They all have trouble adjusting. If they decide to return, they have to start as a novice again."

Casey looked at her watch. "When we finish here, where do you think we should go next?"

"I think Lena has a good idea."

"I admire her for committing to this. She could have forgotten all about these damn things and stayed happily in the States, out of reach of Gleb and Moky."

Al started to speak, then stopped, changed his mind, and said, "I think she has discovered a big hole inside that she's trying to fill." A grin spread across his face. "And she has a way of getting me to think outside the box."

"She should talk to Brandt. He says our hearts and souls are born looking like Swiss cheese. Our job is to fill the empty spots."

"He sounds like a shrink or a priest."

"He's a CIA floater and an artist. Isn't that enough?"

"A provocative mix of interests. It either balances his life or screws it up."

"He worries about the contradictions. I'm afraid it keeps him from being happy."

"He mentioned his struggles to me."

"His sister is a therapist. She's made Brandt her life's project. She hasn't realized he ignores eighty percent of what she tells him."

"And the other twenty?"

"He just forgets it." She looked toward the altar doorway. "Here comes Tig."

Tig had his respirator mask in hand. "There's a problem up top. Couple of Polish generals are making demands. Brandt said to stay down here until he comes for you."

18

It took Brandt and the Delta Team two hours to get the chamber ready for the generals. Forty-five of the weapons had been moved and stacked behind piles of old, torn tarps, rusty mining tools, and machinery. Then a final layer of loose bones, boxed bones, and bones in barrels, enough to fill a church graveyard, formed a five-foot wall across the chamber. To get to the stacked weapons, the generals would have to make their way through or over the wall of remains.

They removed the carriage frames from the other nine weapons and then piled them three high like beer barrels along one wall inside the entrance. Brandt had removed the locks from these nine, so the holes would be visible. The frames were disassembled and added to the debris like arms and legs from robots.

Bronfman came down then. "The generals are getting itchy. I'm not sure how long I can hold them off."

"Almost done," Brandt said.

Bronfman watched him cut the skull and crossbones symbols from biohazard signs with scissors, peel the backs off, and attach them to the barrels. The leftover pieces ended up inside hazmat suits. Brandt and the soldiers then spread dirt and dust on the barrels.

"I think we're ready. Put the generals in suits and respirators. The lights will be turned off in the shaft, but don't give them head lamps. I want them to struggle on the rails behind your light to get here. I'll have one lamp lit in the chamber. That's all."

Brandt sent the Delta Force back to the truck with Bronfman. If they were standing around, he had no doubt the generals would order them to move everything out of the way so they could get to the back wall. He wanted their focus on the SADM barrels by the entrance.

Bronfman brought the generals down. Brandt could hear them stumbling through the shaft. When they got to the ossuary entrance, the vinyl masks that were part of the respirators had begun to fog up like he hoped. Plestvi said something to Straginsky that sounded like a frustrated curse.

Brandt held the lamp and was the first inside. He stayed to his left, next to the barrels, and let the generals step past.

They stopped at the barrier Delta had built, and Plestvi turned to Brandt. "We need to see everything. Have some men move this out of the way so we can get past."

"General, the men have exceeded their safe time limit for today. You'll have to wait until tomorrow for them. I had one man climb over the mass yesterday. He said there's more bones and barrels like these." Brandt lifted the lamp over the barrels. "His suit was ripped in the process and we had him flown to Ramstein. We're afraid those in the back might be more dangerous than everything in here."

"You have more men. Have them help move it," Straginsky said.

"If I do that, then they will use up their safe time and I won't be able to remove these today," Brandt said.

"The EU gave me one day to clear the mine," Bronfman said. "I'll have to ask for an extension. They might insist the mine be closed until we're done. You know what could happen to your tourist visits if that gets out. It might not be worth reopening it."

"What about these barrels? What's inside them?" Plestvi moved to one and looked down the hole where the lock had been.

"I wouldn't get too close to these," Brandt said. "He pointed to the skull and crossbones symbol. "These were gas canisters the Nazis used in Auschwitz. We have to take special precautions with them. We're concerned the barrels in the back might be full."

Plestvi turned to Straginsky but said nothing. They stood in silence, scanning the ossuary. First the mass barrier of bones, then the barrels.

"We'll stand by the truck and inspect what's loaded," Straginsky said.

Brandt had hoped they would give up and leave. He had to think fast. "Of course. You'll need to keep your suits on to watch, and we have to put everything in here into special biohazard containers. We can't risk spreading an unknown dangerous disease. So all you'll see is the containers." He figured he had two chances for success: the generals wouldn't want to open the containers hiding the SADMs, or they wouldn't want to hang around in suits to watch.

Bronfman stretched out an arm and gently guided Plestvi away from the barrels. "Let's not take any unnecessary risks."

The action was perfect. Just enough reminder of the danger for the generals to call it quits. Bronfman had added Oscar-winning director to his resume.

"Okay. I doubt the deputy minister wants to stay here all day anyway," Plestvi said. "But I intend to tell NATO headquarters what happened here. They can assess the contents and send a report to Warsaw."

Brandt held back a sigh of relief. They'd pulled it off.

§

Gleb was flat on the ground on a knoll above the mine entrance. Moky rolled to his side and handed the binoculars to him.

After a quick observation, Gleb said, "Those containers might have our SADMs inside."

"Look at the suits. They could be biological weapons."

"What do we do?" Gleb said.

"Try and count them. See how many they bring out."

"Is Lena there?"

"No sign of her."

"How about the others?"

"I've seen Casey Stephens. In the hazmat gear, it's too hard to identify everyone."

Gleb became jittery. He had trouble holding the binoculars steady. "Should we hijack the truck?"

"Six Black Berets against all those Delta Force, and without orders from Moscow? I don't think so. We'll track the Americans from here. Maybe we'll have a chance to look inside the truck."

§

After the minister and generals had left, Brandt put the locks back on the nine weapons and left the rest of the operation to the Delta Team. Bronfman said he hoped to have the truck and escort on the road by six that evening. Tig stopped at a rare Mexican kiosk for burritos and German beer. Brandt brought the food, Tig carried the beer, and they all ate in the car.

In the common room, Lena was waiting by the fireplace for their return. A Benedictine postulate and novice brought her tea and set a bottle of the monastery's pear brandy and some glasses on a table below a row of Polish icons. Brandt was first in and went straight for the brandy.

"How'd it go?" Lena asked.

"It took a bit of magic, but we're finished here," Brandt said, then sampled the brandy. "Where do you think we should go next?"

"Dresden. It's a bit of a long shot, but it's close. I can't be sure what we'll find, but Petrov went there and was very secretive about it. Didn't want me to know he'd even been there."

"Then how did you find out?"

"In his kitchen, I saw a coffee mug that said, *Guten Morgen, Dresden.* It had to be new. When he saw me looking at it, he quickly put it away and said a neighbor had given it to him. I knew it was a lie."

"I'll let Deke know," Casey said, then went to her room to make the call.

"Dresden, huh?" Brandt smiled. "A travel agent friend told me about Hotel Eckberg. Said I had to stay there sometime. An old castle converted into a five-star hotel. I'll try and get us rooms."

"Are we searching a monastery there?" Tig asked.

Lena replied, "I'm sorry. I don't know where to search. The monasteries were permanently closed. All I know is Petrov was very tight-lipped about Dresden . . . very suspicious. I'm not certain if this means anything, but Putin was a KGB officer there before reunification. He's very proud of the years he was stationed there."

"You think Petrov is working with Putin?" Tig asked.

"I think when it comes to Putin and Petrov, anything is possible."

"We should warn Deke. If Putin's connected to Petrov, Langley needs to know," Tig said. "We'll need some cover-our-ass insurance."

"Not yet," Brandt said. "The State Department will get involved if we tell Langley. Equivocation is the gold standard there. They never met an issue they couldn't sidestep with a smile."

Al was next to sample the brandy. "Petrov went to Dresden for a reason. Maybe on Putin's orders, or maybe because he knew something. That's enough for now."

Tig picked up a Bible on the coffee table, thumbed through it briefly, set it down, and looked at Al, then Lena.

Casey returned with a sly grin. "Tech Service came up with a plan to ditch the Gagarin surveillance. When we leave in the morning, we'll drive to the Galeria Kazimierz Shopping Plaza in Krakow. There's a deep underground garage there. An agency decoy team resembling all of us will be waiting on the third basement level. We'll transfer our gear and weapons to their car and leave for Dresden. The decoy team will wait forty-five minutes, then leave in our Escalade for Budapest."

19

Hotel Eckberg was a castle in the Teutonic tradition: three tall watchtowers standing Prussian military straight, high walls with etched parapets, ivy-covered loggias, and medieval stone masonry. A castle fit for a movie but too small for *Game of Thrones* and too Gothic for *Downton Abbey*. Perfect for *Camelot*. The garden tree wells were still filled with snow, but the lawn had a dewy fresh growth. The rooms had a modern Euro touch but kept the feudal heritage by the use of walnut instead of chrome. All the halls needed were suits of armor posed as sentries. The owners were proud enough of the castle to have the outline printed on the pillow covers and gift shop tee shirts.

Brandt had reserved a suite where they all could meet in private. Casey squirmed into a barrel chair in the sitting room. Brandt flopped on the sofa and extended his sock-covered feet onto an oval coffee table.

"Where do we start?" Casey said. "We really don't know where to search."

"According to the brochure, there's a dungeon and wine cellar. Bet they have a tasting room. Could be a place to start."

"Deke's got Langley digging into the Cold War records. Maybe they'll turn something up. He has an old contact here that might be able to help too."

"Lena suggested we drive by the old KGB headquarters," Brandt said. "See if anything could be hidden or buried in there."

Casey read a text from Lena. "The hotel concierge is in the south tower giving a short talk on Dresden. Beer, wine, and the hotel's special hors d'oeuvres. Al and Tig are already up there waiting for us."

§

The curved stairways corkscrewed up the tower, granite steps passing under iron torch holders left over from the days when servants would scurry to light them. Electric heaters in the circular wall kept the guests warm while they watched the Elbe spring runoff threaten the riverbanks. The hotel was perfectly situated above the Balcony of Europe—the guidebook name for Brühl's Terrace, a lengthy esplanade that had once served as long riverfront fortifications. The concierge's name was Anna Marie, and she had an updo of coal-black hair and an accent that could be traced to Verona.

Brandt sipped a local brew and prodded Al. "See anything Moscow would be proud of?"

"Paved streets maybe. Ivan was never known for creativity. They did rebuild a lot of Dresden after the war. Mostly hideous bridges and unsightly housing. Their love of dismal gray cement and loathsome windows are like a sign saying, 'Help me.' We can be thankful the Germans have found ways to bring them to life."

"Putin lived in one of those apartments," Lena said.

Tig laughed. "Should we check the basements there?"

Anna Marie pointed out some of the city's major sights. "The Frauenkirche dome and steeples are the pride of Dresden," she boasted. "Destroyed in the 1945 Allied firebombing, the church was rebuilt through community and Lutheran church efforts in 2005."

Casey read a text. "Deke wants us to meet with one of his old contacts. Nine tonight at a jazz club in New Town. He thinks this guy can help. After dinner, Brandt and Lena will go with me. Tig and Al will wait here."

§

The taxi dropped them off at the corner of Louisenstrasse and Pulsnitzerstrasse; the traffic pouring into popular Neustadt made walking quicker. Cafés, clubs, and beer halls were getting warmed up for the evening. Residents stood on balconies with beer and wine, making evening plans while they watched the crowds form. Like Bourbon Street during Mardi Gras, but with European panache. Artists and peddlers set up displays of their work under streetlamps and hustled tourists with phony discounts. After turning right on Görlitzer Strasse, they stood outside the Blue Note Club watching people enter and leave.

"We're supposed to go in at exactly nine, tip the hostess fifty euros, and ask for booth three," Casey said. "Deke's friend will find us."

The hostess was blonde and blue eyed with a drugged tranquility to her face. She accepted the fifty euros as if it were the retail price for number three. The booths lined opposite walls with a bar along the back and tiny bistro tables in the center. On their table was a promotional brochure of the bands and entertainers booked for the next month.

A paper-thin waitress in pajama pants and a tee shirt came over to take their order.

Brandt and Casey took time to scan the room and see what everyone was drinking, seeing mostly wine, beer, and coffee.

"Please be quick," the waitress said. "Karl comes on in a few minutes, and we're not allowed to serve while he plays."

Brandt ordered beer, Lena and Casey white wine. The drinks came as Karl walked onto the stage with his guitar. One soft light controlled from the bar kept him highlighted and yet partially shadowed. No disco ball glitter. He skipped a hello and went immediately into a medley of jazz guitar standards, including "Take the 'A' Train," "Milestones," and "Tune Up." He played for thirty minutes, adding difficult chord changes and alternating tempo before ending with "Airegin," "Blue Nile," and Coltrane's popular "Central Park West." When he finished, he left as he'd arrived, in silence.

The next act brought a myopic pianist with thick glasses and a blond male vocalist on stage. Johnny Mathis, Phil Collins, and Freddie Mercury in one smooth liquid voice, and a song portfolio of hits from four decades. When the pair announced a short break, the CIA team in booth three stood to applaud.

A man came to their table and said, "That's my son. I'm glad you enjoyed his set."

"You must be proud of him," Casey said.

"I am, very much so. I believe we have a mutual friend."

"If he goes by Deke, we do," Brandt said, then he slid over to make room in the booth.

"My name is Bruno. Deke and I once worked together. You must be Brandt."

Bruno was a large man with an ample stomach, lumberjack hands, gnarly, twisted fingers, and forearms that resembled hydrants. His abundant hair was long, dirty gray, and swept back on the sides in a manner favored by Italian entertainers. A wispy patch of silver curled over his forehead as if it refused to be anywhere else.

"Your CIA recruited me before the Wall came down. I miss that time. We had purpose then. The KGB and *Staatssicherheit* were our bitter enemies. Now Germany's purpose is to provide cheap immigrant labor for the steel mills and auto companies. Only they don't work, just take our handouts and snub their noses at our German culture. The Stasi would never have let this happen."

"I think it's an EU problem," Casey said.

"The EU *is* the problem. It's already ruined Europe. Those of us who were on the wrong side of the Wall got rid of Moscow's oppression only to find the same problem with those lotus-eaters in Brussels!" Bruno's frustration was obvious. He'd subverted and survived a cruel regime only to find the Germany he fought for didn't exist. To him, the promise of the European Union was a perverted fairy tale. "Read the papers. Our women are no longer safe on the streets. Nietzsche warned us in *The Will to Power*. It's like the EU is on mescaline. Merkel is *Gehirnverweigererin*."

Casey looked to Brandt.

"Brain dead."

"How long before your son comes back on?" Lena asked.

"His break is twenty minutes, but he often takes as much as forty. He's popular enough to get away with it, and it keeps the patrons drinking."

"Doesn't the owner complain?" Brandt said.

"I'm the owner, and he never listens to me anyway."

"We have a problem Deke said you could help us with," Casey said.

"The backpack nukes, right? The defiant KGB's scheme to punish the West and keep Russia safe from Kremlin foolishness."

"Petrov's father was behind it. He believed Gorbachev's imprudence would bring ruin to Russia," Lena said.

Bruno leaned back with a grin. "The Russian lady understands. I knew someone would eventually come looking for them." Pajama Bottoms brought Bruno a glass of Jägermeister and a small bottle of apple juice. He added the juice and took a sip.

"You know where they might be?" Casey said.

"If I help you, will the CIA let me put one in Berlin and one in Brussels?"

"Doesn't hurt to ask, but the odds are pretty high," Brandt said.

"The *Bundesnachrichtendienst* likes to keep tabs on me. I'll go to my office in the back. Wait five minutes and leave. Don't worry about the bill. Walk around to the back door in the alley and I'll let you in."

§

Tig peeked in Hotel Eckberg's sports bar and noticed a mandatory soccer game on the flat screen. "How about a drink and watch the game while we wait for everyone to come back?"

Al looked at his watch. "Why not."

They found an empty table close to the TV, and Al ordered alpine sours for both of them.

"That's Bayern Munchen in the red and Borussia Dortmund in the yellow," Al said. "They don't like each other. Both are guilty of dirty plays. I expect a lot of misconduct cards handed out."

"Who are you rooting for, then?"

"I'd like to see them both lose. Sparta is my team."

The waitress brought their drinks.

"I never thanked you for that drone shot in the orchard. You kicked ass." Tig raised his glass for a toast. "To your timely excellent shooting."

Glasses touched.

Al said, "How are things going with Lena?"

"So you noticed my interest."

"I'm a monk, not a machine."

Tig chuckled. "You might not be a machine, but you're not like any monk I've ever known."

"I don't think any of us are in your army. How would you know?"

"Good point. I guess things with Lena are fine. She looks at me like a friend or mission colleague more than anything."

"You wish it was different?"

"I'm not sure. I like being with her. She can be a real comfort to me. But sometimes when I'm with her, I can't stop thinking about my ex-wife, Becky."

"It takes time to grow together, but you have to leave the past behind."

"I forgot. Brandt told me you were married before becoming a monk."

Al became wistful. "I had a son too."

Tig tried to change the direction. "What's an alpine sour, anyway?"

"It's a German digestive drink—Asbach Uralt brandy and Underberg bitters."

"It's very good."

"We monks know our brandy."

"Lena is more relaxed . . . less guarded around you."

"Monks don't raise sexual tension in women. It's the other way around."

"No, I think it's different. She likes being with you."

§

Bruno's small office resembled a student dorm room. Clothes were stacked and piled on chairs, a bra hung down from a hook like a surrender flag. A philodendron with dry, crispy leaves in need of funeral rites sat on his desk next to a glass jar of Hermann's Bavarian raspberry candy. Brandt noticed a double set of dead bolt locks on the door.

"Just put the clothes anywhere and grab a seat where you can," said Bruno. "I don't know who this stuff belongs to. The staff and stage acts don't like to change with the patrons in the bathrooms, so they come here."

"What's wrong with the stage dressing room?" Casey asked.

"Worse. The staff reserves that for other activities. You never know what you'll find there. For me, it's a no-go zone. I'm okay with that." Bruno set a bottle of Jägermeister on his desk and four paper cups. "Help yourself."

Lena didn't hesitate. Brandt and Casey abstained.

"I had to reach back for some of the names when Deke called. I'll walk you through everything I know. Lazar Matveev is at the center. He was Putin's boss and head of the KGB in East Germany then. A real bastard. The kind of Russian that makes Putin look like the pope. When Moscow's power turned into myth, Matveev and Putin decided they needed to do something about the Party's new direction. Their future and the KGB's was at stake. That's when Igor Petrov stepped in with a strategy for the SADMs that could restore Russia's importance. He designed a plan to hide the weapons all over the satellites until the war with the West would start. Putin jumped at the idea. He recognized the leverage nukes would provide with Moscow and the West. Peace or war, the SADMs gave him an edge. It's good intel, from Matveev's adjutant, who was in on it."

Brandt noticed a knee-high safe behind the desk. On top of it rested a 9mm Luger with wood handle inlays, within reach of Bruno. It was a little like sitting with an underground resistance leader.

"The rest is part rumor, part confirmed intel. Matveev and Putin had a close relationship with the Stasi. Putin even had a Stasi ID card. When the Wall came down, the Stasi needed protection from the East Germans who had been tortured. Americans were more than willing to help the victims hunt the bastards down. The Stasi panicked. New identities for them flew out of the Ministry for State Security as if shot from a cannon. The KGB wanted new identities too, and the Stasi wanted in on the SADM plan. Deals were made and records were conveniently lost."

"We're trying to find out where they are now," Casey said.

"I'm getting to that. Remember, these are all pieces of a puzzle. Conjecture, facts, and half-truths. Horst Brumfelt was the Stasi colonel in Dresden. He and Matveev were close friends. They kept each other in booze and women. As a communist officer in East German State Security, Brumfelt was careful not to flash wealth and abundance. However, his younger brother, Otto, didn't have that problem. Both had deep Nazi roots. Their grandfather was the SS general in Saxony. With the Nazi treasure he confiscated, they stuck a lot of deutsch marks in Swiss bank accounts and used bribes to save the family estate from being seized. Forty-five acres of forest with a large manor house. My guess is Otto has the weapons hidden there or knows where they are."

"Where do we find it?" Brandt asked.

Bruno had everything ready. "Here's the address and the surveillance photos. Drive by and check it out. Otto lives alone now. Horst died soon after unification. Listed as a natural death, but we didn't know about polonium back then."

"Can we get the *Bundesnachrichtendienst* to help?" Casey asked.

"Forget it. Bunch of ex-Stasi and neo-Nazis. Otto takes good care of them."

Casey and Brandt shuffled through the pictures. Otto was tall, with thin-rimmed eyeglasses. Like Deke, he had only wisps of white hair on the sides of his head. He stood next to his BMW in front of his club and stared with contempt at whoever was taking his picture. Brandt knew the Ottos of this world—men filled with checkbook arrogance. Brandt despised him already. A series of estate photos showed a tall iron fence protecting the grounds and a two-story manor home set back from the road. Nighttime pictures had the house and grounds illuminated. Brandt suspected large, angry dogs patrolled the estate. "How do we get in?"

"In the old days, Deke would get a team from *the shop*. Those guys could break in anywhere and steal anything. I don't know who or what Langley uses now. Between the dogs and electronics, I believe you'll need to get someone inside."

Brandt, Casey, and Lena turned toward each other while ideas ran through their minds.

"Otto plays golf at the Dresden Elbflorenz in good weather, then stops at Angel's Tabledance men's club before going home," Bruno said. "It's where I'd start."

Lena nodded confidently. "I can get us in."

20

B randt started to call a cab, but Bruno offered to drive them back to the hotel after his son finished for the night. He drove as if speed limits were an annoyance.

"Deke barely knew about Otto when we were working together," Bruno said. "I kept it that way. If Deke went after him, the Stasi would have made sure his body was never found. There were times I thought it was over for him."

After Bruno dropped them off, Brandt and Casey sat in their room trying figure out all the steps they would need. Lena as honey trap was the easy one; she had what was needed to be in the honey trap hall of fame. If she could get Otto to take her home, all she'd need were a drink and some flunitrazepam to put him out, and then open the gates. The weather would be their cue—golf, then Angel's Tabledance club. The hookup was the question. It had to be subtle and promise something more enticing than a lap dance.

"I think we need to get Deke involved in this," Casey said. "He's run honey traps before. And if Otto has the weapons in the house or grounds, we'll have to be ready to haul them away. Deke can arrange that."

Lena came in with a glass of red wine. Al had a copy of the *Sächsische Zeitung* daily. Tig brought his laptop.

"You have it all figured out yet?" Lena asked.

"The hookup is the key," Brandt said. "We have to assume Otto is savvy and cautious."

"He's got Nazi blood in him," Al said. "So he's careful but corrupt."

"I think the secret is to dangle Lena but let him make the first move," Casey said.

"Someone will have to be a pimp to make it look authentic," Brandt said.

Al rolled his paper into a log. "It will have to be me. He won't trust an American."

Brandt looked puzzled. "What does the Rule of Saint Benedict say about that?"

"Doesn't matter. According to the superior general, I'm now officially a gyrovague anyway."

"Is that a sandwich or a heretic?" Brandt asked.

"It's in the Rule. Look it up. Chapter one, the fourth class of monks. Homeless wanderers, dependent on charity . . . slaves to will and appetites."

"Sainthood is easier than I thought."

"The weather looks good for golf tomorrow," Tig said.

"Act One, then," Casey said. "See what time he goes to the club and be ready for him at Angel's afterward."

"I'll go in first and wait," Brandt said. "After he gets there, Lena and Al will come in."

"Lena will be competition, so the doorman and bartender will have to be paid off," Tig said.

Al was ready. "I'll take care of them. Lena and I will sit at a table. Brandt comes over to seal the deal, then they leave together. I'll follow later. We just need to be sure Otto sees it all."

§

Deke flew in commercial on Air Berlin under an alias and had Brandt drive him to Otto's estate, then past the old KGB headquarters on Angelika Street.

"Bruno busted in there more than once. He had help from the shop—Artie, as good as they come. Best black bag and safecracking expert the agency ever had," said Deke. "Now we recruit hackers and geeks. Give them the front door key, they still can't get in. Bruno copied some code books and directives from Moscow. Stuff like that. Then he and Artie got drunk. Bruno was married then."

"Kinda funny, it's a chiropractor office now," Brandt said.

"Back guy? I wonder if he knows the basement is where they did the torture. There's a bratwurst cart in the plaza. Let's grab lunch."

Brandt pulled the SUV over, and Deke ordered two mettwurst on brötchen with special mustard and beer. They sat on a wood bench in the sun as if waiting for a bus.

"Where did Delta take the Krakow weapons?" Brandt asked.

"Remember that old nuke bunker outside of Nuremburg? The one we found filled with pot plants? We're sticking them in there until Langley decides to tell State about them."

"Any sign of Moky?"

"He followed our decoy to Budapest, then holed up in an old Soviet safe house. We're still looking at the drones."

"Sword of Allah?" Brandt said.

"Could be. Plenty of others too. These mini-drones give everyone capability they never had before."

"Lena and Casey are shopping for the right outfit for tonight. Something that says expensive hooker with class."

"Be sure Al turns him down the first time. We want him forgetting caution. Leave him drooling and frustrated."

"You know Putin could be directly involved in this?"

Deke closed his eyes and sighed. "I wanted to drive by the old KGB office for a look back in time. When I first came here to meet Bruno, I was a new field agent. Yeltsin was the Russian president. Gorbachev was no longer party secretary, but his policies still dominated Moscow politics. The KGB was panicking over the perestroika reforms. Bruno had been working for us since '84 and warned us about Putin even before the Wall came down. 'Keep an eye on him,' he said. Putin was always the last one to leave work. One night, Bruno was waiting with Artie to bust into KGB headquarters and copy a list of Russian agents in Bonn. That night, Putin got into a cab instead of walking home. Bruno got curious about that and decided to watch him closer, see if he could find out what he was up to. Watched for weeks. Nothing unusual. But it eventually paid off. He followed his cab to a small gasthaus in Old Town. The Russians were continually changing curfews in Dresden and few people went out after dark. Putin met Matveev along with a man named Adam who was the Mossad agent in the Communist East. The two were passing on names and locations of underground Nazi groups in Germany to Adam. Some were part of the Stasi. A smart move, covering all the bases, the way things were going in Moscow then. No one in the KGB was safe. They knew they might need help getting out, and Adam had the details about the old Nazi ratline escape routes out of Germany."

"The Mossad and KGB, huh? I wonder what the toasts were like."

"There's more. Matveev was the one to introduce Petrov's father to Putin. According to Bruno's sources, all Putin thought about was the clout nukes would give them. A big bargaining chip if things went bad. Old man Petrov wasn't interested in a strong hand to play. He wanted cities burning as soon as possible."

"And for Putin, not a bad idea to have a bunch of nukes hidden in the West in case the Cold War got hot," Brandt said.

Deke tugged his jaw tight. "SADMs should have been more than a footnote in the SALT Treaty."

"You think Putin knows where they are?"

"I can't see how. If he knew, why all the fuss about wanting help?"

"That's always bugged me about this mission. How did they lose them?"

"The political map of Europe was chaos after the Wall. Every country suffered internal clashes. No one knew who would end up in charge. The left, right, or in between . . . communists, socialists, capitalists, anarchists, atheists, vegans. They all wanted to be in charge. The leery KGB had to watch which way the political wind was blowing and be ready to find new hiding places for the weapons. They were only a phone call away from being sold out and moved from one spot to another like barnyard chickens. They needed help from the Stasi too. Putin lost control during that time. He was back in Moscow trying desperately to avoid being shot and to gather political support. By the time he came into power in '99, he had no clue who had them and where they were."

"Like us."

"Petrov might be the only one who has the answers. My guess is Putin has been happy to leave them in the West he until he needed them, then send the Black Berets after them. He's still hoping to get them first and keep them somewhere in NATO. Petrov and Lena screwed up his plans."

"She forced us too."

"'Cause we dropped the ball. Things got messy for the KGB and Stasi under Yeltsin. Russians hadn't forgotten about what went on in Lubyanka. Double-secret purges with every power swing. The locals in the satellite countries hunted the Stasi and KGB like wolves. 'Save your ass' was the order of the day. Some were defecting, some took a cue from the Nazis and landed in Syria and Egypt, and others went into hiding. Moscow was worried about the big stuff when they pulled out . . . getting the missiles, tanks, artillery back home was the focus. They denied the SADMs existed, and we accepted that."

"Ninety percent of diplomacy is lies. No one cares as long as they get invited to the parties," Brandt said.

"You know these weapons better than I do. Any idea what Putin could do with forty or so SADMs on our side of the Elbe?"

"Win World War III. Annex Europe. Move Euro Disney to Siberia."

"Jeezus, not Disney!" exclaimed Deke.

"SADMs are miniscule next to an ICBM, but their strategic value is being able to place them exactly where they would do the most damage. Even with forty, he could take out enough political and military targets to neutralize Europe."

"We'd launch. He'd still lose."

"Would we? With no missile paths to track?" asked Brandt. "All the evidence they were Russian weapons would be destroyed in the blasts. We couldn't be sure who was responsible. The false flag disinformation would come first. Supply bogus evidence with some terrorist names on it and scream how NATO failed to protect its members. Moscow rushes in to save and defend what's left. By the time the politicians decide what to do, Putin's in charge of Europe."

Deke let his hand with the mettwurst settle into his lap, then looked at Brandt. "The Stalin playbook in East Europe after Hitler."

"Only bloodier. Putin knows Petrov is the key. His bugout with the tritium raises the stakes. None of us know what he's planning."

"It's why we got Moky and the Black Berets. Let's hope we find the rest here in Dresden. I didn't say anything to Sturm about it yet. I don't think he expected any of the SADMs were left in Germany. If he knew, he might feel compelled to tell Berlin. The media would be all over it in hours."

"You think Otto really has them?"

"Who knows? After Matveev went back to Moscow, he had Putin tying up loose ends. A dose of polonium or a shot in the back of the head were the methods of choice. Took out dozens. Even some who had gone back to Russia. He had Horst Brumfelt eliminated. Bruno thinks Otto is the place to start. We'll go with that."

"How about the Mossad agent? Could he help?"

"He was the biggest loose end. If word got out the two were helping the Israelis, they'd be shot the same day. Putin either had him killed or did it himself."

"The Mossad followed us to Krakow."

"I know. Adam was Aaron's father."

21

The first attempt to lure Otto went well. Al walked in the club with Lena and handed the bouncer and bartender hundred-euro notes. Lena stood next to him in white slacks that matched her curves without being tawdry, a yellow eyelet lace-up top that angled across her chest, leaving her left shoulder bare, a leopard-skin jacket draped across one arm. On Lena, an outfit that could raise the dead. For makeup, not too much but not too little. Al was in a black sport jacket and one of Brandt's black turtlenecks. They could have been on a date or on a hustle, which served to boost curiosity. Tig grabbed a table in the rear where he could watch Otto and the bait.

The stage had three dance poles with reserved tables nestled up to the edge for priority customers with cash to stuff. A petite blonde ended her routine to the music of "Hot Child in the City." A bouncer gathered up her discarded outfit from the patrons as she exited. A redhead stood in the shadows, waiting to start her act. A waitress brought the mandatory cheap champagne, and Al and Lena settled in to watch the dancers. Brandt waited to be sure everyone had noticed Lena, then came over and slid a chair to join them.

"This is fun," Lena said. "There's a place inside of every woman that wants to be naughty. *Very* naughty. Life for us is how we handle it. Some struggle with it. Some let it all out. Makes life interesting for men, I guess."

"I'll pretend I didn't hear that," Brandt said.

"I don't know if Otto is watching or not," Al said.

"He is. I can feel his eyes," Lena said.

"Then we should make our move while he's watching," Brandt said.

"Count the bills, then fold them and slide them to me. Then get up with Lena and leave."

"Wicked Games" was the redhead's music selection. She swung around the pole with one arm, then wrapped both legs around it like a snake and let go with her arm. Brandt reached into his pocket and thumbed through a thick fold of euros, then slid them across the table to Al. They both smiled and nodded. Brandt rose and helped Lena up with his right hand, and they made a quick exit, pretending to avoid anyone noticing.

Twenty minutes later, the petite blonde pole dancer sat with Otto. After a round of champagne, they walked to a room in the back.

§

The sitting room in the suite had a gas fireplace and a small bar with two tiny stools. An ice bucket and wine cooler rested on opposite corners of the bar top. The walls displayed black-and-white photos from nineteenth-century Germany—the beards were long and bushy, the dresses full and corseted, the Prussian expressions grim. Tig sprawled on the sofa with a glass of wine. The success of the first day brought laughter and giddy faces.

Deke ignored the Ardbeg scotch on the bar and walked to the sofa. "What's your assessment, Tig?"

"Otto took the bait. He tried not to stare, but he kept shifting attention toward Lena. At one point, he turned around to look at the bartender, who shook his head up and down with a grin."

Deke smiled with an affirming nod.

"Tomorrow's forecast is rain, so no golf. Do we lay low here?" Tig said.

"Negative," Deke said. "Al and Lena will go back to Angel's today. I'll be the customer this time. We want the bartender and bouncer to back us up as noticeable regulars. Nothing more." He went to the bar, took a carton of milk from the mini-fridge, and poured a glass. His face, crunched in a wad as if he were about to drink hemlock, said he wasn't happy about it.

"What's with the milk?" Brandt asked.

Deke glanced at the Ardbeg resting on the bar. "Doctor's orders. Stomach problem. He wants to stick a camera down my gut when I get back. No booze, coffee, carbonated drinks, or cigarettes until then."

"Tea?" Casey asked.

"Doc's English, said tea is fine."

"Try a Moscow milkshake," Lena said. "Vodka and milk." She smiled and walked out on the balcony to smoke.

Al was quick to follow her out.

§

"That wasn't the first time for a pole dancing strip club for you, was it?" Lena asked Al.

"Guilty. I was a major in the Czech Army before. They were popular with my men."

"It's why you were selected for this mission."

"In part. I was a Czech custodial officer for the Russian nuclear weapons. My wife and son were killed by the KGB because of my job. I pray for them every night. There is nothing I want more in life than to get these weapons away from whoever has them. I'm hoping it will give my family's death some meaning. If a few KGB are killed in the process, I'll have no regrets, but I'll pray for their souls."

"Doesn't sound charitable."

"It's why I can't bring myself to make final vows. The desire for revenge is my demon . . . it has long claws. It means I'm not ready. I'm hoping this will put an end to it."

"We have something in common. We've both suffered a tragedy at the hands of the secret police. My lover and I made plans to be married, only the FSB interfered. I believe Leonid committed suicide to save me from them. You might pray for their souls, but I want them all to rot in hell. Especially Petrov."

"The man inside me next to the monk would agree."

Lena's gaze drifted to the statue garden below the balcony. The fountains were ready for summer, with splashy shows and misty sprays. "How old was your son?"

"Seven. Just a boy. Even now I have to fight to hold back the tears. He was truly beautiful . . . beautiful in every way." Al's eyes moistened into a glaze.

"I'm sorry, Al."

"I'll never understand how someone can murder a child."

"I don't know. Maybe your God gives you answers. I never hear any. Maybe you can talk to Him for me."

§

The next time Otto went to Angel's, Tig was the customer. The same procedure followed, but after Tig and Lena left, Otto talked to the bartender, then sat next to Al.

"Your friend is a beautiful woman. I would like the opportunity to meet her."

"I'm sorry," said Al. "We don't know you, and my friend doesn't like strangers."

"That can't be true. I've seen her leave with people she just met here."

"I'm afraid you misjudged us. Those are prearranged business meetings."

"Yeah, sure. I'm sorry. Perhaps I could negotiate such a meeting."

"My friend only does home meetings where there isn't a wife."

"I'm not married, and I have a beautiful home."

Al gave Otto a long, measuring look before answering, "I'll need your name and address."

Otto handed him a calling card.

Al studied it as if committing it to memory, then turned it over and wrote the number of a burner phone from the car stash on the back and handed it to Otto. "Call this number after eleven tonight. If you check out, maybe something can be arranged."

§

Moky couldn't hide the confusion and anger he felt. The broken glass on the floor was proof. The satellite had sent him following the Americans to Budapest, but now he was ordered to race to Dresden seven hours away. No explanation. He would be told more when he got there. And he would have to drive—Gleb and Karyi were too drunk.

§

After Al's report, Brandt turned on the gas for the suite fireplace and sat on the sofa with a glass of sparkling water. There was nothing to do now but wait for Otto to call. Casey was with Deke and Lena, assembling the outfit Lena would tempt Otto with and formulating the plan for the meet.

A warming fire and solitude opened the door to mental flotsam, nuggets of unrelated thought rushing to fill his brain's frontal lobes. The thoughts felt at home there. Most were words he wished he'd said—comebacks, put-downs, apologies, embarrassing mistakes that plagued him—followed by images that popped up on their own. It had happened before. It was as if his unconscious needed to clean the attic. Boxes and cartons labeled *personal history*. Open a box and get the details. Childhood was a gray box: white for mother, black for father. Adolescence was always a red carton. He blushed like a strawberry with his first kiss, a real high point. Marissa was hotter than a blacksmith's fire. The low points were the bloody noses from the locker room fights he lost. Too many. He only counted his wins. College and army were abstract, multicolored, enclosed wood crates. If there was a theme to those years it was: no theme. Shit just happened. Some good, some not so good. Destiny gods had their phasers set on stun in those years. Marriage and children were white cubes with patches of gold foil along the edges. Small letters said *fragile, handle with care, open with warm, delicate thoughts*. The travel business was a perfect brown box. At some point, *Amazon* appeared on the side and wouldn't go away. If he tried to stack the boxes, they looked like the work of a four-year-old, never straight and neat, edges chipped and overlapping. Some boxes were thin with rounded corners, others thick and square. Anne's death and his depression took the shape of a cold, icy-black monolith.

His glass emptied with the monolith, and he went to the bar and added ice and a drop of scotch to the sparkling water. In a way, Ardbeg scotch was Deke. Rough on the edges, silky smooth inside. Life was simple to Deke. No boxes or red cartons. Reality was a river you negotiated—calm waters, eddies, rapids, and waterfalls.

Sometimes a gentle flow. Sometimes a rushing flood. Brandt knew his stacked boxes life path was crash-and-burn risky. One piece could bring it all down. Depression would follow. Deke's approach to life had merit. No boxes, never look back. Learn to swim with the current and depend on yourself. His logic was difficult to refute. But when Brandt tried to look at it that way, all he could see was a log ride at an amusement park. Four people sitting in a hollowed-out log, building nothing together—just along for the splashy ride.

Casey called with a question. "I think Lena should be armed for this. Deke says no. What do you think?"

"Street hookers usually have something like a knife or small pistol. But expensive high-class hookers? I dunno. I'm thinking no."

Casey wasn't a box but a huge gold ingot of psychic matter and emotional experience waiting for life to finish shaping it.

A text from Lena said she liked Al in Brandt's turtlenecks and wanted to know where she could get some. Lena would like his blocks. Scientific theory and hypothesis were perfect for building life stacks. And Al did look good in the black turtleneck. He was like Deke, a river guy. He had been swimming, trying to keep his head above water since his family was slaughtered. Casey was also a swimmer, an Olympic swimmer—breathe under water, sprint on the surface, and the anchor on a relay team.

§

Brandt spilled some of his drink when he heard the gunshot from Lena's room. Tig and Deke beat him there and were trying to get the massive oak door unlocked. Tig had a Glock in his hand. Deke fumbled in his wallet and pulled out a CIA master room key card with a fake Marriott logo. He held it next to the lock screen and watched green dots flash along the top, searching for the code.

22

Casey had just stood to leave Lena when the attack came. The wineglasses were empty, a plan for Otto was in place. Deke had already left. She was ready to say good night when two men dressed in black and ski masks rushed in from the balcony. The tallest one went to grab Casey, who knew what to do, but so did he. When his right hand reached for her, she parried it with her left arm and tried to jab knuckles into his throat. He moved his head to the left to avoid the thrust, then tried to head-butt Casey, who slid away in time. He reached for her again, and Casey formed an X with both arms between his and tried to push them aside. He still managed to grab her neck with his right hand, and she began to kick at his groin. He used his knees to block her kicks and tried to punch her with his left hand. She lurched away, avoiding the brunt of the blow, but his fist grazed her ear. Her right palm aimed for his nose, but he was too quick and the blow glanced off his chin with little effect.

The second man was thickset and had Lena in a choke hold with an arm across her neck, dragging her toward the balcony while she twisted and struggled. He tried to bang her into the wall, but Lena went limp and set her feet in time to push him back into a chair. They both fell to the left, shoving a side table and lamp into Casey's attacker before hitting the floor. That enabled Casey to land a groin kick as he stumbled.

They were still in trouble—neither attacker made an effort to leave. Lena used the fall to break free and crawl to her purse. Scared snakes and crabs never moved so fast. She pulled the PSM pistol out and shot her attacker in his hip as he stood up. The shot brought a third man inside. He dropped the zip ties he was holding and began to help his wounded partner out to the balcony.

Deke's electronic master key card finally clicked the door unlocked but the chain still was attached. Casey moved to release it, but the delay allowed the attackers time to escape to the balcony. Tig was first in with his Glock. The tall man was already climbing over the rail. Casey checked on Lena, then went out to the balcony in time to see the rope hanging down from a tower above and the last man reaching the ground below.

"Are you both okay? Anyone hurt?" Deke said.

Lena stood with her pistol in her right hand. "Yeah." She nodded. "I'm okay."

The hotel night manager came in with a security guard. "We had reports of a gunshot in here?"

Tig quickly stuffed his Glock in his waistband, under the back of his shirt. Deke put his foot over a spot of blood.

Lena had tucked her pistol behind her; she thrust her chest out. "No. Nothing like that. I was trying to show my friend a difficult yoga pose and we both fell and knocked over a table. I'm sorry about the lamp. Please add the cost to our bill."

The security guard inspected the room in silence.

Tig reset the table and lamp and did his best to bend the shade into its original shape. The manager examined the table, then switched the lamp on and off. The guard checked the bathroom, then looked out on the balcony but said nothing about a rope. No dead body or blood left the manager happy. A smile returned to his face. "You're both okay, then?"

"We're fine. Our friends heard the noise and came to check on us." Only then did Casey notice Brandt was missing.

The manager glanced at the guard, who nodded okay. "Then good night. I'm glad you're both safe. Please enjoy your stay with us."

The pair left.

Lena collapsed into a chair. "I would love a scotch."

Brandt walked in with the Ardbeg and closed the door behind him.

"You are a saint. How did you know?" Lena said.

"This stuff has healing powers. I know from experience."

Casey asked, "Where were you?"

"I figured they climbed up the east side away from the spotlights, an easy free climb up the rough stonework. Rappelling down to Lena's balcony from the tower gave the best access. I wanted to be sure there weren't any more up there. I pulled the rope up. It's in our room."

Tig went back out to the balcony and looked up from the third floor and back down toward the statue garden.

"Any idea who these guys were, Casey?" Deke asked.

"Russians. Definitely Russians. Spetsnaz is my guess. The guy who attacked me was well trained in Systema. I'm not sure I could take him."

Lena grimaced. "Black Berets again."

"I thought Moky was in Budapest," Casey said. "How did he find us?"

"Could be a backup squad," Tig said.

Deke had a guilty look. He dropped his gaze toward the floor. "It's me. Had to be me. Moscow Center must have people watching the Brussels airport. They must have seen me board the Dresden flight and sent Moky here."

"How about grabbing a flight to the Falklands?" Brandt said. "Stay until New Year's."

"You think they know about Otto?" Tig asked.

Deke shook his head no. "It's Lena they want."

§

They gathered in the suite, waiting for Otto to call. Al sat on the sofa and stared at the burner phone on the coffee table in front of him. He knew what to say; they went over the plan until he nodded and said, "I got it." Deke was calm; he had been through this before. Casey kept glancing at the phone as if afraid they might miss the call. Brandt relaxed in a wing chair, sketching the scene in abstract shapes and colors. Moving colored pencils helped pass the time.

The phone lit up at 11:01 with Otto's number.

Al said, "Yes."

"This is Otto. I'm hoping to make arrangements for tomorrow night. I can pay whatever you ask."

"I'm sure you can, but I'm afraid my friend says no."

"*No?* I don't understand. Everyone at the club will tell you I can be trusted."

"You're not the problem. It's your dogs. My friend hates dogs. She's petrified of them. She won't go inside your gates, even in a car."

"I'll put them away. She won't even see them."

Al paused. "Wait while I talk to her."

Deke gave a thumbs-up sign after Al pressed the hold button.

Brandt whispered to Casey, "We're close."

"He's quite anxious. I think he'll say yes," Al said. He counted to forty in silence, then went back to the phone. "Okay, but no dogs and no alarm and the gates stay open. She'll have a man in a car just outside the gate. He'll be there to be sure everything goes well."

"That's too much. I can put the dogs away. But the alarm and the gates, it's asking more than I can agree to."

"Suit yourself. You're a new customer, and she feels safe that way. The guard is there to protect you both. If there's no problems, maybe the next time it will be different. The dogs will never be okay."

There was a long pause. "Let me think about it. I'll call you back."

"Five minutes. That's all. If you weren't a regular at Angel's, we wouldn't even be talking." Al hung up.

"Nice touch with the Angel's thing," Brandt said.

"He'll call," Deke said. "Let it ring five times."

Otto called back in four minutes. "I agree as long as the bodyguard is there for both of us."

"Not a problem. That's why he's there. The fee is two thousand euros for the night. Champagne, wine, schnapps . . . anything is fine with her. You supply breakfast. Low-fat strawberry yogurt, a hard-boiled egg, and half a fresh bagel. Her bodyguard will drive up to the door and pick her up at nine a.m. I suggest a generous tip. You'll be happy to do it. Angel's, tomorrow night. Same time." Al hung up and leaned back in the sofa as if struggling with what he had just done. "My superior general might not be pleased with my actions. I'm not sure how this would be considered service to God or man."

"Remember the end game," Casey said. "It's why you're with us."

Al's face sparkled with amusement. "Monks in Italy have a saying, 'Too much goodness ends up in the trash.'"

§

When the Clandestine Imaging Division's 3-D schematic of Otto's estate and manor arrived, they met in one of the hotel meeting rooms where they had access to a big screen and privacy. Al wasn't with them. He had no role in the operation after the phone call but stationed himself by the door. The PowerPoint 3-D image displayed the manor house floor by floor—sixteen rooms, fourteen thousand square feet counting the basement. A long driveway from the gates to the Baroque entrance.

"If the weapons are there, Delta Force is waiting in Klipphausen with a truck. I brought six men in and stationed them around the hotel to watch in case the Russians come back," Deke said.

"Where do we start to search?" Brandt said.

Deke turned toward the screen. "The house comes first, then the outbuildings. The basement is big enough for all of the missing SADMs." He picked up a chrome pointer and with its tip circled a room on the screen. "We believe this is a shooting range at this end of the basement, a small utility room next to it, then two large rooms, either of which could be ground zero."

Deke looked to Brandt first. "Those two are for you, me, and Lena." He turned to Casey and slid the pointer to a first-floor room. "I want you and Tig going through his office, see if he has anything that can help—files, notebooks, diary, address book, calendar, discs, thumb drives, photo albums. Check the usual hiding places. The stuff you learned in training. Anything that tells us about the SADMs or who he is and who he's involved with—all his connections, past and present. We'll take his phone and computer with us, but see if he's got backups hidden somewhere. If he has a shredder, bag the contents and we'll send it to Langley."

"He's probably got a safe. What about that?" Casey said.

"Safes aren't really my expertise," Brandt said. "And I imagine any nukes in the basement are behind a vault door."

Deke nodded. "I expect that's true. If the vault locks are digital, we have the right stuff. Langley went through his credit card statements. They think they're biometric locks installed three years ago."

"That helps," Brandt said. "You bring the Phoenix?"

"Affirmative, and the Black Box for biometric. If they're old-style combination locks, you can give it a try. If you can't do it, Delta has a plasma cutter."

"What's Otto gonna do when he wakes up and finds he's been invaded and violated?" Casey said.

"Try and run like hell is my guess. If we find the weapons, we'll turn him over to an interrogation team."

"What if the place is clean? No nukes, just a world-class wine cellar and lots of sex toys?" asked Brandt.

"Because of his SS grandfather, there are some title issues concerning ownership of the estate. Bruno has the details. We don't think he'll want to attract any attention with Berlin. If he does fuss, I'll have to bring Sturm in."

"He probably doesn't want his connection to his Nazi grandfather and Stasi brother posted on social media," Casey said.

"Someone will need to search the outbuildings and especially the kennel. Good hiding spot with those dogs. Batman would think twice," Tig said.

"We might have to bring some steak with us."

"Or donuts. They're police dogs," Brandt said.

"Once Lena opens the front door for us, Tig will go in with the electronics. The more security he has in place, the better the odds he has our SADMs. I expect intrusion switches and motion detectors at a minimum. Otto is smart, so no wire on Lena. I expect he will turn off the security on the entrance and main floor. But if entry to the basement is protected, he'll probably leave those alone."

"Probably hot-laser sensors, infrared, or microwave," Tig said. "Disarming them could take some time."

Lena raised her hand. "What if I suggest a little target shooting? He'll have to turn the security off for the basement then."

"That," said Deke, "is an excellent idea."

§

Lena was weaponized. A close-fitting black dress with a long side slit, sleeveless with a high choker-style neck and a revealing oval cleavage gap. Inside the house, Otto led Lena to a softly lit oak-paneled lounge with the ambience of a retro beer hall. The photos on the wall were like the Third Reich genetic code—black-and-white 1930s pictures of Munich's popular breweries, Ernst Röhm waiting to be executed by his fellow Nazis, and Hermann Goering with a predator's grin before obesity set in. Lena focused on a shadow box display of historic medals—Hero of the Soviet Union, three versions of the Nazi Iron Cross, and an Order of Lenin. Otto opened a bottle of Krug champagne.

"We almost refused you when we found out you are a gun collector. Guns bring authorities," Lena said.

"I have some influential friends here. I let them come and use the range and my collection sometimes."

"I would love to see it."

Otto's grin spread to his ears. "My guns bring me joy. I would love to show you." He opened an oak wall panel, exposing a control board, and began pushing buttons and flipping switches.

Lena used the time to drop the drugs into his champagne.

The shooting range was like a bowling alley with only three lanes, modern and well lit, the envy of most police forces. Electronic sighting aids and computer target scoring, state-of-the-art gun range ventilation. Hanging on a back wall was an armory fit for an oil prince, with all the big names—Colt, Walther, Glock, Heckler, SIG Sauer, Springfield, Smith & Wesson, Beretta, Ruger. Some nickel plated, some bronze, colorful handles of ivory, pearl, or exotic wood grip inlays.

"This is amazing. It makes me tingle all over," Lena said.

"I'm glad you like it. A toast is in order." Otto raised his glass. "Prost."

"To love and pleasure," Lena said, and drained her glass. "Would it be possible to hold one?"

"Of course." Otto's face reflected bliss, his eyes like silver dollars. "This could be a memorable night." He finished his drink and set it down, then removed a pistol from the wall. "Try this one." He handed Lena a Beretta Nano. "It's one of my favorites. Fits in a coat pocket or purse. I don't even need a holster."

"Can I shoot it?"

"Of course." Otto's grin widened. He loaded the pistol for her. "Here's the safety."

Both put on ear protection, then Lena emptied her clip at the stiff paper target. The gun smoke was sucked away by the powerful ventilation fan. The electronic scoreboard said Lena would never be an expert marksman. Otto took a Glock and destroyed the center of the black image. They tried different guns. Lena never got better. Otto began to miss the center. The special mix of CIA drugs worked quicker than the street versions of GHB and Rohypnol.

Otto put down a Colt and turned to Lena. "I don't feel well." His speech was slurred. He had to steady himself by grabbing the table, then the wall. "You drugged me, you bitch." His knees began to buckle.

She left him on the floor, climbed up to the entrance, and flicked the entry lights off and on twice.

Tig came in first and swept for more alarms, then announced, "All clear."

Casey sent Tig to search the lounge while she went to Otto's office.

Lena guided Brandt and Deke to the basement.

"Any problems?" Deke asked.

"No. But I think he's the biggest creep since Caligula."

Brandt and Lena moved on to the vault doors while Deke left to check on Otto.

"Biometric locks. Langley was right," Brandt said.

Deke returned. "Otto's out but breathing normal. I always worry the lab will OD someone."

"Langley got the locks right. We need his fingerprints. Did you bring the tape and paper?" Brandt asked.

"Got 'em."

Brandt went with Deke and helped get Otto's fingerprints on sticky tape and transfer them to a piece of special paper. "Let's try door number one," Brandt said.

"You work the sequencer. I'll do the prints," Deke said.

"Okay, give me a second to attach it." Brandt placed leads on the lock and looked at the LED screen readout to be sure. "I'm good."

Deke pressed the paper with Otto's fingerprints on the lock screen and waited. Lights flashed on Brandt's device. They both held their breath.

"Six, two, zero, six," Brandt said.

Deke punched the numbers in a keypad, and the lock clicked. "We're in."

Brandt swung the heavy vault door open, and Deke stepped in and turned on the lights.

Lena waited until she heard, "Holy shit."

§

"Didn't expect anything like this," Brandt said.

On the left was a rack of uniforms. Some brandished swastika armbands. On others, Soviet red stars decorated shoulders. There were four seasons of camouflage suits from Moscow and Berlin. Past the clothing racks were stockpiles of laptops and electronic gear from state-of-the-art night vision headgear to computer-aided surveillance radar. Then came the armory—small arms from NATO, Russia, and Israel, enough RPGs to destroy a shopping center. The big find was surveillance and combat drones, partially assembled or hanging from the ceiling.

"This explains a lot," Deke said. "Otto and his friends are getting ready for war."

"No SADMs, though," Lena said.

Brandt didn't look worried. "We still have the next room."

"Doesn't appear to matter to Otto if you're a fascist or a communist," Deke said.

"Grandfather SS, brother an officer in the communist Stasi—an interesting bloodline," Brandt said. "Dracula must be in there somewhere."

Lena shook her head up and down. "This is what brought Petrov to Dresden. I'm sure of it. A chance to bring Nazis, Stasi, and KGB into his plan."

"I dunno. Seems like a stretch to me," Brandt said.

Lena didn't budge. "Not really. Think about it. If you were Gestapo, Moscow recruited you for the Stasi. Just change uniforms. The KGB, Stasi, Nazis . . . they're like cockroaches. They're in every corner of Europe, scheming, planning revenge. Hoping to turn back the clock and get control again. Perfect recruits for Petrov's plans." Lena dropped a Nazi armband on the floor and mashed it with her foot. "The Twelfth Directorate has file pictures of the Stasi and KGB partying with Nazis at Oktoberfest."

"The Nazi party in Germany has been outlawed, but even Berlin admits it can't eliminate it," Deke said. He opened a file cabinet and scanned a thick folder. "They're all here. Maybe you're right. Every nutjob group from fascists to the Marxist left. A few crazy anarchists too." He read more, then added, "Kranz and Ulbricht, the old tyrants of East Germany, are circled in red. No tears shed when they died. They must be in this file for a reason." He kept flipping through the pages. "The prince of darkness must have been working overtime to bring assholes like this together. Ideologies don't fit."

"*Pathologies* fit," Brandt said.

Deke looked up from the file. "Like a glove. A timeless formula. Join forces to defeat the common enemy. When it's done, destroy the partner."

Lena steeled her eyes. "They came together to wage war against Joshua. Psalm 83."

Deke read more, then his voice rose. "Here's your link. Heinrich Schmidt and Rudolf Craener. Schmidt is married to Otto's sister. He was the Stasi chief in Brandenburg. After the Wall came down, he was tried and acquitted for torture and murder of civilians across East Germany. His lawyer was Craener, the grandson of the Gestapo chief in Bavaria."

"So Matveev, the Brumfelts, Schmidt, and Craener are all hooked up," Brandt said. "We can walk this back all the way to Brussels. Grayson. The drone attack. The RPG ambush in Poland. We need to connect them to Petrov."

Lena inspected the rack of uniforms. "They must be the ones who pulled the weapons out ahead of us. Petrov could tell them where to look."

"True believers, psychopaths, and sadists with nukes. What could possibly go wrong?" Brandt said.

Deke pulled out a second folder labeled *Mitgliedschaft* and scanned through the pages. "Jeezus. We need to get these files and laptops to Langley ASAP. They're all here. Front-page political names, government officials, oligarchs, the heirs of the SS elite. If this membership list gets out, we're looking at a European political train wreck."

Brandt had a caustic look—eye half-cocked and a crooked grin. "Does this group have a name we can pass on to Langley?"

Casey walked in. "How about the *Leipzig Autorität*?"

"Leipzig Authority? Never heard of them," Deke said.

"There's notes on his calendar listing 'LA.' Didn't mean much until we got into the safe. It was locked, but the combination was taped to the bottom of a bookend on a shelf. There're minutes from meetings going back over ten years. Otto must be the secretary. The finance minister is in Hanau."

"The leaders?"

"Looks like two, in Berlin and Munich."

"Schmidt owns a printing company in Berlin's Mitte district," Deke said. "Craener is active in charitable organizations in Munich."

"I'll have Tig run Leipzig Authority through the Langley database," Casey said. "See if they're on our radar. The Langley Operations can check the money end."

"How does Putin figure into this?" Brandt asked.

"Probably as surprised as we are," Deke said. "I think Lena's right—the group sort of melded together over time. A couple of KGB knew some Stasi who knew some Nazis. A common need for protection, secrecy, and a desire for revenge brought them together. Dodging reprisals became a way of life for them."

Brandt reached up to touch the wing of a drone. "Petrov's father became the catalyst, and vodka and Jäegermeister the glue. Slap a name on it, and all of a sudden you have an organization with a sense of purpose."

"We have Otto's laptop and a flash drive hidden in a desk lamp. A cell phone but no backups," Casey said.

"Keep searching. We need it all."

Deke moved to a second file cabinet and found a metal box containing false IDs for Czech BIS, Polish AW, German BVF, French DGSI, and the FBI. Another drawer held a heavy carton of blank passports for all of Europe and North and South America. Otto's group could play "catch me if you can" on three continents.

Brandt continued inspecting the drones. A large one with familiar fangs and claws and an Uzi attached hung above the smaller surveillance model he had just touched. Then he poked through wooden crates of mortar shells, RPG warheads, and Soviet hand grenades.

"I've seen enough," Deke said. "I sent a roster photo to the counter-terror group. I'll get Delta in here to take videos and load this stuff up. The laptops and files need to go to Langley first thing. Let's see what Otto has next door."

Brandt and Deke repeated the process and opened the next vault, where a second, interior vault door hinted at the importance of what might be inside. The procedure again gained them entry. Their hopes were answered. SADMs were stacked one on top of another. Their only disappointment was the numbers—twelve—leaving seventeen still unaccounted for.

"If you open one up for me, I'll check for tritium," Lena said.

Brandt stuck a picking tool in the slot and started on the first one. Twenty minutes later, it was open.

Lena attached her nozzle and turned on the gauge. "This one is hot. Here's our connection. Petrov has been here."

"The new locks are in the car. I'll send Tig to get them. Start on the next one," Deke said.

Brandt opened the next one in under ten minutes. Lena noted the presence of tritium. Two hours later, the new locks had been installed on the armed SADMs.

"I'll have to bring Sturm in on this now. See what he wants to do with Otto. I'm hoping he feels the need to check with Berlin first. They'll have to toss this around for a few days and find a way to keep a lid on it."

"Will Berlin keep us out of it?" Brandt said.

"Can't say. It would look better for them if they discovered it, but they need to figure out a story the press will accept and that leaves us and the nukes out. Langley's top interrogation team will be here by first light. We want some time with Otto before the Germans decide what to do with him."

"Sturm will be pissed we didn't inform him first," Tig said.

"Why? We didn't know if Otto was involved with anything other than the Angel's club until we got down here. It could have blown up in our faces. We were only trying to save him embarrassment."

"Sturm is of no concern. We need to find Petrov," Lena said. "He has the rest of them."

23

Before returning to the hotel, Deke watched Delta load up the vault contents and waited until the interrogation team arrived. The others had already gone to their rooms for showers and a few hours of sleep before the late afternoon meeting. He lay on his bed, not expecting sleep. There was too much going on, too many phone calls to make and too many to answer. A chaos drill in Langley.

He wondered about the Leipzig Authority leadership and imagined Schmidt with a huge stomach and heavy jowls, his co-leader Craener, a sweaty Nazi plutocrat in Munich. After a couple of beers at lunch, Schmidt would light a cigar and try to decide between a nap or a quickie with the tart in shipping. The bald Bavarian would be going over what he planned to say to the Museum Board during the night's dinner meeting. When the calls from Dresden came at 6:30 p.m., the *scheisse* would hit the fan. The tart would be forgotten, the dinner meeting canceled. Craener would call Schmidt in Berlin first, then his wife to tell her to pack their bags. They had to fly to Hanau for an emergency meeting. His wife would understand. She was a good Nazi. After arranging the private charter flight, Schmidt would have to choose between his Stasi mistress, his wife, or his assistant for work. He would decide on the mistress, uncertain if he would ever see Berlin again. He would tell her to bring her passport. After a drink from his schnapps bottle in the bottom desk drawer, Craener would call his wife again and instruct her to bring the large blue bag from the closet safe. She would understand what that meant. She would pack a photo album then. When he hung up, he would probably shake his head and say in an audible voice to himself, "That fucking Petrov. Why couldn't he wait?"

§

The team sat at conference tables covered in white linen after fixing plates from deli trays of meat, cheese, rye toast, and brötchen Casey had ordered. Brandt asked for a pot of coffee.

Deke finished a call to Langley while the group reviewed the day's success and snacked. "We're heroes in Langley now," he said. "The Terror Research desk has been trying to gather intel on the Leipzig Authority for years. Quite a puzzle to them, very secretive. Professionals with money behind them makes them especially dangerous. When I mentioned some of the names on the roster, they didn't seem surprised. They'd always suspected the group had friends in high places. They're trying to figure out what to do about Schmidt and Craener."

Al scoffed. "Friends? More like protection."

"Research believes Leipzig Authority is responsible for political assassinations across Europe, including two retired deputy ministers garroted in Paris who were French war heroes. What has had them scratching their heads is some of the kills were Russian politicians. Gorbachev's and Yeltsin's advisors. Last night should help them make the connection now."

"Is Otto talking?" Brandt said.

"He's in a mood to bargain. Seems he prefers a warm climate in air-conditioned Gitmo to a German prison where the ice never melts."

No shock to Brandt. Otto knew what to expect—in an open cell block, the shelf life of a Stasi colonel's brother would be hours.

"Petrov?" Lena said.

"He was here four months ago with trucks. Loaded up all the SADMs that would fit. He told Otto he was only moving them to a safer location and would be back for the rest. After he left, Otto got suspicious. He checked with the leadership and found out no one approved the move. Petrov did it on his own."

"Did he say where he was taking them?" Brandt asked.

"He said he'd tell him when he came back for the others. He had some rough-looking immigrants to help load the trucks, so Otto backed off."

"Jihadists?" Brandt said.

"Could be," Deke said. "The groups that would like these make up a long list."

Casey winced. "Is he selling them to terrorists?"

"Petrov would never sell them," Lena said. "If he's involved with jihadists, it's because he needs them for his plan."

Tig's face turned sour. "If he got mixed up with Ali Baba, he might be dead now and they have the weapons."

"*That* possibility is sending the director to the White House for a briefing," Deke said.

"So we're back to chasing Petrov?" Casey said.

"According to Otto, the last time he talked to Petrov, he was in Berlin and insisted he needed money. He gave Otto a Bundespost account number to deposit it in."

Lena quickly added, "Petrov spent a lot of time in Berlin. He has a friend at the Max Planck Society. Uwe Deist."

"You know him?" Deke said.

"Yes, but not well."

"It's a place to start. I'll have him checked out, then you and I will go see him."

"What about us?" Casey said. "Can we go back to London? I have a hair appointment coming up."

Deke chuckled. "Langley wants you in Austria—Kitzbühel. They have some raw intel about a group meeting in Berchtesgaden that could be connected to the Leipzig Authority. KGB, Stasi, and neo-Nazis. Sort of a meet-and-drink for the deeply depraved and morally bankrupt."

"How about the old Nazis? They haven't forgotten the war," Brandt said.

"They went underground in Bavaria," Deke said. "We watched them until they started to die off. We know they stashed weapons in the mountains, waiting for the next führer."

Brandt grinned. "The Hitler Youth must be in nursing homes now."

"We have an agency floater living in Kitzbühel with her Austrian husband who might be of some help. They own a *pensione* and she keeps an eye on the political groups and sends in traffic reports on the smugglers. Maybe she's seen or heard something."

"What about the Russians?" Casey asked.

"Without Lena, Moky must be desperate." Deke turned to Al. "I'm not sure you're needed anymore. I can have Sturm arrange for you to go home."

Lena froze.

Al replied, "Since I'm now a gyrovague anyway, if it's all right with you, I'd like to be sure we have all the weapons before I go back. And I'd love to see the new Berlin."

Lena relaxed.

24

Al agreed to stay with Deke and Lena at the Regent on Charlottenstraße. Five-star hotels were becoming a fixture in his life, and he wanted to see the modern, reunited Berlin. His one visit to Berlin was in the old communist east and he had never been to the west side. The Soviet-built wall that divided the city then made an impression, with guards in watchtowers trained to kill, machine guns, and searchlights that could reach the moon. An East German major had been his guide, and he acted proud of what they had done to prevent defections.

"I need to meet with our Chief of Station here about Schmidt," Deke said. "I'll ask him about Petrov and see what he has on Uwe Deist."

"Al's never been to the new Berlin. Is it okay to show him around?" Lena asked.

"Sure. But take Tig with you and keep an eye out for Petrov."

The last time Al had done anything like touring with a woman was when he'd taken his wife to see Loket Castle outside of Karlovy Vary. She had never been outside of Prague. Travel had always been restricted by the communist government. The trip had not gone well; traveling for the first time and leaving their son with her mother unsettled his wife. They bickered over small things—where to eat, what to eat, what to see next, what to bring home. They ended up leaving early and in silence.

This tour promised to be different. Lena was an issue on her own. She raised difficult questions within him. Somehow his higher and lower selves merged like river currents when he was with her. Being well out of his monkish comfort zone, dressed as a civilian in some of Brandt's clothes didn't help.

"We should start in Pariser Platz," Lena said. "Brandenburg Gate is the soul of Germany."

Al relaxed. His issues with her disappeared when they were actually together.

"I got your six," Tig said.

Lena felt mixed about Tig's presence. He was a comfort as a guard and a pleasant admirer, but a complication to her hope to have some time alone with Al. She'd felt drawn to the monk from the beginning, yet not certain what he meant in her life. A spiritual guide? A friend who also had been wounded by life? Or a man she had become deeply attracted to despite—or because of—being unavailable? Wanting what she couldn't have had always been a problem for her. There were times when her obsessive drive worked, such as when her career focus helped her become a leading physicist in Russia. But when it came to a deep relationship, the loss of Leonid was the final straw, another broken heart, and she'd been left with a reminder of never getting what she wanted most. When Al was in Brandt's clothes, it was easy to picture him giving a speech or signing autographs in a crowd. That made him a desire and a threat—another unfulfilled dream.

Berlin was cold, with a hint of snow in the air and the perpetual grayness of cities close to the Baltic. Deke had embassy security drop them off at the Soviet War Memorial in Tiergarten Park, leaving them with a short walk to the monument and plaza. A kilted Scottish band played "Amazing Grace" on bagpipes in Pariser Platz. The dark sky had the Polizei prepared for rain or snow in green Gore-Tex coats with bright reflective strips and buttons. Americans and Asians made up the majority of tourists. Europeans considered the historic monument a symbol of a Germany best left behind.

"I found it surprising Brandenburg Gate survived the bombing. The damaged horses on the top and bullet marks were repaired so quickly it almost feels like a German warning," Lena said.

"I remember seeing the horses and chariot on top from the East Berlin side," Al said. "The monument was much taller than the Wall."

"The Germans are proud of Berlin now. Everything rebuilt as a modern city. Proof of what the German ethic and pride can accomplish," Lena said.

"Brandt hates it," Tig said. "No charm. Just steel, drab cement, and beer steins made in China."

"He has a point," Al said. "But before reunification, East Berlin was full of broken concrete and twisted steel in the street for nearly thirty-five years."

Lena slipped her hand in Al's and tugged him toward the river. "Let me show you what's left of the Wall. It's a memorial now."

§

Brandt was familiar with Kitzbühel. A-list celebrity skiers in search of anonymity and indulgence chose Kitzbühel over St. Moritz and Aspen. The owners and restaurant patrons ignored them,

paparazzi were taboo, the formidable ski area was one of the best in
the world, and they avoided Switzerland's punitive drug laws.

Edna and her husband, Klaus, operated the Zum Adler *pensione*
on the edge of the resort town. It was shoulder season in the Alps:
skiing was over and the snow on the trails was too deep for hiking.
Edna, thrilled to fill a room in the empty *pensione* with the CIA,
welcomed them. She was slightly bigger than a forest elf, with
silvery-gray hair tied in a bun, dressed in a Bavarian boiled wool green
jacket and riding boots that lifted her tiny frame an inch. The frail
appearance was a lie. She moved luggage like a forklift.

A black-and-tan shepherd stayed by Edna's side as she led them
into a barn filled with the scent of aged wood and absent horses. "The
Austrians and Germans have bugged all the guest rooms. We haven't
bothered to remove them. We hope if they hear something that's a
danger to Klaus and me, they will warn us,"

"We're interested in any unusual movement and activity in town
and across the smuggling routes," Casey said.

"A lot for this time of year. The passes still have snow," Edna said.
"They're four-hundred-year-old trade routes from when smuggling
was a way of life. The Germans closed them up during the war. The
KGB started using them again to supply the communists in Italy
after the war."

"Who uses them now?"

"Mostly jihadists and drug smugglers. Klaus calls it the Balkan
Beltway. The Serbians, Croats, and Albanians are regulars. Counter-
terror is concerned about the weapons. They like to track the
shipments all the way to the radical cells. Something changed this
year. Not certain why. We had obvious vehicle traffic despite the
snow. Klauus went up to take a look. Some truck got stuck heading

south, then a convoy of snowcats and winter-equipped SUVs took over. Truck is still up there."

"We'd like to see it," Brandt said.

"Klaus can take you to it. He's in Zurich now but will be back day after tomorrow. But there's something else—the caves." Edna had them all climb a ladder to the barn loft, where she had a tripod-mounted telescope stationed. Her shepherd whined and danced circles around the ladder base. "I was scanning the routes after the truck got stuck and saw rope lines hanging down to two caves. Snow makes it difficult to move weapon loads, so the jihadists wait for the roads to clear. They avoid the villages and stay in the caves in summer. When the snow is gone, they can walk to them. Not this year, with that truck stuck up there. Someone had to use ropes. They're gone now."

"Any pictures?" Casey asked.

"The videos show dim lights at night and shadowy figures. SOP is to send an alert to Langley. I was hoping for the usual satellite help but never heard anymore. They must have figured there was too much snow for anything important."

"Can we get to the caves?" Casey asked.

"Klaus has climbing gear you can use."

"We'll wait for him then," Brandt said.

"Let me show you to your room. It's the only one with a private bath. Remember, someone is probably listening. After you unpack, come back to the barn. There's a patio and bar outside. Very private."

Their room had pine walls, a sink, a separate toilet without a bidet, and a tiny shower. The outside window boxes faced north and still had a layer of snow. In summer, they would be bursting with red geraniums.

"Cozy, huh?" Brandt said.

"A little too chilly to be cozy." Casey shivered.

"You'll like the *federbetten*. Nothing is cozier than a feather tick cover and bed."

Brandt chattered aimlessly, covering Casey's search for listening devices. She found one on the nightstand made to look like a screw head and two hidden in electrical outlets but left them alone. She stepped to the sink and turned on a faucet to wash up.

"Let the water run to get it warm," Brandt said. "These places are great for charm but stingy with hot water."

When she finished, she read a text and motioned to Brandt to go back outside. They moved toward the barn but stopped halfway there. "Deke's text said be sure to read the article in the *Post*. The reporter is digging into our past."

"I know. Some guy from the paper contacted Cybil asking about me. Probably got the name from someone in Langley for the price of a lunch. He should know better than to talk to an art agent. As soon as he said he was with the *Post*, she hit him with how my work is outside the box, New World, cutting-edge abstract art. All the bullshit. When he finally got to his questions, she blew him off."

"Nice that Cybil believes you still do travel stuff," Casey said.

"The whole thing makes my head ache," Brandt said.

They joined Edna on a large stone patio Klaus had built on the far side of the barn with a view of the snow-capped Kaiser Mountains, furnished with outdoor tables, chairs, and a crater-sized stone fire pit for guests to enjoy après-ski and alpenglow sunsets. The burning logs were big enough to heat a warehouse. Edna had circled chairs around the warm flames and put out a bottle of Riesling.

"We're fine here. Patios in snow zones aren't good for electronics," Edna said.

Brandt poured them each a glass of wine.

Edna sipped coffee as the shepherd settled next to her chair. "We keep our horses in a heated barn outside of Salzburg for the winter." She dropped a hand to scratch the dog's ear. "Heidi misses them. We'll be bringing them back soon. Tomorrow I'll drive you around Berchtesgaden and show you where the lunatics meet. Their leader is Günter Mungst. He keeps to himself, low profile."

"What are they up to?" Casey asked.

"Well, you never know about them. Until recently, they just talked and talked. More boozing than anything. But with the all the political unrest across Europe, they've become more secretive. Langley asked me to try and get someone inside. So far, no luck."

"Could the truck be theirs?"

A sound or scent of something unfamiliar caught Heidi's attention; she raised her head and let out a muffled woof.

"Klaus thinks so. The truck thing is odd. The smuggling we see in summer is heading for Munich. Jihadist weapons and loads of illegals. This truck was heading toward Italy before the passes were clear." She shook her head. "Weird for this time of year."

§

Deke arranged a lunch meeting with Lena and Uwe Deistin the rooftop Käfer restaurant in the new Reichstag. Deist had gray goatee and mysterious dark gothic eyes. A light spring snow covered Berlin's city's parks and sidewalks. Locals knew it could snow into June.

"It's good to see you, Lena. What brings you to Berlin?" Deist said.

"Petrov. I'm afraid he's in some trouble. We're hoping you might be able to tell us where he might be."

"I can't help much. But it comes as no surprise he may be in trouble."

"Why do you say that?" Deke said.

"Petrov was different when I saw him last. Obsessed about something. He showed me a list of names and asked if I knew where they might be."

"Were you able to help?" Deke asked.

"Not really. I recognized a handful of the names. A few forgotten Stasi the police were hunting after the Wall was destroyed. And some old Soviet secret police. The KGB colonels in Berlin and Frankfurt were on it—Krostov and Bejjein. I remember how they refused to go back to Russia over perestroika. Car wreck on the Frankfurt autobahn killed Bejjein. Krostov left Berlin long ago."

"Did Petrov say why he wanted them?" Deke said.

"I asked. He said unfinished business and made it clear he didn't like the question."

As the heavy, starchy luncheon special of fried potatoes and roast pork was served along with beer, Deist asked, "How long will you be in Berlin, Lena? Maybe you and I could discuss the new research in particle physics while you're here."

"I'd love to, but I'm more interested in spiritual life than physics now. I have a monk instructing me."

Deist's face dropped like space junk. "Well, if something changes, I have presentations from the Edinburgh conference I'd love to share with you."

Deke signed for the check, and they stood up to leave.

"Something else just occurred to me about that list," Deist said. "Couple of names that didn't seem to fit with Stasi or KGB."

"Do you remember them?" Deke asked.

"Yes. Speer and Peiper . . . old Nazis." Deist shook his head. "I'm sure they're dead now."

In the car, Lena asked Deke, "You knew those names?"

"Yeah. Speer doesn't matter, but Peiper is a scary name for us. A Nazi to the end. He was the officer responsible for the Malmedy massacre in Belgium. His wife worked for Himmler."

"But he must be dead too."

"A French revenge team took him out after the war. His men worshipped him. They wouldn't be the kind to let things go. Part of the fascist gangbangers that created the Leipzig Authority. If we checked, I'd bet the two French war heroes who were garroted were on that revenge team."

25

Edna stopped the car in front of the Hotel Edelweiss in Berchtesgaden. "The meetings take place in the basement. There's one scheduled for tomorrow. Klaus and I alternate shooting their pictures from his nephew's place on the corner. We send them to Langley if we see a new one."

"We'd like to see the pictures," Casey said.

"No problem. Langley has ID'd most as KGB and Stasi. Some suspected Nazis too."

"Any of these names mean anything to you? Leipzig Authority? Otto Brumfelt? Petrov?"

"No. But there have been a few fresh faces. They went to a couple of meetings, then stopped."

"We want to see those pictures first," Brandt said.

On the drive back, they passed the empty car park in front of the Eagle's Nest ticket office. Brandt had taken tour groups there before. He leaned over to get a better look up. The snow was almost gone on the road to the tunnel. The mountaintop hideaway boasted a restaurant, great views, and Hitler's fingerprints, a must-see stop for history buffs. Specially designed buses had to be used to take tourists up the mountain on twisty roads to the tunnel entrance. From there, a famous brass-lined elevator took them to the top of the six-thousand-foot mountain and a look back into the Third Reich. When Brandt was working tours, he'd always let the on-site guides explain how Hitler hated the spot due to his fear of heights.

"I think we're being followed," Edna said. "Gray Audi. Picked us up as we left town."

"You recognize them?" Casey said.

"Not yet. Could be two of Mungst's men. I'll stop in Schneizl-reuth. My friends operate Cafe Neu Meran. We can have lunch there and see if they stick with us."

§

The restaurant sat on a steep hillside with a sloping parking lot above a creek filled with sheets of ice and rushing snowmelt. The Audi pulled into a space in the bottom row, and two men followed Casey, Brandt, and Edna inside. Both hung green alpine felt fedoras and leather coats on pegs in the wall and sat at a table where they could make a quick exit. They were tall, grizzled gray, overfed, and dressed like Bavarian bureaucrats in white shirts and ties. In lederhosen, they would look like tuba players in the oompah band.

"Either one familiar?" Casey asked Edna.

"I sent their pictures to Langley."

One of them answered his cell and tried to avoid looking at Edna's table. He hung up and whispered to his partner.

"Where are the restrooms?" Brandt asked.

Edna wagged her head toward the back. "Down the hall, past the kitchen."

The waitress brought oxtail soup and black bread lunches for the three. They ate in silence, trying to ignore the men.

"Any ideas what to do?" Brandt said, putting his spoon down.

Casey winced. "I guess we need to be prepared for anything."

"Nothing here. Whatever they're planning will be out on the road," Edna said.

"I have an idea, but it requires a diversion," Brandt said.

"Like what?" Casey said.

"Anything. Anything to keep them occupied until I come back."

When they finished eating, a waiter cleared their table and accordion music began to play in the background. Edna turned toward a speaker, then rose quickly and sang along. "*Polka mein schatz, Polka mein schatz.*"

She went on singing the words to the "Liechtensteiner Polka" as she danced around the tables. Brandt stood to give her room and slid casually toward the restroom. He shifted past the coat rack, then stepped back as if to watch Edna dance. Casey flashed a big smile and began to clap. An elderly couple in a corner laughed and clapped with her. Edna grabbed Casey's hand, and the two danced together. Brandt dipped his hand into the men's coat pockets until he found the Audi's keys. A cook came out and joined a waitress clapping. Brandt slipped past some of the kitchen staff coming out to watch the dancers, then exited out the delivery door. He raced around to the parking lot to the Audi. The engine started immediately, and he released the brake, then shifted it into neutral and turned it off. The slope to the creek was steep, without a guardrail, and it didn't take much of an effort to get the Audi rolling into the stream. He ran back inside as the song ended.

Edna and Casey did a stage curtsy and received applause for their efforts. Brandt dropped the keys back in the coat, and they left the restaurant together, ignoring the demands for more.

As she sped out of the parking lot, Edna said, "Klaus will be upset I did that. Everyone knows me there."

§

Outside the barn, Brandt tossed a hard rubber ball for Heidi to chase. The ball would disappear in the snow, and Heidi would have to sniff, search, and dig to find it, then race back for him to throw it again.

Casey walked up. "I just talked to Deke."

Brandt picked up the ball Heidi had dropped at his feet and threw it in a high arc to sink deeper in the snow. "Any luck in Berlin?"

"Nothing much. Petrov was gone. He went there looking for old Nazis, KGB, and Stasi. Like looking for rats in a cheese factory. No lead where he might be now."

"Lena and Al? Something is going on there. Did he mention anything about them?"

"Deke? He'd have to be hit with a brick to see it."

"She's like an electron orbiting his proton, hoping for a collision." Brandt couldn't resist the physics allusion.

"I don't know if I can forgive you for that."

"You know me. I'm all about science." Brandt faked a throw when Heidi returned with the ball. Heidi didn't fall for it and waited until he threw it again.

"Al has to be aware of her interest. It must cause him some conflict."

"As an expert on conflicts, I can confidently say Al has a big one. Why do you think he hasn't made solemn vows?"

"Full of doubt?" asked Casey.

"The Benedictines can't give him what he really wants. His old life back." Heidi dropped the ball again, stepped back, and waited.

Brandt used an underhand heave, forming an even higher arc to have the ball sink deeper in the snow.

"Kind of late for that now."

"I think he's operating on a sense of hope, as if there's a larger meaning for him to be on this mission."

"What? Finding missing nukes that threaten the world isn't large enough?"

Klaus walked behind them into the barn with a bucket, and Heidi ran after him with the ball in her mouth.

Casey smirked. "Klaus is back. We'll have a look at the truck and caves tomorrow."

Brandt was pleased the conversation had turned back to the mission. Al's problems reminded him of his own. He didn't want to deal with them. He'd had the dream again the night before. The first version, where the little boy stepped from behind a rock carrying a handful of artist brushes and a bouquet of flowers. The boy looked to be nine years old and wore eyeglasses. The same age Brandt was when his teacher had wanted his vision tested. The dream repeated three nights in a row, until he remembered the flowers—forget-me-nots. The second version had appeared the night after Cybil agreed to be his art agent. Same boy, same flowers, but the brushes were gone, replaced with a Glock.

§

Klaus had a Germanic accent as thick as clay. His hair had turned from blond to ashy gray, but his eyes retained a mischievous liquid blue sparkle. He was warming up two touring model snowmobiles outside the barn. Brandt and Casey were zipped up in one-piece heated winter suits.

"It will take us an hour to reach the truck," Klaus said, handing Casey and Brandt helmets and goggles. "Just follow me. The helmet radios are synced. Speak up if you have a problem. Be careful in the meadow. Stay in my tracks as we cross. Be sure not to move above me." Klaus flashed a wicked smile.

"Avalanche risk?" Casey asked.

"In spring, the meadow is famous for wet slab avalanches." Klaus stowed a climbing rope and gear in the storage compartment. He mounted the tracked vehicle, turned to wave to them, then started across open country toward the truck at full speed.

Casey climbed behind Brandt on the second snowmobile and they followed. The freeze/thaw cycle had made the top layer of snow thick and crusty, and the powder below erupted in clouds of glimmering white crystals in the morning sun. Klaus broke trail all the way to the smuggler's road. The old route was a ledge wide enough for two medieval carts to pass. The edge to the right was an irregular drop that varied from steep and deadly to an easy, gradual descent. The snowcats had dug deep tracks into layers of snow.

Klaus was the first to reach the truck. He used a wrench from his toolkit to bang open the frozen handles on the rear. The empty cargo area gave no hint of what the load might have been. The driver's-side window was open a crack—just wide enough to allow weather to cover the inside in frost and light snow.

Casey opened the door and scanned the interior.

"You won't find anything in there," Klaus said. "Everything was taken to the Mountain Safety Office. Nothing helpful. Food items and water bottles."

"German or Russian food?" Brandt said.

"No borscht, if that's what you're hoping for. Chicken bones and bread wrappers. Some cheese labels. Water bottles from Munich."

Brandt's face turned sour. Could be anyone from anywhere in Europe. "I guess we should check the caves."

Klaus pulled an equipment bag from the back of his snowmobile and extracted the gear they would need. "Have you done any climbing before?"

"It's been a while, but sure. At one time I was pretty good," Brandt said.

"Really? You don't look like it." Klaus's eyes were like a split screen—austere on the right, playful on the left. "I would never have guessed."

"Be nice, Klaus."

"Here's your crampons and harness." Klaus secured the rope to his snowmobile and waited.

Brandt put on the gear, threaded the rope through twin carabiners attached to his waist harness, tied an overhand stopper knot for safety, and nodded to Klaus. "Ready."

"The first cave is about eight meters below where you're standing. You should have no problem rappelling down. But try not to get lost. You'll either need to climb back up, then down again to reach the second cave or do a pendulum traverse. I only have one ice axe for the climb back up, so I suggest the traverse."

"How far to the mouth of the second cave?"

"Six or seven meters. You can judge better when you get there."

"One axe, huh? When I do the traverse, make sure your snowmobile is between the caves."

"Hmph, giving orders now."

Casey watched Brandt extend his body over the edge, then disappear. Klaus leaned over the rim, gauging his descent. When Brandt reached the mouth of the first cave, he turned on his head lamp. A few steps inside, he felt disappointment run through his veins. He'd never said anything, but part of him had hoped the weapons might be there. What he did find concerned him—piles of tubular steel, the metal used for SADM container frames, enough to build a pipeline or a moon rocket . . . or to hold seventeen weapons. He took some pictures, grabbed a two-foot tube, and then walked back to the entrance and paused to adjust to the fading sunlight.

"I'm ready for the traverse," Brandt yelled up.

"Hurry. It's getting cold." Klaus untied the rope and moved the snowmobile, then threaded the rope twice through a carabiner.

Brandt gave the rope a tug. "Take up the slack before you secure it again. Wow! That's enough. When you feel my weight on the pendulum, try giving the rope a little help."

"Ha, that's a good one."

Brandt walked to the far edge of the cave mouth and used his crampons to dig into the snow and move even farther away from the opening. He tried to judge how far he would swing on the first try, hoping for six to eight feet past the first entrance. He moved as fast as his crampons would allow, then launched himself out toward the second cave. It took three attempts at swinging like a pendulum to reach the second cave entrance. Brandt stuck his crampons and the ice axe into the snow to hold him above the cave mouth.

"This is good. Slack now," Brandt said.

Klaus let rope out slowly.

When Brandt's feet touched, he asked for more slack. This cave was wider and deeper than the first. He unhooked from the rope and began his inspection. The floor of the cave entrance was icy in one spot, suggesting a camp stove might have been used there. No metal tubes, no SADM parts, but two frozen bodies twenty feet inside. He flashed his light on the rear of the cave before advancing any farther. Rolled-up sleeping bags and some ski poles lying like matchsticks were all he could see.

The bodies were face up, stacked one on top of the other. They had frozen together, and Brandt had to kneel down and pry and push to separate them. Their faces had a snow globe pallor, and frost crystals coated them head to toe. A six-inch metal crucifix was frozen to each chest. Brandt removed a glove and gently brushed the crystals from their faces. The lifeless, frozen flesh had a pinkish-gray tone. A black hole in each forehead explained the cause of death. Brandt used his phone to take pictures.

The climb back up brought memories of his ice climbing days in the Sierras. He used the ice axe and steel tube over his head for balance, crampons for footing, and climbed with his legs. Klaus was belaying the whole way. Casey gave him a helping hand when he reached the edge of the road.

He took a second to catch his breath. "We have a problem. They must have removed the SADMs from the carriages." Brandt wiggled the tube frame as evidence. "They probably cushioned them in the back of the snowcats and hauled them away. Maybe Deke can see if a Langley satellite can tell us where they went. The second cave has bodies. Two of them."

Brandt showed the pictures to Klaus, who said, "No one I've seen. Maybe Edna can help."

Casey took a look as well and shook her head no. "I'll send them to Langley when we get down."

§

Edna was outside waiting for them by the barn. Silver-and-blue Austrian police cars could be seen driving away with their blue lights flashing.

"What did the Polizei want?" Klaus asked.

"Help. The bodies of the men from lunch yesterday were found in the larch grove outside of town. Sounds like assassination. Head shots."

Brandt wondered if Kitzbühel had a morgue. A large one, like LA or New York. Two in the cave, two in the woods—four extra bodies could be too much in a tiny resort town. A fellow travel agent once told him the morgue in New Delhi had two floors: one for Hindus, one for Muslims. And space for over two hundred if the alley dumpsters for the untouchable Dalit were included.

Edna said, "They were asking if I saw anything that might help them. I told them I hardly noticed them at lunch."

"An execution over a failed assignment?" Casey said. "That's crazy. Even ISIS doesn't do that."

"Stalin liked to do it," said Brandt. "Called it a 'Tartar reward.'"

"I just can't see Mungst killing his own men like that," Edna said.

"Who else would have a motive?" Brandt said.

"That group has plenty of enemies but no one to resort to murder."

"How about the new faces? One of them maybe?" Casey said.

"I've got their pictures on my laptop. Meet you in the barn," Edna said.

Klaus pulled the vehicles in the barn, then left. Brandt covered them with tarps. Edna brought her laptop and set it on a workbench next to the tack room. Heidi maintained patrol, sniffing around the corners of the barn.

"These are the new faces. The first photos show them going into the meeting. Not great shots. Those with Mungst leading them out are better. Full or partial facials." Edna lingered over each one and looked at Casey's and Brandt's blank expressions before moving on to the next picture. She advanced through eleven photos before stopping. "That's it. All the new faces. I don't see a motive in any of them."

Brandt shook his head from side to side. "Nothing." He nudged Casey. "Anything?"

"One or two appeared in nightmares."

Brandt silently agreed.

Casey pulled her phone out and looked at a photo. "Go back to the next-to-last shot, please."

It showed two men leaving the building. Casey pointed. "Zero in on him. The tall guy in front, next to the one in the hoodie." She focused on the screen, then her phone. "It's him. Ivan Krostov. Moscow's KGB man in charge of Berlin. The picture Deke sent is old, but it's clearly him."

"His name isn't Krostov. That's Günter Mungst," Edna said.

"Mungst is Krostov, huh?" Brandt looked at Edna and then Casey, who was beginning to shake from the cold day on the mountain. He remembered that in Iowa, every barn had a liquor bottle. "You have any schnapps out here?"

"In the tack room. Shelf on the left behind a bucket. Paper cups in the cabinet. Bring the peach."

Brandt brought the peach schnapps and set cups on the table. As he poured Casey a warm-up drink, he asked, "Did Krostov, aka Mungst, have them killed?"

Edna shook her head, then poured herself a schnapps. "Maybe, but it really doesn't fit. Even crazy drunk, I can't see Mungst ordering it. Why murder them over a meaningless mission?"

Klaus came back in. "It's all over Vienna, Munich, and Zurich TV. They're calling it a Mafia hit."

26

The mountains were past sundown, but the moon's reflection on the snow was bright as if the snow were coated with luminous paint. The celebrities had left for the beaches in Portofino, Cannes, and Monaco. The ski shop windows promoted sales of Völkl and Rossignol. In the fashion displays, embroidered sweaters replaced imported Scandinavian furs. Deke flew in on an agency jet with Lena, Tig, and Al, nearly filling Edna's *pensione*. They all stood around the bonfire after Klaus added chunks of logs to boost the blaze.

Edna brought out a steamy pot full of Glühwein. "This will warm your insides. Klaus's family recipe." She ladled a glass cup with a cinnamon stick for everyone except Deke.

Casey sat down with Edna's laptop and said to Lena, "Time for the lineup. Tell me if you recognize any of these people."

Lena appeared in a black shearling coat that had been outfitted in Berlin with a pocket for a lighter and cigarettes and a secret pocket for smuggling. She looked over Casey's shoulder as she scrolled through pictures, ending with the five newest. When Casey reached the hoodie-shadowed face next to Mungst, Lena's eyes lit up. "Petrov. That's him." She looked up at Deke and Brandt. "Is he here?"

"We don't think so," Brandt said.

"Are you sure it's him?" Deke said. "Our pictures of him are awful."

"I've seen him in that hoodie enough. It's him."

"How about the others?" Casey said.

Lena scanned the rest again. "Never seen them." She grabbed a blanket and sat down.

Deke leaned over Casey and studied the picture. "That's it. The weapons were here and so was Petrov."

"He hasn't been to any of the meetings for some time," Edna said.

Brandt stomped his feet and spread his hands toward the flames to warm them. "Two fresh bodies in the woods, two frozen cadavers on the mountain. I can see the headline now. 'Four Murdered in Kitzbühel.'"

"Any ID on the mountain bodies?" Deke asked.

"Not yet. Edna's waiting to tell the locals about them until we hear from Langley," Casey said.

Deke's glare held a question; his lips made a squeaky sound. "Did the police say much about the scene when they talked to you, Edna?"

"They said the bodies were stacked on top of each other with a crucifix on their chests. They asked about cults. Wanted to know if I knew about any local groups."

"Just like the mountain bodies. Some weird sect on the loose," Brandt said. "Black magic or worse. Does Leipzig have a religious connection?"

"Nothing in the files," Casey said.

"A hollow-point .22 Ruger in the back of the head and stacking the bodies. That part could be Moky." Deke's face wrinkled. "But a crucifix? Can't see Gleb or Moky doing that."

"Why stack the bodies?" Casey said.

"An old Red Army practice," Al said. "Troops would line up Germans, shoot them, and stack the bodies. The highest stack earned them vodka and a medal from the general. During the war, the communist partisans in Italy came up with a variation. Stack the bodies to please Moscow, then place the cross to claim they were doing God's work by killing Germans."

"Weird stuff, but it's all connected to Petrov somehow." Brandt wondered if Petrov was trying to confuse God.

Casey closed the laptop. "Where's the motive? Without a reason, it's just blood lust."

"Mungst would send his mother to hell to get those nukes. It's a message from Petrov . . . keep away," Deke said.

Lena nodded. "He would have someone else do the killing."

"Crucifixes on the bodies? C'mon. That's worse than the mafia," Brandt said.

Deke looked at the pictures Brandt had sent him of the two in the cave. "I think Aaron would be interested in these."

"You thinking they were Mossad?" Casey said.

"Even iced up, they're familiar."

"They're linked to the truck. We know that much," Edna said.

Lena buttoned her coat for warmth. "Where was the truck headed?"

"South, deeper into the mountains," Brandt said.

Casey looked puzzled. "Is he looking for a place to hide them?"

"It's not the mountains. He's hauling them somewhere," Lena said.

"He's taking a chance moving those weapons in winter because he has a schedule to keep," Deke said. He sat down next to Lena. "Where else did Petrov go on his trip?"

"He went to Italy, but I'm not sure where. I asked about Venice, and he scoffed, so I let it drop."

§

Brandt and Casey helped Edna clean up after the others left, then lingered over the smoldering logs. He picked up a six-foot iron poker and tried to stir some life into the fire. Sparks mixed with renewed hypnotic flames brought a flash of heat. He stared at the glowing logs as they continued to pop and fizzle before lifting his eyes toward a hazy moon shining through the clouds. Then he settled into a chair without speaking.

Casey wrapped a blanket around her shoulders and sat down with a second blanket covering her lap and legs. "You looked like you were searching for something. What's up?"

"Still trying to figure out if I'm wrong for this job."

"Brandt, the truth is none of us are right for it. The people are horrible. The governments are dirty. And we can't help getting some of it on us. It is what it is. Get over it."

"I wish I could."

"If it will make you happy, quit. Go home and paint."

His dream hit him like a slap in the face—boy, canvas, Glock—like pieces of a jigsaw puzzle without a picture as a guide. "Hmph. Sounds simple enough, but I don't feel like I belong there either. Look at my sketchbook. Can't draw any better than a five-year old."

"Go back to California and spend time with your sister until you get yourself sorted out."

Al joined them by the fire. "I have a feeling I came at a bad time."

"Grab a seat. Brandt is just whining about not knowing where he fits in the world."

"Be patient with him. It's difficult and painful. Not something you wish on anyone."

Casey's eyes widened in surprise at Al's sympathy. "I wish he'd just decide."

"He will. When he has an answer. But it's not the kind of answer that comes from the head. It comes from a much deeper place, where head, heart, and soul merge."

With a mix of ire, Brandt said. "What do I do then? Stomp HELP in the snow until an angel comes?"

"Couldn't hurt. Wait . . . relax. Your soul will tell you what to do next. Be patient. That's what I'm doing."

§

Klaus cooked breakfast for everyone. Brandt leaned against the kitchen doorframe, watching a cigarette dangle from Klaus's lips while he rinsed and dried a fry pan.

"We're having an English breakfast. Fatty bacon and burnt toast," Klaus said.

A smoky odor rose from the toaster oven. Smoldering rye bread lay in the sink.

"Is there a donut shop nearby?" Brandt asked.

"Munich, across from the old SS Kaserne." Klaus turned around and put out his cigarette stub in a pottery dish. "Beans are in the oven."

"Black pudding too?"

"I'm not a sadist. How do you like your eggs?"

"Basted."

"Sorry. I like them scrambled and runny."

Deke came in. "We're having coffee on the patio. Grab a cup and join us."

"Klaus shouldn't be left alone."

Klaus reached to light another cigarette. "Go. You're like a damn Swiss banker watching me."

The aroma of strong coffee and uncertainty hung over the flagstone plot. Lena brought Casey a Norwegian wool sweater to fight the cold. They both looked as if they were awaiting the jury verdict. Guity, not guilty or hung jury. "We're waiting to hear from Langley on where to go next," Casey said. "They're checking satellite surveillance, looking for Petrov's trail."

Brandt grabbed a mini croissant, then poured his coffee. "I'm hoping it's Sorrento. Spring is wonderful there."

Deke looked at a text, then Casey. "It's Milan. Let's get the details."

After they left, Al said, "Milan is wrong. It has to be Tuscany."

"What makes you think that?" Tig said.

"From my days in Monte Oliveto Maggiore Monastery. Petrov wouldn't have any trouble finding help in Tuscany. After World War I, the port of Livorno was the birthplace of the Italian communist party. Nothing's changed. The leftover Soviets in Moscow are still the center of the universe to them. Devoted communists to this day. The Russians used their help to smuggle supplies to Cuba and North Vietnam."

Brandt nodded approval. "Yeah, I can see that. Red Star flags wave in their soccer matches. Florence is an hour away. Plenty of communists and synthetic radicals there."

"More monasteries to search?" Tig said.

"Maybe one. But there's plenty of old Medici and Petrucci villas capable of hiding SADMs."

Edna brought out fresh coffee and a pitcher of juice while they waited for Deke, then began helping Klaus set up a buffet in the barn with warming lights, chafing dishes, breakfast seasoning, and condiments. She dropped Heidi a pet treat for patiently sitting and then went back to the kitchen.

Deke and Casey came back, their faces crunched with concern. "We got a good trace on Petrov from the satellites," Deke said. "He had some help, five of them. Ditched the snowcats outside of Innsbruck and rented trucks. Picked up new ones in Liechtenstein and passed through the San Bernardino tunnel to Lake Como. He stopped at a lakeside villa in Lierna belonging to a defrocked Dominican friar who goes by the name Girolamo Discussa."

"There's our religious connection," Casey said.

Deke leaned toward Al. "The name mean anything to you?"

"I know the name, but not the person. It's a historical reference. Girolamo Savonarola was a Dominican Renaissance radical. A real firebrand. He wanted to turn back the clock—destroy Renaissance progress, reform the church, and purify art. He had the Medicis imprisoned. An error in judgment that cost him his life."

"Sounds like Petrov's kind of guy," Brandt said.

"Here's some real Italian irony," said Al. "Savonarola organized the first bonfire of the vanities. His followers forced residents to surrender their treasures to the vanity flames. When the town turned against him, he ended up burned at the stake in the Piazza della Signoria."

"There's a plaque in the plaza stones where they lit him up," Brandt said.

"The 'Discussa' surname is adopted—a subtle threat. It's Latin for 'reawakened.'" Al turned to Lena and asked, "Where was Petrov born?"

"Saint Petersburg. Why?"

"Savonarola claimed an invader from the north would trigger the reform."

"Jeezus. More of that Nostradamus bullshit," Deke said.

"Is Petrov still in Lierna?" Brandt said.

Deke turned glum. "Naw. He left after three days. We tracked him to Milan and lost him."

"There's caves around the lake," Brandt said. "Big ones. A couple big enough to hide the trucks and weapons. The resistance used them to hide from the Germans. Be a good place to check."

Deke looked at his phone. "I need to take this," he said, then hustled back into the barn.

"Those bodies with the crucifixes . . . they could be Girolamo's work," Al said. "He's rumored to have a team of enforcers."

"Don't they all," Casey said.

§

When Deke finished with the call, his head shook so much his bones rattled. "Sturm—what an asshole. I'll kill him myself when I get to Brussels."

"I can help," Brandt said.

"The call was from Rick Dowling, the agency liaison to NATO. Sturm went to the secretary general and bitched that we aren't honoring the agreement and are keeping the Russians out of the hunt. Left out them trying to kidnap Lena, of course. A meeting is being scheduled with Dowling, the secretary general, Sturm, and the Russian ambassador. Sturm's angry I pushed him aside in Dresden. He's trying to even the score."

"That's bullshit," Casey said.

"We finally have a solid trail to follow, and Sturm pulls this. The secretary general wants us to stay in place until the meeting is over."

"Bad idea. We need to get moving," Brandt said.

Deke nodded. "We'll leave together. Dowling can handle the NATO heat. We don't take orders from them."

"How soon can you get us a plane?" Casey said.

"Forget the plane. Sturm will find out and raise hell."

"A rental car will be easier to avoid the Russians and Gagarin," Casey said.

Brandt had mentally passed on a car. "Takes too long, and it's risky through the mountains this time of year. I can get us a plane. Swiss Air has a private jet charter service I used in our travel business."

"Book it for Milan, where we lost Petrov," Deke said.

"Tig and I will head to Como after we land," Brandt said.

Klaus came in and whispered into Edna's ear. She nodded, then said, "We have some fresh faces watching us."

"Either Sturm's guys or Russians," Deke said. "He can't keep his mouth shut."

Edna and Klaus came up with a way to avoid the surveillance. Starting around four a.m., the group dressed as staff and slipped out to the barn. Around five, the bakery and dairy deliveries began to arrive and unload there. They split into two groups and climbed in the back of each truck for the ride to the airport.

§

Brandt had to reactivate his travel account with Swiss Air. As far as the airline knew, he still owned the family travel business. The plane had to be the oldest in the airline's private jet fleet and carried airy remnants of seven continents. The seats had lost their plushness and the carpet was worn slick. The pilots ignored them, in the same manner as bus drivers.

On arrival in Milan, Brandt and Tig drove to Lake Como in a rental car to search the caves. Deke had a consulate driver take him to the Army-Air Force intelligence center in Vicenza for help in locating Petrov. Everyone else hid in the Four Seasons Hotel in the Milan fashion district.

The Y shape of Lake Como forced Brandt to draw on memory and a folding map to locate the caves outside of Lecco. When he found the well-traveled dirt road leading to the entrance of the first cave, he knew the weapons wouldn't be there. Regular traffic had rutted the dirt road, and when he and Tig arrived, they found an explorer group getting ready to enter the cave.

"Girolamo's villa is in Lierna. Let's take a look," Brandt said.

"Where's the next cave?"

"East side of the lake. We'll take the ferry across from Varenna. It's just past Lierna."

Girolamo's villa grounds stretched across three hundred meters of the west shoreline of Lake Como. Tig parked illegally in the town square, and they took the narrow sidewalk to the villa for a closer look. The limestone path turned to rubble at the pale stone-and-iron fence protecting the property. On the other side of the fence was a red brick Liberty-style villa with separate guest housing, a lakeside gazebo, and a series of fountains. Girolamo's gardens were in spring bloom—boxwoods and topiaries trimmed, azaleas flowered in white and pink. Three fast boats were moored at the dock. The electronic gate began to swing open for a limo, and Tig moved to dash in behind the big Mercedes.

Brandt grabbed his arm in time. "Don't. He's only a distraction. The pope and Carabinieri can deal with him."

"Maybe he knows where Petrov is?"

"Forget it. Girolamo sounds like the worst kind of true believer. You'll never get anything out of him."

The limo pulled in front of the grand entrance where a footman rushed out to open the limo door. The man who got out wore a long white religious tunic, matching zucchetto skullcap, and a black shoulder cape. Two men dressed in black suits left the villa to greet him, and they began an intense discussion. Arms and hands gestured in an Italian practice, but voices stayed constrained.

"That's either Girolamo or some visiting Dominican?" Brandt said. "The two in black could be anything."

The men turned toward the dock with one man pointing, then they all nodded in agreement. The footman opened the limo door again, and a short man in jeans and a dark hoodie exited.

"Fuck! That's Petrov," Brandt said.

"I knew we should have snuck in. What do we do now?"

"We need to see where they take him." Brandt turned and ran back toward the square with Tig on his heels. He stopped at the car, grabbed his backpack, then followed a narrow maze of cobblestone steps down to the waterfront promenade. The boat with Petrov had left the dock and began picking up speed as it crossed to the east side of the lake.

"Where are they going?" Tig asked.

"Not sure yet." Brandt fumbled to open his pack. "If it's Menaggio, it's Switzerland, probably Lugano. Bellagio, could be anywhere." He handed Tig binoculars from his pack. "Watch them while I call Deke."

Deke was surprised to find Petrov in Lierna. "AISI and the carabinieri won't touch Petrov unless he's with the SADMs. He hasn't broken any Italian laws."

"How about smuggling nukes into Italy?"

"Where's the proof?"

"If Rome blows up, they'll have their proof."

"Milan won't care."

"We have any assets on the east side?"

"In summer, plenty. Only a part-time floater now. Maybe Edna can get him to help."

"By the time we get a water taxi, Petrov could be long gone."

Brandt hung up, and Tig handed him the binoculars. Brandt focused on the boat slowing down. "Bellagio . . . looks like the Serbelloni."

"How do you know?"

Brandt lowered the binoculars. "I've stayed there. The Grand Hotel Serbelloni . . . the faded lemon buildings are a landmark." He took one more look through the binoculars. "Sits on the edge of town, away from Bellagio's trashy tabloid crowd."

"We need a boat."

"The water taxi is run from the Ortensie Inn by the pier."

It took five minutes for the owner to find the water taxi driver, who smelled of grappa and buttery garlic. Brandt handed him a hundred-euro bill, and he was all smiles. The boat was a clean fiber-glass model, not the luxury teak-and-mahogany taxis that attracted tourists. When they reached the halfway mark to Bellagio, a heli-copter lifted from the pad behind the Serbelloni.

Brandt reached Deke again. "A chopper just left. I'm afraid Petrov is on it. Get somebody to track it."

27

eke called Brandt from Vicenza. "I got some help from the Air Force down the hall. They tracked Petrov's chopper to the grounds of an abandoned convent on a hill above Florence. According to Langley, he got in a minivan that took him across the Arno but stopped before entering the ZTL, which is a limited traffic zone. He met three people there, and they all walked to Piazza Santa Croce. We lost them in the tourist crowd. They're checking the ZTL and CCTV cameras."

Brandt groaned. Catching Petrov was like grabbing smoke. "We're headed back to Milan to pick up everyone. See if you can get us a safe place to stay in Florence."

"Is the whole third floor of a Petrucci villa on Ricasoli good enough for you?"

"That's close to the Duomo and in the ZTL."

"You're worried about the tickets?"

"Parking too."

"We pass the ZTL tickets on to NATO, and it has underground parking."

Underground parking was a winning ticket in Florence. Like scoring an empty seat on the space shuttle. "Al was right about Tuscany. I'm hoping he can help there."

"We're close. I can feel it," Deke said. "I'm bringing in the Rome Chief of Station to boost our assets. He hates Sturm more than I do."

"Anybody I know?"

"Danimo Lucelli. Family owns six restaurants in Philly."

"Is he connected?"

"Isn't everyone in Philly?"

"Well, it rhymes with Sicily."

"Call him Dano. He hates that."

"He's not a Corleone or Gotti, is he?"

Too late. Deke had hung up.

§

Al was surprised by how he felt returning to Florence. Wistful? Nostalgic? Worried? The right word had to be *contorto*. The Abbey Monte Oliveto Maggiore would always stand out as a turning point in his life. A hospital for his damaged soul. The bleeding had stopped and scar tissue had formed. The abbey monks had helped him recover and taught him to search for a place of peace in the world. It was in sight—all he needed was to accept a new beginning. Whatever that was. But his path was no longer as clear as it had once been.

He'd always believed when the desire for revenge left, he would be ready to make the final vows. The demon would be exorcised. But now, feelings were interfering. He had the same problem as Brandt—the *choice between two goods*. Trouble was, the scale between the two kept shifting. As soon as they found Petrov and the SADMs, he would go back to the abbey for prayer and counsel with the abbot. He would have to think of how to bring up Lena.

§

The third floor of the Ricasoli Petrucci villa had been converted into six small apartments. This was the first time they all would be occupied. The agency kept all six on the books to be sure the others would never be rented out. The three overlooking Via Ricasoli had to contend with the tourist noise below. The Accademia Gallery Museum up the street, home of the seventeen-foot white Carrara marble masterpiece, *David*, drew large crowds. When Brandt and his wife owned the travel agency, they would attempt to sell clients Italy tours with, "The Duomo is Florence's Notre Dame, only more colorful. Michelangelo's *David* is its *Mona Lisa*, only larger. Consider it an upgrade. Give up French haughtiness for Italian cuisine." The three apartments in the back were the rooms with a view. Each terrace overlooked a simple courtyard but also gave a spectacular view of the basilica's exterior: green and pink marble panels accented by white borders surrounding Brunelleschi's famous dome. On a sunny day, visitors who had climbed the 463 narrow steps to the top of the dome could be seen circling the cupola beneath the crown.

Al's contact in Florence had better intelligence than Langley. He arranged a meeting with an old friend who knew more than the Carabinieri about Florence's malevolent population. Tig was assigned to stay with Lena while Al took Casey and Brandt to the meeting.

"Pilgrim House Firenze is a ten-minute walk . . . an old convent operated by an oblate order of nuns as a guest house," said Al. "Dante will be in the courtyard."

"Dante, huh? A real poet or just pretending?" Brandt said.

"He's a Dominican priest. Goes by Dante to stay alive. He operates a website exposing illegal activities, subversive groups, crimes, and corruption."

"So everyone hates him."

"Grudges and revenge are part of the genetic pool here. He'll have a bodyguard with him. I asked him to locate Petrov for us."

§

A German spring meant summer in Italy, a dry, dusty summer. The leaves on downy oaks and field elm had a sandy grit. The purple and yellow iris beds were past their Tuscan glory. Pilgrim House's fourteenth-century stucco walls reflected medieval austerity and stayed windowless.

Florence triggered memories of Brandt's final guided tour after his wife's death. Then Haystack intervened, and his life took a huge detour. A good one, a life-saving one. In Florence, he was preparing to drop from the Ponte Vecchio and disappear in the Arno. Deke's need for bait to tempt Sword of Allah rescued him. Now he looked at Florence as a continual flash mob. Crowds everywhere. Its Renaissance provenance was the problem. Utopia for art historians and more a life-sized medieval diorama than a modern city. A Medici-era novelty frozen in time with the advantage of online ticket sales.

Dante was seated on a weathered poplar bench in a shadowy corner. He stood and greeted Al with a hug. Both dressed as tourists in jeans and polo shirts, but Dante carried a Delphic aura that brought instant respect. Al sat next to him. Brandt and Casey found chairs on the other side of a stone table from the two friends. Brandt searched for the bodyguard. Two candidates caught his eye. Either the broad-shouldered young nun—her modest but modern religious habit was still able to hide a weapon—or the ordinary laborer sitting by the courtyard entrance who instead of smoking kept his hands open and ready. A toss-up. Dante looked sallow and sleepy, with cheerless yellow-green eyes.

"Politics as usual in Tuscany?" Al asked.

"Left, right, and center squabble like dead philosophers. Talk, talk, talk . . . never any progress. Gives them something to argue about over a coffee. The polizia and Mafia enjoy picnics together, so all is quiet with them. It's an extreme religious group that the church is concerned about. Keeps the pope and me from a good night's sleep."

"What about Petrov?" Casey said.

"I'm not sure if it's him, but I have heard of a black Russian. Is he African? There's Nigerians staying across the river at Moscow's Lumumba University."

"No, but he wears a black hoodie all the time."

"Must be him. Short for a Russian. He's trying to make contact with a dangerous group of zealots, the *Riformatori*. They claim to be reformers and crusaders. But they're more like gangsters."

Brandt sighed to himself. More Orwellian fanatics, more anti-fascists that terrorize like the Nazi brownshirt fascists. "What's with them?"

"From a religious standpoint, it doesn't get much worse. Call it a profane marriage of two evil sects. A defrocked Dominican is their leader."

"We know about him," Al said.

Dante clenched his chin in a display of ire. "The *Riformatori* are the rebirth of Savonarola's *Piagnoni*. Different name, same ruthless approach. Then some excommunicated wild-eyed Brazilian Jesuits joined them. Liberation theology wasn't enough—they want to burn down the house. The *Riformatori* are capable of anything, I'm afraid."

So is Petrov, thought Brandt. That's why he was trying to make new friends. He wondered if burning down the house would lead to nuking the Vatican. "Do you know if Petrov managed to hook up with them?"

"I can't say. They're a very secretive group, but I'll keep checking."

"Where can we find them?" Casey asked.

Three nuns left the convent guest quarters carrying, towels, mops, and buckets. They stopped to talk to the sister who came with Dante. He waited until they finished, then moved on. "They hide all over the city. Always changing where they sleep. But you can usually find one or two standing around the Duomo. They'll be the ones with clerical skullcaps and large crucifixes hanging down from their necks. They carry a sign offering guided tours of the church and baptistery for donations. If you look wealthy, they'll suggest a place for lunch or dinner where you'll be certain to be robbed."

"Are they in Livorno too?" Al said.

"If by that you mean, are they friendly with the communists there, the answer is most definitely yes."

"If you hear any more, please let me know," Al said.

Dante left the courtyard first with his two bodyguards. Brandt smiled his approval. Two meant security was taken seriously. Al stood and waited for Dante to pass through the wooden gate, then moved to shoo away a magpie sitting on a courtyard wall. It flew off, cackling angrily.

"Magpies have been a sinister omen in Europe for hundreds of years. We don't need any of them watching us."

"Let's see if any *Riformatori* are around the cathedral," Casey said.

The plaza around Santa Maria del Fiore Cathedral reminded Brandt of a crowded airport. An international mix of tourists mingling, standing, gazing up and down, looking both impressed and bewildered. Some looked lost. Most had cameras or selfie sticks in one hand, a gelato in the other. They reminded Brandt of a queue at a Kennedy airport counter. The lines to enter the basilica or baptistery were longer than a rush hour TSA security check.

When they reached the gap between the church steps and baptistery, Al pointed to a man with a clerical collar and a large crucifix hanging across his chest who was talking to a family of five. "That must be one of them," Al said.

They paused steps away, sneaking glances. The family eventually moved off. When the Riformatori saw Al, he hurried away.

Al nudged Brandt. "Head for Piazza Signoria. We'll see if he's joining his friends guarding the plaque."

When they reached the piazza, the renegade from the cathedral was in excited consultation with two Riformatori standing by the plaque.

"Stay back," Brandt said. "If they leave, we can follow them."

"Negative." Casey was anything but reticent. "We're after Petrov, not some religious wackos."

"If Petrov made contact with them, it would be useful to know where they meet," Al said.

They walked around the plaza pretending to read outdoor seating menus while keeping an eye on the three Riformatori talking. Finally, all three fanatics left the piazza together and headed toward the river.

"Al, the one in front of the Duomo recognized you Drop back and stay behind."

Brandt and Casey followed at a safe distance. They dodged past tourists window-shopping along Via dei Calzaiuoli, with Al hanging back.

"They turned on Porta Rossa, so they're headed for the bridge," Brandt said. After another turn onto Calimala, the Ponte Vecchio was in sight.

The crowds became thick and pushy as they neared the choke point at the foot of the historic span. The three Riformatori chose to split up there: one stepped on the bridge, one followed the river to the left, the other went to the right.

"I got the one turning left," Casey said.

Al hurried up. "I'll go right."

"Okay," Brandt said. "Meet at Cellini's fountain."

Despite height that allowed him to see above the crowds, Brandt was only able to keep up with his target for a few minutes. It wasn't long before he lost him in a shoulder-to-shoulder crowd with tour guides waving signs and flags. He suspected his man knew an entrance to the second-floor Vasari Corridor stretching above the bridge jewelry shops. By modern standards, the corridor looked like condos stacked atop retail. Once a way for nobility to cross the river, now it was a way for officials and religious to avoid the tourists. He pushed his way to the other end of the bridge in hope of catching him coming out, with no luck.

He texted Casey and Al. "Burned."

Al texted back, "Me too. Lost him in Novella station."

There was no word from Casey.

Brandt jostled his way back to the three arches in the center of the bridge, the only open area to view the river and both banks. Cellini's fountain was under the center arch on the east side. Tourists waited patiently for their chance to touch the fabled healing fountain water.

Brandt stood next to the crowd while he waited for the others and looked at the railing guarding the river, the exact place he had been planning his jump. Tourists had blocked his path to the edge that day, and the delay probably saved him. While he waited, he thought of Gino's addictive donuts, two minutes away. He decided he should have one more. He finished crossing the bridge to Gino's, where he ate two glazed and then a classic chocolate cake donut with sprinkles. Suddenly his life didn't look so bad.

§

Deke called from the basement garage and Brandt met him at the door. Deke had two bottles of Tuscan Chianti and a bottle of milk with him.

"I think the pace is about to pick up," Deke said. "We can expect Moky to be here soon."

"What?" Casey said.

Deke grinned. "The Russians have locals on the payroll at the base. We tap their phones. They put Gagarin on me. It's why I ditched the car at the airport."

"Couldn't shake it?" Brandt said.

"Didn't see the point. The tap said Moky was already coming here."

"How did he find out?" Casey said.

"Had to be someone in Vicenza passing reports to him."

"The Russians have too many dedicated communists in Italy willing to help," Al said.

"It worked out. We got Moky's phone signature that way, and we get all his calls and texts now."

"You're limping again," Casey said. Deke had been wounded in each leg—one Iraq, the other Afghanistan.

Deke shrugged. "Long car rides in a squishy Fiat 500 will do it every time. Where's Lena?"

"On the terrace with Tig."

"Ask her to come in."

Lena entered and immediately sat next to Al on a love seat.

"Lena, can you think of any reason Petrov would come here?" Deke asked.

"Not really. He never showed any interest in religion or history."

Deke pursed his lips. "Anyone? He has help here, but it has to be more than that. Why Tuscany?"

"I'm not sure if this helps," Lena said, "but after he left, the FSB came and took his computer. I was afraid he might have written something about me. . .personal stuff. Embarrassing pictures, political complaints that could get me in trouble. So I asked a friendly minister if there was anything on his hard drive I should be worried about. He laughed and said there were no bedroom photos. I was greatly relieved. The only thing Petrov deleted were maps. The rest he left for everyone to read. His political manifesto. How Moscow was weak and pathetic and he would punish the West and restore Russia's position of importance."

"What about the maps?"

"The maps were easy to pull off the hard drive. All seaports and marine routes."

"Europe?"

"The world."

Deke read a text. "Dano just parked. He's coming up the elevator."

"Petrov needs the port in Livorno. That's why he's here," Brandt said.

§

Believing he had the lead on the CIA now, Moky relaxed for the first time since Brussels. The villa they were staying in was a huge leap up from the usual safe house. The Moscow oligarch who owned it was in trouble over taxes and offered its use without a complaint. Twelve rooms spread over three floors with a view of the international iris garden and the Arno. The men took off their weapons and began to pass vodka around. Moky took a large swig and handed the bottle to Kraspov. No more catch-up. Losing Lena no longer mattered. She was in Florence, so was Petrov, and Moscow Center had plenty of communist friends there to help him.

"You should go to Livorno and speak to our man in the union," Moky told Gleb.

"Not until I have a *bistecca*."

"That's for two people," Moky said with disgust. "After you gorge yourself, take Kraspov with you and go see Garbinelli. Find out if Petrov has been to the port. See if he knows anything about Genoa too."

"Kraspov can get his own steak."

"It's because of Russians like you that people think we're all pigs."

"Maybe we are," said Gleb, "but if you say that again, I'll slit you open like a pig."

"Threaten me once more, and Moscow Center will get a box with your pieces in it."

Kraspov grabbed Gleb by the bicep. "C'mon, let's go. We'll eat, then find some whores. Garbinelli can wait."

Moky's eyes narrowed over what he saw as typical Black Beret insubordination. It wasn't how Spetsnaz operated. The Black Berets were different, more like Mongols. Then he thought calling them Mongols was an insult to Mongols. The Black Berets were Neanderthals, only better armed. He decided he'd better call his operation controller in the Center for an update.

"The two agents and the monk visited a guest house this morning," his controller said. "Our men were unable to see who they met there. Then they walked to the tourist bridge and split up. They didn't appear to be worried about anything."

"They're probably waiting for Deke Hamilton," Moky said. "Is the monk still with them?"

"Yes. With his contacts here, he could be a problem for you."

"See if he knows Dante." For the moment, Moky decided against saying anything about Gleb. They were close to Petrov and the weapons now. He would wait until he was back in Moscow to file his report.

28

Dano Lucelli could have been an actor in a movie—one about an Italian love triangle full of deceit, lurid escapades, and betrayal. He was taller than Fellini, with the same dark, brooding eyes, yet still able to brandish Mastroianni's glimmering visage. His flaws never seemed to stick with women but rather rolled off them like raindrops on a slicker. He hadn't lost his physical appeal after three divorces and seventeen years under the damaging rays of the Mediterranean sun.

"Meet the team," Deke said. He made the introductions and made sure Lucelli knew that Casey and Brandt were together.

Lucelli's gaze fixed on Lena, trying to meet her eyes. Then he said, "Brother Al, you might be in danger. According to our tap on Moky's phone, he's worried about you and your contacts."

"Is he planning something?" Deke said.

"Not directly, but it's on the table."

Al never blinked. "Is Dante in danger?"

"His name didn't come up. The Russians think you're all complacent, acting like tourists."

"Do we have Moky's location? Maybe you could put some of your men on them," Brandt said.

"He's in a Russian oligarch's villa across the river, near Piazzale Michelangelo. I have men posted at the bridges and three around the villa. As long as Moky has his phone, we have him."

"What about Petrov?" Casey asked.

"*Niente* . . . nothing."

Brandt showed Lucelli to his unit across the hall.

"Small and dusty," Lucelli said. "Doesn't Milan have anyone clean these places?"

"You would know better than me. Tig swept it for bugs. It's safe." Brandt walked to the window and looked down. "Think that might be one of Moscow's men having coffee and keeping an eye on us?"

Lucelli stood next to him. "Looks like one of them."

"The table and chair were in front of the coffee shop before. The guy moved them so he'd have a clear vision of the front door."

"Can we slip past?" asked Lucelli.

"The parking garage has stairs that join with the gelato shop and the alley. We can take the elevator down and slip out with customers or duck into the alley."

Lucelli checked the rest of the setup. He tested the mattress with one hand, then switched a light on and off. He stared inside the tiny refrigerator and said, "You're the director's full-time floater friend. London, right? Under Deke?" His tone carried a mixture of hypothesis and innuendo.

"Don't know who told you all that. I've never met the director or even been past the auditorium. I work for Deke when he wants me."

Lucelli closed the refrigerator door and turned to Brandt. "Sounds simple enough. But I have an ex-wife who works in Langley finance. She caught a guy from the travel section digging into your file. She ran him off but looked at the screen to see why he was so interested in you. Kind of an odd arrangement, even for the CIA."

"Did she say how little I'm paid?"

"No, just you're the only full-time floater the agency's ever had. She thinks it's a cover, that you're really some sort of superagent."

"I think you've probably put that to rest by now."

Lucelli smiled. "Anyway, I just thought you should know someone was curious about you. I'd appreciate it if you kept this to yourself. I don't want her to get in any trouble."

Deke came in with a laptop in his hands. "Langley analyzed the shipping data for Livorno. Mostly a cruise ship and roll-on/roll-off port. Cars and trucks. Container shipping is low volume. The RoRo traffic is tightly run by two companies. Quick port turnaround. In and out in no time. Doubt that would work for him."

"If Petrov booked passage on a cruise ship, where are the nukes then?" Lucelli said.

"He had help and support in Germany and Austria. But in Livorno, he has a population of sympathizers with port access. It has to mean something," Brandt said.

"Are we tracing the container ships?" Dano asked.

"They're working on that. But it will take some time. The port has up to five leaving each day. If we go back to when he left Austria, that's a lot of ships to track."

§

Lucelli made Al look even better to Lena. The knowledge was painful, depressing. Lucelli dripped Lothario. She'd had her fill of those. Al was more like Don Quixote and just as out of reach. She went back out to the terrace and fixed her gaze on the basilica's great dome.

§

Al was next to go across the hall. He held his phone in his hands. "I just got a text from Dante. He has some information that might be helpful. He wants to meet us at seven tonight in Mercato Centrale in the second-floor dining area."

"Is it safe?" Deke said

"Big crowds then. Easy to hide. Six exits plus the underground loading docks. He'll be eating in the kitchen of Savini Tartufi. Dominic will let us in."

"We'll slip out in pairs," Deke said. "I'll go with you. Casey goes with Brandt. Tig stays here with Lena and Lucelli."

Brandt knew the place well. It was a favorite for all his tour groups. Foodies looked at it the way a Muslim looks at Mecca. Some refused to leave. The outdoor leather stalls encroached and crowded the building entrances. The first-floor shops were a series of individual butchers, seafood stalls, cheese shops, and bakeries. The cluster of people around the butcher displays were there for more than dinner; in Italy, butchers dispense advice with sage-like wisdom. A popular adage said, "Confess to a priest, but bring your problems to the butcher." Mall food court counters in America were a defective copy of the second-floor eateries. The mall version equated to *we're selling food.* The Mercato rendition translated to *food is life, enjoy it with us.*

§

Brandt led the team up the stairs to the second floor of the busiest central market in Northern Italy. Throngs of tourists mingled with locals on their way home from work. Savini's was popular for its authentic pasta dishes and low prices. Dominic did duty as cashier, waiter, maître d', and busboy. Recognition crossed his face when he saw Al; he took a moment to see if anyone was watching, then led them back into the kitchen. The office had a long meeting table and desk crammed in a room big enough for only the desk or the table. Dante sat alone at one end of the table. His two guards perched on a metal prep table outside the office.

"I didn't expect to hear from you so soon," Al said.

"Your Petrov made a big impression with the Riformatori. Word spread quickly. They were excited to take him to Livorno."

"Anything said about nuclear weapons?" Casey asked.

"Nothing mentioned. Is that why you want him?"

"There's a possibility," Deke said. "Nothing definite."

"I assumed he was trying to book passage somewhere," Dante said.

"There are a lot of people across Europe looking for him. He can't just grab a flight or a ship out of Italy."

Dante nodded. "Finding help in Livorno wouldn't be a problem for him."

"How about cargo? Any kind of shipment arrangements?" Brandt said.

"It's why I texted Al. The Riformatori helped him send large containers to Naples under the name Savonarola."

Casey looked at Brandt. "Why Naples?"

Brandt shrugged.

Deke's face lit up with hope. "You have the name of the ship?"

"It's a coastal barge. No name, but the tug is called the *Po*. Left port yesterday with the early morning tide."

"Petrov must be on it too," Casey said.

Kitchen staff came in with baskets of bread and bowls of fettuccini, linguini, and calabrese sausage. Dominic brought two bottles of wine and added, "Bon appetit."

Dante said a pre-meal prayer, then Al started the bowls around the table.

"I wonder why Naples instead of Rome," Casey said.

"Sixth Fleet headquarters is there," Brandt said. "Could be a target."

Deke hung up from Langley with a satisfied look and sat down to eat. "The *Po* is due in an hour from now. I've got the Navy on their way to meet them. We should know something by the time we get back to Ricasoli."

When the table was cleared, Brandt left five hundred euros and thanked Dominic for the help and the pasta. They escorted Dante down the back stairs to the loading dock, where the wide doors were open for trucks to back in and unload. A mob-sized group of laborers and truck drivers sat on the ledge, crates, cartons, burlap bags, or stood waiting and smoking. A loud shout brought a dozen men to their feet with nightsticks and truncheons.

Casey and Brandt barely had time to prepare for the assault as Dante's two guards were overwhelmed by five men. Casey put one man on the floor with a nose punch and her favorite groin kick, then defended a nightstick attack by moving inside the arc and sending her knuckles to his throat. Brandt retreated and grabbed an empty crate to use as a shield against the three swinging weapons at him. Al grappled with the three men attempting to drag Dante away. Deke's painful legs kept him well behind the others out of the stairwell, giving him time to retrieve his Glock. He fired the first shot into the cement ceiling. An attacker turned from Brandt and rushed Deke; his second shot took the top of the man's head off. The men not part of the attack scattered like crows. The rest turned and ran. Dante's nun had one arm hanging loose from a club blow to her shoulder.

The male guard had a bloody mouth and ear. Dante was on the floor, and Al helped him up.

"I'm okay. Look after my guards," Dante said.

Casey scrounged some tissue and dabbed the wounds on the bleeding guard. Deke was going through the dead man's pockets.

"We can call an ambulance or take you both direct to the hospital," Brandt said.

The female guard looked to Dante.

"She doesn't speak English," Dante said. "The Carabinieri will take them both to the hospital. They're on the way."

Brandt wondered about authorities coming after Deke's shot.

Dante pointed to the body. "Don't worry about that one. Tomas is Carabinieri. He will explain what happened. Nothing will be said."

Brandt understood then. The local polizia were too corrupt. It was up to the national police to keep Dante safe.

Deke stood up with a leather ID packet from the body. "A union member. Red star stamped on it. They were after Dante. Our Russian friends probably sent them." He showed the ID to Dante. "If he knew we were with you, Moky would have sent the Black Berets."

Two hours later, they were back on Ricasoli, still waiting to hear from the Navy. When the call finally came, Deke's face turned bleak. "Nothing. The tug and barge were clean. I thought we had Petrov and the weapons."

Groans came in unison, as if from the victims of a bad joke.

"What happened?" Casey asked.

"The Italian Coast Guard and our Navy boarded the tug at the harbor entrance and forced it to the police pier. They tore the boat and barge apart. No Petrov, and the containers were either empty or loaded with dry goods."

"So Dante's info was bad," Casey said.

"I don't know what to say. He seemed convinced it was good intel."

Brandt asked Lucelli, "Are there any ports they could have snuck into?"

"We watch Rome's Civitavecchia twenty-four seven. A big ocean barge would have been noticed in the small fishing villages and tourist towns."

"What do we do next?" Casey said.

Deke checked his phone. "Good question. Langley wants us to stand down."

§

Lena wandered back out to the terrace and leaned on the railing. The sound of the Duomo carillon bells gave time a deeper quality, like a kind word that goes straight to the heart. The basilica dome was like a magnet to Lena—an outer shell of beauty and strength protecting an inner spiritual presence. Much like martyrs and saints. Al was like that.

Casey came out and settled on the railing next to Lena. "You've been quiet since we got to Florence. Is something bothering you?"

Not much, thought Lena. She pulled the last cigarette from a pack and lit it. "Just everything about my life."

The more some parts of her life worked, the more they seemed to stuff the other parts into a dark corner. It scared her. There was a danger of living only half of life, being a one-dimensional woman with only a successful career to point to. She knew she needed the other half, and it wasn't just a man or a child. She was past that. She needed someone who could shine a beacon on the parts of herself that needed to be awakened. Unlived parts. A deeper sense of self.

Parts she sensed were there but didn't know how to bring them to life. When Al was with her, she felt them stirring, as if sunlight was searching for them.

Lena continued, "What can I say? This mission has been a failure so far. I haven't helped you find the weapons or Petrov. And the fates keep teasing me. Waving what I want most in my life at me." Her tone began to fade. "Then jerking it away."

Casey responded with tenderness. "It's Al, isn't it?"

Lena paused, then said, "I knew you would see it. Al is like the person to light up my soul. You and Brandt do that for each other. I want that too."

"Does he know that?"

"How can I tell him? He's a religious monk. Forbidden fruit."

"I wish I had an answer for you."

"It's like I'm fighting God for him, and neither side is willing to quit."

29

Dowling called and explained the NATO meeting details to Deke and Casey. The Russian ambassador complained with boozy Slavic vigor. Sturm moaned about CIA ignoring the agreement. When the secretary general found out they were in Florence and so was Moky, his mood changed, and he proposed the two teams should work together again. Dowling refused, citing Moky's treatment of Lena and the need to protect their own intelligence sources. The meeting ended with a decision for both sides to stand down. Langley agreed. The Carabinieri and AISI would take over until the secretary general, Russian ambassador, secretary of state, and the director could work something out.

"What do we do?" Brandt asked.

"It's out of our hands. Langley says wait on the diplomacy Never ends well with them. The director is testifying in a closed-door Senate committee meeting the next three days. The DO will brief him when he can."

"So we sit?" Al said.

"Until someone shoots Sturm."

"Moky won't quit," Lena said.

§

The call came from one of Lucelli's men stationed inside the main entrance to the residence building. A man delivering three pizzas that no one had ordered triggered an alert that brought out Glocks and a Heckler machine pistol.

"He says Brandt Swindon ordered them," the guard phoned.

"Send me his picture," Brandt answered. He checked out the photo. "It's Aaron. Send him up."

He met Aaron in the hall. "It must be tough times for the Mossad if you have to deliver pizzas."

"Food is what we do best," Aaron said.

"Forget it. You can't touch the Italians when it comes to food."

Lucelli sent Tig with two pizzas for the building guards and kept one to share with Lena. Brandt opened a bottle of shiraz, and they all sat around a glass-top table in the small kitchen. Lena removed pepperoni from each of her slices.

"What brings you to Florence?" Brandt asked. "I thought the Med was outside your AO."

"This started in Austria," said Aaron. "Deke is right. The two bodies in the cave outside of Kitzbühel were my men."

"What happened?" Casey asked.

"I have an informant, a sympathetic German in a terror group in Berchtesgaden. A biblical mix of evil—Nazis, Stasi, and KGB. I'm sure you're familiar with them."

"Satan's minions," Brandt said. He wondered if Aaron had made the connection between Putin, the KGB, and his father.

"A Russian was brought in by the group leader. The Ivan claimed he needed some help moving contraband to Italy. He'd pay well. Swiss francs or euros. My informant suggested two of my men. Something happened crossing the Alps that got them killed."

Heads sank over their deaths.

Deke spoke first. "Do you know what the contraband was?"

"You mean the KGB nukes?"

Casey and Brandt smiled.

Deke shook his head yes and didn't mention the stand-down order.

Aaron continued, "I only found out yesterday. The AISI keeps a close eye on the Riformatori. We have a man in the Rome office who picked up on it."

"What did he say?"

"The Riformatori was split on helping the Russian. The Dominican rebels argued no. But once they found out there were nukes involved, the bad-news Jesuits prevailed. They used their contacts in the Livorno communist party to arrange the shipment. Just like you, we found out too late."

"We've been a step or two behind every place."

"I need to go before that guy sitting in the chair watching the door gets suspicious. I'll let you know if we can find out what happened."

After Aaron left, Deke said, "Time to pack up and get drunk." Gloom accompanied each word.

"Why so down?" Casey said.

"I expect Langley to pull us out. We lost Petrov and the weapons. We have no leads, and we're caught in the middle of a diplomatic pissing contest."

§

Casey woke up early to go for a run and found Brandt on the sofa drinking coffee, his laptop sitting on his legs. "Why are you up so early?"

"Couldn't sleep. I had this weird dream that woke me up. Never got back to sleep."

"The boy with glasses dream again?"

"Not really . . . but it seems connected. The big rock was there, the Glock was there, just lying on the ground. Same with the paint brushes . . . just lying there. But the boy wasn't in it. Missing."

Casey poured coffee and sat at the table. Her run would be delayed. "What do you think it means?"

"Not sure. That's what I've been trying to figure out."

"I think it's good. You've moved on. Left all that behind."

"I dunno. Doesn't feel right. A bit too simple for a dream."

"I know. I know. Everything is always gray for you. Nothing is black and white."

"I can't help it. I always see things from every angle. My brain just operates that way."

"Deke loves that you pick up things he misses. But sometimes I need a simple answer from you."

"Like what?"

"Oh, like what do you want for dinner? Is there a restaurant you want to go to? What movie do you want to watch? The exhaustive analysis I could do without."

She was right. And that pushed Brandt to get lost in thought. Dreams had become a big part of his life since his wife's illness and death. They weren't the plug-in, "you will meet your eternal love today" variety, like astrology. No fortune-telling carnival tricks. His were rare but important—the big dreams that Jung said offered guidance. The wise old man and wise old woman dreams were the most important of all of them; the bottomless crystal clear pool they guided him to was a place that offered help. He always hoped for a typed-out answer, like a text, but what he got instead was more of a feeling that wouldn't leave him. *Don't go this way—go that way.* His dream little boy was missing. Brandt hoped nothing bad had happened to him. "You're right. I'll try not to overthink everything."

"I'd love you even more if you did."

Brandt looked down at a page on his laptop. "Oh my God. Someone in Langley threw me under the bus!"

He startled Casey enough that she spilled some coffee. "What happened?"

"Front page of the *Post*, accusing the director of using taxpayer funds to pay for a friend to move to London with his girlfriend, then gave him a special contract that has never been done before. 'Part-time work with special privileges,' it says."

Casey pulled up the article on her phone and read word for word. "He left the low pay out."

"Yeah, that part doesn't fit the narrative."

"The *Post* is definitely after the director's ass."

"I'm collateral damage," said Brandt.

"They didn't use your name. That helps."

"Hit man journalism. Keep them wondering who and put the name in the next hit piece."

"Isn't it against the law to expose a CIA agent?" asked Casey.

"Only prosecuted once—light sentence. Not sure if it covers floaters anyway. The agency haters will be out trying to doxx me."

"Can't Deke do anything?"

"It's tricky now," said Brandt. "A hint of a cover-up would make it worse. He'll have to let the director set the course."

"Deke's never been media savvy."

"Sports and comics, that's it. But I'm sure he'll be calling in IOUs to find out who is doing the leaking."

§

Later in the morning, Aaron suggested a coffee bar along the Arno to meet. Deke took Lucelli with him. They skipped the outdoor tables set for tourists and stood at the bar like locals. Lucelli and Aaron sipped espresso with a dusting of cacao. The crowds spread along the narrow river sidewalk and protective wall across the street. Two large tour buses drove past and skillfully negotiated tight parking in the small square.

"Why here?" Deke asked.

"Friendly owners," replied Aaron.

"You find out what happened to the weapons?" Lucelli asked.

"With some satellite help and your DEA. The *Po* idled on the windward side of Elba. The nukes were in containers and transferred to a commercial trawler out of Corsica with the help of the Marseille drug network. Contract smuggling doesn't come cheap with them. So the Ivan has access to funds."

"The Leipzig Authority has plenty," said Deke.

"According to the DEA, they were off loaded in Bastia, and then trucked to the airport and flown to Palermo, then on to Cairo."

"Jeezus, Cairo. Are they headed for Tehran?" Deke said.

"Tel Aviv isn't willing to take that risk. The PM has already met with the SSC and talked to your president. The defense minister is preparing mission plans. We're trying to get surveillance on the airport warehouse."

"What will you do with them if you get them? The Russians want them back."

"That's not up to me. The PM will make that decision."

"The State Department won't like a wrong one. Cooperation only goes so far."

Aaron said, "I saw the *Post*. I'm sorry Brandt's getting worked over."

"So am I. I got him into this mess."

"I'm hoping to hear something about Cairo tonight. The PM is trying to get permission to intercept Iran Air flights out of Cairo."

§

A gentle late-morning rain drove everyone inside from the terrace. Someone had moved chair cushions under the portico overhang. Lucelli shook Deke's umbrella out and propped it up next to the cushions. Deke gathered everyone around the glass-top table, which was strewn with empty coffee cups, leftover bagels, and yogurt containers. On a narrow wall hung a two-year-old calendar with a picture of the Grand Canyon and Christmas Day circled in red.

Deke was all grins and wry looks. "The stand-down doesn't matter now. We can finish packing for home. Thanks to the Mossad, I think we're done."

"Where are they?" Brandt asked.

"Cairo. Petrov always seems to have another card to play. The Marseille drug mob helped get the nukes there. The Israelis are worried they're headed for Iran and are going to take it from here."

"Is Petrov with them?" Lena said. "I still can't see him with the Iranians."

Deke picked up a bagel slice. "Nothing was said about him, but I can't see him walking away and just letting Tehran have them now."

Brandt leaned the chair on the back legs and rocked slightly, his face taut with doubt, his arms folded across his chest. "I dunno. I don't get Cairo. If they're headed for Iran, Beirut makes more sense.

It's the obvious choice. Weapons move in and out of there like bread in a bakery. Hezbollah runs things, and they take orders from Tehran. So why Cairo?"

Deke set his bagel down. "Is this another of your *everything is gray* ideas?"

"I suppose it is. But so far we've been like Wile E. Coyote chasing the Road Runner. Let's look at other options before the dynamite blows up in our faces."

"Langley's robots agree with the Israelis," Deke said. "The algorithms assign a seventy-eight percent chance to Iran, eleven to Syria, six to Cuba, and four to China, and one the rest of the world."

"I'd call that confirmation," Lucelli said. His hand smoothed back a bristle of hair off his right ear.

"Okay, maybe it is Iran, but then maybe it's not. Arab solidarity is bogus, no more than an old Bedouin myth. Shia versus Sunni is the rule. Ban the Muslim Brotherhood like Egypt did and feel the Ayatollah's wrath. Some real tension there." Brandt rocked back and forth on his chair again. "If it was me, I'd want the safer choice: Beirut. The question we should be asking is, Why did Petrov pick Cairo?"

Al had sat and listened with his hands spread on his thighs, as if in meditation. "Forget the algorithms. Listen to Brandt. If getting these to Iran is Petrov's plan, there are safer ways than Cairo. Moscow used professional smugglers out of Belarus to send weapons and contraband to Iran for years. Petrov's father would have known about them."

"He'd have to find a way through Poland to get them to Minsk." Lucelli said it like he was the only one who could read a map.

Casey chuckled. "Easier than doing a Hannibal across the Alps."

Lucelli glared at Casey as if she could cast spells.

Brandt leaned his chair down on all four legs and tensed up. Something in his mind was threatening to become conscious. Like a name of someone he couldn't remember. He closed his eyes to ward off distractions and sat still. Then it came to him. "The Odessa. . . the Nazi ratline. Has to be. It fits. After the war, Cairo was the Odessa's gateway to the world. Heathrow airport for the SS and Gestapo."

Al couldn't contain himself. "He's right. The Odessa. In Prague, we all knew the Nazi escape network had the KGB's blessing."

Brandt leaned back in the chair again. "Once the Odessa got the panicky Nazis to Egypt, they spread out, hoping to avoid capture. They hid all over. We have them. I'll bet you can find Nazis in the Cairo phonebook now."

Deke twisted his lips in uncertainty. "We gave up on the Odessa. Never found any proof the organization existed."

"Well, the SS got out without buying tickets," Brandt said.

"They're all dead now anyway," Deke said.

"The Leipzig Authority makes a fine legacy."

Brandt's argument triggered silent evaluation around the table. Even he wondered if he was right. Algorithms were supposed to measure all the factors with unassailable precision. Whatever that was.

Al broke the silence. "The KGB and Stasi have been in Cairo for years. Started when Moscow helped Nasser build the Aswan dam. With glasnost, Egypt was flooded with KGB and Stasi. They opted for safety, sun, and beaches." His words seemed to move the discussion in Brandt's favor.

One of Lucelli's men came in and waved him out to the hall. When he came back, his face had a pale look. "I've been ordered back to Rome."

§

After the meeting broke up, Brandt went silent, trying to process it all. Fight his way through everything gray. The nukes were in a Cairo warehouse awaiting the next leg of their journey. The software and Mossad said Tehran. The Israelis didn't wait for permission—*consult, inform, then act* helped them exist. If they were successful, Brandt would be back in London, with the contradictions plaguing his life coming with him. The *Post* series might be a force for change. The director would have to act. No more missions with Casey threatened to be the future. Maybe they both could deal with it, maybe not. Still, he didn't like the decision being taken out of his hands.

And what about Moky? Did the Russians know the nukes were in Cairo? Did Moscow approve of their SADMs going to Khomeini? They supplied them with almost everything else. Intel reports indicated Putin wasn't keen on Iran having nukes. Had he changed his mind? Had Moscow Center finally given up? If the plan had always been to recover them and secretly place them in strategic spots across Europe, Cairo put an end to that idea.

Brandt could see that sun had replaced the light rain falling on Florence. Puddles filled the low spots in the terrace tile. Lucelli and the rest of his men were heading back to Rome. Lena and Al had gone up to the roof together where Al could point out Florence history. Tig had gone shopping for something to bring his ex-wife, something leather that said Florence.

Brandt started three emails to Cybil, telling her he would be back at the easel in a few days. Something always held him back, and the emails were never sent.

Deke spoke with Aaron throughout the day, but it was evening before he shared the news.

30

The Israelis had deliberated too long. The plan was complete. The special trained assault force was at the helipad waiting to board the silent-flight choppers for the two-hundred-fifty-mile trip to Cairo. The prime minister was advised by his staff to clear the mission with the Knesset leaders. Six hours later, the PM regretted the meeting. Eight party leaders had been invited, and he ended up cursing each one to himself. Eight leaders, fourteen plans, none of which made practical or military sense. The meeting ended when he received the message that the SADMs were gone, loaded on an aircraft now in the air. When he relayed the information to the leaders, no one accepted responsibility for causing the delay. Two said it was the PM's error for having the meeting. If the nukes ended up in Iran, it was his fault for bringing them into it. If there was a shiny side to politicians, he failed to see it.

§

Deke didn't wait for everyone to reassemble. He came to Casey and Brandt as soon as he hung up from Aaron. They were on the terrace, resting under the spell of the basilica dome. Scaffolding for

the never-ending exterior cleaning rounded a corner of the dome as if connecting the past and present.

"You were right. It's not Iran," Deke said. "Our spotters in the Cairo cargo terminal came through for us. They're on the way to Buenos Aires. The manifest listed them as Hazardous Material, Radioactive Medical Equipment and Supplies, loaded on Aerolíneas Argentinas flight 012."

"I think we both know where they're going to end up," Brandt said.

"Bariloche, thanks to the Odessa."

Casey had a puzzled look. "Where's that?"

"Patagonia, the Argentine side of the mountains. A piece of Germany in the Andes foothills," Deke said. "The last stop on the Nazi ratline out of Europe. Walking down the street, you think you're in the Black Forest. Better cuckoo clocks than Munich."

"Jesuits have a nasty history there," Brandt said. "Fighting among themselves and stirring up tribal wars. I think they were upset over missing the Crusades. Eventually they got kicked out of the country. If you're looking for wild-eyed, crazy missionaries bent on burning down the house, this is where I'd start."

"You've been there?" Casey said.

"We did tours there. Couple of days in Buenos Aires, a taste of Patagonia in Bariloche, then Pampas balloon rides." He remembered those as the beef-and-wine tours designed to let tourists sample excellent steaks from the local ranches and famous Mendoza Malbecs. There were concerns too. Gauchos were a licentious bunch, and the women needed to be warned.

Deke wagged his head. "Too bad we're done. You could have been useful."

"Probably kicked out before then anyway."

"The director knows what to do. Don't worry about it."

"I've learned when you say that, it gets ugly."

"The KGB and Stasi knew about Bariloche," Deke said. "Got the routes and names of who could help from Aaron's father."

"So what do we do? Let Langley work it out with Buenos Aires?" Casey said.

Deke's laugh was bitter. "Not a chance. The government there would love to be the first nuclear power in South America. The country's flat broke. Having nukes would be a huge morale boost."

Tig was the first to return, carrying a bag with both a brown and a black leather waist jacket for his ex-wife. Deke filled him in on the Israeli mission that never happened. Tig exhaled in a huff, then fingered his earring and shook his head. "Not like the Israelis to fuck up like that. Bet the troops are really pissed."

Al and Lena came in with smiles designed to hide what they were really feeling. When Deke told them the mission might not be over, Lena's smile became real.

"Just chill for now," Casey said.

Tig was not one to sit still. The terrace half wall was peeling stucco, the gray undercoating mixing well with the pinkish walls, creating a camouflage print fashion design; he picked up the pieces of displaced stucco and built a pile for the trash. "I think Petrov is nuts," he said. "Why take them to some whacked-out city in Argentina full of demented Russians and Germans? I mean, what can he do with them there? Nuke some llamas?"

"Petrov is smart," Lena said. "He knows what he's doing."

Brandt understood. It was all about logistics. Terror logistics. Without NATO, Moscow, and the German GSG 9 on his ass, Petrov would get whatever help he needed in Bariloche, a government willing to look the other way, cooperative locals with military assets, international flights, money, and a choice of passports. He had Perón to thank. In '45, Perón told the Nazis, "Come on down." At some point, Matveev realized Bariloche was safer than Moscow and stepped in with cash, gold, and new identities for the KGB and Stasi.

Brandt let out a sigh that sounded more like a groan. A bunch of obsessed psychotics with an attitude that would intimidate biker gangs had managed to acquire nukes. It couldn't be real, had to be either a nightmare or a video game. He stood at military attention and clicked his heels. "The Germans there still wear SS uniforms on Hitler's birthday." He wasn't sure if that was comical, farcical, or a made-to-order Monty Python skit, but diabolical fit in there somewhere. He wondered how they all got along. Old Nazis, neo-Nazis, Stasi, and KGB. Vodka, Steinhäger, Lugers, and Kalashnikovs made a potentially lethal mix. Festivals must be like Dodge City in 1870—no guns allowed.

Lena was more than anxious; she fumbled to light her cigarette. "Can Langley help us? Get some agents to the airport to intercept them?"

"Too late for that," Deke said.

"I know we're supposed to sit on our ass and wait for the big boys to tell us what to do," Casey said, "but Argentina isn't part of NATO. Why worry about Sturm and the Russians now?"

Brandt bobbed his head in agreement. Brussels was seven thousand miles away from Argentina and stuck in a diplomatic dance. A delay could be tragic. "We can't be sure what Petrov plans to do or when. Maybe I should just go after him. No one cares what a floater does anyway."

"Forget it. These aren't a handful of Bosniaks. Alone, you won't have a chance." Deke frowned, then rose from his chair, snarling, "This is the kinda crap that pisses me off. Sometimes we can't get out of our own way. Diplomacy at State is like an invitation to self-destruct." He stood quiet and motionless for a moment, then walked inside, deep in thought. He folded his arms across his chest and looked down at the Ardbeg scotch bottle on the counter. An empty milk glass sat next to it. He picked up the scotch for a closer look.

Brandt's eyes met Casey's.

Lena turned to Al in silence.

Deke set the Ardbeg back down and returned to his chair. "There isn't another way. We have to go."

Lena smiled.

Brandt stiffened like a tree trunk. "You sure? Flipping off the big guys has consequences."

"Maybe so. But everyone knows we have an authority problem. We find the nukes, they'll get over it. But we'll be on our own. No help from Langley until the pissing contest is over."

"What if we can't find them?" Casey asked.

"Well, there's some merc outfits hiring."

"Mercenaries, huh? They pay well," Brandt said. He felt like a gypsy on the run. He remembered when he and Deke had been on their own before. Tight spots battling wildfires in the West and beer garden brawls in Germany came to mind. Sometimes it worked out.

31

Casey sat next to Brandt in Rome's Fiumicino Airport VIP lounge while they waited to board their flight to Buenos Aires. Tig sat next to Lena at the bar, shielding her from a stream of hopeful Italian men. Al was searching for the chapel.

Brandt knew travel websites touted Buenos Aires as the Paris of South America—the usual tourist hype about wide, tree-lined boulevards without mentioning the pickpockets, winos, and hookers. He admitted the Nueve de Julio Avenue was wider than Paris' L'Esplanade des Invalides, but without its parks and manicured lawns, it was just another noisy boulevard with the mandatory obelisk at one end. Tourists gathered on Santa Fe Avenue to shop, but it lacked the glamour of the Champs-Élysées names: Givenchy, Dior, Saint Laurent, Armani.

The differences didn't end there. Politics was a big one. Unlike Paris, where happy hour bounced between love, work and elections, Buenos Aires bars left politics at the curb. It was easy to understand. As far as good government, Argentina set the bar low. It misread the Greeks and morphed democracy into demagoguery. Perón instilled it, and a long series of clueless leaders perfected it. The demagogue answers to financial problems were lies and peso devaluations. They arrived like clockwork. Brandt thought if there was a connection to Paris, it was the traffic—intense, frantic and chaotic. The way the populace saw it, maybe it was true but they still had the tango.

Deke sat down across from Casey with a bottle of water. "Jessie Taub is the Chief of Station. She knows we don't have Langley's authorization on this but agreed to help anyway. We'll meet her at Recoleta Cemetery, away from embassy eyes. I knew her when she was a field agent in Oslo. She created her own cover when she was promoted to Buenos Aires. Very imaginative. She's the embassy facilities manager. None of that phony attaché crap that fools no one."

"Why the cemetery? Place is full of locals and tourists," Brandt said. "Eva Perón's crypt is like a shrine."

"Part of her job is purchasing and distributing fresh flowers in the embassy. They get changed twice a week, or sooner if there's an event planned. She loads up the extras and hands them out to people to lay the flowers next to Recoleta's crypts and mausoleums. She's a fixture there, talks to everyone and picks up gossip, rumors, and government plans that way. It's like having the whole city wired and tapped."

Casey leaned back in her chair. "That's brilliant."

Lena left the bar and sat next to Casey. "I would like to see an old friend, Diego Marquez, when we get there. One of the giants in the physics world. He's been involved in every important physics discovery in South America since the fifties."

"Fifties. How old is he?" Brandt said.

"He's over ninety now. Never retired, mind still as sharp as a needle. Still lives alone. He was seventy-eight when he wrote the bible on the spin tune of polarized protons. He can't wait to see me."

"Should Tig go along?" Casey asked.

"Just Al. I'd like for him to meet Diego."

Deke nodded an okay. "Jessie is trying to get us a current map of the Nazi compound in Bariloche. Langley's is twenty-five years old. When the Nazis arrived after the war, they were certain the Allies would come after them and prepped for war. They turned the compound into a fortress—bunkers, machine guns, and concertina wire. Perón eventually made them remove the barb wire and put away the weapons."

"Now they're only worried about the Mossad," Brandt said.

"Do they live inside?" Casey asked.

"Not anymore. They started moving into town before Perón was kicked out. The compound has become an administrative and cultural center. A place for festivals, celebrations, and an old museum full of disturbing Third Reich crap. There's also a maze of underground bunkers she thinks would be perfect to hide nukes."

Casey exhaled, feigning relief. "That should make this easier."

"Don't bet on it. These guys were resourceful. The old photos show tanks reassembled from parts shipped from Germany. Perón took all but one away. A scout tank is parked next to the museum as part of the display."

Brandt winced. "Tanks, huh? No telling what the KGB and Stasi added to the mix. Weapons, Soviet tech, satellite access."

"I'm afraid you're right," Deke said.

§

Because the Alvear Palace was the place where heads of state stayed on official visits, Tig swept for bugs before they unpacked. Due to its special status, the Recoleta area was scrubbed clean of hookers, beggars, con men, and drug dealers. *Keep your distance and we'll leave you alone* was the unofficial message. The exception were the dancers who made their way from the Almagro tango district to Plaza Cárcano to show their artistic moves to an appreciative public. The flagstone stage was a short walk from the hotel in a shaded plaza where dancers circled the statue of a Herculean man holding up the thick branches of an old gum tree. The music came from the chords of bandoneon accordions. The air was filled with hopes and dreams—a sparkling performance might launch a career.

"No one followed us from the airport. That's a good sign," Casey said. "I like the room. Reminds me of the king's residence in Versailles. Enough pale blue and gold cording for a throne."

Brandt peered intently at a painting on the far wall next to the bar. He smiled. It was good stuff. Nothing subtle about this artist's palette. South American culture took the colors from jungle parrots and spread them on homes, commercial buildings, private cars, and taxis. He moved to the window and watched guests arrive. "The hotel computer system is connected to the police and SIDE inteligence headquarters. Langley helped them install it. They know every guest and room number. Petrov's friends in Bariloche probably have hacked in."

§

In the morning, Lena and Al left to meet Marquez. Tig went out for a run, and Brandt led Deke and Casey to the cemetery. It was fall south of the equator and the jacaranda tree leaves warned of the approach of winter. The park green in front of the cemetery had been mowed, clipped, and edged until it looked like the grounds of a royal estate. Boys were playing catch and throw with Frisbees, trying to impress the girls sitting on fountain steps with their athletic skills.

Jessie was waiting for them by the entrance to Recoleta Cemetery. She had the look of a Wall Street banking executive on casual Friday:

navy fitted slacks, white canvas footwear, white turtleneck, and a locally tailored blue leather coat. She was tall, too tall for heels, and her brown hair was streaked, wavy, and long enough to reach a marbled looped scarf. Her flowers had already been distributed. "There's a coffee shop in the plaza across the park. It's a good place to talk," she said.

They moved past two police officers mounted on chestnut horses, protecting the park. One of the officers was cleaning his sunglasses.

Jessie waved to the police as she talked. "Where's the Russian and the monk?"

"Meeting a friend inside, and Brother Al wanted to see the cemetery," Casey said.

"You should see it too. Most visitors look for where the celebrities are interred, but the architecture is what's so unique and creative about the place. Miniaturized basilicas and castles. Some as large as the egos buried inside."

Jessie was right about the egos. If you were important or had money, Recoleta was the place to be buried. All that Brandt's tours had been interested in was Eva Perón's crypt, and the tourists were disappointed with its simplicity next to the other monuments.

"Were you able to get us an updated map of the compound?" Deke asked.

"I'll have it tomorrow. But I'm not sure how much help it will be. I was there for Fasching two years ago, and it all looks pretty normal now. Just a modern city with the usual urban problems. The local Germans are more interested in economics than politics these days."

"What about the underground bunkers?" Brandt said.

"You should focus on them. Supposedly commercial wine cellars for the vintners. None open to the public. Any areas off limits to the tourists should be our focus."

They sat at a table in the shade. Jessie ordered a traditional tea-like *mate* with mint, Brandt a plain *mate*, Deke passed, and Casey had a Colombian brewed latte.

"What about getting in?" Casey asked.

"Still working on that. There's a guard with a weakness for women and bad soccer bets."

"Assets?" Deke said. "What do you have there?"

"A couple who own a souvenir shop and a clerk in the *intendente*'s office. The Mossad has some floaters, and Chile owns an inn they staff with agents."

Brandt was surprised at the lack of assets. Usually, the more critical and sinister the place, the more agents Langley wanted in place. Bariloche wasn't Brussels or Moscow, but it wasn't Vatican City either.

Jessie said, "The ambassador has rules about CIA operations here. If he knows I'm part of your team, we can keep it from Langley."

Lena and Al exited the cemetery, accompanied by a third man with a cane, shuffling along like an advanced geriatric. Brandt pointed for the others to see.

Deke asked Jessie, "You recognize that guy?"

"Never seen him before."

Casey saw recognition flicker in Jessie's eyes. It was a lie.

§

Casey had been worried about something the last day in Florence, and it carried over to Argentina. It was the kind of worry that is difficult to pin down. Something was wrong, but she was not certain what. The nagging unease had grown after the meeting. There was something about Jessie that kept her insides churning. It went past the lie. Casey had a sixth sense when it came to female agents—she had warned Deke and Brandt about Anna's duplicity as part of the Oleg defection.

She waited until they were back in their room to bring it up. "Jessie didn't seem to have a lot to offer. I mean, no current map. The place is full of Nazis and KGB, and she hasn't been there in *two years*. Hard to believe."

"I would have thought she'd be camped out there. Fill the town with agents and floaters," Brandt said. "These aren't the kind of people you can turn your back on."

Deke wrinkled his nose for effect. "I smelled it too."

"She recognized Marquez with Lena. Why lie about an old man?" Casey said.

"Marquez probably knows too many important people here and where all the bodies are buried. She might be afraid he knows some dirt on her," Deke said.

Casey's face turned sour. "And now she wants to be part of the team."

"A little too close to the Mossad here, I'm afraid. Her comment about only a few Mossad floaters doesn't cut it. They probably have more agents in Bariloche than Beijing."

Brandt grimaced. "A priest, a minister, and an Israeli mole walk into a bar."

Deke looked down in thought, then back up. "You may be right. She's probably helping the Mossad cover up their activities across the region. After all the bad press they got for grabbing Eichmann and putting the trial on TV, they got smart. They organized special *Kidon* teams to eliminate Nazi war criminals."

Aaron tried once to explain to Brandt how hanging Eichmann in 1962 had changed Mossad tactics. Brandt hadn't listened. He hated hearing anything about the sixties. Boomers and media glorified the time as America's awakening, as if everything before and after was meaningless. The way he looked at it, by the eighties, the country was asleep again. He was certain disco had something to do with it.

"How about the skinhead stuff in Germany? It must have Tel Aviv concerned," Casey said.

Deke grumbled. "Compared to this place, Germany is a toothache. Bariloche is rectal cancer."

"The Leipzig Authority?"

"Bad DNA," Deke said. "Aaron didn't find out about the SADMs in Italy like he said. He knew about Petrov all along."

Brandt had a look of agreement. "He knew everything in Brussels before we left and moved in right behind us. We had Lena and Al, so the Mossad was happy to tag along and see if we found them. Florence could have gone either way, so Aaron decided to make contact."

"What do we do about Jessie?"

"Nothing. Keep her out of the loop as much as possible. When this is over, I'll let the South American director know she may be tainted."

Brandt answered the door and let Al in.

"Where's Lena?" Casey asked.

"She's having a glass of wine with her old friend in the courtyard," said Al. "She thought she could get more out of him if I disappeared."

32

When Lena came in, she had everyone's attention. There was an excitement about her, an auctioneer's rapid speech with an unlit cigarette swirling in one hand. "I believe I know where they are. Diego . . . he told me where to look." She paused to catch her breath. "I asked him where he would hide nuclear weapons if he had them. He didn't hesitate. The Huemul Project."

The name drew blanks: Deke thought of Fort Knox, Casey a dam, and Brandt hoped it was a new luxury resort.

"Sorry," Lena said. "It's a physics story. Physicists make bad jokes about it. An embarrassing failure to develop nuclear fusion. An Austrian opportunist, Ronald Richter's brainchild. He convinced Perón he could power all of Bariloche with a Thermotron and a gallon of water. Perón funded a massive concrete research structure on Huemul Island in Lake Nahuel Huapi based on Richter's promises. Now it sits empty. The locals are wary and keep their distance."

"Is it guarded?" Deke asked.

"I sat there while Diego checked with his nephews for me. For years, it's only been a couple of local private police. Now, it's more like a multinational security force. Storm troopers, not mall cops. No one in Bariloche talks about them."

"Petrov's doing," Casey said.

Deke looked like it was Christmas morning. "Langley foots the bill for the DEA chopper at the airport. They'll be happy to loan it to us."

"Jessie sure made a point of steering us toward the bunkers inside the old compound," Casey said. "I wonder if she suspects they're in Huemul."

"Ties in with her concern about Marquez. Either way, her job is to stall us," Brandt said. "Buy time for the Israelis until they figure out what to do."

Deke nodded. "It's a delicate problem for them. We're supposed to be their backup. If they can't get them first, they want to be sure we do. Nukes with ex-Nazis in Bariloche scares the hell out of them."

"I think we need to bring Langley in this now," Casey said. "Get Randy and his Special Ops team here."

Deke didn't hesitate. "I'll make the call."

§

Randy and his nine man Special Ops team arrived in Bariloche in the middle of the night on a military C-40 Clipper with *UNESCO* painted on the fuselage. Deke and Tig met them at the gate and guided them to the luxury lodge on the shores of the lake where Brandt and Casey were waiting.

Randy was dressed in jeans and a blue sweatshirt. The rest of the team could pass for bearded construction workers or gym rats in their street clothes that failed to hide wide shoulders, veiny biceps, and slim waists.

"The pictures you took from the chopper weren't much help, but thanks for the effort," Randy said. "Just a concrete block house.

Lotsa vines and trees. I'll take three of the guys and do a night recon tomorrow. If it looks good, I'll leave two to keep watch and we'll flex in the next night."

"Jessie is the Chief of Station here. We need to keep her in the dark on all of this," Deke said.

"Interesting," Randy said. "We're not even here."

"We expect the guards to be ex-KGB and Stasi, but we can't have any casualties. The government doesn't know anything about this," Casey added.

"You're full of good news. Tasers and gas, then. Anything else?"

"We have to get there before the Mossad."

"How many nukes?" Randy asked.

"If we're right, there should be seventeen SADMs," Brandt said. "Probably in shipping crates. I'll have to open them up and let Lena test them before we move them."

Randy squeezed his lips. "Then you'll have to work fast. We need to be gone by first light."

Brandt massaged his fingers as if warming them up to pick a lock.

"Tig and I will find a boat to haul them off the island," Deke said.

"We'll need a box truck to hold them. Something with a name on the side that won't draw attention at the town loading dock."

"Tig can take care of that."

Randy met everyone's eyes. "It's a start. Rack time. Get some sleep."

§

Al and Lena had breakfast inside while Randy joined the rest on the heated patio.

"I've got Karp and Bones finding a spot to launch the rafts," Randy said.

"From the chopper, I saw a cove about two klicks south, if that helps," Brandt said. "End of a drainage, lots of cover."

"Bones will find it. The rafts and gear are still on the plane. Roark is waiting to hear where to bring it." Randy drained his coffee and poured another, then handed the carafe to a server for a refill. "No moon tonight helps. I figure forty minutes across the lake to the island. Another thirty to the structure. I'll leave Mongo and Bruce there to keep eyes on it and time the watch changes. Unless there's a battalion or more spread across the island, we should be a go for the next night."

"Don't forget Lena and me," Brandt said. "We have a job to do too."

"Second raft. Karp will bring you and the Russian over." Randy hesitated. "You think they're really there?"

"They're there," Deke said. "We've been chasing these things all over Europe. They're there."

Randy looked at Lena sitting inside the dining room, then at Brandt. "We'll be using a chemical agent tomorrow night, and you and her might need protective masks. I don't have extras, so we'll have to fit you both on the fly with two from the others."

"What kind of gas?" Casey asked.

"Dream Boy-2, an extract of Kolokol-2B that the Russians used on the Chechens in the Moscow hostage crisis. Something the lab cooked up using the Russian α-methylfentanyl base. No one is supposed to die from it now."

"Is that the stuff Putin uses to eliminate dissident journalists?" Brandt asked.

"That's Novichok-10. You're dead before you hit the ground."

"And Dream Boy-2?"

"Knocks you out before you know what's happening."

"Has it been tested on humans?"

"Langley says so. Roark gave some to Mongo and he went out like a light."

Bones sat down at the table.

Randy flashed a knowing smile. "A cove, right? Two klicks south."

"Roger that," said Bones. "An old log road for access. We'll need a truck with high clearance."

"Rent something at the airport for the rafts and gear then. Help Roark get them to the cove at dusk."

Casey handed Randy their picture of Petrov. "We believe he'll be with the weapons. If he's there, he comes back with you."

"High value?"

"An important Russian. Lena can ID him. Gas him, Taser him, stun him, kick his ass . . . whatever. Just bring him back in one piece."

§

After breakfast, Al and Lena left for a walk. Chalky-gray clouds kept the mountain sun in check. They laughed over the silliness of the street names seventy years after the end of the war: Aryan Strasse, Reichsboulevard, Kaiserplatz II. Unreality found a home in Bariloche.

"Do you think this is the end of the mission?" Al said.

"Looks like it, but I'll feel better if we capture Petrov when we get the weapons."

"Will you go back to Oak Ridge when this is over?"

Lena stopped in front of a store window selling handmade wooden toys and ornaments, taking time to form an answer. "I really don't know. This has been so different. I'm not sure I know what I want to do after this. If it's a new direction, I don't know what it is."

"New paths, new directions. God's way of keeping us humble and close," Al said.

Lena's voice lost its tenor. "Maybe. But I've never found Him to play fair."

"The Greek philosopher Thales walked around looking up at the stars for life's answers."

"Did he find them?"

"We don't know. We do know he fell into a well once."

"Probably bumped into walls too."

"He claimed the cosmos likes to put us in situations where we need to make a decision and if we get it wrong, it does it again and again until we get it right."

"Is that what Brandt is struggling with? Getting it right?"

Al looked at Lena with uncertainty.

"Casey told me all about his issues," said Lena.

Al slowed his steps. "For men, it's always about our place in the world. We think we know who we are and where we want to go. Then life happens, and we have to adjust."

"Climb out of a well?"

"Or worse. We either let go and listen to our souls or go crazy. Brandt calls it bobbing and weaving through life while trying to keep our head above water and feet on the ground."

"He would know. Casey said he almost gave up after his wife died."

"Sometimes we have to go to the edge before answers arrive."

"Not exactly comforting."

Two local residents stopped on the sidewalk in an animated discussion. The man spoke German, the woman Spanish.

"What are the odds of them settling a bilingual argument?" Lena said.

Al gave a noncommittal shrug. "I'm in one of those difficult situations too. I've been in it since I met you. I'm very afraid of making the wrong choice."

"Me too . . . sort of. What do you plan to do?"

"When this is over, I'm going back to Florence. It's where my life began to change. I'm hoping you might go with me, but I don't know how to ask."

"I think you just did. But I'm not sure why."

"I went to the Benedictines to hide from the KGB. I found that a monk's life is like being in hiding all the time. Our clothes hide everything but our faces. A good part of our life is dedicated to solitude and silence. 'Cloistered' is even another word for 'hidden.' Being with you has forced me to look deeper. I'm just not sure what it means."

Their eyes met in a tactual, intimate way, like the feathery touch of an infant's fingers.

§

Randy was at breakfast on the patio again after the night's recon mission, devouring a lumberjack-size steak with four eggs over easy. Brandt and Casey sat down with him—coffee for Brandt, latte for Casey.

Deke stood in front of the pastry table full of indecision, then finally joined them with chunks of filet and scrambled eggs from the hot buffet. "The boat and truck are all set. An old forty-two-foot fishing boat the owner is too old to use and can't sell. Titanic class, but it runs and floats. Tig picked out a DHL truck at the airport to borrow."

Casey looked to Randy. "How does the mission shape up for tonight now?"

"A timing issue, but nothing we can't finesse. There are twelve guards. No problem with them. Six on each watch. Four shifts. Changes starting at 2100. We want to hit them close to 0100 when they won't be as alert. The six off watch sleep in a makeshift barracks in the trees about fifty yards away. We can slip the chemical agent under the door and between some loose panels to take them out."

"And the other six?" Deke asked.

"Two who patrol the grounds. Two with night vision gear who guard the entrance. That's where the only two windows in the building are. The last two stand watch inside. With no other windows, we can't be certain where."

"Probably guarding the weapons room," Brandt said.

"The rain in the forecast is a plus. Mother Nature's noise suppression. Makes the night vision gear almost useless too. We'll use Taser pistols and stunners to keep them out until we can gas them."

"What's the timing issue?" Brandt asked.

"The chem agent. Dream Boy-2 will only keep them out four hours. That's not much time for this. How quick can you open them up, do the test, and put the locks back on?"

"Depends. If they all have different combinations, it will take longer."

"Won't work. You have to be quicker. First light is 0547 and we need to be on the quay in town with the truck by then."

"Can't you gas them again?" Casey asked.

"Too risky. Second time with that stuff could kill them. That's too many bodies. If we run out of time, we'll have to take the weapons *as is*. You can finish up on the plane."

"They used the same combination before. Maybe we'll get lucky," Brandt said.

"Because of the short time, the rafts will be separated by only five minutes. I doubt there'll be much late-night lake traffic in bad weather. Lena will go with me, Roark, Ely, and Goochie. You'll go with Karp, Bones, and Fast Eddie. You'll be paddling too. Karp will hand you both rain gear after dinner. I'll tap on your doors tonight when it's time."

33

Brandt knew operations never went as planned. Cadets were taught that at West Point, Sandhurst, and École Saint-Cyr. Randy and Deke knew it too. Brandt had a sense they were in for a surprise on the night's mission. He hoped whatever it was wouldn't result in casualties. Randy's team, armed with only Tasers and small arms, would be poorly armed if a real firefight started. He decided to ask Randy for something other than his Glock to take along. One of the Hecklers would be good. If the shooting started, he wanted to be an asset.

Casey finished her shower and came out wrapped in a towel, then looked at Brandt and froze. "Something's bothering you. What is it?"

Brandt tried a bluff. "Nothing specific. Just some mission anxiety. Helps to get me focused."

"Bullshit. What's really bothering you?"

"Okay. Something vague bouncing around in my gut that tells me this isn't going to go the way we hope tonight."

"Paranoia rears its ugly head. You afraid it's a trap?"

"That's only one of the crazy thoughts that has raced across my mind. Mushroom clouds were the scariest. I'm wondering if we should leave Lena behind. Let the AEC check for tritium."

"She'll go. You can't stop her. She's the one to ID Petrov too. I think she wants to meet him face-to-face while we haul away his SADMs."

§

Sheets of rain that obscured vision started a little after 1600, then a light rain, followed by another blinding downpour. One of Randy's beautiful storms—impairing hearing, reducing vision, and eroding alertness. Langley's weather forecast said it would be rainy until midmorning.

Brandt and Casey had planned to walk to a restaurant in town for dinner, but the weather kept them in the lodge. The dining room was a combination of the rustic and the elegant—the work of a gifted decorator. The flat-sided log walls were chinked with a three-inch plaster mix between the timbers. Crystal chandeliers suggested a subtle grace. In the middle of the gray-toned jacquard tablecloth, a six-inch crystal pillar held a simple tea light.

Al and Lena joined them at the table, Brandt ordered a popular bottle of the Malbec.

"Randy and Karp brought my rain gear," Lena said. "Yours is in your suite. Karp instructed me on the raft procedures. The main thing is that if someone says 'deck,' get as flat as possible. Don't show a silhouette. It's all very exciting."

"I was thinking if we shipped the weapons straight to Sandia Labs, you could stay here warm and dry, sleeping comfortably," Brandt said.

"Not a chance. I wouldn't miss this."

Tig came in with Bones and Fast Eddie and walked up to Brandt while the other two found a table against the back wall, facing the entrance. "I talked Randy into putting me on tonight," Tig said.

"How'd you do that?" Brandt asked.

"Technically, I'm your bodyguard and should be along with you."

"Then you're doing the paddling," Brandt said.

After Tig joined Randy's men at their table, Casey said, "Not sure Tig going is such a good idea. If there's trouble, there's a chance he might freeze up again."

"Randy doesn't have his background. Can't blame him for adding an extra combat vet."

"Are you going to say something to him?"

"Naw . . . probably just cause a bigger problem. I'll keep him close to me."

"Just be sure Tig isn't the source of your worry."

34

Randy tapped lightly on the doors. Lena came out dressed in camo rain gear with the sleeves and legs rolled up and duct-taped to her wrists and ankles to make them fit. Brandt's fit well and he was ready to go. Randy was in combat camo, only the minimum equipment and weapons. Silent approach was the plan.

"I believe I have your rain gear on," Brandt said to him.

"Remember, I was a SEAL. We were always wet. Karp's in the truck. Let's go."

Tig was waiting for them by the rafts in the cove. His earring was gone, and his face was blackened like the others'. He applied the two-toned waterproof face paint to Lena, leaving Brandt to do his own face and hands.

Lena could hardly contain herself. She turned to Brandt. "This is so exciting I could pee my pants."

Ely and Goochie helped Lena into the raft, and Roark loaded her test gear and two Heckler submachine guns. Brandt was impressed with how silently the first group slipped into the water and moved toward the island.

Karp checked the time and said to Brandt, "You'll sit in the middle rear of the raft." He then handed Brandt a folding-stock AR-15. "Here's your weapon. Full magazine. Here's the safety."

"No Heckler?" Brandt said.

"Randy didn't like the idea of you with anything full automatic."

"Afraid I'd shoot him?"

Karp smiled. "You get the drift." He moved on, inspecting the raft chambers for leaky softness, then looked at his watch again. "Lock 'n' load. We're up."

Once they left the cove, the dark, rainy night became a black curtain. Karp guided the raft as if it were daylight. He had amazing night vision. Brandt, on the other hand, couldn't see the raft ahead or even the island. He focused on the lake surface next to the raft to measure the rain. Light rain created small dots, steady rain overlapping circles, heavy rain turned the surface into geysers. He turned back toward the lodge; the lights had only a faint, hazy glow.

Roark met them at the shoreline. Randy walked over with an equipment duffel and pulled out body armor for both of them. Brandt put his on while Karp switched the protective panel inserts to adjust to Lena's figure.

Mongo whispered, "I love this shit," to Brandt and grinned. He was a "snake eater" ex-Green Beret with a scuba-size cylinder holding the Dream Boy agent trapped to his back and no rain gear. He was the smallest man on Randy's team, the size of a department store mannequin, and had given up his rain suit for Lena.

The rain paused briefly and clouds thinned enough for a glimmer of moonlight. The team assembled around Randy, and after a comm check, team members inspected each other's gear, securing any battle rattle. Tig checked Brandt and his weapon and then gave a thumbs-up. Brandt moved next to Lena and gave her hand a squeeze. She was so excited she hardly noticed, then smiled at him. When Randy saw everyone was ready, he looked at his tactical GPS with Bruce, and they headed out without a word. The rain started up again as everyone filed behind.

The pace was quick at first, but as they neared the structure, Bruce in the lead moved slow and silent. The rain covered every noise they made. When Bruce stopped the team, the Fusion Center was nowhere to be seen. Brandt looked at his watch—it was only 2350. They had an hour to kill. He sat with his back against a tree to wait it out. Roark carried an infrared device and glided softly to the right with Goochie, then disappeared into the gloom. Karp tapped Brandt on the shoulder and waved good-bye. He and Mongo melted into the woods to their left. Bones unraveled a rain poncho and spread it over Lena for an extra layer. The furry outline of Maitén branches was all that was visible. When Brandt fixed his eyes on them for more than a few seconds, they seemed to move like a wooly mammoth, so he had to keep looking away.

It took only moments before a mental wave crashed in and his bad feeling returned. He told himself: *So far, no problems. No ambush. Stop worrying.* Then he realized that with the four men moving off to their assignments, they sat there, a weakened force if an attack came. His hand moved to the AR-15's safety. He wished Mongo were still with them. He remembered in Bosnia he had combat balls as big as melons.

Lena crawled over to him and whispered in his ear, "I'd love a cigarette, but Al took them away from me before I left."

"Randy would have thrown them away."

"Thank God he let me pee when we got off the raft."

Brandt helped Lena move closer so they could share body warmth, and she spread the poncho across them both. The temperature had fallen since they left the lodge, and the damp rain began to chill them. When Lena's teeth developed a chattering click, Randy came over and gave Brandt two book-size chemical heat packs to help. Brandt snapped one at the center to get it started and gave it to Lena, then broke the seal on his, stuffed it next to his chest, and rested his trigger hand on it.

It was 0035 when Ely and Fast Eddie moved off.

Bones slid next to Brandt and whispered to them both, "It's time. Saddle up and get the blood flowing. Roark and Goochie Tasered the guys on patrol and are putting on their uniforms. As soon as we know the shed is gassed and safe, they'll zap the two by the entrance." He stuck a five-inch strip of luminous tape on the tree above Brandt. "If there's a serious fuckup, this is our rally point. Try and make it back here."

Randy stood whispering and gesturing to Bruce and Bones. Then he muttered in his headset, turned to Brandt, gave a head shake, and they all moved forward. Minutes later, they reached the clearing where the Fusion Center was located. The ground became soft and squishy; rivulets of rain had grooved canals in the turf down from the structure. As they moved forward, Brandt could make out Karp and Goochie waiting under the overhang for them. The rest were already inside.

When they reached the door, Randy said, "Wait here. We're searching the rooms and halls for the last two."

Brandt looked through a foggy window. Mongo was inside with the tank from his back resting on the floor. Fast Eddie was positioned in front of what appeared to be a storeroom where the guards were probably stashed.

Randy addressed them in a normal voice. "Bones is bringing one up from the basement to join his friends. The nukes are down there. Forget about the masks. We didn't need to gas the inside. Roark and Ely are chasing the other guy on the second floor. Shouldn't be long before they drag him down. You can get started then."

Brandt began to let go of his bad feeling. Casey was right. Paranoia.

"How about Petrov?" Lena asked.

"No sign of him, but if he's here, we'll get him."

Lena went limp in disappointment.

Randy handed Lena's equipment to Bones. "Take them to the nukes when Ely has the last one. I'll come down when we're finished up here."

Ely brought the last guard, bruised and bleeding, down from the second floor. Mongo forced a pill in the guard's mouth and handed him a bottle of water, zip-tied his hands, and set him inside the storeroom with the others.

Brandt and Lena, both filled with anticipation, took off their rain suits and followed Bones to the steps leading to the underground level. Brandt began to think of the nukes as the anti-Holy Grail they had been chasing all over Europe.

"I pray they find Petrov," Lena said. "He must be hiding somewhere in here. I don't believe he would leave his precious SADMs."

Brandt's first look gave him a jolt—the nukes weren't locked up in a separate, closed-off room. Instead, they were lined up loose, like brewery barrels, against the wall of a wide corridor. At the far end were large double loading doors where a delivery truck might be waiting to load them. Brandt's heart sank with the next revelation. There were only fifteen weapons pushed against the wall. Two short. He gazed at Lena. "What the fuck?"

Lena counted again. "This can't be!"

"They must be around here someplace," Brandt said. "Bones, call Randy and tell him we're missing two and look for them."

Lena's face nearly touched the ground. "He won't find them. They're not here. Petrov has them."

"Where?"

"I have no idea."

Randy came down the stairs. He looked at the weapons and raised a finger to count them. "Fuck. Fifteen. You sure there's supposed to be seventeen?"

Brandt gave him a look that answered yes.

"I'll send Bruce to look in the shed. The rest can scour the building."

Brandt started on the nuke locks, wondering what this meant to the mission. He began with combinations from the nukes in Otto's basement. These were the same. He had them opened in less than thirty minutes. Lena found tritium in all of them. Petrov had them ready to use.

35

Casey, Brandt, and Deke stood together on the boat Deke had rented. "Only fifteen," Brandt said. "Mongo told me to 'embrace the suck.'"

"No one got killed. Just an inventory discrepancy," Deke said.

"Two missing nukes. Nothing to worry about, huh?"

Tig and Randy's team hauled the SADMs one at a time down to the quay and loaded them onto Deke's boat. With two short, there was extra room.

"When we get back to the lodge, I'll call Langley," Deke said. "See what they want to do."

"Langley will say, 'We'll get back to you,'" Casey said.

Roark and Tig loaded the last of the fifteen and climbed aboard. They were tasked with loading the truck and getting the SADMs to the plane.

When Tig started the boat moving, Deke grabbed a rail to steady himself. "We can't leave the nukes sitting at the airport. Once Randy is back with his team, they'll escort them to the States. Get a shower and some sleep. I'll knock on your doors when I know something."

§

Brandt sat on the room balcony wearing a lodge robe with a red, white, and blue logo shield next to his heart.

"You think this is over?" Casey asked.

"Hard to imagine anything other than a 'well done' and they close the book on this."

"Yeah, I'm afraid you're right."

"Lena doesn't believe we have them all. She's certain Petrov has the other two. I believe her."

"We don't even know where to look."

"Doesn't matter. NATO will call it off, move on to fighting with State about who gets to give them back to the Russians."

Deke came in with a basket of energy bars and fresh muffins. Tig was right behind him, juggling water bottles.

"We're done," Deke said. "The DEA chopper to Buenos Aires, then commercial flight back to London."

"What did they say?" Casey asked.

"Langley is sitting on the fence. They like all the nukes in the world accounted for. NATO said eighty-seven wasn't written in stone . . . only an estimate. Nothing is missing."

"Till one goes boom in DC or London," Brandt said.

"What can I say? Lena's probably right, but NATO doesn't think so, and Langley is scratching their asses. I just hope if one goes off, it's not a three kiloton."

"Lena thinks Petrov would want the three kilotons."

"Have you talked to her yet?" Casey asked.

"Before I came here. She wasn't surprised. It was obvious she'd been crying a lot. When I left, I could hear her sobbing again."

Casey's eyes became moist too. "What does she plan to do next?"

"I didn't ask."

"Between Petrov and how things will work out with Al, she's dealing with a lot now," Casey said.

"I booked her and Al to London with us."

"Not sure that will happen," Brandt said.

"We'll see. I reserved a meeting room for later today. Snacks and wine. No champagne. Doesn't have the feel of a celebration. We can do the after-action report together and try to relax. Leave the adrenaline rushes behind."

§

In Moscow, Moky argued with Grushenko, a one-time general who'd been awarded the final Order of Lenin before the honor was ended in 1991. Now he sat behind a desk in a civilian blue suit fitted in Beijing. Moky thought the argument was pointless. Bureaucrats made a career out of being a roadblock. Pleading for Gleb to be reassigned or sent to a Siberian reeducation camp outside of Novosibirsk was like flapping your arms to circle the globe. But it was worth a try.

Grushenko just grunted. "Gleb serves a much-needed purpose. Maybe *you* need reeducating how to lead our brave troops."

Moky knew that ever since Grushenko had surrendered his uniform and all its glitter, he'd also surrendered his spine. As a Moscow apparatchik, he could be pushed now. The hard edge that had made him a successful general was lost. "Hmph. If you think Gleb is so important, why don't you introduce him to your daughter?"

Grushenko rose up. Unlike other ex-generals and bureaucrats, he'd stayed lean and sturdy. He glared at Moky with eyes that could melt iron. "Enough! Your intelligence is only exceeded by your insolence. Don't let your ego get in the way of this mission. It can also get you sent to Novosibirsk."

Moky wasn't fazed. "Let me remind you we had Lena Averin until Gleb allowed her to escape."

"Doesn't matter. Sometimes Gleb's methods are needed. We're finally ahead of NATO. Go back to using care and good judgment."

Moky bristled at the insinuation that he had come up short when Gleb was the one at fault. He wanted to reach across the desk and grab Grushenko by the throat. Instead, he sighed and slumped in his chair. "Okay, but we split the team into three groups. And no Aeroflot flights. They're watched too closely and too many accidents. Put us on British Air, Air France, and Lufthansa."

§

A sadness tinged with fear and combined with a sense of relief enveloped Brandt when he came into the meeting room. Mixed emotions on steroids. The sadness came from realizing it might be the last time he could speak with Al, and maybe Lena. He was itching to ask Al what his plans were but kept silent. Al would let him know when he was ready. The relief was the result of the mission ending despite the unanswered questions. The fear was more complex. One glance at Lena reminded him that Petrov was still out there and so were two nukes. Added to that, he was going home unsettled, without any idea in which direction to take his life. Maybe Casey was right—go back to California and sort everything out. If the reporter from the *Post* kept after him, it might be his only move.

Cybil's email was also a concern. Damn critics. Apparently the Swedish art critic he'd reproached was out for revenge, crusading against Brandt's work with his London art friends. The critic had managed to generate a review in the *Guardian* referring to Brandt's work as banal. It almost made him laugh. Art critics lived and breathed banal. It had to be in their blood. Trouble was, after the column, some of the paintings sold in the Nottingham show were being returned. Cybil was concerned. She wanted him to do damage control and apologize to the dumb Swede. He told her he'd think about it.

He grabbed a chair on the right side of the rectangular table and looked at Deke talking with Tig. Deke had a glass of milk, Tig held a large sandwich. They appeared ready to return to London. Catch up at home and prepare for the next assignment.

His own future had too many question marks. CIA? Artist? His sister would advise him to be *malleable*. She loved that word. Everything was malleable to her. Life was a series of events that required adapting to change, best approached with an open mind and a flexible attitude. According to Casey, he took it one step further. He didn't just adapt, he reinvented himself. His sister wouldn't understand—to her, every step in life was a simple decision. Look at choices, engage brain, and go. Don't sweat the small stuff, and it's all small stuff. His experience was different. It came from a different place inside. It had to have a soulful quality. Right now, neither CIA or artist had any of that.

Deke walked over and sat next to Brandt. "I have some good news. You're off the hook with the *Post*."

"They find a better target?"

"I told you the director had you covered. He took care of it."

"The reporter euthanized?"

"In a less violent way. The director invited the two ranking members of the Senate Intelligence Committee to lunch in Langley. He told them everything about you. Haystack first. How you stepped up to the plate as a civilian and risked your life to prevent nuclear war. They knew about Oleg. He's a star with them, but they didn't know you were the one to bring him in. The director showed them your file and how the reporter was coloring everything to show something that wasn't there. Told them how you refused to be a field agent and the only way to keep you was send you to London as a floater. All official. After lunch, the senators made a call to the *Post* owner. Told him the truth. No more stories."

"I hope I get a glowing obituary then."

Deke grinned. "The agency has a policy about those."

Brandt wondered why the news left him flat. Another confusing message from his heart and soul. From the joy on Casey's face, Deke must have already given her the news.

In a small surprise, Lena and Al didn't sit together. After Deke left, Al settled next to Brandt with slices of beef on a roll. Lena sat beside Casey, showing her pictures she'd taken in town. Casey as mission supervisor sat next to Deke to jot down notes for the report.

Al whispered in his left ear, "I wanted to tell you myself. Lena and I will not be going to London with you."

"I'm not surprised. Where are you off to?"

"Rome, then a train to Florence. I need some time in my old monastery."

"Will Lena be on the train too?"

"Your questions always have a delicate subtlety."

"I have to be a counter to Deke's bluntness."

"You both rush through life like cavalry waving sabers. I was like that once. To answer your question, Lena *is* going with me to Florence."

"A convent for her?"

Al shook his head. "Mission over, back to smartass, huh?"

"Think of it as a gift."

"We're hoping you can get her a suite at the Westin on the river. I suspect she'll be a familiar face on Via de' Tornabuoni."

"Gucci gulch."

"I think you know what I'll be praying about," Al said. "These feelings are threatening to a monk. It won't be an easy decision. I owe the Benedictines more than my life. They've been my salvation. But having Lena come into my life has brought changes I never expected."

"I'll put in a word above for the both of you. I don't want to see Lena hurt."

"All prayers are welcome."

"My only advice is remember your Pascal. *The heart has its reasons of which reason knows nothing.*"

Al's jaw dropped. "That's pretty good coming from an accidental agent. I'll ask God to guide you in your decision too."

"Tell Him to hurry up. Doors keep opening and closing. Just confuses me."

Al flashed a devilish grin. "I think I'll miss you, but I can't imagine why."

"Likewise."

36

Casey stayed busy in London. She finally got her hair done and caught up with Eric's school progress, sports, and social life. The decorator came by with a new color palette. Her mother went from excited to feverish over her roses after underplanting them with salvias. Brandt perfected a listless moping. A phone call to his sister sent him walking.

"All day if you have to . . . and alone," Casey said. "Just do what I say. Eventually your mind will clear. You'll know what to do."

Their townhouse was on Rochester Row in Westminster, only minutes from the cathedral. At first, he walked to the expertly groomed Saint James Park, meticulously royal despite the tourist crowds passing through to Buckingham. The pelicans managed to ignore them, but Brandt tired of the multilanguage chatter and changed his route to walk along the river. The US embassy was a short stroll across Vauxhall Bridge. He went past it once; seeing the Marine guards in battle dress that day, he kept walking. He had been traveling the same route every day for a week when Deke waved to him as he turned at Lambeth Bridge. He could have been coming from the embassy, MI6 in Vauxhall, or MI5 headquarters two minutes away.

"Casey told me you'd be here," said Deke. "She's packing up for another assignment."

"I'll miss her."

"I was hoping you'd come along."

"Not sure it fits my busy schedule."

"She also said you got things squared with Cybil. How did you do that?"

"Piece of cake. I called the asshole in Stockholm. I told him Fyodor Brusinski loved my work and owned three paintings. Then I told him how disappointed Brusinski was to read the savage review in the *Guardian* and wanted to know who was responsible, that something needed to be done about it. I could hear him shaking over the phone. I dropped Fyodor's name one more time to be sure he knew who I was talking about. Took only seconds for the asshole to come around. An apology, letters, and phone calls to his friends quickly followed."

"Brusinski? I can't see him as an art lover."

"Wouldn't know. Just dropped his name. No way some third-rate art critic was calling the Swedish head of the Russian Mafia."

"So you're back to painting now?"

"Haven't picked up a brush. Casey is thinking about turning my studio into a guest room."

"Are you through with the agency?"

"That's another brush I haven't picked up."

"You're going to have to decide what you want to do before you piss everyone off."

"Well, my sister screams at me now," said Brandt.

They stopped at a corner and let a standard black London taxi turn off Millbank.

"You haven't asked about the mission," Deke said.

"I figured you'd get around to it."

"We believe Petrov is in Paris."

Brandt froze and fixed his eyes on Deke. "The nukes?"

"The Russians think he's got two SADMs with him."

Brandt looked away and continued walking. "How good is the intel?"

"Moky changed his phone in Moscow, but we had his team's phone info by then. Used it to get Moky's again. They skipped Aeroflot and flew in separately. Moky has them staying at the Vendome Renaissance."

Brandt stopped again. He could see the embassy across the river. He asked himself: If he got involved, would this mean he was making a commitment? "Who's going besides you and Casey?"

"Just Tig. Wild Bill in Paris will back us up."

"Lena?"

"Casey is calling her. Not sure how that will go."

§

Lena hung up and walked out to the balcony. The much-prized view of the Ponte Vecchio barely registered. Her mind was elsewhere. She had a problem to solve, an example of Heisenberg's Uncertainty Principle—quantum theory in her gut. She lit a cigarette, and the smoke dived and then twisted toward the Duomo. Casey had said she hoped that Lena would come with them to Paris, she could be crucial if they found Petrov, but Casey understood why being in Florence was important to her.

Lena sighed and muttered, "Fuck." Al was out of touch, in prayerful seclusion. She was afraid if he left the monastery and found her gone, he would assume she'd moved on without him. That frightened her. God hadn't been interested in bringing good men into her life. She had hoped this time would be different.

But the lure of seeing Petrov wrecked and ruined was powerful. She would have to leave a note for Al explaining the need for Paris. He would understand. The desk in the suite had note paper. She took her time writing, careful with every nuance in the English language. She ended the note with: *If I never see you again, know that I love you deeply and wish you a remarkable and joyful life.* She meant it too, every word.

She took the envelope down to the concierge to address it in Italian to be safe. She gave him fifty euros and another fifty for the messenger to take it to the abbey. She doubted they would give him the note until he was done with his ascetic retreat. Privately, she hoped a vision of their life together would strike him.

§

Brandt thought "Paris" could be the only word in a song. Pop, country, rap, or opera. It didn't matter. The effect was the same. Just the name released an ardent mood powerful enough to threaten celibacy. But with nuclear weapons in the hands of Petrov, it wasn't the city he had come to love. The lights seemed dimmer, the traffic worse, and the gaiety didn't seem to fit with specter of mass death.

The team landed at Orly airport in the European Director's Citation jet. Tig had escorted Lena to London—an extra precaution with Moky on the loose. They were met by a parade of black SUVs: embassy American Yukons and French Peugeot 508s. Standing on the tarmac waiting for them to exit the plane was Colonel Emile Firnacourte, the head of the Direction Générale de la Sécurité Intérieure (DGSI), and his aide, Axel.

"*Bonjour*, Deke. Welcome to Paris," Emile said. "The president is most grateful for your help. He's anxious to meet with everyone."

Deke made the introductions.

"We'll take you to your hotel after a stop in our headquarters operations center," Emile said.

"Levallois-Perret is outside Paris? Don't you think we should be in the city?" Deke said.

"I agree. We're arranging a secure place in Les Invalides. It should be ready in the morning."

Deke looked at Brandt.

"Should be good," Brandt said. "Ten-minute walk from the Montreux across the Invalides Bridge."

"I see you're familiar with Paris," Emile said to Brandt.

"Comes from getting lost a lot."

Emile brought them to the eighteenth-century villa that served as DGSI headquarters and directly into a large room with a parquet floor that was once the Grand Estate ballroom. The ceiling was painted with angels with trumpets floating on clouds. The ivory walls had the shadowy outlines of mirrors or paintings that had been removed. Ghostly reminders of a more opulent age. Staff members sat in cubicles at two ends. The area in the middle contained large tables with three-dimensional models of Paris neighborhoods. Axel offered them coffee, tea, or champagne while they looked over the displays. Lena and Casey chose champagne, Brandt and Tig coffee. Deke passed.

When Axel left to get the champagne, Emile started the briefing. "The only reference we have of the Leipzig Authority is the information you sent on Otto Brumfelt. Nothing on Petrov. We wonder why he chose Paris. There must be other targets. Brussels or London seem more obvious."

"Operation Seduction, that was the headline in *Le Monde*," Lena said. "Petrov had it taped to his bathroom mirror. It had nothing to do with sex. The Petrovs were incensed over Gorbachev's yielding to Mitterrand on arms control. They believed the meeting led to the downfall of Russia. It all began in Paris, according to them."

"I see," Emile said. "A sick mind. As far as Nazis in Paris, they don't survive here. We have long memories. A few ex-KGB are around. They brought gold and money with them and are enjoying an excellent carefree life in France. Occasionally they even help us out with sticky problems involving Russia."

"So Petrov can't expect help here," Deke said. "That's a plus."

"I only wish that was true," Emile said. "France may have the worst terrorist problem in Europe. There are any number of groups with members willing to sacrifice their lives to destroy Paris. I sent the current report on those groups to your Station Chief this morning. Wild Bill has been here a long time. He'll understand."

Deke let out a small laugh. "I hope he reads it."

"Stopping Petrov is our top priority. The president assured me I can have anything I ask for. We're searching Bastille today. Everyone tries to hide there. No one asks questions."

"And the terror cells?"

"That's trickier." Emile moved to the largest table. "There are six Muslim neighborhoods in Paris." He began pointing to areas on the models. "These four are happy to help us with any investigation. These two in the Chapelle-Pajol district, overlapping the tenth through eighteenth arrondissements, have more militant residents, mostly the youth. You in America call them 'no- go zones.' We send the Foreign Legion in when we want to search. It's just for show. We haul out a dozen or so suspects for questioning. Some of those are informants. It's our way of gathering information and keeping them safe. We sent the Legion in as soon as Deke told us about Petrov. Nothing productive so far."

"No Petrov means we're left guessing," Casey said.

Emile frowned. "That's what I said to the president."

§

Brandt's contact at the Hotel Montreux was unable to get them suites or a view of the Champs-Élysées below. Brandt did use his connection to get three rooms at half off the nine-hundred-euro rate. A tall, dark-haired receptionist came from behind her table and handed out the electronic keys with a flight attendant smile. Tig and Deke would share. The staff had their bags waiting for them in the rooms. Brandt was lying on the bed playing solitaire on his phone when Deke knocked. Casey let him in and returned to unpacking her cosmetics.

"The French are taking this serious," Deke said.

"Wouldn't you?"

"Emile usually blows us off." Deke walked around the room as if he was looking for a door to a bedroom. "The suites we had last time came with a cool bar and stools. You do something to piss them off?"

"They weren't willing to tell the Windsors it was time to leave."

"Shame. Those were nice."

Casey finished unpacking and sat on the edge of the bed. "Emile didn't seem confident about finding Petrov."

"Can't blame him. Big city. Huge ethnic population. One small Russian. Terrorists have been caught here with as many as twelve false IDs. Emile'll need luck," Deke said.

"How did Petrov get here anyway? I thought we were on his ass from Kitzbühel to Bariloche?" Brandt said.

Deke started to rest a butt cheek on a spindly antique white writing desk with gold fleur-de- lis insets on the legs. Casey winced, and he stopped in time. "Langley thinks they know now. He stayed in Italy after the barge pulled out. Bariloche was just a safe place to store the rest. The Riformatori helped him back to Lake Como. I had Milan send some floaters to watch the villa after we left. They reported comings and goings, mostly ex-priests, monks, staff. The only thing that stuck out was a panel truck that came late one night. They couldn't see much, but the license plate had the Swiss flag shield in one corner and the last two numbers were 44. It stayed two hours before driving off."

Casey had a knowing look. "There's room for two SADMs in a panel truck."

"I think we should get Lena to join us," Brandt said. "She knows Petrov better than any of us."

Casey sent her a text. "She's been trying to call Al since we got off the plane. She's hoping to hear from him."

Lena arrived with her phone in hand. The first thing she said was, "The French won't find Petrov. And you don't have the man power. Our only hope is to stop him once he sets his plan in motion."

"Any ideas?" Casey said.

"I know how he likes to analyze problems and solutions. With the Twelfth Directorate, he gave classes on targeting. That's where we need to start."

"If he's looking for a big splash, he's got either the Eiffel, Notre Dame, or the Louvre," Deke said.

Brandt sat up in the bed. "I doubt it. The Eiffel has too much security and too much thick steel. Too big a job for SADMs. Even a three-kiloton nuke would just pretzel the base. As for Notre Dame, it's an icon but still only a badly damaged church. A meaningless target to Petrov."

"While those targets are dramatic, I believe Petrov is more ambitious," Lena said. "He wants to cripple France. It has to be bigger."

"The fallout could be catastrophic," Casey said.

"Devastating, deaths in the tens of thousands in the neighborhoods close to ground zero. But not city wide, no Hiroshima or Nagasaki," Brandt said.

"What could be bigger?" Deke said.

"Something that hits France like 9/11. Something that wounds the nation's very soul," Brandt said.

"Langley has a program that will show the effect of a nuclear blast in an area for various size weapons," Casey said.

"It's part of the SALT agreement," Lena said. "The Twelfth Directorate has the same one, Petrov would be familiar with it."

"I'll load the program, but Brandt's the one to do this. He's the expert on Paris and nukes." Casey opened the laptop on the writing table.

Deke answered a text. "Wild Bill is coming up. He wants to take us to a new restaurant."

"Good," Brandt said. "He might have some ideas."

Wild Bill Medson could pass for an NFL lineman—girthy gut, shoulders that challenged doorways, and fingers too thick for a standard keyboard. "You and Emile figure everything out?" he said.

Deke responded, "You know better. Anything in the reports Emile sent to you help?"

"Nothing new. I think we have the same informants. They're all blowing smoke up our asses."

Brandt sat down and opened the program. "You know France better than any of us. Where would you use the nukes?"

"How big are they?"

"Probably three kilotons."

"Depends on your goal. I'd look at Brest. They keep three of their four nuclear subs tied up in port. Country's too broke to put more than one out to sea at a time. It's a joke here. They have more nukes than anyone but the US and Russia and only one sub out there to deliver them."

"Something less military?"

Bill paused in thought before answering, "If it were me, I'd try to isolate France. Put one at De Gaulle airport and one in the channel tunnel. Choke their commerce and cut them off from the world. Just like 9/11 did to us."

"Less strategic. Something symbolic that tears at the French psyche like the Twin Towers did," Brandt said.

"Stick with the first arrondissement then. The heart and soul of France. Quite a bit there for tourists and Parisians. Look at damage estimates and fallout zones. Placement will be the key."

Brandt was getting hungry. "Where's the restaurant?"

"By the opera house. We should leave. I have an embassy limo waiting."

"Go ahead," Brandt said. "I'll catch a cab and meet you after I look at a few things."

"Here's the name." Bill handed him a card with the name in French. "It's on boulevard des Capucines."

After they left, Brandt displayed a professional guide's map of Paris on the screen. All the important tourist sites with their visiting hours, ticket costs, walking distances, taxi stands, and metro and bus stops were in front of him. Bill was right—placement was the key. The right spot could even cross over to the Left Bank. The Pentagon targeting map enabled him to place the detonation of each SADM anywhere he chose. The casualties from blast radiation and the amount of destruction were estimated, and by entering wind speed and direction, a fallout map created. A three-kiloton detonation at the Arc de Triomphe could kill thirty-eight thousand and injure ninety; Notre Dame, thirty-one and eighty-two; the Place de la Concorde, forty-two thousand dead and ninety-eight thousand injured.

For the next two hours, Brandt forgot his hunger and tried to be Petrov. The problem was that central Paris had too many targets. A five- or ten-megaton missile warhead could destroy all of Paris. Three kilotons had limits. Casey called to ask if he was still coming to dinner. He answered no and asked if she could pick up pizza from Del Popolo on rue de Rivoli for him.

He was approaching the third hour. The team was not back yet, and his eyes were getting tired from looking at color-coded blast, fallout, and casualty diagrams. He had assumed Petrov would try to take out two targets and deploy each SADM independently. But what if he placed them in proximity to each other? What would that do? He tried several methods: overlapping blast areas meant lower casualties. Too much separation had the same results. But when the blast radiuses just touched, casualties and damage shot up as if multiplied. By the time everyone was back from dinner with his pizza, he'd found the best spot to set off a pair of three-kiloton SADMs.

"I know where I would detonate them. I just don't know if Petrov will come to the same conclusion."

"Show us," Lena said.

Brandt folded a piece of cheese pizza and began stuffing it in his mouth. He moved the cursor as he chewed and swallowed, then stuck a digital pin on the screen map along the Promenade de Champs-Élysées, across the garden from the president's Élysée Palace residence. "Here's number one." Then he moved the cursor straight down the path and through Tuileries Garden. "The second is by the Place du Carrousel."

"Outside the Louvre entrance?" Casey said. "Why not by the pyramid?"

Lena was quicker with an answer. "Because the buildings that surround it on three sides would absorb too much of the blast."

"Exactly," Brandt said. "The open areas help the blast cross the river to the Left Bank."

"They will certainly take out the heart of Paris," Bill said. "Besides Champs-Élysées glitz, the president's crib, the US embassy, the National Assembly, more museums, monuments, historic bridges, and two more palaces . . . finish off Notre Dame too."

Brandt grimaced. "Nothing left but radioactive rubble, and like the Eiffel, a radiation kill zone. Arc de Triomphe is probably too old to survive."

"Fallout?" Deke asked.

"Caesium-137 has a half-life of thirty years, so the first arrondissement will be a deadly exclusion zone for nearly fifty years," Lena said. "The rest depends on the wind and direction. A fifteen mph wind means extensive fallout in the suburbs and countryside. Could eventually reach England."

"What are the casualty figures?" Casey asked.

Brandt hit some keys on the laptop. "A hundred thousand dead in the blasts. Over two hundred thousand injured."

"A good many of those will eventually die too," Lena said.

Brandt settled back in his chair and looked directly at Lena. "Since Petrov had access to the same program, what are the odds he picks the same locations?"

"He knows it all—targeting design, the enhanced effect of two in proximity is greater than the sum of the parts. He led seminars in quantum damage, casualty acceleration, RAD absorption, and fallout drift. Your points might not be exact, but they're close enough."

"Bill's right. We stick to the first," Brandt said. "The right bank."

§

It was barely dawn when Deke answered a call from the Paris CIA tech surveillance room. "Bill said to call you if we see the Russians moving. They split up. One team headed for Bastille, the other Montmartre."

"Thanks. Any voice or text traffic to report?" asked Deke.

"Some personal traffic. Mostly in Tajik. The translator says it could be code in case we're listening. We're trying to use the GyrFalcon program to track them."

Locking on to Moky's phone was a combination of tradecraft and luck. Deke expected they would dump the phones and go to backups soon. Too bad. The Bastille team was obvious. Montmartre, less so. Tourist tacky and no place for a Russian fugitive to hide. Maybe Gleb was checking out the nightlife and hookers.

A text from Emile came next, short and full of misspellings and typos, but it was clear they were headed for Versailles today.

37

Bill sent an embassy Yukon to take them all to Louis XIV's country palace. The early morning traffic was stalled on the Pont de Saint-Cloud, and it took more than an hour to reach Versailles. The Main Gate, Sailors' Gate, and Saint Anthony's Gate were closed and guarded by gendarmes. Axel was waiting for them at the Queen's Gate and helped them past a larger security force that included Legionnaires and French Intelligence Special Ops.

"The news media is going crazy over closing Versailles today. The interior minister is preparing a statement," Axel said.

"What will he say?" Deke asked.

"Natural gas leak. They hope to have it located and fixed by the end of the day."

"Where's the truck?" Casey asked.

"Down by the delivery bays, parked along a fence."

"You sure it's Petrov's?"

"Swiss plates ending in 44."

"How did it get in? The gates are locked and guarded at night," Brandt said.

"Came in yesterday. They claimed to be making a delivery and talked their way in, but instead of joining the queue, they drove around before parking it and leaving."

"Cameras?" Deke said.

"Emile is reviewing them now. I'll take you to him."

"Take us to the truck first."

Deke circled the truck as if looking to buy it while Brandt examined the interior. Plenty of room for two SADMs. Tig copied the VIN number and sent it to Langley. The canine unit arrived, and the dogs began sniffing around and inside the truck. After the inspection, Axel took them into the palace. The security force took up three back rooms on the first floor, separated from the royal apartments and the visitor area by a permanent wood partition. Emile was in the surveillance room going over the CCTV tapes of the previous day with the security commander.

"Anything helpful?" Deke asked.

"I'm afraid it's more than I feared. We see them entering Queen's Gate. Two men inside. But they didn't go directly to the delivery bays. That's the part that has the minister panicking. They drove around on the service roads for hours. The van was able to duck out of camera view by pulling into the bosquets where the trees and tall shrubs hid them. We're searching those areas first."

"Didn't any of the workers or security notice them?" Casey asked.

"My men are questioning everyone. But you have to understand, the garden has many vendors and contract workers here every day. Delivery vans, flatbeds, and pickup trucks would not be out of place."

Deke looked disappointed. "Let's see what you have."

The men in the truck made no attempt to hide from the camera. Deke had the operator skip ahead to when they parked the truck and left. After leaving it, they joined a tourist group walking to the exit.

"We have good pictures of them and should be able to ID them soon," Emile said. "We have over a hundred men searching the grounds. Fifteen of my men are questioning employees."

Tig took a call. "The van was rented in Lugano, Switzerland. Langley is trying to get the camera feed."

"Is there a place we can get coffee?" Brandt asked.

"The café. Limited service while the staff is being questioned, but I'm sure they have coffee ready."

The café was down an Italian marble floor with a private entrance for security. A waiter quickly brought cups and a carafe of American coffee. Deke skipped the coffee and asked for tea.

"Lugano is just across the border from Lake Como," Brandt said. "From there, they could drive back to Menaggio in less than an hour, take the ferry across the lake to the villa, and pick up the weapons,"

"I don't get it. Why Versailles? They could have dumped the truck anywhere," Tig said.

"I'm thinking the same thing," Casey said. "Maybe Petrov was doing a test. See if he could get a truck in without a search."

"Then he succeeded," Tig said.

"But why that specific truck?" Brandt said. "He could have used any truck. And why leave it? We're missing something."

Axel came in from the kitchen with a basket of French pastries. "Axel, your men ID'd the truck from the Swiss plate information we gave DGSI. What would have happened if it had a different plate?" Brandt asked.

"I imagine security would tow it away and try to contact the owner. Cars left overnight in the visitor parking area are taken to a gendarme storage area."

"Then the palace would have opened as usual," Casey said.

"I believe so."

Emile joined them. "We have the names of the two from the truck. Islamic terrorists from Molenbeek, a no-go zone in Brussels."

"Brussels! Jeezus. NATO and the EU," Deke said.

"We'll have to warn Sturm," Casey said.

Deke looked down and nodded.

"Then Paris is safe?" Emile couldn't hide the hope in his voice.

"I'm afraid not. It's classic Petrov," Lena said. "He found out what he needed to know."

Brandt nodded in silence. Lena was ahead of them, but he was catching up. "Used some KGB-style misdirection too."

"I don't understand," Emile said.

Lena spoke with confidence. "Petrov knows we were close to him in Kitzbühel and Florence. He didn't know if we were looking for him here. That could alter his plans. If we knew about the truck, we probably knew he was here with the SADMs. How the French reacted to the truck was what he was looking for. If the truck was just towed away, he was safe. Closing Versailles told him we know he's here. Probably with two nukes."

"We had no choice. We had to close the palace," Emile said.

"Petrov knew you would have to. Any other truck wouldn't have worked. He'll change his location now and speed up his plans," Lena said. "Brandt figured out the rest."

Brandt said, "He expected the two from the truck would be ID'd. Now that he knows we're on his ass, he's hoping to send us to Brussels."

§

Al continued to have faith he would be guided to the right path. But what distressed him was the way the answers flipped over the course of the day. Each morning, he awoke believing his path was clear, blessed by God. When he left the chapel after evening Compline, the direction had changed again, as if the forces of heaven were toying with him. "Two roads diverged in a yellow wood." Robert Frost's poetic words. Frost chose the road less traveled. Al envied Frost's clarity.

The abbot had turned Al's counseling duties over to Monsignor Trevelli, a gentle man with a permanent warm smile that gave him an aura of having one foot in heaven. The last session with him struck Al in a different way. Trevelli told him, "Life is meant to be uncertain. A daily challenge for laypeople. Living in a monastery shields us from much of life's problems, but monks aren't exempt from difficult choices. God is more creative than that. He brought you to this point in your life for a reason. Look at that in your prayers."

What he learned was that he didn't know the right path: *Life was uncertain.* Not knowing would always be a part of it. Faith was what was needed. Like Frost, he would only know the right road long after walking it.

§

A convoy of SUVs and military vehicles from Versailles pulled into the Court of Honor in front of Musée de l'Armée, the military museum and the largest building in the Les Invalides complex. Emile and Alex waved everyone through security and then climbed stairs to the third floor. Technicians were still working on the computer, flat-screen, and communication installation. Brandt thought the room had been converted from attic storage. Long, cold, dusty, and dark, much

like a Paris catacomb. The floors, of an indeterminate wood, had the
character that only time and soldiers' footsteps could create. Probably
late eighteenth century for Napoleon's dragoons and cuirassiers. A team
of maintenance workers cleaned windows, briefly eliminating some of
the room's dinge until the security shades were installed.

Emile, his face folded in disappointment, made a brief announce-
ment. "The president has authorized drone surveillance in Paris for
the first time. One of your army's Predators. It will be stationed above
the first arrondissement and flown by our pilots in the flight control
center next door."

"Just one?" Brandt asked.

"That's right. If the press gets word, he'll be crucified."

"You need at least two more," Deke said. "Surveilling the no-go
zones are our best chance to find Petrov before he can blow the city up."

Emile looked away. "I'm afraid one is all the president will accept.
Because of all the yellow vest demonstrations, our camera coverage
of the first has been extended. Streets, sidewalks, parks, metro stops,
and tunnels all have surveillance. He believes that should be enough."

Brandt's voice turned gruff. "What happened to 'anything you
want'?"

"Does he know the risk he's taking?" Casey said.

"I tried." Emile looked embarrassed. "I sent my family to stay
with relatives in Strasbourg."

Deke moved to sarcasm. "So it's just one? Paris isn't that important, I guess. Well, maybe we'll get lucky and Moky and Gleb will
find Petrov in time before Paris is in ashes."

"Moky brings up a tricky question," Casey said. "Without the
Russians, we wouldn't even be here. Maybe we should be sharing intel
with him. He might have a lead on Petrov we don't have?"

"I think we have him covered," Deke said. "Bill has the tech guys using digital voodoo on them. They can't take a leak without us knowing."

Emile looked at his watch. "Lunch will be brought in at twelve. We have time to walk over and look at the target area while they finish up here."

"I have some things to check. I'll stay," Lena said. She switched on a table lamp in a dusty corner of the room and opened her laptop.

Emile escorted everyone else across Pont Alexandre to the Champs-Élysées quarter under a layer of smog and patchy clouds. They turned left down the famous avenue, past the Montreux, and under the neatly trimmed horse chestnut trees. Brandt didn't believe people actually shopped on the Champs-Élysées—the famous-name storefronts seemed more like an advertising billboard. When they reached the traffic circle, they crossed to the other side and walked up to the arched entrance to the palace grounds. Ceremonial guards flanked the iron gate, but a permanent security detail in battle dress was visible in the courtyard. An armored car was parked on the Avenue de Marigny next to the palace garden.

"We plan to flood this area with Legionnaires, gendarmes, and DGSI plainclothes for the day of attack," Emile said.

"Petrov would have a tough time putting anything this close to the palace," Deke said.

"You said, 'day of the attack.' How do you know that? Casting runes in Élysée Palace?" Brandt said.

Emile gave an agreeable laugh. "That's for the Swedes. We French have a different history. We take our assumptions and pretend they're unshakable fact. The General Staff and ministers believe we have a month. Bastille Day, that's the day of the attack, when Paris presents the optimal target for Petrov. We have to capture him before the fourteenth of July."

"Has Macron considered cancelling the celebration if Petrov hasn't been caught?" Casey asked.

"A difficult decision for the president. A cancellation would be a huge blow to a country that uses pride to cover its flaws. But the reality is that too many French lives would be lost. His staff is trying to develop a way to cancel that would lessen the impact."

They entered the Grand Ailee of Tuileries Garden that led toward the Louvre. Parisians had started to occupy the chairs surrounding the Basin Octagonal. A breeze from the east created a gentle ripple on the basin pool. Women smoked with their feet resting on the basin ledge and raised skirts to tan their legs. Men in scarves read papers and peeked at the women. Short lines formed at the food trucks selling baguette sandwiches, croissants, drinks, and treats for children.

Brandt recalled the Medicis had had a hand in Tuileries' birth. They seemed to have had a finger, hand, or arm in everything in Europe in those days. Marriages were like NATO treaties—strategic and loveless. Catherine de' Medici's wedding to Henry II had been no different. The accidental death of her husband set in motion the creation of an Italian Renaissance garden that became Tuileries.

Emile said, "Good weather or bad, this area will be crowded on Bastille Day. The French love pageantry, and the parade is the biggest of the year. If we have to cancel, the metros and streets will be blocked off as if the yellow vests were coming to protest. There's nothing we can do about the local residents and visitors staying here short of a total evacuation."

"Petrov is a visitor," Deke said.

"We're checking the hotels for Petrov. Airbnbs and Bastille rooms are not as cooperative."

They reached Place du Carrousel and looked up toward the Louvre and back toward Concorde.

"Did any of you see some good places to stick a SADM?" Brandt asked.

Emile looked around again before wagging his head no.

Casey shrugged. "Good question. How does he hide them?"

§

Lena stayed in her dusty corner while the flat-screens were being connected to the city's CCTV cameras. They would fizzle and pop when the operator switched scenes. Technicians were trying to connect one large screen to a drone feed without success. She understood their French curses. The email from Al she was hoping to read hadn't arrived. To calm her anxiety, she pivoted her thoughts to Petrov and the weapons. Brandt had done excellent work on the targeting question. She agreed with his choices. That left the other big question—*When?* She was hoping Emile would be able to answer that one. The French would assume Bastille Day the perfect choice, but it was over a month away. She knew Petrov wouldn't risk waiting that long.

Casey waved hello when Emile brought the team back to a crowded room of lunch caterers and installers still working on the drone screen. Emile was upset about how long it was taking and threatened the men with transfers to the French Djibouti garrison if they didn't get everything finished ASAP.

Casey walked up to Lena. "The French think it's Bastille Day. You know Petrov. What do you think?"

"He'll never wait that long. Especially now that he knows we're looking for him."

"How soon then?"

"If he has the help he needs, he could do it any time. Tomorrow. A week. The French are right about this, though. He'll want a day that has special meaning. Other than the large crowds, Bastille won't work. It has to be special to *him*."

"You know him better than any of us. Try to figure out when."

France was like Italy when it came to honoring special days. Religious and government holidays coupled with public strikes created mini-vacations. In Russia, vodka determined those. Lena decided to skip the list of French holidays and go to the Russian calendar. Fewer and less Catholic, but with the May Day celebration past, nothing stuck out. Birthdays were important—when was Petrov's? It took her ten seconds to come up with February 21. A dead end. Petrov had always ignored hers, so that was even less likely.

A bank of espresso machines, coffee makers, teapots, and porcelain cups with a French flag imprint had been set on a shiny metal table. She walked over and dialed a bold espresso into a machine. Petrov never drank it. He complained it kept him awake, but his father scoffed at sleep as a waste of time and savored espresso all day.

A thought struck Lena like a club to the head. Maybe Petrov's father was important. Their relationship had been unique and intense. Petrov hated his mother, who lived for vodka, but worshipped his father. Together they'd mourned the end of the Soviet Empire and plotted its rebirth. She rushed back to her laptop to search his life and obituary. Igor Petrov was born March 16 and died June 10. That was easy. June 10 was the day Petrov planned to blow up Paris in his father's honor. It was less than twenty-four hours away. She grabbed Casey's attention with an excited wave.

"You find something?" Casey said.

"It's tomorrow, June 10. That's when he plans to destroy Paris."

"How did you come up with that?"

"It's the anniversary of his father's death. The only day each year Petrov would get drunk."

"You sure?"

Lena nodded without a word.

"We need to tell the others."

Brandt, Deke, and Emile were in front of the big screen, waiting for the techs to finish with the drone camera. Emile stood watching like a prison guard.

"We have only hours," Casey said. "Lena figured it out. Tomorrow is Petrov's Nuke Paris Day."

"Why tomorrow?" Deke asked.

"It's the anniversary of his father's death. Paris will no longer be Paris after that."

Emile's jaw hung loose.

"We're fucked. It's Whitmonday. Pentecost," Axel said. "The Seine boats . . . the gardens . . . the Eiffel . . . they are always popular on spring holidays. Tuileries will be filled with families having picnics."

"The six churches in the first will be full for Pentecost services. Louvre will have long lines," Emile said. "I'll tell the president we have to evacuate."

Brandt looked at Deke. "Too late for that."

38

E mile brought Deke along to an early evening meeting with the president and General Staff. The president entered the room dressed in a white tuxedo shirt with a red diplomatic sash angled down from his shoulder to his waist. The generals were in dress blue uniforms bordered in red, with chests full of medals even they couldn't explain.

President Macron opened the meeting. "Emile has reported he believes we have only hours to find Petrov or evacuate. While I'd like to believe we could accomplish an evacuation, I don't believe it is possible with so little time." His mood turned brackish. "I'm charging this group to find Petrov or find a solution. France is counting on you. Do your job. Save Paris." Macron moved to leave, and they all stood.

Deke listened to the staff debate and only spoke when he was specifically addressed. The brass stuck to Bastille being the target. The same plodding thinking that believed the Maginot Line would stop Hitler. They came to a consensus that an evacuation was the best idea but impossible with so little time. Transport would be overtaxed and as many people would be coming into the first arrondissement to help relatives, protect businesses, and gather belongings as would be leaving. Panic and clogged transport would be impossible to avoid. Deke agreed. The only thing worse than a French clusterfuck was a Greek protest. The Legionnaire garrison commander asked Deke what the Americans were planning to do.

"The embassy will be closed and the State Department will issue a red alert terror travel warning and suspend Paris-bound flights. Those living in the first, sixth, and seventh will either stay with friends or be flown to London early tomorrow. Staff living outside will be given the London option or encouraged to stay indoors. The rest of us will be huddled in the underground communication center."

After three hours of analysis and planning, an adjutant was writing up the official report for the president. The General Staff concluded Bastille was still the most likely target, but the risk to Whitmonday couldn't be ignored. The document outlined the broad strokes for the various staffs to use for guidance. A warning of a possible terror attack in the First would be released without mentioning the SADMs. Leaves and vacations would be cancelled. Legionnaires, special ops commandos, and gendarmes trained in counter-terror would flood the area. The Minister of Health would quietly prepare for nuclear casualties. Emile could have two more drones to search the no-go zones, and Macron would leave for his home in Tours after the evening reception.

39

Silvery mist rose from the Seine on the cold, damp early morning of June 10. The faint cabin lights of the tour boats and batobus moored along the *quai* emitted a pious quality, as if humble candles in a church. Brandt and Casey knew the Whitmonday holiday would be different. Pentecostal prayers in the cathedrals would be needed. Forget the City of Light—it was now the city of dark shadows and murky lanes threatened by a perverse and punitive Petrov. In the predawn hours, extra security had already been deployed. Brandt and Casey were stopped by two Legionnaires under a streetlamp along the Seine walkway and asked for identification. NATO documents earned them, "*Bonne journée.*"

"I watched the security film of last year's Whitmonday with Deke," Casey said. "A rainy day, and the area was *still* crowded. The lines at the Louvre were hours long. Maybe the terror alert will thin the crowds."

"Don't count on it," Brandt said. "The French issue terror alerts like parking tickets. Fourteen already this year. No one pays attention to them anymore."

Two prostitutes leaned against the stone half-wall with a leg propped to expose a thigh and a thin smile. They giggled to each other as Brandt and Casey passed by.

"Legionnaires' disease," Brandt said. "With Uber, working girls are very mobile."

They continued at a slow pace up to Pont du Carrousel. From the middle of the bridge, they could see the shadowy outline of the bell towers of roofless Notre Dame in the morning gray light. "Something my sister said to me when I told her I was coming here has stuck with me. She said she was glad I was going and able to take a small step toward committing to something."

"Was she screaming at you then?"

"Down to a screech and a howl."

"What do you think she meant by that?"

"I think she was referring to how Anne struggled with me at times. I never really wanted to join the army. But she convinced me the travel would be fun and there weren't any real wars then."

"That was the time you hooked up with Deke in Germany after college."

"Yeah, that worked out great. She got me to commit. I don't think I ever gave her enough credit." Brandt thought of the list he'd made while Anne was in hospice. Things he wanted to tell her, things he wanted to thank her for, things he'd said or done that he was sorry for too. Giving her credit for pushing him at times was also on that list.

They watched a tug pull a barge underneath the bridge before continuing to the Louvre. The first rays of sunlight mirrored off the glass and metal pyramid above the museum entrance.

"I'm afraid a lot of that glass could be flying around today," Casey said.

"The local guides love to mention all the size and dimension statistics. All I remember is there are over six hundred glass segments."

"The travel business was also her idea, wasn't it?"

"Yeah. I hemmed and hawed about that one too."

"Are you seeing a pattern here?"

"You sound like my sister."

"Answer the question."

"Yeah, I do. Elaine told me this back-and-forth between the CIA and painting was a symptom of something deeper. She's right. It's the commitment thing."

"Are you ready to commit to one now?"

"Yes and no."

"You are totally fucking hopeless."

"It's not what you think. I never know when to look back for direction or when to look ahead. Sometimes it feels like I'm stuck in a whatever-was-whatever-will-be place. Just a top spinning in a cosmic circle. Yet when I let go and relax, I remember I was the happiest going to work when we owned the travel business."

"But you sold that after she died?"

"Yeah, I did. I had to. Anne was like a ghost there." He remembered hearing her talking to him from her empty desk. He'd turn around to say something, expecting her to be sitting there, and be hit with a wave of grief. "Maybe I'm past that now."

"I think I see where this is going. A London travel business."

"When I saw *Swindon Travel Adventures* on the side of the SUV in Brussels, I felt my soul stir."

"So CIA and art were never that important."

"Hmph. I guess not. I just didn't see it."

Casey laughed so loud she turned heads. "You know. Elaine is right. You really can be a dick."

Emile and Deke waved to join them as they neared the Place du Concorde entrance to Tuileries. Emile looked as if sleep was no longer part of his life. Unshaven, his eyes circled in red, his clothes rumpled, an apocalyptic fear spreading down from his forehead to his chin. A Michelin two-star food truck pulled onto the open area near the garden entrance, and the occupants began opening service windows and spreading an awning. A colorful second truck offering Italian pastries, espresso, pizza, and calzones parked in its designated spot.

"The SDAT is searching all the food trucks and concession trailers," Emile said.

"How many food trucks will be here today?" Casey asked.

"On a holiday like today? Could be as many as twenty spread from the Place du Carrousel to avenue Matignon. Unlicensed vendors trying to take advantage of the crowds will be turned away. Delivery trucks will have special ops with them until they leave the arrondissement."

Military personnel vans and trucks offloaded troops and gendarmes in Place du Concorde. Officers sent them on assignments toward Élysée Palace and the Louvre.

"We're hoping the military and police presence is large enough to scare Petrov off," Emile said, but he didn't look confident. "The men have stop-and-search authorization. Special event traffic laws are in effect. Anyone who tries to evade the barricades will become target practice."

"However it ends, it's a sad day for Paris and France," Casey said.

Warmer temperatures and bright blue sky promised to fill the area with Parisians. Deke shaded his eyes and looked up. "Can either of you see the Predator?"

"Too high," Brandt said.

"We were hoping to get the CIA version instead of the military. I've been told it can count the hairs on your chin."

"I always thought it should be called Voyeur instead of Predator," Brandt said.

Deke failed to laugh. "I guess it's time to head to the embassy." He met Emile's eyes and spoke in a slow, weighty voice, as if they were soldiers under attack and about to run out of ammunition. "After this is over, I hope we can have dinner together tonight."

Emile forced a Parisian smile, part honor, part warmth, part deception. "I'll make the reservations. I know a place even Michelin hasn't found."

"Axel?" Brandt asked.

Emile looked wounded. "I told him to stay home today. I wouldn't be needing him. And on such a gorgeous day, I want to enjoy a walk across Pont Alexandre one more time."

§

Wild Bill, Tig, and Lena met them at the embassy entrance. A bus was leaving for the evac plane without her. Marine guards were covering ground-floor windows with metal plates and stacking sandbags at weak points.

"I'll bring these guys and the roof snipers inside soon," Bill said. "I plan to have this place locked up tight and everyone in the command room or bomb shelter by nine thirty. The French are moving one of their Renault six-wheeled tanks here and one at the palace."

They followed two marines to the basement and down a long corridor. Four marines with a sense of urgency were rolling racks with M4 carbines and shotguns out of an armory and lining them up against the wall for quick access. The command room was a scaled-down copy of Langley's Europe ops center. Three very large high-def flat-screens, ten smaller sized, and nine operators stationed theater-style. Behind them, two communications specialists in front of a control panel and, below, an elevated position for the officer in charge.

"We've had twenty-four-seven satellite coverage of the First since you guys arrived. The drone link is in the center, the satellite pictures on each side," Bill said. He pointed his head to the right. "We brought in extra chairs. Make yourself comfortable. Coffee and snacks in the hall. MREs if we get stuck down here. The embassy has some nuke radiation suits stashed somewhere. I've got the guys from protocol trying to hunt them down."

Tuileries was starting to build a crowd. Early picnickers were securing the best spots.

"What are we looking for?" Casey asked.

"A small Russian with a large backpack," Deke said.

"You guys probably won't notice anything," Bill said, "but my people are trained to pick up danger signs . . . a furtive look, a nervous walk, a vehicle that slows or stops in a strange place. Anything out of the ordinary pretending to be ordinary."

"What about the Russians? What's Moky up to?" Casey asked.

Bill hunched his shoulders to answer. "He sent two teams to nose around the no-go zones today. Then he went off on his own to meet with some ex-KGB living in Bobigny."

Casey turned to Deke. "That mean anything to us?"

Deke pushed his right hand against a spot on his stomach. Pain creased his face. "We think it was social. Looking for info on retiring here."

"Or defecting," Brandt said.

A yellow light flashed next to a brunette operator. The officer in charge walked down to talk to her and looked at a small screen on the wall with her. After a short discussion, he walked up to Bill and Deke and said, "Sandra is always the first to notice something strange. She's got the best instincts here. Picks up details the rest miss. She saw an ambulance parked in Concorde with the insignia of the 2nd Foreign Engineer Regiment. The legionnaires posted here are from the 1st Foreign Parachute Regiment. Probably nothing, but Emile is checking it out."

Food trucks were lined up to be inspected—Italian pasta and gelato, Spanish paella, Greek souvlaki, German bratwurst, and a wine-tasting van from Bordeaux. The drivers got out, lit cigarettes, and waited impatiently in the queue. A full-bearded man pedaling a bicycle ice cream cart tried to skirt around the column. A red light flashed on a control room desk. Four soldiers in camo fatigues rushed at him. He was quickly shoved to the ground and handcuffed. An officer came over to inspect the cart. Satisfied the cart only contained ice cream, the police put him into a van to wait out the day.

By late morning, the right bank became crowded from the Louvre to the Roosevelt Metro stop and overflowed to the Left Bank. Minor threats resulted in quick action by the security force, and a cautious calm began to spread through the embassy.

By midafternoon, Brandt was beginning to think Whitmonday was a false alarm. "Maybe we dodged a big nuclear bullet," he said.

"The French could be right about Bastille Day," Deke said.

Brandt shook his head as if to agree. "The extra time would be a blessing. I've been sitting here trying to think how I would try to sneak a SADM in here. Too big for a child's stroller or motorbikes . . . maybe a pedicab."

"I thought the ice cream peddler definitely had one," Casey said.

"I'd put them in the bratwurst trucks. Just another beer barrel," Tig said. "Have a beer, then blow up Paris."

"Jeezus," Deke said and met Brandt's stunned glare. He asked Bill, "How many German beer trucks are there?"

"Two. One outside the Louvre entrance and one by Élysée Palace."

"Call Emile," Brandt said.

A red light began to flash on the bottom of the drone screen.

"Emile is sending men to inspect the beer trucks," Deke said. "What's with the red light?"

"Damn drones," Bill said. "The Predator has identified a small one flying two hundred feet above Tuileries."

Brandt's eyes narrowed and the lines on his face turned grim. He grabbed Tig's arm. "Come with me."

Brandt raced to the weapons rack and grabbed an M4. Tig did the same, and they climbed up to the entrance. The doors were barred and locked. Tig used the butt of his M4 to free the bars, then Brandt shot the lock open. The courtyard was bathed in bright sun and it took ten seconds for their eyes to adjust.

"We have to shoot that small drone down. Petrov is using it to detonate the nukes," Brandt said.

They moved to a shaded stretch of lawn.

"You cover twelve to four. I'll take eight to twelve," Tig said.

Brandt switched his safety off and focused on the sky. Ravens and gulls confused and distracted the search. He saw a dark object flying toward the Louvre at treetop height. "There it is . . . two o'clock." He raised his weapon and fired.

Tig had selected full automatic and fired a short burst. Legionnaires ran to the embassy iron gate and pointed weapons at them but hesitated to shoot inside the embassy grounds. Brandt continued to fire, and Tig unloaded a second burst. The drone stopped in midair with a puff of smoke, then fell to the ground in pieces. The crowds scattered in a panic. Whitmonday was over.

Bill peeked from behind the door, then entered the courtyard with Deke and Casey close behind. "A drone? Should have guessed."

"Nice work for a floater," Deke said. "Paris will still be Paris."

"And you saved Macron's ass," Bill added.

"I'm pretty sure I missed. Blame Tig."

Deke finished talking to Emile on his phone. His face almost glowed with the news. "The Legion stormed both beer trucks. Some hand-to-hand was all the resistance. The SADMs had *Hofbrauhaus Maibock* stenciled on them."

40

L e Petit Chateau was an intimate restaurant in a creaky post-Renaissance home with a living room converted into an inviting dining area with three tables and a fireplace for ambience. The faint scent of past meals infused the walls with French culinary promise. To seat Emile and the Americans and Lena, the restaurant staff joined two large tables together. The owner, Alain, never printed a menu. The dining offerings changed daily with what ingredients he found appealing at the market each morning. The evening guests were invited into his kitchen to see what he'd prepared and make their choices. Alain then selected the appropriate wines, and his wife, Michele, served. The dessert menu was simple—one item, Michele's *mousse au chocolat*.

Emile offered a ceremonial toast, thanking the CIA for their help and success.

Brandt thought those were as rare as politicians refusing bribes. "How did you find this place?"

"Since Alain never advertised and his regular clients were part of the criminal world, we suspected a money laundering and tax-avoidance scheme We found no evidence of money laundering, and the food was too good to worry about tax avoidance."

Brandt folded his hands as if entering a cathedral. "I understand. Avoiding taxes is like a religion here."

"I bring Paris prosecutors here to make sure they leave him alone."

"The gangster types?"

"They love the food and the privacy."

Deke looked at his phone and excused himself, missing the lentil soup course.

"Macron wanted to join us, but I told him no. He and his staff don't need to know about Alain," Emile said.

Deke returned in time for his *coq au vin* and mousse. He waited to break the news from the call until they were back in the hotel. He was hunched over in an attempt to ease his stomach pain.

"You okay?" Casey asked.

"Just a little gas. Hated to miss the soup."

"What about the call?" Brandt said.

Deke sat down on the bed and sagged. "We're not cleared for home yet. I had two calls. The first was from Moky thanking us for finding their nukes for them. You can expect a congratulatory text. He was smug as hell. Hope he gets a nuke up his ass. State and NATO are making arrangements for the official return ceremony."

"All of them?" Tig asked.

"Yep. Putin agreed to destroy them. We demanded to be included. Anyone care to bet on how that will work?"

"A handful of liquored-up diplomats watching the Russians destroy oversized nesting dolls," Brandt said.

"The second call blew my drawers off. Petrov."

Lena was the most surprised. Her head jerked as if yanked by a rope.

Brandt copied Deke. "Jeezus!"

"What's he want?" Casey said.

"He wants to come in. He's screwed big time and knows it. Putin has put a five-million-euro reward on his head. Moky was in Bobigny to tell the expats about the money and get them to help find him. He can forget about any assistance from Leipzig Authority too."

Brandt credited Otto for the end of Leipzig. He must have realized that lie, squirm, and weasel was the wrong approach. He'd be dropping names and places as if they were radioactive.

"The money's been cut off," Deke said. "Berlin, Prague, Europol, and Interpol are rounding them up like a cattle drive. Without Leipzig funds, Petrov can't move."

"The Riformatori?" Casey said.

"No nukes, no help. He wants asylum, a new identity, a house, and a BMW."

"Why not let the Russians have him?" Tig said. "We got the nukes." There was a growing confidence in his voice. The Bariloche island mission had put him back in battle dress and the drone shooting back in action. Tig sounded like a soldier again.

Deke turned to Lena. "What can Petrov offer?"

She had been peeking out a curtained window at the wall of windows across a courtyard. "More than enough. Proof Putin had KGB and Stasi agents killed. His ties with the Mossad in Dresden would be treason to the old guard. He can't let any of that get out."

Deke stood up. "Langley and the White House would love to have Putin in front of a firing squad in Red Square."

"I dunno," Brandt said. "Doesn't seem right. Petrov was trying to kill thousands and we give him a 'Get out of jail free' card?" Over the course of the mission, a kaleidoscope picture of Petrov had formed in his mind. Caesar was vile and devious. Petrov cloned him. Napoleon had a messianic sense of mission in his DNA. So did Petrov. Attila had an army. Petrov had nukes. That made him infinitely more dangerous. Was it his father's influence or something in the Russian character that set him off? Cultured Western Europe had always looked down on Russia. They feared Peter the Great but made cruel jokes about Catherine, and it seeded a Slavic self-hatred in Russia. Was Petrov a result? Or was he attempting a cure? There was no question that Stalin would have smiled his approval.

Casey appeared defiant, her arms folded across her chest. "If Brandt didn't say it, I would have. He had eighty-two others to blow before we stopped him. He's as evil as they come."

"What does it say about us?" Tig said.

"I'm not saying it's right. It's realpolitik. Pragmatism and ratio-nalization for the greater good. Every country does it," Deke said.

"More Machiavelli," Brandt said.

"Diplomats again. There has to be a limit," Casey said.

"Just how much are we willing to rationalize?" Brandt said. Right now, he needed Al with them as much as Lena did. Al had the soul and background for this kind of discussion. There were at least a dozen quotes from famous philosophers, mystics, and saints he could draw upon.

Deke turned to Lena. "Jump in any time."

Lena took a regal pose. "Alive, Petrov is valuable. Death serves only justice."

Brandt let her words hang, quick and accurate but with a serrated edge to them. He admired Lena's ability to speak truth with an economy of words, scientific certainty, clarity, and emotional strength. Lena could do it all—Mensa physicist, warrior, fashion maven, and one-time playgirl who regretfully slept with Moky. She had more facets than a polygon.

"There's no sense debating this," Deke said. "It's not our call anyway. Langley said they'd get back to me."

§

Deke was sitting with Wild Bill in his embassy office when Langley called. Lena and Casey sat on the sofa drinking tea, listening to Langley's decision. Brandt and Tig were on their way up from the basement Command Center. The instructions were clear. A team from the Russia desk was coming to interrogate Petrov in London. Get him on an agency plane as soon as you can.

Brandt and Tig joined them in time to hear Petrov's call.

He sounded as brazen as a dot-com billionaire. Asylum for him was going to be another run at keeping the game going. "Have Lena stand by the Point de Rencontre sculpture in Châtelet Station at six p.m. today. Just her," he said.

"Can't happen. Even if she even agrees, I won't have her go alone," Deke said.

"She's either alone or you'll never see me."

"With Spetsnaz and the Black Berets looking all over Paris for you, I'm certain that's true."

"They'll never find me."

"Well, good luck then. Call if you find work."

"Wait." Petrov needed a moment. "Send the floater with her." Then he ended the call.

"Petrov knows what he's doing," Brandt said. "Châtelet is the busiest station in Paris. Easy place to hide in the big crowds. The Point de Rencontre is in Correspondence Hall. It's a meeting place all Parisians use."

"Where do we take him?" Casey asked.

"The Russians watch the embassy twenty-four-seven. There's a safe house across the river in Saint-Germain we can take him to," Bill said. "Ten minutes by metro. I've got some floaters I can put in Correspondence Hall for backup."

"Petrov will notice them. Leave them out," Lena said.

"You have anyone who can help us with disguises?" Casey asked.

"Not a problem. Who do you want to be?" asked Bill.

"Lena."

"You won't fool Petrov," Lena said. "Remember, we were lovers at one time."

"We need to fool the Russians. We can't have them following you and Brandt."

"She's right. Moky will be hoping we lead him to Petrov," Deke said.

"A wig, heels, some makeup, and a quickie boob job, and *voilà!* I'm Lena. Then I can walk out with Deke and Tig. Brandt delays ten minutes, leaves alone, and waits in Élysées park for Lena to come out looking like cleaning staff. It will be quitting time, so she can mix in with everyone as they walk out. Meet Brandt and go to Châtelet together."

"I'll send some marines along to make it look they're protecting Lena. Moky won't even get a good look at you with a marine escort," Bill said. "My team can ride line four metro between Châtelet and Saint-Germain all evening if they have to. Once we have him, we don't want to lose him."

Deke asked Lena, "You sure you're okay with all this?"

"Since the day I came to Brussels."

41

Lights and mirrors were brought into Bill's office to assist with the disguises. The cosmetics went well, but Casey found the thick-padded bra cumbersome and the wig hot and sweaty. A knotted blue scarf hung down like a noose. Lena was dressed in loose slacks, a billowy top, and cloche hat, and had gray circles added to her eyes.

"I'm not sure Petrov will recognize me looking like this," Lena said.

"I picked the biggest marines to screen Casey walking back to the hotel. Even in civvies, there's no mistaking them," Bill said.

Lena moved the pistol she'd fired in Dresden from her leather bag to the cloth bag that was part of her disguise.

"Lena, we can't have you shooting Petrov," Casey said.

"I'd like nothing better than to see Petrov dead, but I have no intentions of shooting him."

"Maybe you should leave the gun here anyway," Deke said.

"Let her keep it," Brandt said. "We don't know what Petrov has in mind."

Bill rose from his desk. "Skip the metro to Châtelet. There's always taxis out front. Châtelet can be confusing, so have a map ready on your phone When you get to Correspondence Hall, you'll be on the metro cameras all the way to line four platform. We'll be watching."

"Get off in Saint Germain?" Brandt asked.

"The safe house is a hundred meters from Saint Sulpice Station at 174 rue Madame. I'll have agents there waiting for you."

The four marines accompanying Casey were standing by the repaired main door. She put on sunglasses, and they left for the Montreux with Deke and Tig behind. Brandt and Lena waited, then grabbed a cab to Châtelet.

"What are you going to say to him?" Brandt asked on the way.

"I don't know. I'll let the moment tell me."

Brandt decided the bronze characters of the Point de Rencontre Brandt sculpture gave the two abstract figures the appearance of being hatched. The pointed, curved panels surrounding them resembled broken eggshells. Parisians stood and looked at the time while they waited for someone. As soon as they reached the sculptures, Brandt noticed Petrov standing by an entry passage. His clothing charade was part Bart Simpson, part tech nerd. It might fool Russians, but never an American. He'd dropped the black hoodie in favor of a bright purple Lakers jacket, khakis instead of baggy jeans, old PF Flyers for shoes, and an orange beret.

"I see him by the entrance. He's waiting to be sure it's safe," Brandt said.

Lena reached into her shoulder bag.

"Lena, don't. He's not worth it."

She extracted her phone. "I just want a picture of him dressed like an ass."

Brandt chuckled, then scanned the room for threats while she finished. Parisians were in a hurry to go home or to see their lovers. The businessmen carried flowers and briefcases, others had a messenger bag draped across a hip and a phone in one hand attached to earbuds.

Petrov posed with a cocky smile, then walked to them. He ignored Brandt and addressed Lena, his face full of smirk. "It's good to see you again, Lena."

Lena didn't hesitate, her right hand slapped his cheek hard enough to jerk his head to the side. The sound brought curious stares from the crowd.

"That's for Leonid. I only wish it could be more."

Petrov rubbed his cheek. "I guess that means you won't be coming to New York with me."

"Only if I can push you in front of a subway train," Lena said.

"Leonid was weak. But I never expected him to kill himself."

"Let's go," Brandt said. "We've attracted enough attention."

§

One of Wild Bill's men joined them at the line four metro platform while they waited for the next train. Brandt recognized two female Paris agents, Jeannie and Celia, sitting in the car when they boarded. Brandt sat with Petrov, and they observed the common metro travel silence. Lena was sending texts, including one to let Casey know they were on the train. The trip took twelve minutes to Saint-Germain, then all three agents became a tight escort to the safe house. Inside, Petrov demanded American whiskey.

"Okay, but forget a toast," Brandt said. He searched until he found some Jim Beam in a kitchen cabinet and poured some for Petrov. "We'll be going to the airport when the car gets here."

Jeannie overheard him and said, "Car's caught in traffic but on the way."

"Where are you taking me?"

"London. Some of our people want a little chat."

"Not for long, I hope. I'm anxious to see New York."

"If I were you, I'd stay out of Brighton Beach and Sheepshead Bay."

Petrov laughed but failed to hide the malice in his voice. "My BMW should be the M6. In black."

"Not my job. If it was up to me, you would be on the way to Lubyanka or Gitmo."

"But I'm not."

"Our bad."

"Someplace warm I hope, like Southern California."

Jeannie said, "Car's finally here."

Lena was first out of the house, and Jeannie and Celia flanked Petrov on the way to the car. Brandt was steps behind. The driver sat behind the wheel of a cream-colored Escalade. An agent exited the front seat and opened the back seat door. The group paused to let a running club dressed in matching blue uniforms pass by. The last man in the group slowed to a stop as if to say something. He quickly covered his face with a Club Français logo cap before spraying a heavy mist in Petrov's face and speeding away. Petrov brought a hand up too late, coughed twice, then slid to the ground as his body convulsed.

There was nothing they could do for Petrov. He was finished.

The agents hustled Lena into the car. Brandt let his eyes linger on the body for a moment. Burial plots were for the wealthy in Paris. Petrov would be cremated and his ashes put in an underground church storeroom for the unknown and unwanted. Brandt felt tired—no joy or sadness, just tired. They left the body on the sidewalk and drove off. He called Deke.

"Novichok-10. Had to be," Deke said. "Fucking Moky."

"Don't forget Aaron. Randy says the Mossad has one just as lethal."

"Doesn't matter now."

The drive to Orly was stop-and-go. The car was heavy with a sense of decay. Lena said nothing after the attack. Her head barely moved as she stared out the window.

Brandt assumed she was in shock. "You okay?" he finally asked.

She opened her phone to messages and handed it to him without speaking.

Brandt scrolled through her texts. The latest one was to Moky, with the picture of Petrov she took at Châtelet and the address of the safe house. His head sagged on the seat headrest, and he closed his eyes and sighed softly. After a few minutes of reflection, he deleted the last message and handed it back to her.

42

B randt sat behind his new desk. It was the only furniture in the recently opened Swindon Travel Adventures in Piccadilly. He had spent most of the day calling airline executives, tour operators, cruise lines, American Express, and his old travel connections on both sides of the Atlantic. Casey came in, put the mail on the desk, then sat on a folding chair. Starting a new business was like building a baseball diamond in a corn field. Put an *Opening Soon* sign in the window and they will come. Internet services, advertising agencies, money to loan, travel companies, good deals on rental cars. Go with us, and we'll make you wealthy. Among the stacks of letters, brochures, and invitations was a postcard of the iconic blue-domed church in Santorini, Greece. He quickly flipped the card over.

Pascal was right. Choose the lighter one.

It was signed *Al* with a hand-drawn smiling emoji labeled *Lena*.

THE END

ACKNOWLEDGEMENTS

A uthors are quick to admit their books are a team effort. Mine, more than others. Gratefully, the staff at HMB Press and Book-side Manner are gifted with patience. I can't imagine releasing a book without the editorial work of Kelly Cozy and a nod from my friend Kristen Tate. Dr Andrea Bonanomi and his charming wife Alessandra guided me through Florence's secrets and delights. There were many, starting with the famous Bistecca. Proof he is more than a gifted healer who saved my life in Venice. Special thanks to Kimberly Moreland, Pam Jacobs, Kay and Randy White for pushing me to get the book finished. Every author needs friends like them. The Benedictine monks of The Monastery of Christ in the Desert, an isolated New Mexico canyon sanctuary, deserve my deepest gratitude. Much of the story and many of the words are theirs.